THE DUCHESS OF IDAHO

MEREDITH ALLARD

Cover design by Jenny Quinlan

Copperfield Press

www.copperfieldpress.com

ISBN: 978-0-578-28534-4

The Duchess of Idaho/Meredith Allard – 1st paperback edition 2022

{1. Fiction. 2. Time Travel—Fiction. 3. American Western—Fiction. 4. Oregon Trail—Fiction. 5. Westward Expansion—Fiction. 6. Paranormal Witches—Fiction. 7. American Historical 19th Century—Fiction.} I. Title

CHAPTER 1

IDAHO

*E*veryone has secrets.

      Secrets are the things we keep tucked inside, just ours, for no one else, even those we love the most. Sometimes we keep secrets for reasons the holder might find embarrassing, like the middle-aged woman who calls herself Mrs. Eggers though everyone knows there has never been a Mister. Sometimes we keep secrets for reasons the holder knows will get them into trouble, like the man who says he's across the country on a business trip when he's really with a woman who is not his wife a few miles down the road.

Sometimes we hold onto secrets for reasons the keeper doesn't entirely understand, truths we can't yet face or truths that may spark reactions we cannot bear. Some things are simply better left unsaid. At least, that's what Grace Wentworth thought. There were so many things about her life she didn't understand, and James and Sarah, her parents, were less than forthcoming.

Grace had known since she was small that her parents had secrets together that they shared with no one. She also knew that James and Sarah were different from everyone else she knew—

they were in the world yet distant from it, happy with their simple life, content in each other. It wasn't that they were cold toward others. James and Sarah Wentworth hadn't an unkind bone in their bodies. They had a smile for everyone, even if they didn't socialize much, preferring to keep their own company. Doctor James Wentworth was a respected professor emeritus of literature who finished his academic career at UC Berkeley. Sarah had also retired from her librarian's job at the university. James and Sarah were both young to retire—James was 50 and Sarah was 52—but together they decided it was time to leave their work behind. They bought a home in the picturesque town of Carmel-by-the-Sea along the California coast and they settled into a slow life, enjoying the little things—reading and writing for James, cooking and gardening for Sarah. If there were two people more content on earth, Grace had yet to meet them.

Grace thought a lot about her parents' secrets as she drove from Carmel to Portland, Oregon. As she traveled along the highway she watched the landscape morph from urban sprawl to rural beauty back to urban, still wondering about her parents and their intense connection to one another. Whatever secret knowledge they shared, Grace thought, they would take it to their graves.

Shortly before her road trip, Grace brought the subject of her parents' secrets up with Olivia Phillips, the woman she called Grandma.

"It's only right, Grace," Olivia said. Olivia's hoop earrings jingled as she nodded, and Grace smiled at the sight of her dear friend on Skype. At 82, Olivia still looked every bit the gypsy with her billowing blouses and peasant-style skirts. Her hair was more silver now than red, but the white-gray streaks suited Olivia's mystical energy. "James and Sarah have been through a lot, and married couples should have some secrets together." Grace nodded, unsure what to say. "Your turn will come, Grace. You'll see what it's like to have secrets with someone you love soon enough."

Grace laughed. "I don't think my turn will ever come, Grandma. Only a few people are lucky enough to have what Mom and Dad have."

"How do you know you're not one of those people?"

"I suppose I don't for sure. But what Mom and Dad have is special. Something about the way they gaze into each other's eyes, something about the way they lean toward each other when the other's talking. It's as if no one else exists in the world. Sometimes they even forget Johnny and I are there."

"How is your brother? On his way to Europe?"

"He landed at Heathrow yesterday."

"How are your parents taking it?"

"They're worried, but he's 18 and they have to let him do his thing."

"Indeed, they do. I'll call Johnny tomorrow." Olivia moved her face closer to her phone's camera and Grace couldn't look away from the steel-gray eyes that seemed to see through her despite their physical distance. "Actually, Grace, you're right. What your parents have together is very special. I know the way your mother's eyes light up from a simple 'Hello' from your father. I've seen the way your father glows when your mother walks into the room. You're a young woman now, and I hope that at 22 you're old enough to realize how lucky you are to have been raised by parents who love each other so completely since they've shared that infinite love with your brother and you. Your parents are *beshert*, Grace."

"What does that mean?"

"If a husband and wife are meant to be together, they're *beshert*. It means the husband and wife are soulmates and it's inevitable that they end up together. It's destiny. And you, my darling granddaughter, I wish the same for you. I wish for a soulmate as perfect for you as your parents are for each other."

"I just wish they would tell me their secrets," Grace said. "I know they're hiding something from me."

3

"Everything in its own time, Grace. We learn everything we need to know in its own time."

"But to keep secrets from their own daughter?"

"Nothing is ever what it seems. You'll learn that for yourself soon enough."

When Grace packed for her road trip, she thought she had found a way to broach the subject with her mother. Grace was at her parents' turquoise-colored house near the Carmel shore, and she was pulling her t-shirts and jeans from the closet and laying them out on her bed. The gently slapping sound of low-tide waves breezed through the open window. Sarah was helping Grace pack by rolling the shirts and jeans and slipping them into the rollaway bags Grace would take with her.

"I'm surprised your mother has asked me to come to Idaho to visit her," Grace said. "I only remember her visiting us that once before Johnny was born."

"Annabelle is full of surprises, Grace. But she's asked to see you and it's nice of you to go."

"You mean she's asked me to help her clean out her house."

"Yes, that too, but she's making contact and that's a good sign."

Grace sat at the end of the bed. "You and your mom don't really get along, do you?"

Sarah twisted the blue t-shirt in her hands and sighed. "My mother and I, I don't know, we're just very different people. She's very sociable, Annabelle, and I've always been more of a bookish introvert. My father, your Grandpa Miles, you would have liked him very much. He and I were much more alike. I don't know how he stayed married to your grandmother, honestly."

Grace pulled a backpack from the closet and filled it with toiletries and her hairbrush. "Isn't she nice?"

"She's…"

Grace's father, James, stood in the doorway, his hands in his trouser pockets, his eyeglasses low on his nose. "An acquired taste."

Sarah laughed. "Yes, thank you, James. Your grandmother

Annabelle is an acquired taste. But she is your grandmother, and maybe it's time you got to know her."

Grace marveled at how her parents had hardly aged. Sarah Wentworth was 52 and she was as beautiful as she had ever been. Her chocolate-brown curls were largely silver now, her curves rounder than when Grace was younger. There was a stillness within Sarah's dark eyes, a wisdom, as if she had lived ten life-times. James was 50 now, still tall, still strong-looking, his hair still largely gold if graying at the temples. They looked right together, James and Sarah—two halves of a whole.

"We moved to Boston when I was young," Sarah said, "but I remember that house in Idaho very well. And Boise has grown a lot since I lived there. I used to have such vivid dreams when I lived in Idaho."

James leaned his tall frame against the wall. "You had vivid dreams in Massachusetts too, as I recall."

Sarah tried to swat her husband with the t-shirt. "I've always had intense dreams. It's just that some were more meaningful than others."

"What kind of dreams did you have?" Grace asked.

Sarah shook her head. She reached into the closet for a hoodie jacket and began rolling. "I don't remember the dreams from when I was a child in Idaho, exactly. I remember that I woke up in the middle of the night certain I had come back from somewhere, but I couldn't have told you where. Then when I moved to Salem I felt as if I had lived in that seaside town my whole life though I had never been there before." Sarah and James glanced at each other, that secrecy between them.

"Sounds like something Grandma Olivia would love," Grace said. "She's into dream interpretation, mysticism, and all that sort of thing."

Sarah set the hoodie into the rollaway bag. "My dreams were so vivid in Salem I even kept a dream journal to keep track of them."

"Was this when you met Dad?"

"As a matter of fact, the dreams became more powerful after I met your father."

"What dreams, Mom?" Grace grabbed Sarah's hands. "Mom?" She looked at James. "Dad?"

"It was nothing, Grace," Sarah said. "I've always had vivid dreams."

"Do you still have that dream journal?" Grace asked.

James shook his head, just enough. "No," Sarah said. "I don't think I kept it. After a while I didn't need it anymore."

Grace sighed. "Mom, I know you and Dad are keeping something from me."

"You make it sound like a conspiracy," James said. "Your mother and I have only ever wanted the very best for you and your brother. You must know how much we love you. For every single one of your 22 years, Grace, you have been our miracle. And you always will be, no matter what the future brings."

"But..."

Sarah brushed a gold curl from Grace's blue eyes that perfectly matched her father's. "There's nothing you need to know, Grace. I promise you. Everything is fine. Our family is fine. And if you do have strange dreams in Idaho like I had in Massachusetts, then you should keep a dream journal too. You never know what you might discover."

"I can't remember a single dream I've had in my entire life," Grace said.

"You're definitely my daughter," James said. "I don't remember my dreams either."

In the morning, James and Sarah loaded Grace's luggage into the back of Sarah's white Subaru Forester. Grace's first stop was Oregon to visit friends from Portland State University. It was June now, only a month since she graduated from PSU with a degree in American History. She had returned home to attend

Berkeley for a Master's and she was looking forward to it. After all, she and Johnny had practically grown up on the campus. A week after returning to California, though, Sarah's mother called to say that she needed help cleaning out her house in Idaho and she wondered if Grace would be willing to help.

"I still don't understand why Annabelle asked for me," Grace said as James set the last rollaway bag into the back of the Subaru.

"I offered to go, but she wanted you," Sarah said. "She and I agree that since you're a budding historian you may like her house. Who knows? Most of what she has stashed away is probably junk, but you may find some treasures too. Your Grandpa Miles used to love to go up to the attic and read the books and papers that have been in our family for years. The house isn't as old as our place in Massachusetts, but it's seen more than a century pass and your grandmother has a lot of antiques. Her stove is authentic from the nineteenth century."

"Doesn't it smoke her out of her house?" Grace asked.

"She's had it modernized so it's electrical now. Her sewing machine is from the early 1900s. She loves the old-fashioned life, my mother. She loves to garden, bake bread in her old-fashioned oven, ride her horses, and quilt."

"That's not so different from how you and Dad live now."

"There's something peaceful about quiet," James said. "Sometimes you don't know how beautiful silence can be until you don't have it anymore."

James slammed the back of the car shut while Sarah put her arms around her daughter.

"What you're doing for Annabelle is a wonderful thing, Grace. While she is an acquired taste, as your father said, she is getting older and it's good for her to get to know her only granddaughter."

"If you ask me, she'll outlive us all," James said.

Sarah shook her head at her husband. "I think she's using the cleaning as an excuse to get Grace to come and see her. After all, she's lived in that house her whole life and all of a sudden now she decides to downsize!" Sarah stepped back and looked seriously at her daughter. "You don't have to go, Grace. It's nice that she's asked for your help, but don't feel obligated. Or I can go with you if you'd rather."

"It's okay, Mom. I don't mind. I need something interesting to do this summer and maybe you're right. Maybe as I rummage through her house I'll find some antiques worth something. We can get an appraiser to look at them on Antiques Roadshow."

"Sounds like a deal."

Grace hugged her mother again. She was about to step into the car when her father stood in front of her.

"Say good night, Gracie."

"Dad, seriously?"

"Say good night, Gracie."

Sarah laughed. "Just say it, Grace. Your father won't give up. He never has yet."

Grace stretched her arms toward James. "Fine. Good night, Gracie." She hugged her father, glanced back at the turquoise-colored house with the bay windows facing the ocean, and got into the driver's seat. She turned the ignition, pulled into the road, and waved good-bye.

After Grace spent a week with her university friends in P-Town, she drove six hours, taking the I-5 North to the I-84 East through Oregon into Idaho.

Once she was surrounded by the rural landscape there wasn't much scenery to occupy her thoughts, nothing but grass, mountains, and spindly trees. Her car was the only vehicle on the road until she neared the farmlands—long green patches populated with haystacks and horses. Grace smiled at the raw yellow ochre and emerald green angles of Van Gogh's pastoral scenes.

After a while she felt lonely, as if she were the only person in the world. In the distance she spotted an open-back potato truck, but it was moving so slowly she had to pass it before she began driving backward. Soon she encountered other cars, but the sense of isolation remained. In California, the freeways were five lanes wide and everyone drove as if racing to cross the some imaginary finish line. Here, there was one lane in either direction. Motorists, unconcerned with the unruly spuds that occasionally rolled onto the highway, continued at a snail's pace. Most were older, retired, and driving well under the speed limit, their cars older models that needed a good wash.

Finally, the town of Nampa appeared on the highway signs. As Grace neared her exit she noticed a fire-engine red farmhouse sitting by its lonesome in a field of tall grass under a jewel blue sky, similar to another painted scene, perhaps from Monet. Loitering near the farmhouse were some brown cows, content with their lot as they chewed the cud. Grace enjoyed the impressionist-like scenery, but instead of feeling comforted she thought she had descended on some unknown world where she would never quite feel at home.

She tried to shake off the heaviness as she took the exit for North Franklin Boulevard. The weight returned, however, when she realized that she wasn't sure what to expect when she came face to face with Annabelle Alexander, her grandmother by blood though she had only set eyes on the woman once in her life. Grace didn't know much about Sarah's mother. Grace knew her age, 85, and she knew Annabelle's maiden name was Emerson. Grace had that one vague memory from when Annabelle had come to California for a visit around the time Johnny was born. Grace knew that Sarah and Annabelle had never been close. Mother and daughter shared a brief phone call on holidays, and Grace and Johnny knew to expect an envelope from Annabelle with a $20 bill on their birthdays.

Well, Grace thought as she turned down Happy Valley Road. I guess Annabelle won't be unknown much longer.

The GPS voice said to make a left near the gas station with the dinosaur logo, and Grace found her grandmother's home in the cul-de-sac at the end of the road. Sarah had told Grace that she couldn't miss the house, and there it was, a two-story structure that looked like something out of *Little House on the Prairie* with its front-facing brown bricks and wooden log walls. The shutters and awnings were forest green, and the slate-gray front door faced the road at a caddy corner. Grace parked on the gravel driveway and marveled at the odd shape of the house—a square front with an adjoining rectangle that stretched toward the mountains. The other houses in the neighborhood, newer and more modern, were fairly spread out, allowing for a sense of space between the properties. The loneliness Grace felt driving into Idaho returned, and she wondered if she made a mistake coming after all.

She walked to the white fence in front of the house and saw a backyard with well-manicured grass, flowers, a vegetable plot, and a horse stable with two horses, one gray and one white, both leaning their heads outside as though gauging the weather. Grace made her way to the front door and stopped, unsure what to do. Should she call Annabelle to let her know she was there? Before Grace could decide her grandmother threw open the door.

"Well, Missy? Are you coming in or are you going to stand there like a lump on a log?"

Grace exhaled and stepped past the front door that Annabelle held open for her. Grace wasn't sure what she had been expecting of her grandmother, but this formidable woman wasn't it. Grace had been thinking more along the lines of a bent-over, downward-looking elderly woman in a wheelchair maybe, or possibly someone shuffling along with a walker. Annabelle Alexander pulled her painted-on eyebrows into a frown as she studied Grace. Grace studied Annabelle just as intently, looking for something, anything that resembled her mother and finding nothing.

That wasn't entirely true. Annabelle had dark eyes and a pale complexion like Sarah. But other than that Grace found nothing that marked them as mother and daughter. Annabelle wore her silver and white hair in an ear-length bob that she brushed away from her face as though she couldn't be bothered with it. She was dressed in a navy blue housedress with white flowers under a crocheted beige sweater vest though it was June and warm. Annabelle wiped her hands on her frilly white apron as she pulled her lips into a flat line. She looked as though she was about to speak until someone knocked. Outside stood a young man, maybe in his late teens, holding two paper bags of groceries. The young man's red hair stuck out from under his Albertsons baseball cap, which he pulled over his eyes while he gulped, his Adam's apple bobbing under the strain of Annabelle's gaze.

"What is it with people today? Everyone shows up but no one comes in." The young man stayed where he was, smiling weakly. "So? Are you planning on bringing my groceries inside? If it takes you that long to step over the threshold I can only imagine how long it'll take you to get all the way to the kitchen. Set those down there."

"Yes, Mrs. Alexander." The young man placed the bags on the side table where Annabelle pointed.

"At this rate I might as well have gone and got the groceries for myself."

"Yes, Mrs. Alexander."

"And do something about that hair, boy. I don't know how the manager at your store lets you go running around like you have snakes growing out from under your hat. Who are you, Medusa?"

"Who?"

"All right now, see, there are these things called books. You ought to try reading one someday."

"Yes, Mrs. Alexander."

Annabelle grabbed her handbag and pulled some $20 dollar bills from her wallet. The young man nodded at Grace as if to say it's okay, she does this all the time. Annabelle handed the delivery boy his money, told him to keep the change even if he was late, slow, and strangely Greek-like.

"Go on," Annabelle said. "Be gone with you."

The young man said a polite thank you and hurried outside.

"Hmmp." Annabelle carried the bags into the kitchen. Grace offered to help but Annabelle shooed her away. "We don't put guests to work in this house."

"I'm not really a guest."

"You're my guest. You'll be doing enough for me by helping me clean this place out." Annabelle waved toward the living room with its shelves of bric-a-brac. "The very least I can do is take care of things and cook for you."

"Thank you," Grace said. "But I don't mind helping."

"Suit yourself."

While Annabelle busied herself in the kitchen, Grace noticed the dark living room with the wooden paneled walls. This place looks like it's caught in a time warp, Grace thought. The furniture was old-fashioned, with two tan sofas covered by crocheted star blankets near a matching tan recliner, also covered in a crocheted blanket. A rectangular window at the front overlooked the driveway where Grace had parked while a smaller window near the kitchen overlooked the large backyard. A black cocker spaniel slept soundly on the woven rug near the unlit fireplace. To the right was the kitchen with its olive green appliances. To the left, the rectangle of the house, were the bedrooms, Grace guessed. She peeked into the kitchen and saw the black pot-bellied stove her mother told her about, modernized for electric cooking. In the corner was a breakfast nook with a doily covered table set for two.

"Dinner is nearly ready," Annabelle said. "If you're hungry."

Grace wasn't hungry but she didn't want to say no, thinking it was best to stay in Annabelle's good graces, certain that her grandmother could frighten anyone out of their wits with a single stare. Medusa indeed.

A kettle whistled, and Annabelle gestured for Grace to sit. "You like tea?" Grace nodded. "What would you like?"

"Earl Grey, if you have it."

"As a matter of fact, I do. Earl Grey was your grandfather's favorite."

"It's Mom's favorite too. And Dad's."

"Well well. They have all kinds of things in common, don't they?" Annabelle chuckled to herself, some in-joke only she understood. Annabelle set a box of Twinings Earl Grey, two tea cups, and a porcelain sugar pot on the table. "Let's have a cuppa, as my friends from England say."

Annabelle dropped three tea bags into the porcelain pot and added boiling water. They sat in silence while the tea brewed, and when the air was sufficiently scented with bergamot Annabelle poured the tea into their cups. She sat across from Grace, blowing on the steaming liquid. After a sip she said, "All right then. Stand up. Let me have a look at you, Grace Wentworth."

Grace was going to protest but decided to humor her grandmother. She stood near Annabelle, who leaned close, squinting.

"All right. You can sit. I've seen you. For some strange reason you look like your father to me."

"When Mom and I are together people tell me I look like her, but I always thought I looked more like Dad."

"People really say that? Interesting." Annabelle squinted at Grace some more. "I remember James' gold hair from when I met him at your parents' wedding. He's good-looking enough, I'll give him that, but there's something odd about him. I went to shake his hand after the wedding and he jerked away like I had the plague. He apologized, said he had a cold, but he didn't seem so sickly when he kissed your mother like he was going to suck her lips right off her face."

"We haven't seen you much since then."

"I saw your parents and you that time I visited California. When was that now?"

"Around the time Johnny was born. He's 18 now. He just graduated from high school."

"Has it really been 18 years? Time flies, doesn't it?" Annabelle pulled a packet of Virginia Slims and a blue lighter from her sweater vest pocket. She flicked the lighter, lit the cigarette, and inhaled.

"We might as well start laying everything out on the table since you're here, Grace. I'm sure you're wondering why your mother and I never kept in close touch. The truth is I love your mother, and I know she loves me, but we never got on so well. Your mother is, well, we're not the same. Your mother and her books, you know. And she always had these crazy ideas, and I've had my own crazy ideas to contend with."

"What kind of crazy ideas?"

"Oh." Annabelle flicked cigarette ashes onto an empty plate. "When we left Idaho for Massachusetts Sarah acted like it was the best thing in the world. She was five years old, your mother, no higher than this," Annabelle held her hand two feet off the floor, "and she kept saying, 'I belong in Massachusetts. Massachusetts is my home.' Every time we went anywhere in Boston she was always looking around like she was searching for something. Whenever I asked her what she was looking for she said she didn't know. She'd know him when she saw him."

"Him?"

"Odd, right? Especially for such a little girl. I was worried something was very wrong but we didn't know anyone in Massachusetts and your Grandpa Miles said it was just a childhood flight of fancy and leave her be. It turned out that Miles was right, but it was a strange thing for a little girl to say no matter how you look at it. Then after Sarah finished college she upped and moved to Los Angeles. I still don't know what that was about." Annabelle eyed her granddaughter through the smokey haze. "Don't you know any of this?"

"No," Grace said. "I don't."

"You should ask your mother."

"My mother doesn't like to talk about her past. Neither of my parents do. I wonder..."

"Don't keep us in suspense. What do you wonder?"

"I think my parents are hiding something from me."

"I wouldn't put much stock in it. Your Grandpa Miles and I, well, we had a secret or two in our day. Every family has some secret they have to contend with. Every family is different."

"How is our family different?"

Annabelle sipped her tea as she considered. "We have our own ways. Did you see that red barn as you drove here?"

"Yes, I saw it."

"What did you think of it?"

"I liked it well enough."

"Well enough? Is that all?"

Grace fidgeted under Annabelle's gaze. There was a weight to her grandmother's stare—as though Annabelle pressed her down and held her still without touching her.

"The Wentworths have our own ways too," was all Grace could think to say.

"I gathered as much." Annabelle watched the quiet road through the window. She grew thoughtful as some birds flew past. "Has your mother ever mentioned our family in Idaho?"

"I didn't know we had family here except for you."

"Cousins." Again, that inquisitive stare.

Grace finished her tea slowly to allow herself time to find a topic of discussion where she might actually be able to follow the conversation. "So you moved back to Idaho after Mom and Dad got married?"

"After Sarah married James and they were so wrapped up in each other I decided it was time to come home. I was never much for Boston, and I didn't care a hoot for Salem."

"Why? It's just a seaside tourist town."

"That's what they want you to believe." Annabelle leaned close to Grace, again with that laser-like stare. "You do look like James, though. You have Sarah's curls but you have James' blond hair and blue eyes. That's crazy, isn't it? It's like dogs."

"Like dogs?"

"You know how they say dogs and their owners start to look alike after a while. I'm sure there's a person or two who'd say Casey and I look the same." She nodded toward the sleeping cocker spaniel. "That must be it." Annabelle nodded, satisfied with her answer. "If people and their dogs can start to look alike, then so can adopted children and their parents, don't you think?"

"I don't know any adopted children, Annabelle, but if I ever meet one I'll let you know."

Annabelle leaned back in her chair. "You don't know any adopted children? Good heavens, child." She took a long drag on her cigarette and stood as she stumped out the flame, shaking her head the entire time. "My mahjong club starts at 4 o'clock and it's nearly that now." She put her unfinished tea in the sink and gestured at the stove. "I made spaghetti and there's tomato sauce in that pan. The meatballs are in the oven. They ought to be done by now. Help yourself to anything while I'm gone."

Annabelle grabbed her keys from a drawer near the refrigerator and her quilt bag from a hook near the front door. "Don't wait up. The games can run late, and I'm sure you're tired. You're in the loft bedroom at the top there." She pointed to the staircase at the end of the kitchen. "And don't forget to feed Casey. He may need a walk. He's old but he's spry in his way."

Grace stood near the window and watched Annabelle get into her brown Honda Civic and drive away. Casey, the cocker spaniel, found his way into the kitchen, sitting near Grace's feet and wagging his stumpy tail. He wasn't at all frightened by the new person in his house; in fact, he nudged Grace's hand for a pat, and she was happy to oblige.

"What have I gotten myself into?" Grace said.

When the dog didn't answer, she ate the spaghetti and meatballs in silence. She washed the dishes, then sat on the kitchen floor and pet Casey's long ears, finding comfort in the dog's friendly presence. When Casey wandered off she explored the house.

Kitsch was the word that popped into her mind. The vintage curio cabinets held shelves of Love Is dolls, Merry Mushroom creamer sets, and Berries novelty figurines. In the kitchen, Grace felt the pull of the 1970s even more strongly with the rattan window blinds, orange and yellow flowered wallpaper, and olive green formica countertops that matched the appliances.

Uneasy in the house, Grace decided to see more of the neighborhood. She attached Casey to his leash and walked him around the block. She marveled at the space, the wide sky unimpeded by tall buildings, the mountainous scenery. Back at Annabelle's, she let Casey inside, then walked around back to make sure the horses had hay and water. The horses weren't any more worried by her presence than Casey. She pet the animals behind their ears and they nickered in soft conversation. When the horses seemed fine, she went inside.

Exhausted, with no one to talk to but the dog, who didn't have much to say except a low ruff now and again, Grace climbed the carpeted stairs to the loft bedroom. Instead of four walls, there were three with a railing facing the rest of the house, to keep people from falling down a flight, she guessed. Standing as close to the railing as she dared, she looked down into the living room.

Grace's mind raced with excuses about what she could say to her grandmother about why she had to leave so soon, right this very minute. No wonder her mother never got along with Annabelle. What a stern, strange woman Annabelle is, she thought. She looked for a window to open but there wasn't one and she coughed from the musty air. She imagined the walls of the old house falling down around her while she perished unseen under 1970s kitsch memorabilia.

Grace pulled herself away from the railing and sat on the edge of the bed. She exhaled and reminded herself that everything was all right. The walls were perfectly perpendicular. She was fine. She tried to turn her thoughts to more pleasant subjects and she remembered the cows near the red farmhouse, which reminded her of a story her father told her about the time he moved to Massachusetts with his father. He was born in London, James, although you'd never guess that to hear him speak with his perfect American accent. When James and his father first arrived in Salem, James was surprised at living next door to cows. Everywhere he looked all he saw was cows. He hated the cows, he said, until he found them to be rather agreeable in temperament. Grace nodded because now she was confronted with her own mooing neighbors.

She wandered back to the kitchen and watched the darkening sky through the window. A single car drove past and she sighed. In the distance she spotted the farm with the flatbed trucks stacked with newly harvested, dirt-caked spuds. She jumped when her phone buzzed but smiled at the name on the display—Grandma Olivia.

"Oh, good, dear. I was afraid you were sleeping already."

"I'm here, Grandma."

"What's wrong?"

"How did you know something was wrong?"

"I know you too well, Grace Marie Wentworth. I could feel you struggling, something in your energy feels anxious, but I couldn't make out the problem from here."

"Massachusetts is far from Idaho."

"Nowhere is too far when you love someone. What's troubling you?"

"It still freaks me out when you can tell that something is bothering me."

"What can I say? It's the invisible world, dear. It's magic. Now what's on your mind?"

"I think I'm going to be lonely here."

"Is it that bad?"

"It's not bad. It's…strange."

"Give it time. The strangeness will pass. You're there to help your grandmother, and that's a good thing. Besides, Idaho is full of history, and for a budding historian like you I bet there's a lot for you to discover there. Take advantage of the opportunities being in Idaho will bring. And it's only for a few weeks, after all. You'll be back in California before you know it."

"You're right, Grandma."

"Besides, maybe it's time you had a little adventure in your life. You like to play things safe like your mother, but I know you have some of your father's adventuresome spirit. Johnny has that adventuresome spirit, that's for sure. He loves England. He would, of course, with James being from London. Now your father has settled down and likes to play it safe like your mother. I suppose he's earned it, if anyone has."

"Grandma..."

"All I'm saying is give it a little time before you decide to go home. Will you promise me that?"

"I promise."

"And call me any time, dear, no matter what time it is here in Salem. I'm always here for you."

"I know, Grandma. Thank you."

Grace returned to her loft bedroom and unpacked the larger rollaway bag. The bedroom was much like the rest of the house, old-fashioned and dark, with turquoise, gold, and brown pattered wallpaper while a blue and green patchwork quilt covered the bed. A long chestnut desk and a blue-cushioned wicker chair was pressed against the wall. A wicker bookcase filled with an antique-looking globe and old books stood near a print of farmlands. Grace stopped unpacking when she spotted the small tube television on the dresser. She turned the dial and the television sputtered to life, sort of. It flickered into grainy static.

As she waited to see if anything would show up on the screen she noticed a hatch door in the sloping ceiling. She was curious but too tired to see what was up there. Finally, the TV snapped on. It was a black and white set with only a dial to change the channels. She flipped the channels and found nothing interesting but local news and old movies. She sighed and turned the set off. She heard a whimper and looked over the rail to see Casey wagging his tail, looking up at her expectantly from the bottom of the stairs.

"Come on up, Casey. It's okay."

When Casey whimpered, Grace guessed the problem. She went downstairs, lifted the dog, who was heavier than he looked, and carried him up. He seemed content when she set him down next to her on the bed.

"We'll keep each other company, Casey. What do you say to that?"

Soon Grace and the dog fell into a sound sleep.

CHAPTER 2

*G*race's limbs jolted, a painful flash of static, and she sat up, panting. It took a moment to remember that she was in Annabelle's house. She saw the old-fashioned furniture, the quilt on her bed, the tube television on the dresser, and she exhaled, resting back on the pillow.

"Too bad this wasn't all a dream," she said. "I could have woken up in California."

She ran her hand over the indentation where Casey slept during the night. He wasn't there, so he must have made his way downstairs on his own or Annabelle helped him. Grace groaned with the aches that come from sleeping in a hard, unfamiliar bed. Really, she felt exhausted, as if she hadn't slept at all. She made her way into the kitchen, found the box of Earl Grey, and put the kettle on. Casey appeared, his stumpy tail dancing in greeting. Grace found his kibble in the cupboard, fed him, and gave him fresh water. While Grace waited for the tea to brew she watched the farm down the road come to life while Nampa awakened with a pink line along the horizon.

Still exhausted, she returned to the loft, crawled into bed, and pulled the quilt over her head. Overwhelmed by the strangeness of her surroundings, and upset for some reason by the reminder that she had cows for neighbors, she wept into her pillow.

Grandma Olivia is right, she thought. My parents do like to play things safe. But maybe caution isn't such a bad thing. Maybe it's better to think things through. I should have asked more questions about Idaho, about Annabelle. I should have known what I was getting myself into. As Grace thought about her parents' home in Carmel, she drifted back to sleep.

THE SECOND TIME GRACE AWOKE SHE HEARD ANNABELLE SHUFFLING in the kitchen. Grace wasn't up for any conversation so she stayed in her room. She remembered the tube television on the dresser and turned the clunky dial. She turned from station to station to see if there was anything on, anything at all that might distract her. She passed a quiz show and a cooking show. She saw a classic movie and stopped. She liked black and white films. Her father loved old movies and they had watched many together. Idaho felt a bit black and white to her, like Dorothy in Kansas where everything is rural, ordinary. The film on the tube television must have been from the 1950s based on the actors' clothing and hairstyles. She recognized Van Johnson from an episode of "I Love Lucy" while the screen filled with happy smiles and soft shoe dancing and everyone was having a grand old time.

When the announcer said, "We'll return to *Duchess of Idaho* after these messages," Grace couldn't have been more surprised. Why are people singing and dancing about Idaho? But she had nothing else to do, and she wasn't ready to face Annabelle, so she propped the pillows against the wall, got back into bed, pulled the covers to her chin, and settled in to watch. It turned out that "Duchess of Idaho" is a title Esther Williams wins in a dance contest. But the movie was set in Sun Valley, Idaho, not Nampa, and who would want to be Duchess of Idaho anyway? Duchess of Potatoes is more like it.

When the movie ended, Grace made her way downstairs. Annabelle was resting in her recliner, her eyes glued to a tube television only slightly newer than the one in the loft.

"There's bacon and eggs on the hot plate in the kitchen," Annabelle said. "You can take care of yourself while I watch my stories, can't you? We'll start tackling the house tomorrow. Today I'm taking Daisy out for some exercise. Do you ride? Horses, I mean."

"I rode a pony once when I was a kid."

"That's one more surprise for my ever-growing list. Your mother loves to ride, or at least she did when she was a child. If you want to ride Daisy or Chuck just let me know. They're both well behaved and they'll let you take them for a spin. I'll teach you how to saddle up if you'd like."

Grace thanked Annabelle, said maybe some other time, and left her grandmother in peace to watch the English soap opera that had her enthralled. Grace sat at the breakfast nook, ate her breakfast, and took a bottle of water up to the loft. As she checked her phone she saw a text from her mother asking how things were going. Grace put the phone away, thinking she'd respond to her mother later. When she went downstairs she stifled a laugh at the sight of Annabelle with her khaki trousers tucked into well-worn riding boots, a contrast to her hot pink blouse under a sweater vest of blue and purple flowers. Annabelle was buckling her riding hat under her chin.

"Why don't you come out with me now?" Annabelle said. "You're not doing anything and there's no reason for you to sit around feeling sorry for yourself." Before Grace could respond, Annabelle shook her head. "I've seen that pucker on your face since you got here. Idaho might not be to your taste, but you have to give it a chance, that's all I'm saying. Besides, it might do you good to slow down a little, see the sights, enjoy the simple things.

I'll teach you to cook, and sew, and mend, and quilt too. You never know when those skills will come in handy."

"I can cook a bit," Grace said. "And it's easy enough to buy clothes or blankets."

"Sometimes there's nowhere to buy them."

"Are you saying there are no stores in Idaho? Mom said there's a mall in Boise."

"There's more than that now. But it never hurts to have some practical skills, you know."

Grace nodded. "It would be nice to be better at cooking, and I wouldn't mind learning how to quilt." She gestured at the quilts hanging from a rack on the wall. "Did you make those?"

"As a matter of fact, I did. My mother taught me, as her mother taught her, and her mother taught her, all the way back to when our people first settled here in the nineteenth century. Our family came over on the Oregon Trail. Didn't your mother tell you that?"

"No, she didn't."

"What do you Wentworths talk about all day? And you interested in history and all. I wonder about Sarah sometimes, honestly I do. I used to try to teach her family things that have been passed down the generations but she was never interested. She likes to cook and garden, Sarah, but sewing, quilting, churning butter, now those are skills that will come in handy no matter what life has in store for you."

"Churning butter?" Grace struggled not to laugh. "All right, Annabelle. I'll try some new things while I'm here. Grandma said I should open myself to the possibilities of being in Idaho."

"Grandma? You mean James' mother?"

"No, Dad's mom died before I was born. I mean Olivia Phillips. She's like a mother to my parents and a grandmother to Johnny and me."

"So you call your own grandmother Annabelle and a family friend Grandma? Whatever floats your boat there, Grace. But don't forget that I actually am your grandmother. My DNA runs through your veins. I have some family stories I can tell you, and I may even know a thing or two about you."

"I didn't mean anything by it. It's just…"

"You and I are virtually strangers. You're right, we are, and I'm sorry for it, I am. I've been interested in you since the day your parents brought you home. I wonder if you're the one after all."

"What do you mean by *the one*?"

Annabelle shook her head. "I mean nothing. I'm an old woman talking nonsense. I want to get to know you now you're here, Grace, that's all. Now that I think of it, I insist you come riding with me. I'll settle you on Chuck. He's a nice boy, an easy-going gelding."

"I don't have the right clothes for riding."

"Chuck's no fashionista. He doesn't give two figs what you're wearing. So long as you can sit astride and hold him steady, he'll do the work." Grace tried to think of a good excuse, but Annabelle was having none of it. "Do you have some pressing engagement, Missy?"

"I suppose I don't."

"Come along then. Don't dawdle."

Grace followed her grandmother to the mud room where Annabelle found a second riding hat. Annabelle helped Grace tug on the black riding boots that came to her thighs, big but not dangerously so. Annabelle wondered aloud at Grace's jeans, which might be too tight to ride in.

"Let's see if you can straddle without ripping your bloomers and showing your hoo-hoo to the world."

Grace couldn't help laughing. She was stern, Annabelle, but there was a sense of humor beneath that no-nonsense attitude. They stepped into the afternoon light and the tops of the mountains glowed gold in the distance. Annabelle led the two horses from their stables and saddled them both. She showed Grace how to lift herself up and held Chuck steady while Grace mounted, awkwardly, but she made it on her first try without kicking the horse and startling him.

"All right then," Annabelle said. "Make sure you're balanced and steady up there. Don't be afraid. Chuck's a good boy. Aren't you, sweetie pie?" Annabelle stroked the horse's cheek as she squinted at Grace in the saddle. "Not bad for your first try. Now lean back a little. You look like a wooden board. That's better. You want Chuck to know you feel natural up there."

"I don't."

"But you will."

Grace exhaled and tried to relax her muscles. He was indeed a nice boy, Chuck, waiting patiently for Grace to settle. Annabelle demonstrated how to click her tongue to make Chuck go, how to slow or stop by gently releasing the reins. "After all, the bit's in their mouth and you don't want someone yanking your tongue out when they're ready to stop, now, do you? I didn't think so. When you're ready to stop say 'Whoa' and release your pressure. That's all there is to it. But don't worry. Chuck will follow Daisy and me. You won't have to think too much."

Annabelle and Daisy trotted away, slowly to give Grace time to get going. Grace clicked her tongue the way Annabelle showed her but nothing happened. Chuck thought a moment, as if he were unsure whether or not Grace meant that odd sound as an order. He must have decided it was since he began following Daisy. He took his time with his steps, a nice, slow gait that allowed Grace time to acclimate to the movement and enjoy the scenery. As they trotted along, Grace saw that Nampa was more inhabited than she thought, though she reveled in the rural panorama of farms and mountains. Wisps of clouds floated cotton-like above their heads.

Grace exhaled fully for the first time since arriving in Idaho. "Maybe I don't have to rush home after all," she said.

"You were going to make the great skedaddle, then?"

"I said that out loud?"

"Were you?"

"It's just..." Grace didn't want to offend her grandmother. "It's so different here from what I'm used to."

"But you were in Oregon for college, weren't you? Studying history?"

"That's right, but Portland is closer to what I know at Berkeley."

"You don't feel any connection to Idaho at all?"

"I haven't been here long enough to feel anything in particular about Idaho."

Annabelle sighed. "Look, Grace. I know I'm an old lady, but I am your grandmother and I do care about you, even if I haven't been wonderful about showing it all these years." Annabelle stared straight ahead, as though the conversation hit too close for comfort. Then she glanced at Grace from under the pointed brim of her riding hat. "I'm glad you came, you know. I'm glad I have a chance to get to know my granddaughter. That's all."

"I'm glad I came, Annabelle. It's beautiful here, and I would like to learn those skills from you, I would."

"So, no great skedaddle?"

"No skedaddling. At least not until after I've done what I've come to do, which is help you clean out the house."

"That makes me happy, Grace."

They continued at an easy pace. Cars passed in the distance while children jumped from their school buses with their cartoon character backpacks swinging from their shoulders. Daisy and Chuck trotted toward Old Nampa, the downtown area, and Grace was charmed. With its Art Deco-style brick buildings and brick sidewalks, its old-time Post Office, and charming shops, it had the feel of a quaint life from a bygone era.

"There's music down here sometimes," Annabelle said, "along with food trucks and cafés if you're into that sort of thing." Annabelle nodded toward Grace. "Maybe it isn't as bad as you thought?"

Annabelle nodded at two older ladies, and from the pleasant greeting between them Grace guessed they knew each other. It was nice to see Annabelle in a different light, chatting with her friends. Grace had to admit that Annabelle was growing on her. A bit.

The ladies continued their walk and Annabelle turned Daisy around. "Now let's head on home, Grace. I want to show you how to plant tomatoes and there's a recipe for quick-bake biscuits you should know."

INSOMNIA WAS SOMETHING GRACE HAD DEALT WITH HER WHOLE LIFE. She was indeed her father's daughter.

When her family first moved to California from Massachusetts, they lived near Berkeley since both of her parents worked at the university. Then, when her parents retired they bought the turquoise-colored house in Carmel-by-the-Sea. The whole Wentworth family loved that house, but Grace in particular adored it. When she lived there she never wanted to sleep. She didn't want to miss a moment of the whispering ocean breeze, afraid that if she dozed off even for a moment she'd miss a pronouncement of great importance. Her father must have felt the same. How many times had she crawled out of bed in the deepest night to find him hovering near the bay window, the one with the view toward the water, his eyes far away, the street lamp reflecting like mirrors off his eyeglasses, his head hanging as though his thoughts weighed him down? Other nights she found him at the dining room table, a cup of Earl Grey beside him, his laptop open, surrounded by research for his scholarly tomes about Victorian literature, books he had been wanting to write forever, he said, and now that he was retired he finally had the time. Whenever James saw Grace beside him he smiled.

"You either?" he'd say.

"Not a wink."

James made Grace ginger and turmeric tea, no caffeine for her that late, and they would sit in that comfortable silence they had together.

"Well," her father would say, "I've been a night owl for as long as I can remember and so it seems are you. You are a true Wentworth."

"Isn't Mom a Wentworth?"

"She certainly is. But you're my blood, and while your mother has my heart forever and a day, my blood doesn't flow through her veins like it does yours." He smiled. "Oh, yes, my Gracie. You're a Wentworth indeed."

After Grace finished her tea she would finally feel sleepy. She would wash out her cup and saucer, set them in the dish rack beside the kitchen sink, and smile at her father as she headed back to her room. Every time, without fail, her father said the same words.

"Say good night, Gracie."

And every time Grace would laugh.

"Dad, you've been saying that Burns and Allen joke since I was a baby."

"Say good night, Gracie."

"Good night, Gracie."

After a day of helping Annabelle make biscuits and gravy from scratch and planting tomatoes, Grace felt tired in a good way. As she got ready for bed, her phone rang.

"Grace?" Sarah asked. "Is everything all right?"

In the background she heard her father. "Gracie? Are you sure you're okay?"

"I'm all right, Mom. Tell Dad I'm fine. Why are you asking?"

"I texted you but you never answered back. Then Olivia said she felt something odd in your energy and she felt it again this morning. Is Annabelle treating you all right?"

"Annabelle is fine. She's..."

"An acquired taste?" Sarah asked.

"Yes."

"Stubborn," James said.

"Apparently, I'm drawn to stubborn people," said Sarah. "Grace, I know Annabelle can be stern, but believe me, under that tough exterior is a woman who would give her heart away if someone in her family needed it."

"I think I see that now."

"I'm glad. She and I have never seen eye to eye, as I'm sure she's told you, but I've never doubted that she loved me in her way. Are you sure you don't want me to come?"

"No, Mom. It's okay. I feel better today. Annabelle and I have been horseback riding and we've gardened and baked together. Annabelle wants to teach me to cook and sew, and I did enjoy the horseback riding even if I am a little sore now. It's certainly pretty here in Idaho."

"Yes," Sarah said, "it's very pretty there."

"And it is an interesting old house, like you said."

"Have you found anything for the Antiques Roadshow yet?" Sarah asked.

"We haven't started cleaning anything out, but I wouldn't be surprised if something worth a lot of money popped up."

James' voice grew louder in the background. "Are you sure you don't want to come home, Gracie?"

"Mom, will you please tell Dad that I'm a grown woman and I don't need you two checking up on me every five minutes? How many times have you spoken to Johnny since he left?"

"As a matter of fact, we spoke to him last night," Sarah said. "He's flying to France today. And we know you're a grown woman, but no matter how old you are you will always be our child and we will always worry about you."

"I know, Mom, I do. But I'm fine. I promise. Annabelle can be cranky, but the truth is I'm starting to like her. I want to get to know her better and learn more about our family. How come you never told me our family came west on the Oregon Trail?"

"I should have, Grace, you're right. For me, my life started when I met your father and that was in Salem. Anything before that is, well, before that. If you need anything, anything at all, call us any time day or night."

"I will, Mom."

"I love you, Grace."

Then she heard, "Say good night, Gracie."

"Dad."

"Say good night, Gracie."

"Good night, Gracie."

Grace hung up the phone, annoyed with her parents but thankful for them too. She knew they would be her soft place to fall for as long as she needed them.

CHAPTER 3

Sarah Wentworth found her husband lingering near the refrigerator, door open, staring inside.

"Have you found it yet?" Sarah asked.

"Found what?" said James.

"Whatever it is you're looking for."

James shut the refrigerator. "I don't know what I'm looking for. Perhaps I'm looking for Grace's lost youth, and Johnny's for that matter."

"I don't think you'll find that in the refrigerator."

"I want our children to be young again, Sarah."

"You know better than anyone how time marches on."

"So I do." James made his way into the dining room, pulled out a chair, and sat at the table that seemed empty with their two children gone. He reached for Sarah as she sat close to him. "I think I'm so used to searching for something. For so many years I *was* searching for something. For someone. You."

"You found me. I'm here. And now, more than twenty years later, we're here together, as full of joy as any two people can be. We have our beautiful life together with our beautiful children and our beautiful home. We have peace and quiet. So what is it you're still looking for, Doctor Wentworth? If you tell me maybe I can help you find it."

"I'm not looking for you anymore, and I thank God every day for that. You are my Sarah. My Sarah."

They kissed, passionately. Sarah pulled away first. She felt the tightness in his lips, and his six-foot-two frame looked heavy, as though he would tip over in his chair and knock her down under his weight.

"James? What is it?"

"Are you sure Grace is all right?"

"She's not alone on the moon. She's in Idaho with my mother. I know my mother isn't the easiest person in the world to get along with, but I believed Grace when she said she's beginning to like Annabelle and she's enjoying her time there."

"But why is Annabelle showing this interest in Grace now?"

"She's always asked questions about Grace, wanting to know about her, her interests, wondering if she might like Idaho."

"Then why didn't she ever come to see her?"

"I don't know. But to be fair, we didn't go to see Annabelle either. Once she questioned me about why we named her Grace."

"Did you tell her?"

"Of course not. Can you imagine what someone as logical and straightforward as Annabelle would do with a story like that? But she asked Grace to visit her and I'm glad. Annabelle and I will never be close, but maybe she and Grace can be." Sarah brushed a stray lock of gold from her husband's eyes. "My mother has a lot of interests that she and I never shared. I enjoyed horseback riding when I was a kid, and I learned how to cook and garden from her. I've never enjoyed baking as much as she does, and sewing and quilting weren't my thing. Maybe she's hoping she can leave some of that knowledge with Grace. That's what it sounds like anyway."

"Perhaps. But there's something about this that doesn't feel right to me."

"You sound like Olivia."

James leaned back and rested his head against the chair. Sarah reached for him, and he reached back.

"James, we promised each other a long time ago that we would always be honest with each other. Something else is bothering you. I can see it. You should know by now that you can't hide anything from me."

"I'm sure I'm just being paranoid. After everything we've been through, worries still pop out at me from nowhere. It's as if I can't trust in our joy. As if I'm waiting for something terrible to happen. I think that's it, Sarah. That's what I'm looking for—something bad to happen. We've experienced so many tragedies."

"We've had smooth sailing for a long time now, my love." Sarah smiled as she brushed more gold from James' face, his hair as stubborn as the rest of him, and she settled his glasses on his nose. "I think we've been through the worst of it."

"But that's just it. We can't know for certain."

"Of course not. No one can. But Johnny is doing well, and Grace is doing well. We're doing well, aren't we?"

"Of course we are. You are my life, Sarah. But I'm worried about Grace. It's this feeling I've had. Like we're going to lose her. Again."

Sarah pressed her finger to James' lips. "Don't say that. Please. We went through so much when we lost her the first time. We nearly lost her the second time too."

"I lost the both of you, and I had to live with that void for oh so very long."

"But we're all here now, all happy. And you have to remember one important thing. Grace isn't ours to keep, James. Neither is Johnny. They never have been. You know how they say children don't belong to their parents. Their parents get to keep them awhile, help them find their way in the world, but then they have to let them go." Sarah touched her husband's cheek, and he slid his hand over hers. "Grace is a young woman and we have to let her go. That doesn't mean we'll lose her like we did the first time. It just means things will be different. But we've been through a lot of different together, haven't we? And we've survived it all."

"Yes, we have."

"And whatever this is, we'll survive it too."

Sarah pressed her head into her husband's chest and exhaled, because everything seemed surmountable with her dear and loving husband's arms around her. When she looked into his deep blue eyes she saw that he was still struggling, the mist hovering under his eyelids.

James sighed. "I can't believe how our children have grown, Sarah. Grace is starting graduate school and Johnny is traipsing around Europe." He pulled Sarah closer. "But watching them grow into fine young adults with you by my side is the greatest joy I've ever known. I'm so thankful to Olivia for helping us. For the way she continues to help us."

Sarah sat back so she could see into James' face. "What is it that Olivia says? Everything always turns out right in the end. If it's not right, it's not the end. And haven't things always worked out for us in the long run?"

"Sometimes the very long run." James walked toward the window, seeking some unnamed answer in the darkness. Finally, he said, "What if Grace discovers the truth? About us? About her? I think she suspects something."

"She's suspected something for some time now." Sarah stood beside James. "I think we should tell her."

"I don't see what good can come from that."

"You don't want her to find out accidentally, do you? She'll never forgive us if she doesn't find out from us. We should have told her long ago."

James managed a weak smile. "It never gets easier, does it?"

"No, not that. But this." She took James' hand and brought it to her cheek. "This is worth everything we've had to go through to get to this moment. But I still think we should tell Grace the truth."

"The truth is we are her parents who love her very much."

"And that won't change when she learns about our past."

"If you think it's best. But Sarah?"

"Yes?"

"The thought of it terrifies me."

"I know. But it has to be done. She needs to know."

"You're right, of course," James said.

Sarah smiled. "I usually am."

CHAPTER 4

*W*hen Grace wandered downstairs the next morning she discovered that she was alone. According to the note on the refrigerator, Annabelle had gone to her Thursday Morning Luncheon and Poetry Society. Grace sighed as she glanced at the crammed knick-knacks in the curio cabinets and the shelves of old books and magazines. Tomorrow, Grace thought. I'll start on the house tomorrow.

She made herself some toast and coffee and noticed an oil painting beside the refrigerator of white-covered wagons in the foreground as the western sun dropped in the distance. She covered her ears with her hands, overcome suddenly by sounds— creaking wheels, braying animals, chattering children, and shouting adults. She glanced around to see if there was anyone else there, or maybe a television or a radio had been left on. Casey joined her in the kitchen, but he didn't have much to say and he certainly couldn't bray. She patted his head and grabbed his kibble from the cupboard.

"Did you hear that, Casey?" She looked around again, still

searching out the sounds, as she set his bowl down. "It sounded like a wagon train passing through. How odd." She sat beside the dog while he ate, the linoleum cold on her legs. She realized that she had only learned a little about the Westward Expansion from one of her American history survey courses.

"My area of study is the American Colonial period," she told the dog. "I'm from Salem, Massachusetts, did you know that? Salem was founded in 1626." Casey barked. "That's right. It was a long time ago. My parents have a house in Salem from that time. I practically grew up in that house. We've lived in Salem every summer my whole life, and I've always been interested in the early colonial era. But I don't know much about the pioneers. Annabelle said our family came over on the Oregon Trail. Maybe that's what triggered my thoughts—seeing the painting and thinking of our family's trip West."

Grace spotted the second note near the kettle: "Take Casey for a walk. He likes the red barn this time of morning."

Grace thought, rather unkindly, that Annabelle had asked her to come to Idaho as dog walker more than anything else. After she finished her breakfast, she led Casey to the appointed spot, the red barn she had seen on her way to Annabelle's. It was a well-kept barn, neat and tidy, and the exterior walls looked as though they had been recently refreshened with a coat of fire-engine red paint. Casey sniffed the long grass near the wooden fence that surrounded the property and he woofed at a cow lingering nearby. The cow mooed in response, as if the animals were on friendly terms.

Grace stopped. Another sound. What was it this time? She heard an undertone, a whisper. Something. Or someone. Was it a voice? She checked behind the bushes and walked toward the barn but no one was there.

"I must be hearing things, Casey."

The cocker spaniel wagged his stub in response.

When she heard the sound again she bent her ear toward the

barn, straining, but all she made out was bounding echoes. She turned, again and again, a full circle; still nothing. She grabbed the wooden fence with both hands and studied the serene scene. Farmlands stretched into the distance. More cows roamed about while chickens clucked and flapped their wings as if they owned the place, and maybe they did.

Back at Annabelle's, Grace gave Casey some fresh water. After a drink, the dog contented himself with his spot on the rug, and Grace didn't want to sit around because then she'd have nothing to do but dwell on the strange sounds. Instead, she decided to get out and see some of the area. She started up her mother's Forester and took the I-84 East to Boise.

Grace parked downtown, enjoying the quirky coffee shop and taking selfies at the Capitol building. From there she found her way to Boise State University. She had inherited her parents' love of university campuses. Her parents worked at Berkeley most of her life, though both James and Sarah had worked at various universities before she was born. James and Sarah met when they were both at Salem State in Massachusetts, after all. Unlike other families who visited beaches, restaurants, or museums on vacation, the Wentworths visited universities.

The campus was located near the Julia Davis Park with its blooming roses and Zoo Boise near the Boise River Greenbelt. Grace parked near the campus and walked toward the houses along the Boise River. They were nice houses, certainly, well-tended and much-loved by the look of them, and they had exceptional views of the Greenbelt. She passed one house, then another, and another, admiring the manicured lawns and the basketball hoops over the garages. One house caught her eye, a brown brick house hidden beneath a hanging oak. Grace stopped when she heard the same bounding echoes she had heard near the red barn. There were no lights on inside the house and no cars in the driveway so she stepped closer.

You're being ridiculous, Grace told herself. What sounds do

you think you're hearing? Whose voice would you hear when there's no one else around?

She marched herself to the Boise State campus and found her way to the Student Union for an iced coffee. She neared the Albertsons Library and thought of the many hours she had spent with her mother at the Bancroft Library at Berkeley and smiled. She sat on the grass in the Quad, sipping her coffee and watching the students on their way to their summer classes. She saw an older teenaged girl holding the hand of a small lookalike boy with a lookalike older woman reading a map while pointing out buildings. Grace remembered when her parents did the same for her. On her first day of classes at Portland State, she already had her route mapped out with her parents' help. Suddenly, Grace realized how special it was to have parents who dropped everything to help you even when you were older and maybe didn't need the help but it was nice to have anyway. Grace watched the family turn down a lane between two buildings and disappear.

Others about Grace's age were out and about, some sitting on the grass, some eating lunch, some on a university guided tour. Grace wondered at them. She had always felt different from others, although she could never say why precisely. Somewhere along the way she had gotten it into her head that she was born in the wrong era, that she belonged in some other time in the past. That was the main reason behind her interest in history. Once she had jokingly said to her parents that maybe she was searching for where she belonged.

"What era do you think you should have been born in, Grace?" her mother would ask.

Grace heard the hesitation in Sarah's voice, as if Sarah were afraid of the answer. It surprised Grace that her parents took these silly thoughts so seriously. Surely, such childish fancies were like nonsense poems. On the surface they seemed to make sense, but when you dig down you realize they aren't even words.

Every time her father responded to her whimsy with, "You're a Wentworth, for sure."

Grace stopped in the university bookstore, wandering through the aisles of textbooks, office supplies, and merchandise. She picked up a blue and orange Boise State Broncos t-shirt for herself, a refrigerator magnet for her mother's collection, and some notebooks with the university's logo for her father. As she headed toward the register she saw more stacks of notebooks. She remembered what Sarah had said before she left California, about recording her dreams in a journal. Grace picked up a black and white composition book and turned it over in her hands. She didn't remember her dreams, but something about the idea of keeping a journal appealed to her. She had never been much for journaling before, though her father had kept one religiously for as long as Grace could remember.

Maybe writing down my experiences here will help me make sense of them, Grace thought. Maybe I'll feel less alone while I'm here. She added four black and white composition books and a packet of pens to her basket. It can't hurt, she decided, and if she didn't use them she'd give them to her father when she got home.

When Grace arrived at the cash register the bespectacled woman behind the counter asked to see her ID for her credit card purchase. When Grace handed over her driver's license the woman squinted as though she couldn't see through her glasses.

"You're one of those, then?" the woman said.

"One of those?"

"One of those Californians who come here and buy up all the houses and raise prices sky high. My son and daughter-in-law can't find a single house around here they can afford."

"I'm not here to buy any property. I'm visiting my grandmother."

The woman shrugged as if it were no matter to her, or she didn't believe her, Grace wasn't sure which. Grace grabbed the bag with her purchases, found her way back to her car, and back to Annabelle's.

ANNABELLE WAS LEANING FORWARD ON THE SOFA, INTENT ON THE quilting frame before her, her reading glasses perched at the tip of her nose and held in place by the silver chain around her neck. Casey slept near her feet. Annabelle was stitching what looked like a patchwork quilt in the colors of the American flag. Cobalt blue stars sat stacked on the side table, along with red circles and white triangles. The background was blue like the sky.

Annabelle sat back and squinted at her work. She waved Grace over when she saw her hovering near the door.

"Come in, will you? You don't need an invitation in this house."

Grace moved closer and saw a pattern forming. Azure squares, turned on their sides into diamonds, would make up the larger background while the red, white, and blue shapes would add depth.

"What do you think?" Annabelle asked.

"It's going to be beautiful," Grace said

"Have you ever quilted?"

"I never have."

"Well then. You said you were willing to try some new things while you're here. It's an old family tradition passed down too many generations to count."

"Sure," Grace said. "I'll try."

"Anyone who can use their hands can quilt. It's not rocket science, you know."

Grace sat beside Annabelle and watched as her grandmother pulled the basket filled with colorful rolled materials toward her. Next to that was a smaller basket with odds and ends of every shape and size, pieces that didn't fit where they were intended but might make good for another project. Grace laughed at the sight of the old sewing machine her mother had told her about. It certainly looked like something from the turn of the century: black, bulky, with a large foot pedal attached by a heavy wire. When Annabelle pressed her foot to the ground the needle bobbed haphazardly, as though it had to think every time it moved, it was so very old after all.

"Would you like me to buy you a new sewing machine for Christmas, Annabelle?" Grace asked.

"No, I would not. Those new-fangled machines don't know their front feet from their hind legs. They might be faster than Old Bess here, but they have no character, churned out a dime a dozen the way they are. Now Old Bess," Annabelle pet the creaky machine as though stroking a favorite cat, "knows her business. She can read my mind it seems like. When I need to get a move on she creaks away at a good clip. When I need time to think she keeps her pace slow. No." Grace thought Annabelle was going to kiss her sewing machine. "Old Bess here does me just fine. Besides, she's a family heirloom. She's been passed down for generations."

"Has a lot been passed down in your house, Annabelle? Is that why you keep everything?"

"Like I told you, our family came over on the Oregon Trail. We have a long history here."

"Mom says every family has their stories."

"We have our stories, certainly." Annabelle grinned. "And wouldn't it be something if our family's story turned out to be true?"

Annabelle's reading glasses slipped from her nose. She pressed them back into place, studying Grace as if seeing her for the first time. "I don't know what's what about you, Grace. I truly don't." She gestured toward the living room with its shelves of knick-knacks. "To answer your question, yes, there are many things in this house that have been passed down the generations. But I can see a lot of it is junk and everything needs a good sorting through.

I've always wondered if I could find something to bring to the Antiques Roadshow."

"That's what Mom and I said we should do if we found something that looked good."

"Smart minds think alike." Annabelle shook her head as she considered her belongings. "I used to be better about keeping the house up. After your grandfather died everything got out of hand, I suppose. Now let me show you this quilting. Like I said, it's not brain surgery. You have these pieces of fabric and you decide what sort of pattern you're going to sew them into. It requires a little math but nothing someone with half a brain can't handle. Geometrical shapes are the most common in quilting, but really, the sky is the limit. My friend Beatrice from my Quilting and Bridge Club did a beautiful mural of birds in a tree for her granddaughter and it's a piece of art, I can tell you."

"What should I do?"

"You have to decide. Start by creating a picture in your mind. Close your eyes. What do you see?"

"I see my parents' house. I see the bay, the beach, and the blue sky."

"The house in California or Massachusetts?"

"The house in Massachusetts."

"You're still not thrilled about Idaho?"

"I'm starting to like it here, Annabelle, but it's not home."

"Let's say you could go to California or Idaho or Oregon. Would you choose to come to Idaho?"

"I grew up in Massachusetts and California. I'm going back to California in the fall to go to school. I went to Portland State and I love Oregon. But if I had to pick just one of those places I'd choose California." Annabelle's face dropped. "I have nothing against Idaho, Annabelle. I'm just not sure I would choose to live here."

"California, huh? Not choose to live here? Well well." Annabelle gestured at the baskets with an impatient hand. "So you're going to make your quilt a picture of the bay in Massachusetts?"

Grace searched her mind for a picture that was easy enough to recreate using geometrical shapes.

"I think I'd need a little practice before I tried something like that. I liked the red barn I saw this morning when I took Casey for his walk. It's a beautiful place. I loved the landscape, you know, with the green farmland all around."

Annabelle perked right up. "So there is something in Idaho that floats your boat after all. You liked that barn, did you?"

"I did."

"That barn belongs to our cousins. Their side of the family settled here at the same time as ours after traveling the Oregon Trail together. Did you meet any of them by chance?"

"I didn't see anyone but a cow and some chickens."

"The cow who likes to wander near the fence is Oakley, yes, as in Annie. She's a sweet girl, Oakley. One day I'll take you over so you can meet her properly." Annabelle searched the smaller basket as though she needed something urgently. "I've been meaning to ask you, Grace. Have you had any interesting thoughts since you've been in Idaho? Anything about this house, or the red barn? Anything at all?"

How did Annabelle know about the rickety wheels, the braying animals, the echoing voices? Grace hadn't shared any of that with anyone, not even her parents or Grandma Olivia. For a moment, she was tempted to say something, but Annabelle's features were more severe than usual and Grace couldn't imagine saying something so out there to such a stern-looking woman.

"I just thought it was a nice looking barn," Grace said.

"Hmmp." Annabelle gestured toward the larger basket with the rolled materials. "Take a look and find the colors, textures, and patterns that will help you bring your vision of that red barn to life. You can always use those," she gestured toward a small plastic box with templates of various sizes, "to help you create the shapes you need if you don't want to cut them freehand. But before you start cutting you should decide how big you want your quilt to be.

After you measure things out you'll know how many pieces you'll need of which shapes. You'll probably have to play around with the layout. Quilts should always have symmetry, you see. It should always be equal on every side so no matter which way you fold it the quilt looks the same. That's the part that takes practice. You need to figure it out one square at a time."

Grace searched the materials but was quickly overwhelmed with the amount of possibility. "I need to think about it first," she said.

"That's always the right way. Too many quilts have been messed up beyond repair when the quilter didn't take the time to think things through. It's a life lesson, certainly. I think maybe before quilting I'll teach you sewing. And maybe you ought to know some darning too."

"Darning?"

"You never know. There may come a time when you'll need to mend some clothes. It's always best to be prepared."

Grace sat near Annabelle as she resumed her sewing, nodding in rhythm with the tha-thump-tha-thump of the old-time machine as it heaved and groaned under the weight of the bobbing needle. Annabelle concentrated with a squint at the white thread as it crossed the blue stars. Without looking at Grace, Annabelle said, "So do you want the house?"

"Excuse me?"

"The house."

"Which house?"

"This house, of course. When I'm dead."

"Don't be silly, Annabelle. You're going to be around for a very long time."

"None of us will live forever, and I want to know if you want this house. I know I should leave it to Sarah, but I don't think she wants it. My only child lives in California and never visits." Annabelle's shake of the head was perfectly self-righteous. "It would be a shame if the house didn't stay in the family, that's all.

Our ancestors built their homes with their bare hands. True, over the years they moved the houses around as areas built up. But if you don't want the place I might as well make some money for my golden years." She looked at Grace under lowered eyelids. "So? Do you want it?"

"I'm not sure what to say."

"Because you'd rather be in California."

"I'm just surprised at the offer. I would love to have this house, Annabelle, but you're going to be living here for a long time to come."

"We'll see. I'm doing all right except for some popping joints and a bit of angina my doctor says won't kill me. I have some gas in the tank yet."

"You're far more active than Mom or Dad or me."

"You all like your books."

"Yes, we do."

It wasn't very late, the sun just setting over the west-facing fields in the distance. Grace stood from the sofa. "I'm going upstairs, Annabelle. Is there anything you need?"

"I'm hardly an invalid, now, am I? You want me to make you something to eat to take up there?"

"I can make myself a sandwich."

"You're supposed to respect your elders, young lady. I'll make it for you."

Grace brought the grilled cheese sandwich and a glass of iced tea to her bedroom. She turned on the tube television and ate watching the local news. When the news ended she turned from station to station to see if there was anything else on. She thought about watching a movie on her phone, but something so modern didn't feel right in Annabelle's house. She flipped past the same few channels again, hoping for something different to pop on the screen. The station she stopped on was running a commercial. Then she heard, "We'll return to *Duchess of Idaho* after these messages."

Again, Grace thought? How many times does this station show the same movie?

With nothing else on and unable to concentrate on something like reading, writing, or even texting a friend, Grace propped the pillows against the wall, got into bed, and leaned back to watch the song and dance film once more. She had the phrase "Duchess of Idaho" caught in her head, and she even hummed a few of the songs during the commercial break.

After the movie resumed, Grace once again noticed the latched door in the vaulted ceiling over her head. For a moment she considered pulling the rope so she could explore the attic. Casey barked from the bottom of the loft stairs, so Grace went down and carried him up. She placed him on her bed and stroked his long ears while she kept glancing at the latched door.

"What should we do, Casey? Should we see what's in that attic?"

When the dog didn't seem interested either way, she took matters into her own hands. She stood under the sloping door and pulled on the knotted rope. She tugged once and nothing happened. She tugged twice and the door sprung open with such force she nearly toppled over. Casey barked as if the door were an intruder.

"That is quite a door, isn't it?"

She pulled as hard as she could until the door opened like an accordion into a staircase. When she was confident the stairs were sturdy, she climbed up and looked around.

It was so dark she could hardly see. One round window smirked from the top of the highest wall, and the only other outside light filtered through cracked shutters. She couldn't take a single step without tripping since the floor was strewn with a hoarder's array of books, magazines, newspapers, crates, baskets, trunks, old radios, and other odds and ends. She pinched her nose when the mustiness overcame her. Oh well, she thought. This is what I came here for—to clean up. I might as well get started. Annabelle can look through everything I've set aside later.

In the kitchen, she found a box of black plastic bags under the sink and pulled a flashlight from a drawer. She returned to the loft to find Casey standing on the bed, his nose forward, his short tail back, the perfect picture of a pointer dog.

"What is it, Casey? What do you see?"

The cocker spaniel stayed like a soldier on watch. Grace climbed back into the attic with the flashlight on. She stood for the longest time, looking much like a pointer herself. She had no clue where to begin. For a fleeting moment, she resented Annabelle. Annabelle had asked her to come to help clean out her house, yet Annabelle was gone every day at her Ladies Marching and Whatever Else Societies. Grace exhaled. She reminded herself that she made the decision to come as well as the decision to stay.

She coughed as the dust filled her lungs and she kicked any obstacles out of her way until she made it to the window. She tried to push it open but it was stuck. She coughed some more as she examined her surroundings.

This is all junk, she thought. But then she wondered. Someone at a flea market might be interested in the old magazines. Her father might like to see the old books. He had a collection of first edition classics from the seventeenth century onward. Those books were probably worth a fortune, but she wasn't sure if the ones in the attic were worth anything. They looked too time-worn to be valuable, but you never know.

She noticed an old trunk in the center of the room made of carved wood with scroll-like patterns. It was beautifully made, and Grace guessed it had been hand-carved. Maybe that was something for the Antiques Roadshow. She walked toward the trunk and felt light-headed suddenly, as if she had too much wine to drink. All she had all day was tea, coffee, and water, so that wasn't the problem. Again, she heard that hollow echo, though when she struggled to make out the sound all she heard was Casey murmuring from the loft. She shrugged, climbed down from the attic, and took a bath.

. . .

THE NEXT MORNING GRACE WAS ENJOYING HER BREAKFAST OF EGGS and coffee while Annabelle washed the dishes.

"You need all kinds of skills on the prairie," Annabelle said.

"This is farmland, Annabelle, but it isn't exactly the prairie. Prairies don't have WinCo or the co-op I saw in Boise."

"Maybe yes, maybe no, but like I've been trying to tell you, it's good to have certain skills." Annabelle went to the cupboard and pulled out cornmeal, salt, and sugar along with some butter from the fridge. "Today you're going to learn to make johnnycakes. Everyone should know how to make them."

"What are johnnycakes?"

"What are johnnycakes? What kind of historian are you? Johnnycakes are only one of the most versatile meals ever. You mix cornmeal, salt, sugar, water, and butter, fry them up, and they'll keep you going all day. For each batch you'll need a cup of cornmeal, three teaspoons of sugar, and a half teaspoon of salt. Mix them together." Grace did as she was told. "Good. Now grab a pan and boil three cups of water."

Again, Grace did as she was told. It was easier to follow her grandmother's directions than argue. She stood over the pot, waiting.

"Haven't you ever heard that a watched pot never boils?"

"Annabelle…"

"Now take that butter and cut off two pats."

While Grace cut the butter the water boiled. Annabelle grinned with an *I told you so* expression.

"Now add the dry ingredients to the water and keep stirring so it doesn't all stick together. Add the butter and keep stirring. Keep stirring, girl, before it tastes like the bottom of an old shoe." Annabelle looked over Grace's shoulder and nodded. "That's all right then. Let it rest a bit and we'll wash the dishes."

By the time they were done the cornmeal mixture looked like a thick cake batter.

"That looks good, Grace. You did well. Now put another pat of butter in the pan and form the batter into circles the size of your palm. Now fry them up until they're a nice and deep golden brown. If they're not cooked through they taste like socks."

"This tastes like socks or shoes, huh?"

"You don't want your food to taste like footwear is all I'm saying. Now let's see if you remember how to make those quick biscuits."

Grace watched Annabelle sift the flour, salt, and baking soda together. Then she added some sliced butter and kneaded the batter with her hands until it was more inviting. She added buttermilk, pressed it in with her hands until the dough was smooth, and put it aside. She set the black dutch oven on the front burner of her pot-bellied stove, dropped some butter in, and the sweet aroma filled the kitchen.

"Aren't we baking the biscuits in the oven?" Grace asked.

"No ovens. We're doing this the right way by frying them."

"Like on the prairie."

"That's right. And no sarcasm from you, either. Now it's time to get your hands dirty. Scoop out a handful of the batter, form it into a round, and drop it into the dutch oven. You have to be patient when you fry them like this. Out in the open the pioneers placed their skillets over fires made with coals or buffalo chips."

"Buffalo chips?"

"Yes, it's exactly what you think it is. Don't laugh. They burn well and make good fires. You use whatever is available, understand? Now we're going to make butter."

"I'm pretty sure we can find butter at WinCo, Annabelle."

"I feel like a skipping needle on a record. Everyone needs these skills."

"Churning butter?"

"There's nothing more simple than churning butter."

"I was hoping you were joking."

"I never joke." The way Annabelle said it, Grace believed her. "I tried to teach your mother once but you're more practical than Sarah, I can see that, so you're going to churn butter." Annabelle squinted at Grace as though making a decision. "Just in case."

"Yes," Grace said. "There's always a danger of every grocery store in town running out of butter at the same time."

Annabelle shooed Grace's words away with a swat of her hand as she set out an old-fashioned wooden butter churn and a pitcherful of cream.

"Now on the Oregon Trail the pioneers didn't have to do much to get butter. They'd hang the cream in a bucket inside the wagon and after bouncing around all day they'd have butter by the time they stopped for the night. But if the way's not bumpy enough, or if you're at home, then you churn it like this."

Annabelle demonstrated. She gestured for Grace to try, and Grace couldn't believe how hard it was to turn.

"It's easier if you hold the handle on the dome," Annabelle said. Grace tried it and it did turn more easily. "And you're going to need to turn it faster if you want butter before midnight. It takes some elbow grease."

Grace's arm was sore from the effort, but soon she began to see whipped cream, then a grainier cream.

"Keep churning until you see that the butter has separated from the milk," Annabelle said. "And keep that buttermilk. There's a lot you can do with buttermilk."

Annabelle scooped some of the mixture out with a spoon and examined it. "It's nearly there. A bit more churning and you'll be done." She handed the spoon to Grace, who tasted it and smiled.

"It's actually really good, Annabelle. But I still don't see myself doing this on a regular basis."

"What if you find yourself stuck in the middle of nowhere with no grocery store nearby? Are you going to eat dry bread for the rest of your life? Don't be so soft. That's a problem with you young people these days. You have no can-do spirit about you, no deter-mination."

Annabelle pulled her gray cable sweater from the hook near the door and slid it on. She found her car keys and nodded toward Grace. "You keep that up until you have fresh butter, hear me?"

"Where are you going?"

"To my Crochet and Thai Food Circle." Annabelle looked as though she would say something more but changed her mind. She left, closing the front door behind her.

In a moment of weakness, Grace considered pulling a stunt from an episode of "I Love Lucy" and buying a container of butter and passing it off as made by her own fair hands. But Annabelle was too quick for that. Besides, Annabelle was right. The butter took just another few minutes of churning before it was done. Grace spread some across two slices of toast and she admitted, if only to herself, that her homemade version tasted far better than what she bought in the store. Grace thought about her whirlwind morning baking and churning, laughing at her grandmother's sternness, and she wondered how her quiet, bookish mother survived living with such a formidable woman. And now Annabelle wanted to leave her this house. How quickly things changed.

Grace spent the rest of the day quietly, sitting in the sunshine in the backyard garden with its trellises of pink, red, and white roses. The large shade tree with overhanging leaves was the perfect place to sit awhile. Grace brought a book and a glass of lemonade outside, spread a blanket down, and settled in to read. When Casey barked, she opened the glass door and he joined her, stretching out for a nap in the sun.

Grace lost track of time, enjoying the day. As the sun began to set she heard the phone ringing inside. Before she could get to it the old-fashioned answering machine picked up.

"Grace?" Annabelle called. "Are you there? My friends have invited me to stay for dinner so I'll be late coming home. Have a good night and I'll see you in the morning. Don't forget to take Casey for his walk and feed him his dinner."

Grace was more convinced than ever that she was there as a dog walker. She liked Casey and his friendly companionship, though, so she didn't mind.

CHAPTER 5

*T*he next morning Grace found Annabelle in the kitchen frying bacon in a cast-iron skillet. Annabelle hadn't seen her yet, odd since Annabelle usually noticed things before they happened. Once again, Grace searched for any similarities between her mother and Annabelle Emerson Alexander, and once again she found almost nothing. In profile, Annabelle looked remarkably like the Wicked Witch in *The Wizard of Oz*. If you paint her face green and put her in black, she'd be a dead ringer. Instead of black, Annabelle wore a plum-colored blouse with yellow dots and a flowery gray sweater vest. Patterns, Grace thought. Annabelle loves patterns.

Annabelle shook her head. "There are no buses around here to wait for. Come turn this bacon over."

Grace flipped the bacon while Annabelle grabbed a hunk of bread from the sideboard and sliced it into fat pieces.

"That bacon is done now. Take it out and put it on this plate."

When the skillet was empty Annabelle slid the bread into the pan, allowing the slices to soak up the fat. She turned the flame of the stove high and fried the bread on both sides, leaving a golden brown crust. Grace saw baked beans in the dutch oven on the back burner. Bacon and baked beans weren't Grace's usual breakfast fare, but it smelled good and she was hungry.

Annabelle leaned over the bacon and breathed in. "I'm so hungry I could eat a horse right now. If you tell Chuck or Daisy I said that I'll deny it with every breath in my body. Now let's eat."

Grace set the table with napkins, silverware, and the white stoneware plates she grabbed from the cupboard. Annabelle poured some sweet iced tea into two tall glasses and set them near the plates.

They sat at the table together and Annabelle bowed her head. She had never said her prayers aloud before.

"Lord, thank you for the bounty of this table. Thank you for the shining sun. Thank you for the air I breathe. And thank you for sending Grace my way. Whatever is in her future, please protect her. Amen." Annabelle grimaced. "Don't you Wentworths pray in your house?"

"We never have."

"I knew your father would change your mother's ways. Well, there's nothing to be done about it now."

"Mom used to pray?"

"Oh, yes. She was quite fastidious about her prayers when she was younger. I could tell she left it behind when she moved to Salem, but I always hoped she might have picked it back up at some point."

They ate in silence, the only sound coming from Casey as he drank some water. Grace rather liked the bacon, fried bread, and baked beans. She finished quickly and eyed the food still warm on the stove.

"Do you want some more?" Annabelle asked. Grace nodded. "This isn't *Oliver Twist*, Missy. If you want more, take it. You're my granddaughter and this will be your house one day. It's about time you felt at home in it."

Grace took her plate to the counter and added more bacon and beans with another slice of fried bread. Annabelle's lips moved and Grace thought her grandmother might actually be trying to smile.

"I'm glad you like it. Good, hearty food that fills you to your beakers, that is." Annabelle pointed to Grace's plate with her fork. "There are times when you need some serious sustenance. I was thinking you'd be too California with your avocado toast and green smoothies to eat something as plain as bread, beans, and bacon."

"Are the beans your recipe?"

"It's an old family recipe."

"From the Oregon Trail?"

"You're starting to catch on. Your mother never makes them?"

"No, she doesn't."

"It's like she doesn't remember a single thing I taught her."

Grace washed the dishes while Annabelle dried. When everything was put away, Grace remembered what she had wanted to speak to her grandmother about.

"I went up to the attic and saw some old magazines and newspapers. I'm going to get started today, but I think it will take time to clear it all up."

Annabelle lit the cigarette between her lips. "The attic, huh?"

"I noticed the door and I wanted to see what was up there. Only I'm not sure what you want to keep and what you want to give away."

Annabelle exhaled a thin line of smoke. "I saw this show on TV where the lady said you should only keep what brings you joy."

Grace laughed. "I saw that same show. I'll divide everything into three piles like she said—a keep pile, a give away pile, and a trash pile. I thought you'd like to see if I'm putting everything in the right place. You should be the one deciding what to keep, throw out, or give away."

Annabelle's stern features flattened into odd confusion.

"Did I do something wrong, Annabelle? I thought that's why I was here, to help you clear out the things you no longer need."

Annabelle snapped back to herself. Her painted-on eyebrows pulled into her familiar frown. "No, no, you're fine. I haven't been up there since your grandfather died is all. That attic is full of memories. Our family's memories." Annabelle glanced around the kitchen as though looking for something to clean but there was nothing. "Did you find anything of interest while you were up there?" She watched Casey as he left the kitchen.

"I haven't seen much but old books and newspapers and some old crates. There was one old trunk that looked interesting. I thought maybe it was an antique."

"An old trunk?" Annabelle crunched out her cigarette, pushed herself up from the table, opened the drawer near the refrigerator, and pulled out Casey's leash. "Come here, dog," she called, not unkindly. The dog sat at Annabelle's feet. "It's time for your walk." She seemed to forget that Grace was there.

"Annabelle? Do you want me to show you what I'm throwing out or recycling?"

Annabelle walked Casey to the door. "I trust your judgment, Grace. You should decide what you want to keep." She stopped by the door, her hand on the knob. "An old trunk, huh?" Casey trotted outside, trying to pull Annabelle along, but she stayed where she was. "Come to think of it, you don't need to bother yourself with cleaning out the trunks. Those were your grandfather's favorites. He'd sit up there for hours reading away. But everything else, have at it. It's just collecting dust anyway."

"What's in the trunks?" Grace asked.

"Oh, you know. Old bills and such. Nothing you'd be interested in." Casey won the tug-of-war and Annabelle stepped outside. "I suppose I shouldn't be surprised you found your way up there." Casey huffed as he sat, still waiting. Annabelle looked far away suddenly, her mind clearly somewhere else. Finally, she said, "I suppose you were looking for something to do. It must be dull here for a city girl like you. It's quiet, but that's why I like it. I can hear myself think. It's getting busier, though. A lot of you people are congesting the streets."

"You people?"

"People around here don't like Californians much."

"I guessed that."

"Just last week I had to wait to cross the road because there were five cars coming. I wouldn't go telling people you're from California, that's all I'm saying."

"I guessed that too."

Annabelle nodded distractedly as she watched Casey hopping from foot to foot. "All right then." She let the dog lead her down the road, all the while keeping her eye on Grace.

GRACE MADE HER WAY BACK TO THE ATTIC AFTER DINNER AND THIS time she came prepared, bringing a larger flashlight, more black trash bags, a fan to blow the dust out of her face, a pair of gloves, and a bottle of water. She turned the flashlight on, an old square model that beamed a single spotlight like a film projector. For two hours she set the newspapers and magazines into piles by dates. Her back ached, so she found a small clearing where she could sit against the wall, her legs stretched out, while she grabbed a magazine from the 1940s and read. The women were glamorous with their war-time hairstyles, the men dapper with their wide-shouldered suits. After sitting for an hour she felt sore so she stretched her arms toward the slanted ceiling. She was grimy with dust, but she had made progress and she was pleased.

As she drained her water bottle she spotted the beautiful wooden trunk again. Despite what Annabelle said, she would tackle the trunks at some point. She ran her hand over the ornately carved wood and smiled. If her grandfather found them so engrossing, maybe there was more inside than Annabelle knew.

It was nearly 10 pm and Grace decided she had done enough for the day. She froze as she climbed down the stairs. For a flash, like a flickering image on an old-time screen, she saw an image of herself as though she were posed for a grainy daguerreotype. She wore a simple homespun dress, her hair pulled into a severe bun, and she stared without smiling into the camera. Grace grasped the sides of her head, unable to shake the vision.

She meant to go downstairs for more water but her legs shook and the weakness spread to every muscle in her body. She stretched her hand out to touch the photograph but there was nothing but air.

She had an urge to call Olivia though it was late in Massachusetts. Grandma Olivia was good at things like that, mystical things. After all, didn't she hold tarot card and palm readings at her shop in Salem? Didn't she sell books of magic spells? She was a spiritual person, Grandma, and she had always told Grace that magic explained a lot about life that couldn't be explained any other way.

"But I don't believe in magic," Grace would say.

"Ha!" Olivia would answer. "Your mother said the very same thing when she first arrived in Salem."

"And now?"

"Now you need to ask her. But I'll tell you a little known secret, dear—everything is magic. Poetry is magic. Beauty is magic. Life is magic. Love is magic. The invisible world is magic."

After she sat down, after her breath settled, Grace's rational mind took over. Of course she imagined the daguerreotype. All of Annabelle's talk about pioneers and cooking over open fires and that painting of the white-covered wagons must be getting to her.

WHILE ANNABELLE WAS AT HER FRIDAY MORNING GARDENING AND Tennis Society, Grace wandered through the house, imagining what it would be like if it were hers. The kitchen was nice enough, bright and airy with its large windows though the olive green would have to go. The old black stove sat in the center, giving the room character, and that would stay.

She opened the sliding door and went outside. She liked the garden more every day. The spiky green grass was soft and she enjoyed sitting beneath the hefty tree, resting her back against the trunk, protected from the sun by the overhanging leaves. The black spaniel followed her outside, his stubby tail wagging while Grace pat his back. She found peace in the blue sky, the bird songs, the gentle breeze stirring the roses. That's one thing Sarah and Annabelle have in common, Grace thought—a love for growing things. She breathed slowly, trying to steady herself, but her thoughts kept returning to the house and everything inside.

Maybe that's why I'm uncomfortable here, Grace thought. Cluttered house, cluttered mind. She thought of the rope hanging from the attic door in the vaulted ceiling and wondered if she should attempt to tackle more of the mess. But she was comfortable, and Casey was comfortable, so they stayed.

CHAPTER 6

*A*fter spending the morning under the tree, Grace gathered her supplies, walked up to the loft, pulled the rope, and climbed into the attic. Of course, Annabelle was out—at a friend's for lunch.

This time Grace was even more prepared. She brought two clean pairs of Annabelle's flower-patterned gardening gloves since she still wasn't entirely sure what she would be touching. She also brought two flashlights to brighten the hidden corners and three bottles of water to drown the dust away.

In the attic, spindly light winked through the tattered blinds and dust mites swirled above her head. Grace shivered, afraid that something, or someone, lurked in the shadows. She turned the larger flashlight around and found more stacks of discarded crates. And cobwebs. And possibly creepy crawlies. Hopefully, whatever she saw wouldn't walk away.

She cleared the floor first since that would make it easier to move around. She gathered the rest of the old magazines and newspapers and set them into their appropriate piles, then pushed the crates against the opposite side, coughing the whole time. She was going to do the same with the old trunks. She reached for the beautifully carved trunk in the center of the room and felt an odd push-pull, as though she were compelled toward the trunk and away from it at the same time. Grace shook her head. Push-pull, my eye, she thought as she leaned to open the trunk. She reached for the latch, which was unlocked, and pressed the rounded top open. Nothing. No fireworks. No singing angels. Just a plain old trunk with some white books inside.

"See," Grace said aloud. "You've been imagining crazy things since you got here. There's nothing there."

She sighed as she stepped away. She would examine the contents another time. She removed the scrunchie from her wrist, pulled her hair into a ponytail, exhaled, and sat on the dusty floor. Maybe the next thing I should do is clean, she thought as she wheezed. Grace surveyed the cleared floor and nodded. Her phone buzzed and she smiled at the name on the screen.

"Grace, dear? Are you all right? That strange energy I've been feeling from you was even stronger last night, so strong I felt myself being pulled toward Idaho. What on earth is happening there?"

"I still don't understand how you always know."

"I just do. Now what's happening? Did you go somewhere? I feel like your energy is traveling."

"I haven't been anywhere, Grandma. It's just…"

"Just what, Grace? You have to tell me."

"I feel like everything I've said to you since I've been in Idaho has been ridiculous."

"The worst thing you can do is not let me help you when I can."

"All right, then. I keep thinking I hear these sounds. Sometimes I think they're animals and sometimes I think they're voices."

"Where do you hear them?"

"There's a red barn near Annabelle's and I heard something there. Then there was this house near the Boise River."

"Can you tell what the voices are saying?"

"No. I can tell they're men's and women's voices, but I can't make out the words. Other times the sounds are bounding echoes."

"Bounding echoes?"

"I don't know how else to describe it."

"All right." Olivia was silent while she considered. "Do you have any visions that accompany these sounds?"

"Well, I mean, there's the oil painting Annabelle has of white-covered wagons. Then I had the strangest sensation that I saw myself in an old photograph wearing old-fashioned clothing." Grace waited for Olivia to say something but it was silent on the Massachusetts end. "Annabelle told me that her family came over on the Oregon Trail, and she's been teaching me to cook the way the pioneers did. That probably has something to do with these crazy ideas." Still silent. "Grandma? I don't sound ridiculous, do I?"

"No, of course, you don't. I'm just trying to make sense of what you're telling me."

"This isn't normal."

"I wouldn't worry so much about normal, dear. Everyone's normal is different. You're hearing sounds and seeing visions of yourself in the past. That's your normal right now and we need to figure out what it means. Yes, Annabelle bringing up her family on the Oregon Trail might be triggering your reactions, but what you're describing sounds more intense than the power of suggestion. And you're awake while you're hearing these sounds and seeing yourself in the past?"

"Yes." Grace heard Olivia lock a jingling door. "Are you at work, Grandma? We can talk later."

"Nonsense. There's nothing more important than my granddaughter. I just closed the shop for the rest of the day. People can buy their incense and crystals tomorrow. Now," Grace heard the cash register snap closed, "obviously, I need more information before I can say for certain what's happening, but since these experiences aren't dreams I'd say the past is trying to communicate with you."

"Grandma, that's pretty out there, even for you."

"Is it? I'm always out there." Olivia laughed, and so did Grace. "Oh, my dearest one, there's a whole world you can't begin to fathom. It's the invisible world, dear. It's magic."

"You say that every time you're talking about something that doesn't have an explanation."

"Magic is an explanation."

"If you say so."

"I've told you before that the universe will teach us whatever we need to know when we need to know it, and it will send the message in whatever way it thinks will best get through. The universe tries to teach us every day, but we need an open heart to hear what it's saying. So the question becomes, what message do you need, Grace Wentworth?"

"I don't know."

"I think you do. It may not be obvious yet, but I think what you need is already inside you somewhere, somewhere you don't even know exists. But you're your mother's daughter, and the ability for the universe to communicate with you is strong. We need to be patient, I think, but whatever message you need will make itself known in time."

Olivia was silent again and for a moment Grace thought their connection was lost. Then Olivia said, "How would you like a visit from your old grandmother, Grace? I've never been to Idaho and I've heard it's beautiful there. I'll ask Nancy to run the shop for me for a week—she won't mind. Maybe there's something another set of eyes would spot that you can't see because you're too close to it."

"I'm sure it's just foolish nonsense, Grandma."

"Maybe. But it would be nice to see you. So how about it?"

"Of course. I'd love to see you too. I'm sure Annabelle won't mind if you stay here."

"Wonderful. Now, have you told your parents about the voices and the old photograph?"

"Of course not. They'd never understand something like this."

Olivia laughed. "How little we know our own parents."

GRACE RAN TO OLIVIA PHILLIPS AS SHE EXITED THE BOISE AIRPORT and they hugged tightly.

"Grace." Olivia wouldn't let go. "Every time I see you again it's like I've forgotten that you're a grown woman now. I still think of you as the little girl your mother wheeled into the Witches Lair in her stroller, reaching out to touch everything she saw."

"I still want to touch everything in your shop, Grandma. You promised me a psychic reading the last time I was there. Mom told me you gave her a few readings when she first arrived in Salem."

"How much did she tell you about those readings?"

"You know how Mom and Dad like to keep secrets."

"Yes, I do." Olivia looked the same as always with her comforting, motherly smile, her steel-gray eyes that could bore a hole through to your very soul, the metaphysical aura that hovered over her wherever she went. She was in her usual attire with her silver hoop earrings, billowy blouse, peasant skirt, and Birkenstocks. On the way to Nampa they stopped at a grocery store for some essentials.

Olivia laughed when she saw Annabelle's house in the cul-de-sac. "It's charming, Grace. It's quirky and it has character, which is more than you can say for most of the dime-a-dozen houses you see nowadays."

Grace helped Olivia carry her luggage inside. Of course, Annabelle was out, where, Grace didn't know. Casey trotted over, sniffed Olivia's outstretched hand, and he seemed pleased with the new visitor as he sniffed her skirt and her Birkenstocks. Olivia let out a long, low whistle as she surveyed the curio cabinets.

"My," Olivia said. "There's tchotchkes galore here."

"I don't think anyone has thrown anything out of this house for more than a century."

"Is the house that old?"

"Apparently this house has been moved and rebuilt from the original structure. Annabelle's family remodeled the original house when they moved to Nampa. Originally, they settled closer to the Boise River after traveling the Oregon Trail."

They put Olivia's groceries into the refrigerator and gave Casey his lunch. After a quick salad, Olivia gestured at the curio cabinets in the living room. "We might as well get started."

"You don't need to help clean, Grandma."

"I'm here and I prefer being useful. Let's go."

Grace handed Olivia a large plastic bag and together they tackled the newspapers and magazines on the shelf over the sofa.

"I should get back to the attic," Grace said. "I've made pretty good progress up there and I might as well get it done. Then at least I'll have one part of the house cleaned up."

"Let's finish down here and then we can go up to the attic." Olivia looked through the window at the garden. "That's a nice yard, actually, bigger than mine in Salem."

"It's a nice house if you can look past the mess." Grace flipped through the magazine in her hand, decided it was too ragged to be of interest to anyone, and tossed it into the trash. "Actually, it's going to be my house. Annabelle said she wants to leave it to me."

"Grace, that's wonderful. And very generous of Annabelle. That might explain why it was so important to her that you came to visit this summer."

"You don't think Mom will be upset that Annabelle is leaving the house to me instead of her?"

"Of course not. Your mother will be thrilled, I promise you."

They worked in companionable silence, dropping the ragged newspapers and magazines into the plastic bags. After they finished both shelves they took a break.

"I know we've talked about my parents' secrets before, Grandma, but I want to know—do you know what their secrets are?" The question had bubbled up out of nowhere, but not really. She just hadn't intended to be so blunt about asking. But there it was, and Olivia didn't seem bothered by the turn of their conversation.

"I've known your parents a long time, Grace. I know them pretty well. They still haven't told you anything at all?"

"Once Mom let it slip that she was married to another man before Dad. I couldn't get her to tell me anything else about it. I still can't imagine Mom with anyone else."

"Neither could she, apparently, which is why the marriage didn't last."

"She was married to that other guy for ten years. That's a long time to be unhappily married."

"As someone who has been unhappily married several times, I can tell you it's not always easy to end a marriage even when you know it's the right thing to do. Sometimes, no matter how unhappy you are, there's a voice inside you telling you to stay because to end it would be giving up, and we're taught to keep going, keep pushing, keep at it no matter what. For too many people it's better to pretend they're happy even if they're not. Don't ever do that, Grace. Promise me you'll always live your truth, no matter how hard, no matter what others tell you. Be brave. Your mother was brave to end her first marriage, and then she went to Salem and found your father."

"Her *beshert*."

"Yes. And I want the same for you. I want you to be crazy and creative and bold. I want you to love fully, with your whole heart." Olivia patted Grace's hand as she had when Grace was a child. "Do you promise me, Grace? Do you promise to find the magic in your life and grasp it with both hands?"

"I promise, Grandma. But I still don't understand what that has to do with why Mom and Dad keep secrets from me. And I think I'm a part of their secrets somehow."

"It's not always easy to tell the truth, Grace, no matter how much you want to or no matter how much you love the person. Sometimes we're afraid the truth is so strange that we won't be believed. Kind of like the way you were afraid to tell me about the voices and your vision of the old photograph." Grace nodded. "Come. Let's finish some more in the living room before my old back gives out."

Grace grabbed more black bags, and together they tackled the curio cabinet near the window. As they examined the kitsch pieces, Olivia stopped to look at Grace. "You, dear, are the perfect embodiment of both your parents. You have your father's gold hair and blue eyes, your mother's features and curls. You're logical like your father and intuitive like your mother. You're such a treasure to them. When they found you again, I thought their hearts would burst with joy."

"What do you mean found me again?"

Olivia lowered some newspapers into a trash bag, her eyes firmly on her task. "Forgive me, dear. It's been a long day and I just realized that I really am very tired. Let's tackle some more tomorrow." Olivia dropped onto the sofa and rested her head against the cushion. Grace thought she had fallen asleep until her eyes flashed open. "The answers you're looking for are here."

"What answers, Grandma?"

But that was all she said. Olivia had fallen asleep, gently snoring. Grace kissed Olivia's forehead, covered her in a quilt from the back of the sofa, and she sat for a moment, wondering what to do with herself. She remembered the attic and decided to get more work done up there.

She rummaged through the kitchen for her usual supplies, then checked on Casey, who was asleep in his usual afternoon spot on the rug near the unlit fireplace. Back in the attic, she turned the flashlight on and spotted the open trunk that seemed to be waiting for her like an old friend with outstretched arms.

"All right," Grace said to the trunk. "Let's see what you've got there."

She reached for one of the white books and shouted as a shock rocked her from head to toe. It must be static, she thought, and she managed to lift the book on her second try, ignoring the fact that her fingertips were numb. She turned the book over in her hands, gingerly so she wouldn't feel the throbbing again.

The book was well made—hardbound embossed white leather. Something struck her as familiar as she flipped the pages though she couldn't say what that was. A cursory glance revealed the book to be a journal, possibly a very old one from the way the once-white pages yellowed and loosened from their binding. The budding historian in Grace grew curious and she wondered if this was an important journal, one historians should examine to see if it had anything of value to share.

She wanted to know the secrets contained in those pages. She sat with her back against the wall and began reading. Before she finished the first page she felt lightheaded, unable to concentrate, as if the earth were drifting away from her, or perhaps she was the one drifting away. She felt weightless. And then she felt nothing.

THE FRONT DOOR CREAKED OPEN AND OLIVIA'S HEAD POPPED UP AT the sound. She nodded as Annabelle removed the blue kerchief from her head.

"Hello, Annabelle," Olivia said. "It's good to see you again. We haven't seen each other since James and Sarah's wedding."

Annabelle nodded in Olivia's direction and bent over to pet Casey. "It's good to see you again, Olivia. It's nice that Grace can make time for both her grandmothers." There was something curt in Annabelle's tone that Olivia didn't want to trifle with. "Where is our granddaughter, by the way?"

Olivia looked around the room. "I'm not sure. We cleaned up a bit down here and then I must have dozed off. And then…"

Olivia stood up. Goose pimples covered her neck and arms and she shivered. Something was…what? Something was wrong? "Where's Grace?"

"Is there an echo in here? I just asked that question."

Olivia grabbed Annabelle's arms. "I'm serious, Annabelle. Where's Grace?"

"And I'm serious when I tell you I don't know. I just walked in the house five minutes ago. You saw me." Annabelle's painted-on eyebrows bounced to her hairline. "Why?"

"I'm not sure. Something in Grace's energy is very wrong. I can feel it. We need to find Grace."

"Let's start with her room."

When Olivia and Annabelle arrived at the staircase Casey was sitting at the bottom, his nose lifted toward the loft.

"Grace?" Annabelle called. No answer. "Grace? Where could she have gone?"

"While we were cleaning downstairs she mentioned something about the attic, that she wanted to get back to it because she had been working to clear it out."

"The attic? She went to the attic? Oh, Olivia, we have to get to her first."

"First for what?" Olivia shook Annabelle's shoulders so hard Annabelle's hair combs fell to the floor. "What aren't you telling me?"

Annabelle kept shaking her head, looking up, down, through the kitchen, into the living room. Almost, Olivia thought, as if she had seen a ghost.

"Annabelle?"

Annabelle's pale complexion was ashen and she clutched at Olivia, too unsteady to stand. "I'm fine, Olivia. Just fine. We have to find Grace." She tripped over her own feet as she pulled herself up the stairs. When they arrived in the loft Annabelle was so shaken she dropped onto the bed. The attic stairs were down but Grace wasn't there.

"Grace!" Olivia called. "Grace!"

"She's not here."

Olivia climbed the stairs, coughing as the attic dust squeezed her lungs, squinting to see in the darkness. All she could make out through the hazy light were piles of magazines, newspapers, books, old crates pressed against the wall, and one nicely carved wooden trunk with the top open. A white leather book lay open beside it. She jumped at the sound of Annabelle's voice.

"She's not here, Olivia. I wish to sweet heaven she was, but she's not here."

CHAPTER 7

Olivia awoke before dawn. In truth, she hardly slept. She might have dozed off, but the day before had been too much. Even for Olivia, who was more at home in the metaphysical world than the physical one, it was too much.

Olivia paced to the window and slid the glass open. Idaho was so quiet, or at least it was a different kind of quiet than she was used to in Salem. In Massachusetts, Olivia commiserated with the sea, with the moon, with the arcane light that gave Salem a fae-like glow. Olivia loved Salem's steady flow of magic, a magic she had known her whole life, and her mother had known, and her mother, back to Miriam, her ancestor, who had come to the Massachusetts Bay Colony from England, named as a witch and lucky to make it out alive. Only it was true—Miriam was a witch. She had magic, and she had passed her conjuring skills onto her descendants, down to Olivia and then Olivia's daughter Jennifer. It was only Miriam's magic, and the magic of her sisters, that kept them out of the dungeons and away from the hangman during the witch hunts in 1692.

Olivia looked out the window, saw the empty street, saw the

purple dawn on the horizon. She stuck her head outside and breathed in—manure. Olivia coughed, shut the window, and sat on the bed.

"Well, Miriam," Olivia said to the ceiling, "what do you think of all this? What has happened to our dear Grace? You helped her father, and her mother, and now Grace needs you. I certainly need your guidance."

The thought of Grace squeezed Olivia's heart like a tight fist. She couldn't breathe and grasped her chest, caught in the throes of a terrible panic.

Grace. What has happened to Grace?

Leaving her bathrobe and slippers behind, Olivia ran across the hall, through the living room and the kitchen. There must be some element she overlooked. She stood on the bottom stair leading up to Grace's room and stopped. What was she looking for? She didn't know. She took one step, then another, and another, and stopped again. She heard clattering and saw Annabelle bustling in the kitchen, cleaning the stove top, washing the dishes, trying not to be obvious with her glances toward Olivia. But Olivia had nothing to say to Annabelle, or if she did it included a fair number of obscenities, and it never pays to talk to someone when you're angry. Olivia had seen too many others learn that lesson the hard way.

She went into Grace's room and searched for anything that might give her a clue about what happened. Grace's bed hadn't been slept in. Her belongings were there—her wallet, her phone, her money. The bathroom was empty. The attic stairs were still down.

"Grace?"

No answer.

Olivia's heart pounded a furious rhythm. It was completely out of character for Grace to disappear without telling anyone where she had gone. Oh, my God, Olivia thought. James and Sarah. What am I going to say to James and Sarah?

Olivia climbed up to the attic and looked around, hoping that some magical clue would jump out suddenly, shouting, "Here I am! You missed me!"

She spotted the finely carved trunk again, the one with the dark wood that looked like it had been lacquered but time had its way with it. She saw the one white leather book, glanced inside, and saw several more white books, along with some of far lesser quality made of cardboard and glue. Upon closer inspection, Olivia saw that the trunk was chipped and decaying, but it was holding up well. It was quite dusty, like the rest of the room. Olivia went to the bathroom, wet a washcloth, and wiped decades of dust from the top, bottom, and sides. The box was too large to lift so she sat beside it and pressed her face as close to it as she could, listening, hoping it would whisper its secrets.

"Do you have something to tell me?"

The trunk stayed silent. She admired the hand carved accents, the swirls and flowers along the sides. Someone had spent a lot of time and care creating this. After all this time the swirls held their lines. With a flicker of recognition, Olivia realized that there were initials carved into the lower right-hand corner, well-hidden within the flourishes. The letters had been nicked over time, but Olivia was certain she made out a G, W, and C.

She picked up one of the aged white books, carefully flipped through the pages since they looked ready to fall out, and realized it was a journal. She flipped through the other white books and realized they were journals as well with similar handwriting, so they must have been written by the same person. Something about the handwriting made her pause. She heard two gruff barks, peered down the attic stairs, and there was the floppy-eared dog staring at her.

"Are you spying for Annabelle then?" Olivia picked the dog up, huffing under his weight, and put him down in the attic. "That's all right. I imagine she's guessed what I'm doing up here."

She grabbed one of the journals and began reading. By the end of the fifth page she knew.

"Oh, my God. Grace."

She carried Casey down the stairs and sat on Grace's bed. She closed her eyes. For the first time in her life, she was unsure what to do. She felt some strange pull, like an invisible forcefield circling her. She thought she was being lassoed. She slowed her breathing and tried to empty her mind. She imagined herself using an eraser across a whiteboard that held every thought she had ever known. Usually, that worked when she wanted to contact the spirit world, but she couldn't clear the barrage of images away.

The forcefield moved from the air into her veins. She jumped off the bed and paced the loft, shaking her arms as a way to rid herself of the excess energy. When she felt settled some she sat back on the bed. Again, she tried to still her breath and listen.

"Is anyone there?" Nothing. "Is anyone there?"

The cocker spaniel lifted his ears as he listened. When no one answered he put his head back down.

Olivia shook her fist at the ceiling. "So you won't answer, then? Fine. If you won't come to me then I'll wait for you."

She waited and still nothing. Whatever presence she had felt was gone.

"Oh, Grace." Olivia sank back onto the bed, her hand clutching her chest, pressing hard to keep her heart inside.

OLIVIA NEEDED TIME TO COMPOSE HERSELF. SHE HAD TO CALM down, think rationally, consider what she had learned. She wasn't sure why she was so rattled. Nothing should surprise her anymore.

She made her way back to her room and changed into a brown gypsy skirt, white peasant blouse, and she pulled her close-cropped silver hair back in a flowery hair band. She slipped on her Birkenstocks and steadied herself. There was only one person who knew more about what happened to Grace than she had let on. She also happened to be making coffee and frying bacon.

Olivia walked into the kitchen and pet the top of Casey's head. Annabelle hardly seemed to notice her, involved as she was in watching the coffee drip, splash by splash, into the pot. Olivia wasn't sure what to say so instead she pulled her packaged tofu from the refrigerator.

"Feeding a rabbit, are you?"

Olivia looked at Annabelle. "Excuse me?"

Annabelle pointed her chin at the package. "Looks like rabbit food. You sure you don't want some bacon? There's plenty."

"Oh, no, thank you, Annabelle. If I could just borrow a frying pan so I can scramble my tofu that would be perfect."

"Whatever you wish." Annabelle pulled a frying pan from the cupboard and handed it to Olivia. Olivia chopped the tofu into chunks, set them into the hot frying pan, and whisked them so they resembled scrambled eggs. Annabelle plucked the bacon strip by strip from the skillet and set them on a plate, tapping the slices with a paper towel.

"So you're one of those viggins then?"

"Viggins? Oh, vegans." Olivia laughed. "As a matter of fact, I am."

"Won't find many of those in Idaho."

"I love potatoes so I'm sure I'll be fine here."

Annabelle nodded. She poured two cups of coffee and the two women sat across from each other at the doily covered table. Olivia wanted to ask Annabelle something, anything, that would help her understand what had happened to Grace, but Olivia was lost for words. She looked through the garden window to the green expanse of the backyard, at the the growing tomato plants, the roses lining the border of the flower bed, the large tree with the overhanging leaves.

"You have a lovely backyard," Olivia said. "Sarah helped me get my little garden in Massachusetts going. Your daughter has quite a green thumb."

"Gardening is the only thing Sarah and I ever had in common. Well, that and cooking. Sarah and I would spend hours in the garden together talking about some plant or vegetable or other. She was always good at growing things." Annabelle held the plate of bacon toward Olivia. "Are you sure you don't want some? That doesn't look very filling."

"You're very kind, dear, but I promise you, I'm quite happy."

Annabelle shrugged as if such a thing couldn't be possible. They continued in silence, Olivia taking comfort in the rural scene outside as she thought through various ways to begin this uncomfortable conversation. Annabelle refilled Olivia's coffee cup and Olivia nodded her thanks.

"I suppose you're wondering what I meant last night when I said Grace has gone a very long way away," Annabelle said.

Olivia sipped her coffee. "I've been reading through those white leather journals. I haven't read them all, and they're not dated so it's hard to tell the order in which they were written, but I think I've read enough to understand. A little bit, anyway."

Annabelle fumbled for the green lighter beside her. Her fingers trembled as she plucked a cigarette from the pack and slid it between her lips. It took three tries to light it, her hand was so unsteady.

"Annabelle? How did you know? I mean, without looking into it, without asking questions, you knew what had happened to Grace."

Annabelle's face was hazy through the cloud of smoke she exhaled. "I had, well, I had a hunch that this might happen. We have a family legend about such a thing, and, well…"

"Have you read the journals?"

"No, I haven't. I've always been afraid to read them."

"Why?"

"Because I was afraid of what I'd find. But I've known about the legend all my life."

Olivia slammed her cup onto the table, splattering coffee across her plate. "You mean you knew this could happen?"

Annabelle stumped out her half-smoked cigarette. "I didn't know for sure. I suspected it, that's all."

"When did you start suspecting it?"

"After I saw the photograph. And then Grace arrived and despite..."

"What photograph?"

Annabelle continued as if she hadn't heard. "Despite the circumstances, I thought that if the legend were true it had to be her but I still wasn't sure."

"Until yesterday."

Olivia exhaled. She didn't want to lose her temper, not now. She wiped the spilled coffee away with her napkin, her detective seeking clues look pulling her motherly features into taut concentration.

"I'm just thinking out loud here, Annabelle, but I'm wondering if it might have been a good thing to warn Grace, to tell her that something like this might happen. Only instead of saying something to her, something that might have helped her, you said nothing and now..." Olivia waved her hand at nothing, which is exactly what she thought they had as far as the ability to help Grace—nothing. She poured herself more coffee as she considered. "Your suspicions were based on a family legend. That's very poetic. I'm surprised you considered that it could even be true."

"The story has been passed down the generations, and I know I should have..." Annabelle shook her head. "You're right, Olivia. I'm not into voodoo or magic or hippie dippie anything. When she arrived I saw the resemblance right away but I didn't see how..." She squinted at the air. "If you don't mind my saying, Olivia, you don't seem surprised by the hippie dippie magic part of it. You're worried about Grace, I know, but the rest of it? It's like you already believed such things are possible."

"Of course such things are possible."

"So you're one of those hippie dippie types?"

"I beg your pardon?"

"You certainly look the part with your long skirts and sandals and jangling jewelry. You eat like one with all your viggin foods."

Olivia looked at her scrambled tofu, covered with coffee and untouched on her plate. "It's tasty, healthy food."

"I'll have take your word for it. But you're into that new age madness with the dream catchers and the choclas?"

"Chakras? I don't know if Sarah told you, but I have a little shop in Salem that sells books of charms and spells, tarot cards, candles, and crystals. It's called the Witches Lair."

"No, Sarah never told me. She never tells me anything. But you seriously believe in magic?"

"I believe in magic the way I believe you're sitting before me now. I've felt magic's guiding hand carrying me through my life. I've watched magic bring loving souls together and heal broken hearts. Magic is in the invisible air we breathe, and magic is the invisible love that makes life worth living. I don't need to see something to know it's real, Annabelle. Magic can be as plain as the nose on your face if you take the time to see it."

Annabelle sighed. "It's hard for me to believe in such things. I'm a practical woman, you see."

"I don't doubt that."

"And practical as I am, I think when you get to a certain age you ought to have an ounce of sense about you, that's all."

"I'd like to think I'm pretty sensible. Just because something isn't logical doesn't mean it's not sensible, and deep down I think you know that's true. That's why you never mentioned the family legend to Sarah or Grace. It wasn't that you thought it was rubbish and could never be true. You were afraid that the story *was* true and the magic might happen. And you didn't know how to face it."

Olivia pressed herself upright. She felt frozen, as though her body wouldn't obey her brain. She wanted to pace, to scream, to punch the wall. What could she do to help Grace? Finally, she said, "James and Sarah's souls are intertwined for eternity. They were apart for a long time but they were reunited in Salem. That's why Sarah had to go to Salem—to find James."

Annabelle's stern expression softened into something Olivia thought was sadness. "And you think that has something to do with what's happened to Grace?"

"I think Grace might have a similar destiny as her mother, yes."

"Sarah thinks of you as a mother." Annabelle didn't sound accusatory. She was matter of fact about it—this is a truth of life the way the sky is blue and one and one equal two.

"That makes me happy because I think of Sarah as my daughter and Grace as my granddaughter. I don't mean that as any offense to you, of course."

"I don't take it as offense. Sarah and I have always been different people. She's more like her father. "

Pieces to this puzzle were still missing, Olivia knew. Something wasn't right. Grace's experience was similar to Sarah's but not exactly the same. What was different? She tapped her temples as she considered. And then everything she learned straightened itself out in her mind.

"Oh, my dear Grace." Olivia pointed at Annabelle. "And you knew!" Annabelle reached for another cigarette but her pack was empty so instead she rattled her fork on her plate in an off-beat tune. "That poor girl is probably frightened nearly to her death, right this very minute, Annabelle."

Annabelle searched the kitchen drawers until she found a full packet of Virginia Slims. She lit her cigarette and the flaming red nicotine seemed to soothe her. "I know I should have told her as soon as she arrived in Idaho, but I figured there would be no way she'd find her way to the journals in the attic."

"So the magic is connected to the journals?"

"That's what the family legend says." Annabelle took a long drag on her cigarette, and her hand shook as she knocked off the ashes. "Now look, Olivia, I may not have handled things in exactly the right way, but I did what I could to help her. I taught her to make biscuits and johnnycakes and bacon-fried toast. I was going to teach her to sew but we hadn't gotten to it yet."

"No," Olivia said. "There's something else happening here. Something we don't understand yet. Wait a minute." Olivia stretched her hands toward Annabelle as if she were pleading. "This is all your doing. The only reason Grace came here in the first place was because you invited her. You wanted her to come to Idaho. And then once she arrived you started teaching her about your family on the westward trail and you even showed her some homesteading skills while you were at it. And all along you knew!"

"Like I said, I didn't know for sure. I didn't believe it was possible."

"Is that why you invited her here? To see if the legend was true? And what was that about a photograph?"

"Well..."

"You knew your family legend was very likely about Grace. But you didn't tell her!" Olivia felt her face glow like coals and she covered her eyes with her hands in an attempt to cool her temper. She wasn't used to anger and now she understood why it could be such a dangerous emotion. Anger prompted you into things you knew you would regret.

She would not be lured into anger. She used her magic for good. She helped the preternatural find their way to wherever they were supposed to be. She helped souls make sense of the complex cosmos. Even when she came across the worst the universe had to offer she held onto her sanity because she knew she could use her powers to heal. She tried to settle her breathing again, and again it offered no solace. Instead, she cried. It was some time before she could speak.

"You kept the truth from her, Annabelle. You used Grace like some secret experiment to see if your family legend was real, and now my poor Grace..."

Annabelle's sorrow snapped into petulance as her painted-on eyebrows lowered to her nose. "I wouldn't get all high and mighty about secrets there, Olivia. It's not like you're so innocent in that matter, or Sarah or James either."

"What on earth does that mean?"

"I mean, how come Grace is 22 years old and she doesn't know she's adopted?"

Olivia collapsed into the chair nearest the window. A bird singing from a nearby tree gave her strength. "It's not as simple as that."

"Hey, Grace, you're adopted. Sounds simple enough to me."

"There's more to James and Sarah's story than you know. And Grace's too."

"You don't say." Annabelle stamped her cigarette out on her breakfast plate. She looked at Olivia under hooded lids and pointed her head toward the loft. "There's something I want to show you in the attic."

"The trunk with the white journals? I've seen it."

"Not that one. Another one."

Olivia nodded. Whatever fury had boiled her blood was gone. She only knew one thing for certain. She had to do everything in her power to help Grace.

CHAPTER 8

GRACE

J clutched my head while the world circled away from me. I felt as though I tripped down a flight of stairs and I fell, weightlessly, through a vortex—an all-consuming confusion where I forgot my own name. I tumbled down—down, down, down, forever and ever, until the spiraling stopped and my body ached with the collision. I opened my eyes, then closed them again until everything stopped spinning. I stretched out my arms to gather my balance and managed to stand upright, but barely. Everywhere around me was sparse, rural beauty, a panorama of wide, open spaces.

My muscles spasmed until I was ready to heave. I bent over, my hands on my knees. I tried to settle my breath while I gasped for air. I shuddered but I wasn't cold, and I felt so airy I wasn't sure I had a body. But I had eyes. And I could see. With a downward glance I saw that I wore a long dress of finely spun blue cotton I remembered from somewhere. From a dream? With a touch of my hand I found my hair gathered in a braid that fell down my back and my eyes were shielded from the high sun by a blue bonnet of the same finely spun cotton. I've come dressed for the party.

These must be the ridiculous things that cross your mind when you're dreaming. All right, I thought. Let's see what this dream is about. It ought to be good since I never remember my dreams. When I was steady enough to inspect my surroundings I saw an old-fashioned town square in the distance. Slow-trotting horses clomped along the flat dirt road as their drivers checked the store fronts for the ones they needed. I jumped out of the way of a cart whose driver seemed content to run me over. He didn't even glance my way as he passed.

I slapped my hands to my cheeks in an attempt to keep my head in its place as I searched my surroundings—a befuddled owl turning round and round, trying to gauge everywhere at once. Squat wooden structures lined the dusty road—an apothecary, a barber, a saloon, a general store, a saddler, a harness maker. Nearby were the wheelwrights, the blacksmiths, and there was a tanners further down the way.

Pioneer-looking people bustled about their business, rushing from here to there as though time was wasting away. Hollers from the men buying and selling livestock in an open field wafted over the conversations of those buying weapons and wagons and those leaving the general store with sacks of flour and cornmeal they then shoved into the backs of uncovered wagons. The noise both- ered me most. I tried to block out the shouts, the laughter, the haggling, the whinnying horses, and the bellowing oxen.

One man tried to pull a mule, as stubborn as its reputation, as it dug its hooves into the ground. The man yanked the rope, but the mule didn't budge. The man grasped the harness, but the mule didn't budge. The man yelled something at the poor animal, who was probably frightened half to death by the cacophony of busy- ness and didn't know what to do about any of it.

I understood how the mule felt. I was also frightened into paralysis. Everything around me was so alive, so vibrant, but there was too much of it. With the press of people everywhere there was nowhere to escape. I felt as if heavy hands tightened around my throat, making it difficult to breathe. How do you handle the anxiety of being caught in a dream you don't understand? I gathered whatever energy I could muster and pushed past the crush of people, making my way toward the general store where it was busiest of all, but at least there was a space between that and the barber shop where I could hide and think.

I stayed hidden for some time. Then I realized that I wasn't going to accomplish anything waiting behind the barber shop, so I steadied myself and headed back into the commotion of the square. With all the movement surrounding me, the rolling covered wagons, the herding livestock, the shopping men and women, I realized that I was alone in a sea of people. A man I passed mentioned something to his companion about being glad to see the back of Independence, it was such a dusty place after all, and I decided that must be where I am. Though it didn't feel much like Independence to me.

I had nothing to do, nowhere to go, and no one to talk to, so I walked. The sunlight reflected like mirrors off the rocky ground and I pulled the brim of my bonnet closer to my nose. I caught a glimpse of myself off a nearby window, still amazed by my blue dress. With a modest peek beneath my hem I found undergarments of a cotton chemise, cotton pantalets, a laced-up corset, and two petticoats. Confused is not the word I'd use to describe how I felt. Muddled? Bewildered? I'd need a thesaurus to help me, but I don't happen to have one handy.

Suddenly, over the din, I heard a voice that sounded strangely familiar though I couldn't place it. I searched for the speaker and found him, a dark-haired young man at least a head taller than those surrounding him.

"When are you leaving, Cooper?" a gray-bearded man asked. He was an imposing figure, this gray-bearded man—more broad than tall, and his shirt was so thin his well-worked muscles were obvious. His eyes were small, his features serious.

"In two days, I reckon," the dark-haired young man said.

"Everyone says now's the best time to start and I'm all for starting at the best time. It's been warm for a bit now and the grass has grown enough for the animals to eat their fill along the way, yet it's still early enough for us to make it through before the snowfall in the winter makes the mountains too hard to pass."

From the level way the gray-bearded man held the young man's gaze, I guessed he wasn't one to be trifled with. He nodded as though consulting with himself. "So then the train is sorted?"

The young man nodded. "I thought you've already decided to join our train. We have you listed as one of our wagons."

"Oh, I'm coming. But I have questions. Your brother-in-law's to be the captain, I hear. And his brother Hiram's to be the guide. That ought to come in handy, everything being all in the family."

"Are you implying nepotism, Moses Johnstone?" the young man asked.

"I'm just saying it will come in rather handy for you, Matthew Cooper, and I want to make sure the rest of us are heard while important decisions are being made."

Young Mr. Cooper turned with some impatience toward the speaker. "What will come in handy is making it to Oregon alive. Hiram was a fur trader for some time and he's made it back and forth across the trail more times than he can count. He knows how to get to Oregon. And Amos will be a fine captain. He'll do everything he can to make sure every person in his charge is as safe as can be. He'll make sure we listen to Hiram. Besides, you know perfectly well I'm not the one who hired Hiram. The families in the train decided as a group to hire him. And I didn't vote for Amos to be captain because he's my sister's husband. I voted for Amos because he's the most capable, level-headed person I know. I can't think of two men I'd rather have leading us on this expedition. What we're about to do is hard and dangerous and I for one want to give us every opportunity to succeed." He looked at the others, who stared at their boots. "Unless any of you have other ideas."

"And Amos will listen to the other men as well?" Moses asked.

"He'll listen to opinions and take votes when necessary, but as captain Amos has the final say."

Moses Johnstone crossed his arms over his chest. "Hiram's bringing that wife of his?"

"Yes, Mrs. Wetherfield will be joining us."

Despite his youth, Mr. Cooper stood toe-to-toe with the grizzled Moses Johnstone. He held Johnstone's gaze until the older man turned toward a braying mule, speaking to it with a softness I would not have associated with him. Finally, Johnstone asked, "So who's going to be the officers?"

"There's still some argument over that," Matthew Cooper said. "The final vote is tonight, but right now it looks like Lee Tappertit and Sylvester Banning."

"And you."

"If the others elect me, then yes, I'll serve as an officer."

Moses Johnstone smirked. "It's like I said. It comes in handy having your brothers-in-law as the captain and the guide. Helps make sure you're not palavering about all day, all talk and no work."

Young Mr. Cooper shook his head, but he smiled. "I'm hardly the palavering type, Moses Johnstone, and neither are you."

"Thanks to goodness," said Moses. "Otherwise we'll never make it across in time." His small eyes disappeared while his mouth grew narrow. "And we have to make it across in time."

A red-haired, red-bearded man pressed his way into the center of the conversation. "How many wagons in your train, Matthew?"

Matthew thought a moment. "I'm not sure, Wilbur, but Amos said there'll be about 30 families and I don't know how many wagons and livestock. But things have come together and we're as prepared as we'll ever be."

"I can't believe how many people are here," the red-haired man said. "Independence, Missouri has become bigger than New York City. We should have left from St. Joe."

"Been to New York City, have you, Gridley?" asked Moses Johnstone.

"No, but I can read, can't I?"

"Can you?"

Wilbur Gridley took a step toward Moses Johnstone, who pulled his gun from his holster. Wilbur responded in kind. Matthew held out his arms to stop them.

"Stop it, the both of you!" Matthew exhaled in frustration. "Hiram said it's better to leave from Independence so we're leaving from Independence. Now put your weapons away before someone gets hurt." Johnstone and Gridley backed down, holstering their guns and dropping their hands to their sides. Matthew made sure both weapons were gone before he continued. "Everyone who's leaving with us needs to make sure they have everything—their wagons, their tents, their guns, their bullets, saws, mallets, axes, coffee, sugar, flour, cornmeal, bedding, and whatever other supplies they're taking. Amos is starting wagon inspections today, so everyone better be ready."

Wilbur Gridley scratched his red-haired chin. "The only thing I'm still not sure about is traveling on Sundays. I don't think it's right."

"Hiram says we need to travel every day if we're to make it across in time," Matthew said. "You want to end up like the Donner Party?"

The men shook their heads, their expressions grim.

"I don't think I'll ever be convinced about traveling on Sundays," said Wilbur, "but I'm ready for this journey. I can feel the excitement in my very bones. I can't wait to get started."

"Be careful what you wish for, Gridley," Moses said.

I want to know more about this Matthew Cooper, and I find myself drawn to him for a reason I can't name. I have so many questions. Who are you? What are you doing here? And do you know what I'm doing here?

Wilbur Gridley said, "I don't know nothing about nothing with all this." He removed his wide-brimmed hat and scratched his head.

"Stick with me, Wilbur," said Moses. "I'll show you the way West."

"I thought that was Amos and Hiram Wetherfield's job," said Wilbur.

Moses said nothing, his eyes disappearing as he studied the red-haired man.

"All right then." Matthew stepped forward. "Those of you coming along with our train, have your wagons ready for inspection."

As the men departed I mentally scanned through every American history course I've taken, and the only moment that makes sense is the Oregon Trail. Hadn't Matthew mentioned Oregon? Gathering supplies. Preparing wagons. Going West.

Matthew Cooper passed near me as he headed for his next destination. I couldn't help but notice that he's a striking, handsome man with strong but refined features. As he walked he dodged a wandering cow who didn't seem to belong to anyone and he doffed his hat in amused acknowledgement of the animal. He was so close I could see his sea-like eyes, green like water on a dark day. I wanted to call him back, to ask him my questions, but he was gone.

I WALKED TO WHERE THE LAND OPENED IN EVERY DIRECTION, staring into the distance, following the sun's path toward the western horizon. Shimmering gold threaded through the hydrangea blue sky while waves of clouds winked as though they knew where everyone was headed and they would lead the way.

I had nowhere to go, so I walked toward a city of tents. Boxy green wagons in various states of undress were parked every which way. The frenzied atmosphere was punctuated by the excited shouts of children. Oxen and mules grunted as they grazed as they did in Noah's day, two by two, while the sharp smell of linseed oil, wafting from the pristine white canvas covers, hovered in the breeze.

The men slapped each others' arms while the women stood high-shouldered and tight-lipped, surveying their wagons. Some of the women huddled together, their sunbonnets touching so they could hear each other over the cacophony. Whatever comes, we're in this together, their bowed heads seemed to say.

But there was much to be done. The men, when they weren't checking on their livestock or arguing about one thing or another, admired their neighbors' wagons and helped each other pull the canvas cover over the half-circle bows, commiserating over the steep prices, more than $100 for the 4x10 feet of storage on wheels.

An older man, standing near the back of a brand new prairie schooner, said to an older woman, likely his wife, "I've been dreaming of this for years, Loretta, and my moment's finally here."

"Hurrah," Loretta said, without enthusiasm.

Loretta's husband stared side-eyed at their wagon as though he was certain some fault would be discovered too late. He and Loretta peered into the back of their wagon and examined the supplies inside.

A man's graveled voice called, "Amos Wetherfield will be here any minute now. Be ready!"

Men, women, and children scurried about. I felt displaced, caught in some odd half-life where I'm immersed in the moment but still separate from it.

"What on earth is happening?" I said aloud.

"Who said that?" cried a woman's voice.

"I did," I said.

A tired-looking woman brushed unruly strands of brown-gray hair under her bonnet as she turned toward me. She looked me up and down, shrugged, and went back to whatever she was doing, whispering something to the younger woman beside her, her daughter, perhaps. I shrugged back, thinking of sharing a hand gesture or two, but the woman wasn't paying any attention and it wasn't worth the effort. Maybe this is what it's like to dream—you watch things happen around you, you feel like you're a part of what you see, yet you're not really there.

Everyone around me stopped, listening, expectant, but nothing happened. Some of the men exhaled, the smoke from their pipes wafting near their heads, while others grumbled under their breaths. The women grimaced while the children hopped from foot to foot, ready for something to happen even if they weren't sure what. A mule snorted, a sound of derision, and other animals followed suit.

The ground rumbled and everyone turned. An old, awkward Conestoga wagon pulled into view, nearly running over some poor cow's foot as it slid to a lazy stop. The wagon wobbled and I noticed the iron bolts holding the right front wheel to the axel tipping at odd angles. I guessed they must have loosened under the wagon's heavy weight. I spotted Matthew Cooper nearby, his feet apart, his hands on his hips as he spoke to the nervous-looking man in the driver's seat.

"I knew that was you rumbling along before I saw you, Ezra. Come on now. You know you can't take this old boat 2000 miles across an unsteady path with all those mountains and valleys, not to mention the rivers. Conestogas are too big for this trip. I've told you so a hundred times. Not to mention the fact that this girl here," he slapped the driver's seat, "has seen better days and she's packed too tight. This doesn't look safe to me, Ezra. I'm sorry, but it doesn't."

"What's wrong with old Georgietta here?" asked Ezra.

"You call your wagon Georgietta?"

"Why not? It's as good a name as any."

Matthew turned away and steadied himself. Something about Matthew's smile warmed me somewhere deep inside. The wagon creaked and Matthew waved at those nearby to back away.

"Watch out!" he yelled. "This wagon is going to fall!"

A young woman holding her toddler's hand stepped beside me. I didn't think she heard Matthew's warning and I wanted her and her child away from the accident waiting to happen.

"Look out, please!" I said. "That Conestoga is about to tip over."

The toddler grabbed her mother's apron and the mother nodded her thanks to me as she lifted her little girl and rushed away.

Creak! Everyone turned toward the sound.

"The wagon!" Matthew screamed. "Ezra, you get yourself and your mother out of there this instant!"

The Conestoga growled as it shuddered, lurching once to the right and twice to the left, leaving Ezra clutching the reins while a woman screamed from inside.

"It's all right, Ma," Ezra shouted. "Matty's making a fuss is all. The wagon's just settling."

"Settling?" the woman shouted back. "Looky here, Ezra. This ain't no house. A wagon ain't supposed to settle!"

A woman near me clutched her infant to her chest and ran in the opposite direction while others watched in wonder as the old Conestoga griped and grumbled. Then the wagon jolted forward and back as if it were a seesaw. The iron bolts holding the front right wheel finally gave way and the wagon tipped forward until the back wheels were five feet in the air, dropping the curse-filled driver onto the ground while the woman inside screamed.

When the wagon settled, women stood on their toes and peered through the open back, calling, "Mrs. Quigley, are you all right back there? Mrs. Quigley?"

Two taller men reached around the fallen cover and grabbed the older woman, one by each arm. Once they had her safely out of the wagon, a few of the women checked her for injuries. The women touched her gingerly, afraid she was injured.

"Aw, she's fine," said Ezra. "She's strong as an ox, and don't you let her tell you otherwise. She just rides in that old barrow because she's too lazy to walk herself."

"Lazy? Boy, I'll tell you who's lazy. Now who can get me my little cart from inside that mess of a wagon?" One of the men pulled out a small brown barrow with one large wheel on either side. "You tell me I'm lazy, well, I say I'm smarter than you. Who wants to walk all the way to Oregon, I ask you? I got this nice little contraption now and all I got to do is turn the wheels." To demonstrate, Mrs. Quigley sat inside the barrow, which she used like a wheelchair, turning the wheels with her hands and stopping just short of running over her son. "Now you listen here, Ezra. I'll learn you about letting some wagon settle. I'll hide you til the cows come home."

The oxen harnessed to the wagon tongue were struggling since the poor animals had been knocked forward under the strain of the fallen wagon. One looked like it was choking to death until it was freed. Matthew was among those helping the oxen first and Ezra Quigley second.

"You all right there, Ezra?" Matthew called.

Ezra, perhaps in his later 40s and slightly built, coughed out the dust he swallowed when he hit the ground. He stood and knocked the dirt from his denim shirt and linen trousers. A few expletives escaped his mouth as he surveyed his damaged wagon.

"I'm still alive," Ezra said. "Not so sure about old Georgietta here. What the hell happened?"

Mrs. Quigley shooed away the women still trying to help her, as though needing assistance was an affront to her dignity. "You best watch your mouth, there, Ezra. Don't you go taking like that in front of all these goodly folks."

"I just fell out of the damn wagon, Ma! What do you want me to do, a jig?"

"It's your own fault. Everyone said you picked too big a wagon and packed it too tight. How many times did Matty here say you needed a smaller, sturdier vehicle but you knew better, didn't you?

Stubborn like a mule, just like your pa. Who on earth expects to drive a ruinated old wreck like that across the plains and brings a piano along for the ride? Leave it to your father to leave behind a son who's a half-wit."

"Forget all that, Ma. How in dangnation are we supposed to get to Oregon now?"

"Dangnation? Boy, let me tell you about dangnation. Dangnation is having a good for nothing son who can't tell which end is which."

"Come on, Ma. You can't talk to me like that. I'm 48 years old!"

"Forty-eight in rabbit years."

"What does that mean?"

"It means what I say it means, boy. You've ruinated so many things for me since the time you was born I lost track of them all. Ruinates everything for his old mother. We're headed on a 2000-mile journey West and this corn-pone packs his piano!"

Matthew peered under the lopsided white cover. "There's a piano in there?"

"I thought you liked hearing me play, Ma."

"I do like hearing you play. It's the one thing you do all right. But dangnammit, boy, it's too heavy! What'd you want us to do, eat it on the last leg of the journey? Fried piano, how does that sound to you?"

"Heavens to Betsy." A sturdy-looking man with an impressive walrus mustache, level-eyed and weathered looking, as though he had spent his life in the sun, stood near the fallen wagon. He removed his hat, letting his faded chestnut hair fall about his ears. He stepped into the commotion while those closest moved aside as though this man had a position of respect. He shook his head as he inspected the wreckage. "Well," he said, "at least no one was hurt. Mrs. Quigley could have been badly injured back there. But you know you can't come now, Quigley, don't you? We're moving out at first light, which isn't enough time to get you situated with another wagon and fresh supplies."

Ezra sighed in dramatic fashion. "Yes, Captain Wetherfield. We ain't going nowhere."

"At least it happened before we left," said Mrs. Quigley. "Can you image if this happened once we'd gone? Me and you'd be left out in the prairie to starve to death. People would eat our bones!"

"Nobody wants your old bones, Ma."

"I told you once to watch your mouth, Ezra Quigley. I'll rump your roast in front of every one of these fine folks if you're not careful."

"Ma!"

Amos Wetherfield surveyed the damage once more, shaking his head as though he couldn't believe what he was seeing. Matthew whispered something to Amos, whose eyes grew wide when he spotted the piano under the canvas cover.

"There are still trains leaving in a week or two," Amos said to Ezra. "They're leaving it late, I think, but they're determined to go this year. Maybe you can get yourself settled in time to travel with one of them. Or maybe you can try again next year."

"Next year, fiddlesticks!" said Mrs. Quigley. "My good for nothing son will figure out some way to ruinate that trip for his old mother too. We'll be lucky if we can get back to Ohio from here."

"I'm sure it'll be fine," Matthew said. "Won't it, Ezra?"

Ezra Quigley threw his hands into the air as if he hadn't a clue. He gathered whatever of his belongings he could hold in his arms and piled them together on the ground. He took stock of the mess, his wandering oxen, his broken down wagon, and he muttered several expletives too low for his elderly mother to hear.

The men commiserated with Ezra and the women with his mother until Amos Wetherfield continued his rounds inspecting the wagons. The others followed him with hopeful expressions, certain their own vehicles were well-equipped and safe for the journey.

CHAPTER 9

I was a lost soul, belonging nowhere and needed by no one. It must be time to wake up by now, I thought. An eight-hour night must have passed. This dream has been fun, but now it's time to wake up. Only I didn't.

I wandered around the camp, which had quieted while everyone settled down. The crickets kept their chirrups low out of respect for the travelers. I hovered like a ghost in the background while families lingered near their dwindling fires until they crawled into their tents. From the soft conversations floating across the breeze, I thought there wasn't much sleep to be had. Children whispered to each other. Husbands and wives commiserated. From what little I could make out, it sounded as if the husbands were convincing their wives that going West was the right thing to do for their families.

I noticed a white-covered wagon with Wetherfield painted in red across the top. A woman cooked over a fire and I guessed she must have been one of the Wetherfields' wives. She was a younger woman, maybe in her early 30s, her dark hair parted severely down the middle and pulled into a tight knot at the back of her head, her brown calico dress swinging from side to side as she bustled around.

She was busy, all the women were, cooking, minding the children, mending clothing, and checking and double-checking their supplies. I was standing at the edge of a camp of hundreds of men, women, and children getting ready to travel to the other side of the continent and all I could think was, why am I here? How have I ended up alongside a wagon train bound for the Oregon Trail? If it's a historian's nightmare to dream themselves into the era they study, then surely I should be in Colonial America and not waiting to leave on a trek across the continent. I pinched my wrist as hard as I could to snap myself awake. Instead, I stared at my swelling skin and wondered at the pain.

The night darkened and more people settled into their tents. Muted conversations slipped away. I had nowhere to go so I stayed where I stood, watching the moon's smile fade. I was tired and realized that I didn't have anywhere to lay my head, which was odd, I thought, since I'm sleeping now. Do you feel tired in dreams? I thought of the handsome dark-haired young man, Matthew, and I wondered where he was. And then I remembered that the Wetherfields are his brothers-in-law. I sat behind the Wetherfields' tent, unsure what to do.

Out of the stillness I heard that voice I recognized, like a whisper in my heart.

"Hello."

At first I thought it was my father, who begins every morning with an easy "Hello" for my mother.

"Hello."

The man's voice was more forceful the second time so I turned to meet it. I smiled when I saw Matthew Cooper. The dark-haired young man stood beside me and I looked into his eyes, less like the sea now and more like flashing jade in the darkness. He settled his wide-brimmed hat over his forehead as he watched me, maybe too intently, but I didn't mind his scrutiny.

"Forgive me," he said. "I know it's highly improper for me to speak to you since we haven't been introduced."

"Are you talking to me?"

He looked right and left into the empty darkness. "I should say so, Miss, unless you see someone I don't."

"We haven't met," I said. "We passed each other when the Quigleys' wagon crashed."

"Yes, that's right." He removed his hat, pressed his stubborn dark hair from his eyes again, and bowed in a gentlemanly manner. "We ought to introduce ourselves, I reckon. Matthew Cooper, Miss."

"Grace Wentworth."

"How do you do, Miss Wentworth?"

He knows his manners, I thought. I remembered some of the old-time movies I watched with my father and did my best to replicate the manner of bygone days.

"I'm rather well indeed, Mr. Cooper, thank you kindly. I do hope you're finding your time here to your liking?"

"I reckon it doesn't matter how I like Independence since we won't be here much longer. It's just the jumping off point for the journey, after all." I nodded, unsure how to respond. Should I keep talking like we were in an old western? There was something earnest in his manner that made me think this was no joke to him. "Missouri's a bit over-crowded for my taste," he continued, "but it'll do til we leave, which will be soon enough since we're moving out at dawn." He looked into the distance, then at his boots, then shyly at me. "I saw what you did for Mrs. Preakness and her child when the wagon was ready to fall. You kept them out of danger and I thought someone should say thank you."

"It was nothing. Anyone would have done the same."

"Not anyone." He brushed his hair back once more before settling his hat on his head. "Are you headed West, Miss Wentworth?"

Am I headed West? I felt as if I were trapped in the Oregon

Trail video game I used to play with my dad. He took that game so seriously it was a struggle not to laugh at him. He planned his journeys meticulously, from how much money he should have, to which supplies he'd buy, to what personality and skills his characters needed, to how to make their way across the continent—all with the precision of a chess game. This is what I was doing now—a game of Oregon Trail—and I had to decide how I was going to play.

"Yes," I said. "I'm going West too."

I might as well take the adventurous route while I'm here.

Matthew stepped closer. He hovered just a breath from my face, but I didn't mind. He studied me, and I was just as curious about him.

And then I wondered. Should I continue my conversation with this handsome stranger? The feverish confusion I felt when I first found myself in Independence returned.

"Something is wrong," I said. "I'm not supposed to be here. Something is very wrong."

"Are you well, Miss Wentworth?"

Matthew sat beside me at a courteous distance but close enough to help if I needed it. He allowed me a moment to pull myself together, and I appreciated his silent but friendly presence. Finally, he said, "There's lots of folks feeling the way you do right now, Miss Wentworth. We haven't left Missouri yet, so any one of us can still change our minds and go back to wherever we call home. Going West will be a challenge, but challenges are good, I think. We all need one from time to time." A sadness darkened his features. He kicked the ground with his boot as if to end his thought. "If I may be of any assistance to you, Miss Wentworth, say the word." He snuck another glance at me from under the rim of his hat. "I have the strangest feeling we've met before."

"Like I said, we saw each other when the Quigleys' wagon fell."

"I mean even before today. You look like someone I used to

know, a Miss Gloryanna Winters. Everything about you is the same, even the sound of your voice. You sure you're not her?"

"I think I should know my own name."

Matthew Cooper laughed. "I believe you should, Miss Wentworth."

It had grown so dark I could hardly see him. With the moonlight nearly gone he became a silhouette, a familiar one, as if his likeness had hung on my wall all my life.

"You sound better so I think I can leave you now. You ought to get back to your people before they send out a search party. You can never be too careful these days. Besides, you need whatever rest you can get. We're heading out before first light and we have a big river to cross."

He doffed his hat and made his way into a cluster of tents near the Wetherfields' wagon. He disappeared with one last glance my way as though still wondering if I were Miss Winters after all.

CHAPTER 10

A flat pink line flared across the horizon. Everyone was up and about and the scent of bacon and fried potatoes filled the air. Families sat together for their breakfast and then everyone went to work. Women scrubbed plates, cups, and skillets while men hitched animals, counted their livestock, and checked their wagons. After an intense discussion, the men agreed to travel on Sundays, as Hiram said they must if they were to make good time. To make up for this ungodly travel day, it was agreed that Reverend Aubrey Smith, who was traveling with the train, would read from the Bible Sunday mornings before they departed while each family would be expected to say their prayers every night.

"Our Heavenly Father sees what we're up to," Amos Wetherfield told those who weren't convinced. "He knows we need to get through our journey as quick as we can since we don't want to end up like the Donner Party. The Good Lord will forgive our Sunday travels until we get where we're going."

The men's pained expressions showed that they understood. No one wanted to repeat the poor Donners' experience of being caught in the mountains in the worst of winter with no passable roads and no food to be found. Those who didn't starve to death resorted to cannibalism to survive. Even the men who had been most insistent about not traveling on Sundays quieted down. In the end, every man nodded in agreement except Moses Johnstone, who watched the scene with his hat over his eyes and his arms crossed over his chest.

The oxen and mules stirred impatiently, leaving the wagons in two haphazard lines. The people were equally impatient, their necks craned to see around those in front, their expressions eager, much like dogs anticipating their masters' commands. A bugle's tin-like echo pierced the air and everyone, human and beast, exhaled simultaneously.

"Here we go, everyone," called Amos. "We're on our way home." He waved his hand West to emphasize his point.

After a nudge or two, the oxen moved forward, hauling their heavy wagons at a leisurely pace. The three-mule wagons went faster, but only just.

Without any clues about what I was supposed to be doing here, I followed the rumbling wagons and stayed close to the Wetherfields, guessing that Matthew would be close by. The further we stepped from Independence, the louder the cheers came from those sending the travelers off. Women waved wet handkerchiefs to those they were leaving behind, taking one last glance at loved ones they would never see again.

The travelers turned their attention to each other. "See you in camp!" they cried to family and friends in case they were separated along the way. The children were most buoyant of all, ready for their adventure, because this was an adventure to them.

Oxen, mules, horses, even the livestock behind the wagons, became edgy as they pressed ahead, one hoof at a time. The animals seemed to understand that something long, unknown, and dangerous lay ahead of them. Sunburned men, sun-bonneted women, and children with sunny smiles shouted to each other about how exciting it all was. As we continued, one of the men mentioned the Missouri River and some of the excitement dissipated.

Finally, I saw him. Matthew. He looked fine on horseback, broad shouldered and strong. He rode near Amos while Amos steered his wagon from the driver's seat. Matthew leaned close so Amos could hear him over the shouting voices and rumbling wheels. Matthew removed his hat and his mop of dark curls fell over his blue collar. He grabbed his horse's reins with one hand while he rubbed the gray animal's ear with his other. He leaned forward, sharing words meant only for the horse. The horse exhaled, its muscular shoulders lowering.

We moved at a good clip. Those at the front set a quick pace, and those walking behind, already covered in dust, muttered that if the drivers continued to move at this speed we'll all be dead in a week. Mothers called to their children, saying get alongside this wagon this minute or you'll get lost and we won't ever see you again. Some of the children didn't seem to think that was such a bad thing. Others saw their mothers' stern expressions and did as they were told. The women shaded their eyes against the dust and the sun with their hands, their bonnets not doing much good, and stared straight ahead as though if they squinted hard enough they could see the Pacific Ocean. The air was loud with clanging wheels, baying livestock, and chattering voices, hundreds of them.

"Matthew!"

The woman I saw cooking near the Wetherfield wagon called him. When Matthew slowed his horse by her side I saw the family resemblance. She has the same dark hair as Matthew, and she's taller than most of the women. I remembered that Amos Wetherfield is Matthew's brother-in-law, so I guessed she was his sister. Matthew nodded in my direction after the woman spoke.

There I was, step by step, one foot in front of the other, ready to walk 2000 miles. Why was I following them? I'm not sure I can answer that. I saw the wagon train move out and I went with them. I still felt thin, airy, a wisp of an idea. Here and not here. I had the strangest sensation that I was making the journey for the same reason as everyone else. Is there anything out West for me?

I slowed my pace and fell behind, coughing through dust so thick I could hardly see my hand in front of my face. I hadn't noticed the woman I thought was Matthew's sister walking beside me.

"Excuse me, Miss?" When she had my attention she smiled. "Pardon me, but I couldn't help saying hello. I know you're not Gloryanna Winters, my brother told me so, but the resemblance is simply uncanny. Are you two related somehow? Like her sister or her cousin or something?"

"I'm afraid I don't know a Gloryanna Winters," I said. "Are you Mr. Cooper's sister?"

"Indeed I am. And he's right. You're the spit of her. How strange, and not to be related at all." She smiled, all warmth and kindness. "Maybe you're related and just don't know it." She shifted the weight of her baby, a girl based on the ribbon tied around her head, from one arm to the other. "Well? Who are you then?"

Who am I? Am I even myself here? I told the truth as simply as I could.

"My name is Grace Wentworth."

"Hello, Miss Grace Wentworth. I'm Wilhemina Wetherfield. Him there," she nodded toward the wagon driver, "is my husband Amos and him there as you're acquainted with," she nodded toward Matthew as he galloped at a pace toward the front of the line, "is my brother Matthew. This little one here," she held up the baby in her arms, "is Leticia and those two rascals," she smiled at the small boy with sand-brown hair like Amos and the small girl with Wilhemina's dark hair, "are my eight-year-old twins Paul and Sally." She looked around as though searching for someone and shook her head. "I'll tell you what, Miss Wentworth. If you muddle along at that pace you'll be left behind to fend for yourself and you don't want to cross any part of this trail by yourself, believe you me." She gestured toward the winding horseshoe of the great Missouri River as though that proved her point. "Where are your people?"

"My people?"

"Your family. I thought I knew everyone traveling with our train, but I'm not familiar with any Wentworths."

"I'm..." I needed a careful response. "I have to return to my family."

"Ah." A warm, motherly tone crept into Wilhemina's voice. "That explains it then. You're trying to get home, poor thing." Again, she glanced around as if searching for someone, but everyone else was busy with their own driving or walking, preoccupied by their own thoughts. "Who are you traveling with then? At least you have a maid with you, don't you?"

I wasn't sure how to answer her. The best I could come up with was, "I'm here alone. I discovered this train was going West so I decided to follow along."

"You decided to follow all on your own? By heck, girl, you've got spunk, and that's the truth. It's a good thing too since you're going to need all the spunk you have to get through this, especially if your folks are already West." Wilhemina looked at me to verify this point, but I said nothing. "Your folks are West, is that right?"

"My parents are in California."

Wilhemina's sympathy was evident in her soft expression. "All the way in California? You'll come along with us, then, Miss Grace Wentworth. A young woman out here alone? That will get you some attention you don't want. And you haven't even got a wagon or anything except the clothes on your back from what I can tell. Wearing your Sunday best? That'll be worn out before we reach Oregon. Your folks must have bought that from the general store, being such a pretty blue as that. We'll have to find you something more practical for the journey. I have that green gingham that I brought with me for extras. It'll have to be taken up a bit, but I think I can stitch it so it will fit you fine." She squinted at me. "And as for that corset and those petticoats, well, we brought ours with us, don't you worry about that." She whispered in case there were any men nearby to overhear. "You may want to unlace that corset when you're working out here since there'll be some hard labor for sure. And as for your petticoats and stockings? I'm not sure you're going to need those while we're traveling. But don't tell Mrs. Brownlow I said so. She's determined to dress like a proper New England lady, from her chemise to her stockings, no matter how rough our journey gets."

Wilhemina laughed, and I laughed with her. I wondered at Wilhemina calling my cotton dress my "Sunday best." It didn't seem anything out of the ordinary until I noticed how the women wore dark-colored dresses with fitted bodices, loose sleeves to the wrist, high collars, and long skirts covered by aprons. Their bonnets, which matched their dresses, had long brims.

"So?" Wilhemina looked at me expectantly. "Will you join us on this journey?"

"I'm appreciative, truly," I said. "But I feel like I'd be in the way of your family, and I don't want to impose."

"Nonsense. You're young and spry and I'm sure you'll make yourself useful. With Tish and these fiends," she nodded at Paul and Sally, "I could use all the help I can get. Now stop fussing and come along."

Wilhemina Wetherfield didn't know me from anyone, yet she invited me to join her family on a long trip across a dangerous continent. At some point this dream will end, I know, but it would be nice to have somewhere to belong while I'm here. She shooed me forward and we both quickened our pace until we walked alongside her family's wagon with the red Wetherfield painted at the top. She pointed at a nearby wagon with Wetherfield painted in green.

"That's Amos' brother Hiram's wagon," Wilhemina said. "Hiram's wife is riding inside the back there. You belong to both these wagons now, Miss Wentworth."

"Thank you, Mrs. Wetherfield," I said. "I'm more grateful than you know."

"I'm glad you're here, Miss Wentworth. There's nothing more to be said."

Her husband, Amos, kept turning his head, watching us. I took little Tish to give Wilhemina's arms a break, and her husband gestured for her to join him. She moved to the driver's side of the wagon and leaned her head close to her husband as they talked. Though Amos kept his voice quiet, Wilhemina spoke loudly enough for some of us to overhear.

"What else am I supposed to do, Amos? She's making the journey West to reunite with her family and she doesn't have any people here. She doesn't even have a maid with her. It would be like leaving her to the wolves to leave her on her own. Isn't it the Christian thing to do? Doesn't it say in Hebrews: Be not forgetful to entertain strangers, for thereby some have entertained angels unawares?"

Amos said something I couldn't hear. I felt eyes turn my way and I noticed a group of women walking behind me. My head ached as though their intense curiosity was drilling holes into the back of my skull.

Amos spoke again, and Wilhemina responded, "I am keeping my voice down, Amos. I don't want our business in everyone else's face either." She listened as her husband answered, and her response was slightly lower but still audible while a few of the bolder women crept forward to hear better. "Maybe it's strange that she's on her own, and maybe it isn't. It's not my place to judge, Amos Wetherfield, and it's not yours either. And if I know my Bible, and I think I do, Amos in the Bible showed a heart for the oppressed and the voiceless. This young woman on her own would certainly be voiceless, and I'm not having it, not on this wagon train where the only way we're going to survive is by pulling together. But you're the captain of this train. Of course, the decision is yours."

Amos replied, then called to the mules and they picked up their trot at a jolt. Wilhemina slowed her pace to join me. When she saw the women's prying eyes directed our way, she smiled in a friendly manner.

"My husband just wanted to know what we're having for our next meal. He likes a good meal, Amos."

There were smiles. Several "Oh, of course" responses. The women turned to each other, likely to discuss everything they heard.

Wilhemina shrugged. "Listening to our business like it's any of theirs. I wouldn't expect anything else from that bunch of biddies. That one there," she nodded toward a tall, broad, red-faced woman in a fashionable green dress whose red hair was braided into a coil behind her head, "is Mrs. Anne Brownlow. She's a widow, and so is her daughter there," she nodded toward a small, slight, blond woman in blue, "Mrs. Lydia Carson. They're coming along with Mrs. Brownlow's brother, Sebastian Rood. They have family already settled in Oregon, I hear."

Mrs. Brownlow, the mother, was speaking to the man who must have been her brother since they shared a similar redness in hair and complexion. Her daughter, Mrs. Carson, was strangely doll-like. She was pretty, certainly, with large eyes and pouting lips. She walked three paces behind her mother as if Mrs. Brownlow were royalty.

"Don't pay them any mind," Wilhemina said. "They're both odd ducks who love to tell tales to anyone who will listen. Actually, it's the mother who tells tales. The daughter just nods at whatever her mother says."

"Your husband didn't sound very pleased to have me along," I said.

"Don't worry about Amos. He likes to grumble sometimes, but he knows letting you come along is the right thing and he'll always do the right thing. Besides, I don't think he minds so much, but he worries about the look of it. It is odd, after all, to have a young woman such as yourself make this journey on her own. People might wonder where you came from and why you're here."

"I wonder the same thing. Really, I just want to get home."

"I believe you, Miss Wentworth, I do." She took Tish back and I was sad to lose the pleasant weight in my arms. She saw the way I watched the baby and I almost thought she was going to hand the little girl back but Tish was far more content in her mother's arms, as she should be.

"Are you widowed?" Wilhemina asked. "It's all too common to have young widows and widowers make the journey West."

"No," I said. "I've never been married."

"A pretty girl like you and not spoken for? How old are you?"

"I'm 22."

"Twenty-two and never been married? Heavens, girl, what are you waiting for? Folks will have something to say about that, for sure. But like I said, you can't mind them too much. They have their lives and you have yours. But Amos needs to keep the respect of the men if he's going to keep his authority until we get to Oregon."

"Are you afraid some of the others might decide that your husband isn't in charge anymore?" I asked.

"What I want is for some of them to break off into a separate train, but they signed on here and they paid good money for Hiram's expertise so they'll likely stick around. Hiram knows the way and Amos has his senses about him. The other men know that even if they'll argue about everything. Mrs. Peterson told me that some of the men wondered how you can elect Amos when he's so quiet. How's he going to get everyone's attention when he needs it? But when Amos speaks people listen. Last night they voted on the rules everyone needs to follow. The laws are sound enough to keep us on schedule and everyone in line." She watched her husband slow his team of mules down. "We need to get it right, Miss Wentworth. And Amos and Hiram are the two to make it happen."

A young boy, maybe about ten years old with hair the color of straw, eyes like tourmaline, and skinnier than you'd want a boy his age to be, came slinking in our direction. Wilhemina eyed him suspiciously. He didn't seem to be a child she knew. Then she nodded.

"You're Nancy Billings' boy, aren't you?" she asked.

"Yes, ma'am. I'm Jimmy."

Wilhemina grinned. "What have you got there, young man?"

Jimmy Billings turned the color of the pink wildflowers he held in his hand. "I saw these and I thought the pretty lady might like them." The boy glanced in my direction and I guessed they were meant for me.

"If those are for Miss Wentworth then give them to her. She's right here."

Jimmy handed me the flowers with a gentlemanly bow, and I accepted them, gladly.

"They are beautiful, Jimmy," I said. "Thank you. You've brightened my day."

Jimmy's smile was so keen I thought it would rival the sun. Then he ran back to his mother, two rows to our right, who beamed at her boy but watched me with some suspicion.

"She doesn't look very happy," I said to Wilhemina.

"No, well, Mrs. Billings doesn't look happy about much. But that little Jimmy is her whole world, and if giving the pretty lady flowers makes him happy, then she'll tell him to do it. She and her husband had six girls before they had him, and that little boy is their pride and joy, let me tell you."

"More than their girls?"

Wilhemina clutched little Tish to her chest. "I love my children equally, Miss Wentworth, but sons are more valuable, aren't they? They carry on the family name and heritage in a way daughters don't."

Before I could answer we were at the Missouri River, our first challenge of the journey. Amos and Hiram decided to stop to consider how to best cross. We ate a meal of baked beans and toast, and the night grew too dark to see before we finished eating. Amos set up a tent for himself and Wilhemina and a second tent for Paul and Sally, which I would share with them, but I didn't mind. They are both sweet-tempered children, and I was grateful for a place to lay my head. I stretched out on my quilts and smoothed down my blue cotton dress, briefly wondering how I came to be wearing it. Like everything else about this dream, it simply was.

I untied my hair from its loose braid, slipped off my boots, and closed my eyes. It was only a matter of moments before I realized I wouldn't be sleeping. My mind was racing from the strangeness of my surroundings. This has been a fascinating dream, I thought, but it's time to wake up now. I forced all of my concentration into moving my limbs, from my fingers to my toes, trying to will some awareness into my muscles, but nothing. I was still in the tent with the children.

All right, then, I decided. I'll have to live in this world a while longer. I braided my hair, pulled my boots back on, and climbed over the sleeping children into the drowsy night, the moon projecting its bright eye over the land. I meandered toward the river, which appeared friendly enough, the tippling water making pleasant music. The tents were silver in the moonlight.

I should have been surprised to see Matthew Cooper but I wasn't. He stood near his sister's schooner, new from the look of it, the pristine white cover still smelling of linseed oil. His head was uncovered and his dark hair looked blue in the night. He stood tall, the stance I had already come to expect from him, his feet apart, his hands on his hips. He examined the wagon from front to back, from the top of the white cover to the bottom of the wooden wheels. He didn't seem any more surprised to see me than I was to see him.

"She's a beauty, isn't she?" He nodded toward the wagon.

"Yes, she is."

"She ought to be for what she cost. More than one hundred

dollars. Amos and I went in together. She was one of the cheaper ones, if you can believe it, but she's sturdy and strong and I think she'll do just fine."

"Unlike the Quigleys' wagon."

"Dangnammit!"

Matthew did such a fine impression of Mrs. Quigley's obstinance that I laughed, loudly, then worried that I had woken the whole camp. Luckily, no one stirred.

"We shouldn't laugh," Matthew said, trying but not succeeding to settle his face.

"It is funny," I said.

"Especially since he actually thought he was going to drive that old Conestoga across the plains. He's a good one, Ezra Quigley. He's not always the brightest fire you'll ever see, but he's got true goodness, and that's rare enough these days. You'd think people would be smarter about things in 1850, but they aren't." Matthew ran his hand across the driver's seat. "Do you know much about wagons, Miss Wentworth?"

"I'm afraid I don't."

"Neither did I before we started this. We had wagons on the farm, of course, but it was never a matter of such importance. Amos and I had to learn quick." He pointed to the name Wetherfield painted in red across the top of the white cover.

"I noticed that," I said. "Most of the families here have names or nicknames on their wagons."

"So we can find our way home if we get separated."

"I suppose this is home for the next 2000 miles."

"Indeed it is."

Matthew walked me around our home, a green box four feet wide by ten feel long. He named the various parts, from the five hickory wood bows, the two end bows flaring outward, which held the white canvas cover in place. The cover was threaded through so that it puckered and it could be opened and closed as needed. I was informed that the wooden wheels were bolted together, then greased with tallow and tar so they would run smoothly. The iron tires were heated until they slid into place. Matthew pointed out the jockey box at the front, used as the driver's seat as well as storage space. The long tongue was used to harness the oxen or mules, whichever that family had chosen to pull their wagon.

"Both have benefits," Matthew said. "Oxen have a steadier demeanor and they're less excitable than mules, but they're hulking animals and go at an awful slow pace. Mules may be harder to control and they're easily frightened, but they go at a pretty good clip if they have a mind to." He pointed to the team of three mules drinking from pails set in front of them. "We went with mules since we had them on our farm in Massachusetts and we know their ways. That's Ed, Ted, and Fred. Fred is a molly, a female, but little Paul wanted their names to match so we went with it."

"She could be Fredericka," I said.

Matthew's smile made me happy. He seemed so pleased to tell me about his wagon, and I found the lesson fascinating if only because of my teacher.

He pulled back the white cover to show me inside. I was informed that Hiram had said that most wagons could carry about 2000 pounds of supplies but he recommended keeping the supplies to 1500 pounds to make things easier for the animals pulling the vehicles. Matthew showed me sacks flour and corn-meal. He showed me 70 pounds of bacon, along with sugar, salt, lard, beans, and rice as well as coffee and tea. He opened the sack of flour where dozens of eggs were safely stored inside. Besides foodstuffs, there was 25 pounds of soap along with a washboard and tub stacked into the corner. There were guns, with lead and powder packed separately where the children couldn't reach, farming tools, a butter churn, pots and pans, cooking utensils, bedding, a well-read Bible, and a stack of books. Matthew shrugged. "Paul and I like to read."

"What do you like to read?"

"Adventure stories, mainly. Paul loves Swiss Family Robinson."

"What else?"

"I enjoy some Dickens myself."

"How funny," I said. "My father loves Dickens too."

Matthew showed me how the boxes of food, dishes, pots, and barrels for water are settled near the back of the wagon to make cooking easier. The furnishings Wilhemina insisted on bringing, a family heirloom chest of drawers, some chairs, bed headboards, and a dining table, were pushed near the front near the driver's seat. Between the furniture at the front, the extra supplies such as rope and canteens, and the kitchen necessities was an open center with two featherbeds pressed together covered with quilts.

"This is extra space in case anyone needs a break from walking," he said.

Is this what a dream is, I wondered? To show you the kind of people you would like to know in real life? I would like to know a man like Matthew Cooper, I thought. He cleared his throat, as though reminding me of his presence, then glanced toward the tent from where I had come.

"My sister says you're coming along with us." At my blank expression, he added, "You can't take this trail on your own, Miss Wentworth. It's too dangerous. Even if you are trying to find your way home."

"It was kind of her to offer."

"She'd give her heart away if she knew someone needed it. She's that kind of person."

"I'm grateful to her."

Matthew looked toward the river. He held a few pebbles in his hand as though tempted to skim them, but he must have decided against it and he dropped them on the ground.

"It's quite a big thing you're doing, going West," I said.

"It's the same thing you're doing, the same thing everyone else here is doing, and others have done before us, and more will do after. I know you're going to reunite with your family. I don't know what happened to separate you all and I won't ask. It's none of my business anyhow. For myself, all I can say is I have to go West."

"Is someone holding a gun to your head?"

"No, but that's how it feels—like some great invisible force is pressing me to go. I don't know how else to explain it."

"Try."

He studied the wagon as he considered. "The West calls to me. I can hear it in my sleep, hear it while I'm awake. It's like a siren's song and it's filled me up inside. Something is pulling me toward the sunset. Something I can't describe. I have to go, I just do."

"It's like a fairy line," I said. "An invisible rope that wraps around your waist and tugs you in that direction even if you don't understand why."

"How did you know?" Matthew leaned toward me. "Really, how did you?"

"Because I feel that way myself."

"I was right about you, Duchess. You have a fine way of saying things."

"My name is Grace."

"You're Duchess to me."

His tent creaked as the poles fell inward. He pressed first one pole, then the next firmly into the ground and his tent was upright again. Footsteps echoed in the quiet night and Wilhemina stood beside us, Tish in her arms. She eyed us like a concerned older sister, but when she saw we were a respectable distance apart she relaxed.

"I was just telling Mr. Cooper how grateful I am that you're allowing me to come with you," I said.

"Nonsense. We're happy to have you."

Matthew looked at me, at Wilhemina, at the baby in her arms. He kissed the infant's head. "Nighty night, Leticia."

He disappeared into his tent, and Wilhemina and I sat under

the stars. She gave me a side-eye smile, though her brightness quickly darkened.

"I wasn't always for this trip you know, Miss Wentworth. I was so mad at Amos and Matthew for selling our farm in Massachusetts I could hardly stand to look at them. I thought the trip was a waste of money, a waste of time, a waste of our whole lives. I told Amos I was sorry I ever met him, let alone married him. I told him I'd never forgive him for dragging me down the nine circles of hell."

"I think you only have to cross five of them to get to Oregon."

Wilhemina laughed. "You're probably right."

"It's such a difficult thing to do," I said, "leaving behind everyone you've ever known and loved for some vague idea of how wonderful life could be somewhere, out there, grasping at promise-filled straws which may be real but which may very well not. There's nothing definite to look forward to. Hanging your entire life on building castles on the sand, or farms on unseen land. It's either the bravest or the most foolish thing someone can do."

"I agree with you wholeheartedly, Miss Wentworth. But Amos and Matthew were so set on going and in the end I couldn't say no. I'm more of a mother to Matthew than a sister, really. Our parents died a few weeks apart of consumption when I was seventeen and Matthew was ten. I was already engaged to Amos by then. We married quickly and took Matthew in." Willie smiled, perhaps at the thought of her brother. "So were you born in California?"

"I'm from Massachusetts, like you. We lived there until I was about three and then we moved to California."

"California." Willie whistled but stopped when Tish stirred. "That's a fine thing. You were already West and now you're going again. What brought you back?"

"One day I suddenly found myself here."

"Just like that, huh?" Wilhemina nodded. "I must have sensed you were Massachusetts stock. That's why I liked you from the moment I saw you. We're from the Lowell area, as a matter of fact.

My people have been farming there since before Massachusetts was a state. Whereabouts in Massachusetts are you from?"

"Salem."

"Ah, Salem. Well, we had our troubles in Lowell too." The night was on its way out and silver glimmered in the background. "I suspect we ought to try to get some rest, Miss Wentworth. We've got quite a day ahead of us tomorrow."

"Grace, please," I said.

"Thank you, Grace. You know I'm Wilhemina, but my friends call me Willie."

"Thank you, Willie. For everything."

We stopped outside the tent Willie shared with Amos.

"I'm still amazed at what you're doing," I said.

Willie stared into the late-night sky. "We all have our reasons. Some of us are looking for personal freedom, some are looking for financial freedom, some are looking for religious freedom, and some are just the adventurous type. I think my brother might be one of that last group. He's one of those who may never settle down. Oh, I don't mean about getting married. He'll marry when the time's right." She grinned at me and my cheeks flared. "I mean he'll always be looking for the next new thing, the next inspiration. Hiram's just the same. He left home at 14 to make his way West. He was probably the youngest fur trader anyone's ever seen and he loved his time in the mountains, but he needed some new excitement so his adventure now is guiding people West. Matthew's the same. Right now his adventure is going West. What's next? We'll have to see."

She smiled at the baby sleeping against her breast and she seemed to forget me. It was beautiful to see, a mother's pure love for her child. Then she sighed.

"Like I said, Matthew was determined to go West and then he got Amos caught up in it. Everything you said about the risks we're taking is true, but all Matthew and Amos can see is the good that can come from it. Both of them talk about how wonderful it will be in Oregon with fresh land to farm and no one to answer to. Wouldn't it be great for them to be their own men, they asked me? And Amos is still haunted by everything he lost in the Panic of '37. That was 13 years ago now, and Matthew was just 12 at the time, but when our bank failed Amos near about died. He didn't know where our next dollar was coming from. There was nowhere to turn for credit, and if he couldn't buy seed he couldn't plant, not that there were any markets where he could have sold the crops anyhow." She stopped and considered me. "You know all about when the banks collapsed, of course."

"I was in California then," I said.

"Somehow we managed to keep our farm, but the whole situation left a bitter taste in Amos' mouth, and Matthew's too even though he was young at the time. I think that's why Matthew developed a sense of adventure. He didn't want to be dependent on someone else's bad decisions ever again. In the end, it comes down to the fact that I believe in Amos and Matthew. I believe in their grit and determination, and who knows? Maybe once we're in Oregon we will make a fine new life for ourselves. As for leaving loved ones behind, well, we don't have much family left in Massachusetts." She stopped, rubbing the baby's back, smiling at me in a comforting way. I thought she was waiting for me to share my story. After all, she had just shared something personal with a virtual stranger. But even if I wanted to tell her the truth, I couldn't. What could I say to her about any of it?

Willie nodded. "In your own time, Grace. You'll see that you can trust me and you'll tell me your story. You must be looking forward to seeing your folks again."

"My parents…"

I had been struggling not to think of my parents. Suddenly, all my worries washed over me at once. My main worry? I've had the strangest feeling that this isn't a dream. And if this isn't a dream, I can't begin to guess what that means for me.

I looked into Willie's kind eyes, the same green as her brother's, and I wondered if I would ever see my parents again. How will they know what happened to me? How will they know I'm here? The thought of being gone from them forever, never seeing my mother's smile, never hearing my father's voice, was too much.

"My parents..."

The harder I tried to erect a ring around my heart the more broken I felt. And then, when the dam shattered, I was washed away by wave after wave of grief. I buried my face in my hands, overtaken by fears I couldn't share.

Willie put her arm around me. "Oh, you dear girl. Don't you worry. Amos will make sure you find your way home. I trust him with my very life, with my children's very lives, and in time you'll trust him too. You will go home again, Grace Wentworth, I can feel it. You can believe me too. Takodah says I have a good sense for understanding people."

"Takodah?"

"Hiram's wife. He said he traded a handful of buttons for her."

"That can't be true."

"Hiram does like to tell tall tales. Takodah is Indian, you know. She's planning on traveling in their wagon as much as she can since people are so ill-mannered nowadays. The biddies like Mrs. Brownlow and her daughter, even Mrs. Starkey and Mrs. During-ton, ogle her like she's got three heads or something."

"Takodah can walk with us."

"Of course she can. I've told her so a hundred times but she feels safer in the wagon and who am I to tell her different? You'll like her. She's wise for her age, hardly older than you, I should think, but she knows things."

"What kind of things?"

"Hiram said Takodah has magic. I thought Amos was going to throw a Bible at Hiram's head when he said it."

"A bit of Cain and Abel," I said. My tears dried. The conversation with Willie helped to distract me.

"It's not rivalry, exactly. They're good friends and they get along well enough most of the time. But Amos does read his Bible most regular. Hiram a little less so."

"From what I heard, it sounds like you know your Bible too."

"I should hope so. My pa was a minister in the church in Lowell."

"Do you believe Takodah has magic?" I asked.

"I believe she's a healer who sees things differently than other folks. She is Indian after all, and they must know a thing or two, being around for as long as they have, even if the others around here won't see it that way. But the people here will warm up to her when they realize she can make salves and set broken bones and deliver babies. They'll need her since we haven't got a doctor traveling with us."

Willie was about to enter her tent, but I stopped her.

"Aren't you scared?" I asked. "Of the journey?"

"It'll be hard, but Amos and Hiram will lead the way, and with Matthew by their side we're in good hands. We have everything we'll need, and Hiram says we'll find plenty along the way." She must have seen my pained expression. She grasped my hand. "Wait. I have something for you." Willie went to her wagon and I held Tish while she rummaged through the back, moving objects aside, squinting in the darkness. She reached under a panel along the bottom. "Ah. Here they are."

As I handed her the baby she pressed six beautifully embossed white leather-bound journals and a handful of pencils into my arms. Something about the white books made me pause, but I couldn't think why. When I tried to give them back, she shook her head.

"Please, Grace, I want you to have them. Amos bought them for me when I saw them in a shop window in Independence. I had to have them. I thought I'd be like Mrs. Narcissa Whitman and write grand, detailed diaries of my journey West, telling folks of all the beauties we saw and how amazing our life is in Oregon. I thought my diaries would be published in all the newspapers and everyone would be fascinated by our travels. Now here we are just getting started and the thought of keeping a diary makes me want to pull my hair out strand by strand. These books were expensive and I hate the thought of them going to waste. And I can see that Matthew was right about you. You have a way with words. Are you educated?"

"Yes, I suppose I am."

"I guessed as much. You'd do much more with these journals than I ever could. I'm sure you could write things people would want to read." She pressed them against my chest. "Please, Grace, accept them as a gift from me."

I nodded as I admired the embossed leather covers. "Thank you, Willie. I'll make good use of them. I promise."

"I know you will." She smiled before crawling into her tent.

So here I am, keeping an Oregon Trail journal. If nothing else, writing helps me to think through everything that's happening. Moving my knife-sharpened pencil across the blank pages allows me to turn half-formed thoughts into full-fledged ideas so I can begin to make sense of the odd turn my life has taken.

Only I'm not sure if any of this is real.

CHAPTER 11

The wake-up bugle sounded in the darkness. Men shouted orders and women shouted orders and children squealed and animals howled. After a quick breakfast of scrambled eggs, buttered toast, and coffee, Amos and Willie had our wagon ready for crossing. Willie pointed at Paul and Sally, who were too close to the river for comfort. They were back by her side in a moment.

Mamie Durington didn't have as much luck with her children, also a boy and a girl. She pointed at them as Willie had at Paul and Sally but the Durington children paid no attention to her. She screamed to make herself heard over the cacophony.

"Oliver! Priscilla! You two Duringtons get your behinds over here right now. And you best quit that caterwauling before I make you sorry you ever woke up today."

"Yes, Ma," little Oliver said. He took his sister's hand and led her toward the Duringtons' wagon.

"Good heavens." Willie shook her head as she watched the small Duringtons pass. "We're all so on edge about the children and we're just getting started."

"It's easy to worry about the children," I said. "There's so much happening and it's hard to keep an eye on them when they scatter everywhere." I took Willie's arm. "I'm here to help, remember?"

"I was right about you, Miss Wentworth. I believe we're entertaining an angel unawares."

Sunlight danced across the Missouri River as it waited, wide and steadfast, as hundreds of travelers congregated on its banks. Gold-like ripples winked like friendly eyes welcoming us. Come enjoy the beauty of the water, the river seemed to say. Bask in the coolness on this warm spring day.

I knew what the river wasn't saying. Once we crossed to the other side we were out of the United States proper. Excitement pressed people's expressions to the right and concern pressed their expressions to the left, leaving everyone off-center, like a Picasso painting. A collective gasp bounded from wagon to wagon as each family waited, as though everyone realized that our journey West had truly begun.

"Wait!" I wanted to shout. "This journey is dangerous and so many things can go wrong!"

The travelers already know this. Yet everyone is determined to go anyway—or most everyone. Willie told me that most of the women had to be talked into this journey by their husbands just as she had been talked into it by Matthew and Amos. A few, like Mrs. Darrowby, continue to grumble away from their husbands' hearing. Many, like Willie, have resigned themselves to their fate.

Several of the men, including Amos and Matthew, circled a man wearing too-large fringed leather trousers, a too-large fringed leather shirt, moccasins, and a beaver tail hat. He's leaner and more wiry than Amos but shares the same sharp features. While Amos wears an impressive chestnut-brown walrus mustache, the fringed leather man wears an even more impressive navel-length beard. Someone called "Hiram!" and he turned. While there's something disheveled about his mountain man appearance, he has an easy-going calm like Amos. The men walk along the riverbank squinting to the other side, their heads pressed together so the womenfolk can't overhear. They tug their hats over their eyes while they scan the area for some clue about the friendliness of the water. I inched closer since I wanted to hear what they said, but someone tugged at my sleeve.

"That you there, Miss Wentworth?" Beula Durington asked. "You'd best wait here with us. Let the men take care of men things."

"Men things?"

"Hiram Wetherfield knows his business when it comes to crossing rivers. He's done it enough times he could do it blindfolded."

"Let's hope we never have to find out."

"I agree with you, Miss Wentworth. But we have lots of rivers to cross, and we should let Mr. Wetherfield tell us how to do it. We don't need to get in there interfering."

"I wasn't going to interfere. I just wanted to hear what he said."

"Like I said, we shouldn't interfere. There's nothing we can add to that conversation, that is, unless you know something about traveling to the West the rest of us don't, you being from California and all." Miss Durington nodded, waiting, though I added nothing. "Their job is to make the decisions. Our job is to do what we're told."

"What are you being told to do that you don't want to do?" I asked. "Don't you want to go West?"

"Oh, you know. My brother caught the Oregon Fever and since he's the only family I have left I had no choice but to follow him." She smiled sweetly. "I hear you're headed West to get back to your people." She waited for a response, but still I said nothing. Instead of pursuing her line of questioning, she nodded toward the huddled men. "We're from Lowell like the Wetherfields, and my brother has known Amos and Hiram for some years now. I trust that Amos and Hiram are both good men. Even if Hiram did get himself an Indian for a wife, I still trust him."

Biting my tongue to hold back my reply, I studied the woman. Beula Durington is short with a round face. Her white-gold curls slip out from under her denim-colored bonnet, which matches her denim-colored dress, which matches her denim-colored eyes that seem to take in everyone around her at once while her head constantly turns from side to side, listening to every conversation. She strikes me as an innocent-looking Big Bad Wolf—the better to see you with, my dear, the better to hear you with, the better to gossip about you later.

"Well, I'm pleased to know you, Miss Wentworth. The others don't know what they're talking about. You don't seem off-center to me at all." She said it so sweetly too. Her face was all friendliness as she headed toward the wagon with Durington painted in blue.

As Willie said, there's nothing I can do about the wagging tongues. Instead of worrying about something I have no control over, I turned my attention back to the men. Hiram stroked his beard as he nodded at everything Amos said. Although Hiram is the guide, it's clear that Amos is in charge. After Amos finished speaking, Hiram had his say, and he had much to say. When no one was looking, I inched closer. Willie stepped beside me and we listened together.

"We had this conversation yesterday," Amos said. The men waited while he gathered his thoughts. "I thought we were all agreed with Hiram. Crossing with the ferry is an expense, but we don't want to fall behind schedule, not this soon, and not ever as far as I'm concerned."

"So we are taking the ferry across?" Wilbur Gridley asked.

"Yes, we'll take the ferry across," Hiram said.

Those standing nearest to Amos nodded, but one man in the back cleared his throat.

"I don't mind the idea of the ferry," the man said. "It's the expense, you see…"

"If you don't have the money to do this properly then head on back to wherever you came from." He isn't an old man, Hiram

Wetherfield. My best guess is mid-30s, yet he, like his brother, has a natural authority. "Better to make an easier time of it while we can since there'll come a day on this journey when nothing will be easy and we'll look back on these as the good old days."

The men chattered amongst themselves. They were about evenly divided from what I could tell—half for the ferry and half against.

"Hush now." Moses Johnston stared each man in the eye. "The women and children ain't so far and they'll hear you. They have more sensitive dispositions than we do and we don't want to scare them."

I turned away so I wouldn't laugh. Willie did the same.

"We're gonna ferry with the animals and everything?" Jonas Blackwood's wide expression left him looking younger than his 18 years. "I though we were walking across."

"Who do you think you are," Moses Johnstone said with thunder in his voice, "walking on water."

"I don't mean walking on the water, you fool. I mean through the water."

"The people and wagons will be ferried across," Hiram said. "The muleskinners can show their animals the way and swim across with them. We'll fit as many animals on the ferry as we can, but the rest will have to swim."

"We've got to get a move on," Amos said. "I'm more worried about getting stuck in the mountains in the snow than I am about some expense for the ferry. You all knew you'd have to spend some money making our way West. The ferry is better than making our own rafts, which could take as long as a week, and then we'd get a late start. We don't want the grass gone when it's our turn to pass through. We need to get to the other side of that river right quick if we don't want our journey over before we've even begun."

"I still think we should save the money," Jonas said.

"Hey, everyone," called Lee Tappertit. Tappertit is one of the officers and the others quieted when he spoke. "Ain't you heard of the Donner Party?" Silence, and the men removed their hats and bowed their heads. It seems that whenever someone wants to make a point about crossing in a timely manner they bring up the Donner Party. Even the river slowed out of respect. "You want to end up like them? Freezing to death in them icy mountains with no one to rescue you?"

Jonas Blackwood grabbed Matthew's arm. "I wouldn't look here for a hearty meal. This fellow ain't got enough flesh on him to last one breakfast let alone a whole winter."

"He looks hearty enough to me," Moses Johnstone said with a wicked grin. "Muscle enough to pull the wagon himself all the way to Oregon."

"I still think he's pretty flimsy," said Jonas.

"Whereas you'd feed the entire train three Christmases straight, Moses," said Matthew.

The men laughed, but the decision had been made and we were crossing on the ferry. Even young Blackwood finally agreed. While families waited their turn to cross, men had time to wax their wagons to prevent water seepage.

People, wagons, and animals ambled toward the ferry, waiting as those at the front took their turn. Horses and mules bayed as they were led forward, digging in their hooves, rearing right and left, twitching their ears, shaking their heads, no, we don't want to go, we're perfectly fine here, thank you. The livestock had to be prodded to stay together as they searched for any escape. It was a dry day and already warm before the sun made its full appearance. As the wagons, people, and animals inched forward they kicked mounds of dust into the curling wind and I couldn't stop sneezing. The ferry was now occupied with the Duringtons' wagon and there were still two vehicles ahead of us—Hiram Wetherfield's and the Tappertits'.

Suddenly, a woman's horror-filled scream reverberated through my bones. Men and women rushed to the edge of the riverbank to see what had gone wrong. Willie looked up and down, right and left, worry etched into every line in her face. I held Tish close to my chest while Willie kept a tight grip on Paul and Sally. Amos rushed over.

"Willie, rope!" he yelled. "We need rope and some men who can swim."

Willie handed the rope to her husband. "What's going on, Amos?"

"The Duringtons' two smallest children slipped under the water. They're gone."

"Gone?" Willie stared at Amos, who shrugged as if he had no better answer. "Amos? They can't have vanished?"

Amos gazed at his own children, brushed a hand through Sally's dark curls, and shook his head.

Matthew appeared, as tight-lipped as Amos. "I heard they just slipped right under."

Willie clutched Sally to her chest. "What do you mean slipped?"

"The mother's so beside herself she's not making sense," Matthew said, "and who can blame her. The children were beside her one minute and the next she sees them flapping in the water."

"You have to find them," Willie said, "both of you."

"We'll do what we can," said Matthew.

Amos left with the rope thrown over his shoulder, with Matthew, Lee Tappertit, and Hiram close behind. Everyone peered into the murky river, the mud dug up from the continuous ferry crossings and the swimming people and livestock. Someone yelled "There!" and Matthew and Amos jumped into the water. They swam alongside Mr. Durington, who doggie paddled near the ferry, shouting "Oliver! Priscilla! Oliver! Priscilla!"

Matthew took a gulp of air, ducked under the water, and stayed a few moments too long until he came up empty handed. Again he filled his lungs and ducked under, this time staying even longer, and again he came up empty handed.

"Oh no," said Lee Tappertit. He pointed at something bobbing beneath the waves. Matthew skimmed under the water and reappeared with five-year-old Oliver in his arms. He swam back to our side of the shore where the boy's father waited. Mr. Durington took Oliver into his quavering arms and tried to shake, yell, and cajole the boy awake, to no avail. A small, dark-haired woman with serene eyes and a gentle manner reached for the child.

Mr. Durington snapped his son to his chest. "If you think I'm giving my boy to an Indian!"

Amos climbed onto the riverbank, panting from his exertion in the water. "It's all right, folks," he said after a gulp of air. "That there is Mrs. Wetherfield and she's my sister-in-law. Let her see the child."

Desperate hands thrust Oliver into Takodah Wetherfield's arms. Takodah opened the boy's mouth, swept across his tongue with her finger, and she took in a deep breath and pushed much-needed air into his lungs. The boy coughed and opened his eyes and his mother Mamie, watching everything from the ferry that had stopped midstream, screamed from joy or relief or both. Then Matthew emerged from the water with another child, this one smaller, a girl, but he grimaced as he neared the shore.

"No!" Mamie Durington cried from the ferry. "No! No! Give Priscilla to the Indian. She'll fix her like she fixed Ollie."

The strain on Takodah's face told everyone what Matthew already knew. The girl was gone. She tried, Takodah. She opened the tiny girl's mouth, swept out any debris she might have lodged inside, and breathed into her as she had Oliver. But when Priscilla's chest didn't rise, Takodah shook her head.

"I'm sorry," Takodah said.

"No! No!"

Poor Mrs. Durington flung herself toward the water so violently her sister-in-law Beula had to grab the infant she carried from her arms. On our side of the river, Oliver was crying and squirming but otherwise seemed all right.

The ferry began to drift again toward the opposite shore. Mrs. Durington's screams faded across the Missouri.

Mr. Durington and Oliver caught a ride across with Hiram and Takodah, father and son staring into the water as though afraid it would try to swallow the boy again. Mr. Durington held his daughter's corpse to his chest. When their family was reunited, Mamie Durington took her son into her arms and wept over him. Mr. Durington spoke softly to his wife as he held their daughter's body out to her, though Mrs. Durington wouldn't look. Beula spoke to Mamie as well, to no avail. Lee Tappertit grabbed a spade from the back of his wagon and dug a child-sized grave some distance from the Missouri. He didn't want the body to wash away when the river flooded, he told Amos. He found a sturdy piece of timber, scratched in the young girl's name and age—she was three years old—and banged the gravestone into a nearby tree, high enough so it too wouldn't wash away. Mrs. Durington tried to throw herself into her daughter's grave, but her husband held onto her as Reverend Smith read some words from the Bible about crossing the River Jordan, words meant to comfort the grieving family but went largely unheard, muffled out as they were by the wailing depth of Mrs. Durington's despair.

Finally, it was our turn to cross. Willie had shut down, closing in on herself. She watched Paul, Sally, and baby Tish as though if she lost sight of them for a moment they'd disappear forever, which is exactly what happened to the Duringtons. One moment little Oliver and Priscilla were happily watching the water, the next Priscilla is buried in her mother's linen tablecloth.

Amos stood near his wife, letting her process what had happened. Finally, he said, "We need to keep going, Willie. We need to stay strong."

Willie stared into the river as though it had been sent by Satan himself. "We're crossing our first river, Amos, and already I think this will be too hard."

"Do you want to go home?"

Willie looked at the wagons. She looked at the animals. She looked at the people waiting on the other side, the women crying openly at the loss of the little girl who could have just as easily been one of their own. She looked at Matthew, who waited for her response. Then she looked at her children.

"No, I don't want to go home. I want to go West, Amos. I want these little ones to have a chance at that better life you're so sure we'll find there. But I'm afraid. What good is trying for a better life if you're not alive to live it?"

"It's okay to be afraid, Willie. But if you and I and Matthew and the others here, if we work together, then we'll do everything we can to be safe."

"The Duringtons' children weren't safe."

"No, they weren't. And now we know we have to watch out for the children even more carefully than we did before."

"No one should have to die to learn that lesson."

Matthew nodded. "You're right, Willie, they shouldn't. So let's not let little Priscilla die in vain. Let's take the lesson she has to teach us to help get the rest of us safe and sound to Oregon."

Willie sighed. She looked at Paul, Sally, and Leticia for a long time. "All right then. Let's cross this river."

After an impatient call from the ferry master, Amos and Matthew loaded our wagon onto the flat boat. As they steadied the vehicle, the wind picked up ferociously and the muddy Missouri splattered and swirled, shaking the ferry, nearly tipping it on its side. Visions of the Durington children, happy one moment and fighting for their lives the next, kept us silent and still. I saw Willie's mouth move as if in prayer, and if I were religious at all I would have done the same.

As we floated across the winds flew even faster. If the wagon hadn't been tied down, we all would have ended up in the water, I'm sure of it. We were knocked around, front to back, side to side, so much that it was a good thing we hadn't eaten for hours. I was nearly knocked off my feet twice, and I stayed upright only because an arm caught me around the waist. The water calmed, and my feet settled under me, but the arm around my waist remained. Suddenly, the raucous winds grew in strength again and the tremulous ferry, which wasn't too sturdy to begin with, rocked from high side to high side like a seesaw. I closed my eyes and said aloud, "This is only a dream."

The ferry stopped with a bump and the arm came out from around my waist.

"You can open your eyes now, Miss Wentworth. We're on the other side."

Without looking I knew who the arm, and the voice, belonged to.

"Thank you, Mr. Cooper."

His breath came like a feather against my ear. "I'm here to help you, Miss Wentworth, however I can."

I peeked through squinted lids and saw all of us in the Wetherfield party together, all of us alive. I exhaled, nodded at Matthew, grateful to him for not letting me go. My legs wobbled, but I managed to follow the others onto land. Matthew and Amos grabbed Paul and Sally, lifting them off the ferry and placing them on dry ground. Then they grabbed Willie's hands, then mine, and helped us off the creaking pile of wood. Willie ran to Paul and Sally, clutching them close, while I held little Tish, who gurgled and smiled and seemed none the worse for the crossing.

Even in tragedy, life goes on. I noticed a sound like twittering birds overhead. I pressed Tish to my chest and noticed some of the other women leaning their heads close and whispering while they watched me, rather boldly, I thought. When the mother and daughter team of Anne Brownlow and Lydia Carson passed nearby, I mentioned something about how badly I felt for the Duringtons. At first I thought they hadn't heard me because they kept walking. Then they gave me a long, hard sneer. They stopped near Lenore Starkey's wagon, three heads pressed together, Gorgon-like, until they pulled apart to stare at me some more. After a moment, they huddled back into their conversation, as if they needed me to know that they were talking about me.

Willie pulled me away. "It's like I said, Grace. Don't pay them any mind. Some folks are just fixing to cause trouble."

"What trouble?" I asked.

Willie shook her head, ending any further questions I might have had, for that moment, anyway, since my attention was drawn to those who had crossed on the most recent ferry. They were causing quite a commotion. Loud voices echoed, livestock bleated, and there was some laughter from the back end of the reforming train. People gathered around, men on one side, women on the other, chuckling at whatever they saw.

"What is it?" I asked Willie.

Willie wiped Paul and Sally's faces with a wet rag, they had grown quite muddy, and shook her head. "I'm not sure, but from everyone's smiles it should be something good."

"We could use something good about now," I said.

The crowd parted and Ezra Quigley appeared, hat in his hand, his downcast demeanor unchanged since I last saw him.

"Quigley? That you?" called Lee Tappertit. "I thought you stayed in Independence. What on earth are you doing here?"

"Got hired by the Clarks as a cattle driver," Quigley said, to his boots.

"You were hired as a cattle driver?" Matthew said. "That's great, Ezra."

"Not me. Ma!"

From the distance I heard "Haw! Haw you kine! I'm moving faster than you and I'm not even on my feet! Haw!"

Willlie and I needed to see for ourselves. Sure enough, there was Mrs. Quigley, rolling herself quick-as-you-like in her barrow. She must have come over on the ferry while the livestock swam across. The animals didn't seem scared by her, exactly. They were more amused, as though they thought she was playing a game with them. Whatever she did, and whatever they thought, it worked, and the livestock under her charge were neatly rounded up.

"Leave the livestock be, Ma," said Ezra. "We don't need the

animals to move that far ahead. Let's wait for the wagons at the front to get further along. We don't want dust in our faces."

"Who you calling dust, boy? And who hired you to take care of the animals? No one, that's who. Who'd be fool enough to hire this booby of a boy to take care of anything with eyes, that's what I'd like to know."

Willie stopped near Mrs. Quigley. "I'm glad you came," Willie said. And from her smile she seemed to mean it. "I felt bad that you were going to have to stay behind when I know how your heart was set on going."

"I wasn't going to let that fool boy ruinate this for his old mother. We promised his father we'd make our way West and we're making our way West if I die doing it."

"Don't say that, Ma." Ezra looked genuinely upset at the thought.

"Don't worry, Ezra. I got more old bones to make yet. I reckon I need some grandchildren to help me get through whatever is left of my days."

"Oh, Ma." Ezra, whose face and neck were already red from the sun, now appeared magenta.

"Looky here, Ezra. I'm already old bones and there's no generations coming after you. If you don't pull yourself together and find yourself a wife our family will be finished by the time your bones are done and dusted. Right here on this wagon train there must be some nice young woman..." Mrs. Quigley spotted me and rolled in my direction. She moved so quickly I thought she would run over my toes. "Now how about this nice young lady? She's pretty enough to give me good-looking grandchildren. What's your name, dearie?"

Willie jumped to the rescue, landing squarely between the barrow and me. "Her name is Miss Grace Wentworth, Mrs. Quigley, but I'm afraid she's spoken for."

"She is?" The disappointment in Mrs. Quigley's voice was palpable.

"That's why she's returning West. Her folks have found her a match and she's going home to get married."

"Dangnammit!" Mrs. Quigley shook her head. "Well, if her folks have arranged it I suppose it can't be helped." She spotted pretty Mrs. Carson, the young widow. "Now you're a pretty girl too, and you've been married before so you know what it's about. How about my Ezra..."

Willie and I watched as Mrs. Carson skipped daintily away while Mrs. Quigley rolled after her.

CHAPTER 12

I'm thankful to Willie for many things, but right now I'm thankful for the journals. I don't dare date my entries since I hardly know what day it is. It's still April, I think, and it's 1850. Somehow, out here the calendar doesn't matter much.

First thing this morning, before the others were awake, Willie altered her green gingham dress so it would fit me and that's what I'm wearing now. I've learned that the hems of our dresses are sewn an inch higher than would be considered proper in polite society, but for women on the trail the shorter length makes it easier to move. I've been ordered not to touch my blue dress again until we arrive West. Willie informed me that she has taken one of her finer dresses along for the journey, which she also won't wear until we're safely in Oregon.

Willie has given me her second apron, which I've been instructed to wear daily. Married women always wear aprons since it's correct for a housewife to do so, though here women and girls wear either full or half aprons to protect their clothing. Our hair is braided simply or pulled into a bun. It's more *Little House on the Prairie* than *A Christmas Carol*, where you imagine the fine-looking Victorian women in dome-shaped skirts, petticoats, and crinolines in fashionable fabrics, their hair curled and braided to labyrinthian perfection.

Just as women and girls wear the same types of clothing, so do men and boys. Men and boys wear overlarge, open-necked cotton shirts that give them room to move, loose trousers of buckskin, wool, or blue-jeans fabric, and most wear suspenders to keep those wide trousers in place. Men's coats are made of wool or blue-jeans fabric as well. As the women's faces are protected from the sun by bonnets, the men wear wide hats of straw or felt, their feet protected by simple leather boots with no distinction between the right and left foot. Women and girls also wear leather boots.

"There's no room for fripperies here," Willie said as she scrubbed Paul's trousers in the water. "Everything is practical. It has to be."

I offered to help wash the clothes, and Willie laughed when she saw that I didn't know what to do with the washboard.

"Your folks must be rich enough to hire all the help they need," she said.

Willie showed me how to rub the clothing against the washboard, and then I twisted the excess water away and hung Sally's dress over a nearby bush to dry. Even though my muscles were sore from the work, I felt myself floating, as if I were watching myself from the distance. I'm conscious of being here and there—here on the Oregon Trail and there in my other life. At times I feel myself pulled in both directions—as though the past has my right leg and the present has my left and the opposing forces are tugging me in half like a wishbone.

I tried to remember the little I learned about the Westward Expansion from that American history course. We were taught about Manifest Destiny, how people at this time believed that God had ordained the United States its proper place in the highest order of things as it claimed dominion over the North American continent, spreading the righteousness of democracy from coast to coast. We were taught that people believed it was their duty to go West, and they believed they should expand the United States from sea to shining sea. But as I moved about the camp and chatted with some of the friendlier women, and as I overheard conversations between men, I realized that they aren't so concerned about stretching the United States across the continent. They care about doing the best they can for themselves. They care about finding a better life for their families. They believe in their hearts that they will find something better on the other side. They don't seem to be particularly concerned about an abstract idea of the nation's destiny, although I can't say that's true for everyone making the journey West, only the few I've met.

I also learned that the Native Americans are displaced from their homes in cruel, horrible ways. I learned that the greed for gold and silver will overcome some people's gentler sensibilities. And I learned that the fight over slavery, over which states or territories will be free and which will be slaveholding, will escalate into a bloody civil war, which is, what? Just 11 years from now. I know all this, yet I cannot share it. I wonder if I'm here to bear witness because what else can I do?

When we stopped for the night, the sun, our Western Star for the next 2000 miles, lingered but barely, surrounded by hues of blue-gold-pink. I enjoyed the quiet, which allowed me time for contemplating our crossing. Several of the men set out for the first guard duty of the night. Matthew Cooper wasn't among them.

Willie set a quilt on the ground. She gestured for me to sit beside her, and I did. We sat in companionable silence in the glow of the dwindling campfire as she rocked Leticia to sleep.

"I admire you, Grace, I do," Willie said after the baby closed her eyes. "Making your own decision to go West? I'd never be brave enough to try such a thing. Most folks here find your decision shocking, but I say it's a fine thing when women choose their own path. That takes gumption."

"Sometimes we're courageous because we don't have a choice," I said.

"That's true enough, though sometimes even when we don't have a choice we turn away from what we know we have to do. Oh, Lord. Here she comes again."

A young woman, a girl, rather, in her mid-teens in blue and green calico with her half-apron swaying in her quick movements, was running in our direction, her eyes firmly on Willie. Her chocolate-colored hair was pulled back from her attractive face in a long braid, her head uncovered, and without invitation she sat beside us, pressing a small loaf of bread into Willie's hands.

"Hello, Miss Pritchard," Willie said, holding the bread away as though afraid it would explode. "What have we here?"

"I know how much Mr. Cooper, I mean, I know how much your family likes my molasses bread so I made an extra batch for you. If you could, I mean, if you're so inclined, if you'd like to share it with everyone in your family, why, I'd be most obliged."

"Was this your mother's idea?" Willie asked. Miss Pritchard's neck turned an ungainly beet color. "Don't worry, Miss Pritchard. You tell your mother that I'll share your lovely bread with everyone."

Miss Pritchard nodded in a most serious manner and left toward her family's wagon. As she walked away she glanced around as though searching for one of Willie's family members in particular. Willie sighed as she set the molasses bread on the ground. When Paul inched closer, she called him over.

"Paulie, bring this bread over to the MacNeills. Mrs. MacNeill is near her time and she's likely not cooking much. They'll need that bread more than we do. And tell her I'll send over some bacon after I've made our supper."

Paul did as he was bid. When Willie saw me looking at her, she shrugged.

"Seems like every mother of every unmarried young woman on this train has their eye on Matthew, trying to catch him like he's some kind of squirrly bird. And I suspect an attractive young woman such as yourself will find a suitor or two lingering about. You won't be unmarried much longer if you don't want to be, Miss Wentworth."

"My main priority right now is getting home," I said.

"Of course it is."

Willie's face contracted as she considered me, meaningfully, but I wouldn't hold her gaze. It didn't pay to tell her that I was drawn to Matthew in a way I've never felt before. In fact, I would like him for my own squirrly bird, but I can't have him since I'll be gone soon. I'll wake up, I'll be home, and the strangeness of this bizarre dream will be forgotten.

Matthew will be forgotten.

The realization pained me and I felt an ache in my chest. I hardly know this man and already the thought of never seeing him again is too hard. But he's just a figment of my imagination. Isn't he?

Willie must have sensed that I was struggling. She patted the quilt to see if it was folded thickly enough to suit her. "Seems comfortable enough, though I don't suspect anything will be too homey for the next six months." Tish woke up, and as Willie lifted her the baby gazed at everything with wide eyes, as though astonished by everything around her. Paul and Sally were throwing a ball made of yarn back and forth to each other. Paul threw the ball to me, and I joined in. I enjoyed the simple game, and Paul and Sally are such fun to play with.

The fires have burned away and everyone has settled down for whatever rest they can find. I'm tired enough that I'm doing the same.

CHAPTER 13

*A*t night the men pull the wagons into a circle, a corral, as protection against anyone, human or animal, with a mind to cause trouble. Last night, after a quick supper where we finished the beans and rice from our nooning meal, everyone in the train—man, woman, and child—did their best to rest and gather strength for the next phase of the journey. Instead of resting, I heard the people tossing and turning in their tents. I could feel their restlessness in my jittery joints. This journey will only become more painful the further we go. The most difficult days are ahead of us, as Hiram likes to remind us. We've already seen tragedy, and I worry what else lies in wait for us. I tried to settle myself enough to fall sleep but it didn't work. As soon as I thought about closing my eyes I felt as if my lids were pinned apart.

The two men on watch laughed in the distance as another two headed in their direction, a changing of the guards. I listened for one voice in particular but didn't hear him. I still felt the dust from the day's walking in my lungs and I took a long drink of water from the canteen. I was so fidgety that I tapped my toes to an off-beat tune on the rocky ground.

I had trouble making sense of my thoughts as they spiraled from one synapse to another. I gazed at the sky while the heavens sprinkled eternal light across the darkness, watching the half-open moon, trying to gauge the time. It was late—I guessed that much. Dawn was already on its way since the stars, so bright a moment before, were fading fast.

What is this odd tableaux of pioneer scenes playing out in my head? Dorothy dreamed she was in Oz until she completed her journey on the Yellow Brick Road, traveling all that way only to realize that she had started out where she wanted to be in the first place—Kansas. Is that it? Will I stay in this dream until I complete my journey on the Oregon Trail? My father used chess-like strategy when we played the Oregon Trail game, deciding how he was going to get his avatars across the plains alive. If I make bad choices here, will I die? I screamed inside my own mind, "I'm done with this dream!" I focused on waking up, but again nothing. I'm awake, my senses tell me. My eyes are open. I'm here.

I jumped at the sound of nearby voices, exhaling only when I saw Jonas Blackwood and Samuel Maylie counting the heads of the livestock. Footsteps crunched the ground behind me, but I recognized them and I was glad. His mere presence settles me.

"Duchess."

"Why do you call me Duchess?" I asked.

Matthew didn't answer as he sat beside me, close but not so close. My breath caught somewhere inside at his proximity, knowing I could reach out and touch him. But I didn't.

Instead of answering my question, he asked, "Tell me about your family. They're in California? What does your pa do?"

"My father is a teacher."

"A teacher? Well, that doesn't surprise me. And Willie says you're originally from Massachusetts?"

"That's right."

"But then you all went to California?"

"We did."

"And you came back by yourself?"

"I…" How do I answer him? "I need to be with my family."

There was truth to that, and Matthew nodded.

"Why do you call me Duchess?" I asked again.

"With your quality ways and fine manner of speaking, you sound like a duchess to me."

"You speak rather well yourself, Mr. Cooper."

"My pa was a minster in Lowell and learning was important to him."

"I see." I searched for something to say because I didn't want our conversation to end. "So do you meet many duchesses on the Oregon Trail?"

Matthew laughed. "So far you're the only one."

Sitting next to Matthew felt like a warm embrace. My cheeks glowed hot at the thought, but it was dark and I hoped he hadn't noticed. He glanced upwards as the stars, now dulled under cloud-light. He nodded as he stood.

"Good night, Duchess. You better get some rest."

"Mr. Cooper," I called as he walked away. "I hope when you get out West you find whatever it is you're looking for."

"I wish you the same." He looked thoughtful, as if he wanted to say more, but he disappeared into his tent.

I wanted to run after him and grab his arm. "I have," I wanted to tell him. "At least, I've found something I don't want to lose."

But I can't. It's ridiculous of me to even think such a thing. I hardly know Matthew Cooper, even if he feels as familiar to me as my own heartbeat. Even if it feels like he's always been there, somewhere.

CHAPTER 14

I can't recall a time I haven't walked this land, a time I haven't known the Kansas prairie. There's nothing else in the world but this tall grass, these wildflowers, that endless sky. While the panoramic scenery is stunning—I gasped aloud when I first saw it—by now the pink coneflowers, the blue switchgrass, the golden wheatgrass, and the white pearly-everlastings are the same day after day, too mind-numbing to be noticed. Still, sometimes, even when I think I cannot take one more step, the scenic views refresh me and I'm in awe of the spectacular creation.

Each day at noon we stop for an hour to eat and allow the beasts some rest from their burdens. But we have no release from our labors. For women, there is always something to cook or clean or mend, and if there's water nearby we wash clothes. For men, there is wear and tear on wheels or wagons to tend, the result of the vehicles' constant bouncing through the ruts left by previous travelers. The only way we know for certain that time is passing is when we stop each night for food and rest. I sleep sometimes, but fitfully, a dream within a dream. My father told me once about embedded narratives—stories within stories—and I think this is what is happening to me. I'm living in a world within a world, a life within a life. Am I here or am I there? And where is here and where is there anyway?

THE DAYS OF ENDLESS WALKING HAVE ATTACKED MY NERVE ENDINGS, as if someone pokes my swollen feet with sewing pins. Luckily, the greenery alongside the generous river provides some respite from the hard ground. This morning I took my boots off and let my aggravated legs linger in the ice-cold water, which helped to freeze some of the blisters away. The water is pure, clear, and fresh-tasting. Wildflowers sprout in the tall grass. The plains remain beautiful. Unfortunately, mosquitoes like this scenic area as well and they enjoy feasting on our animals as well as us. Takodah cannot make balm fast enough to soothe our itchy bumps and I keep my hands folded in my apron to avoid scratching myself to my bones. Dry brush scrapes my ankles and burs stick to my dress. Sometimes I have to put my hand out to feel for the wagon, the air is so thick with dust.

TODAY WE HEARD THE EXUBERANT CRASH OF A NEARBY WATERFALL rushing down a ten-foot-long ledge into a shaded pool. Willie and I filled our canteens, jugs, and barrels to brimming. We've already been warned by Hiram that there will come a time on this journey when clean, healthy water will be hard to find so we should enjoy it, mosquitos and all, while we can. Paul and Sally had fun trying to catch the slippery frogs that jumped through their hands. Too soon, we were moving again. The dust was so thick I kept lowering my bonnet over my eyes. The grit embedded itself everywhere—in my dress, my hair, my eyes, my mouth. Even now, after we've stopped for the day, I can't stop coughing.

· · ·

SEVERAL WEEKS OUT AND WE'VE FALLEN INTO A ROUTINE. TWO hours before dawn, Brent Hardisty, one of the night guards, blows off-tune into his bugle and everyone awakens with sore limbs and a grumble. Drivers round up the livestock, who have been left to roam free for their fill of the tall grass during the night. Men unpen the mules. Others harness the oxen. Each morning, while Mrs. Quigley argues with Samuel Maylie about which cow or goat belongs where, Sally is sent to Pruella, Willie's cow, to milk the easy-tempered animal. We drink fresh milk with breakfast, and Willie pours any remaining cream into the butter churn and hangs it on a hook inside the wagon. By the end of the day, after the bumping and jostling, the butter is indeed ready.

I've become known around camp for my johnnycakes. My grandmother's recipe is a good one and the others like them very much. I've been asked by some of the women if I would make a batch for them. Many of the women have been friendly enough toward me, although I've noticed that Anne Brownlow, her doll-like daughter, and Lenore Starkey don't come themselves but instead send Mrs. Starkey's youngest son Thomas to ask for an extra round of johnnycakes if any were left begging. I'd like to tell them where they can stick those johnnycakes, sizzling right out of the skillet, but it's easier to fry the cakes and send them along. It's the least I can do to keep the peace. The truth is, I'm happy to cook the morning meal. I feel useful, at least.

The women who have asked for johnnycakes share their corn-meal, salt, sugar, and butter with me so I'm not using up all the Wetherfields' supplies feeding other families. Those who are not a Brownlow, a Carson, or a Starkey thank me for taking care of breakfast while they tend to the cleaning, the packing, and the children. Everyone who passes my cooking fire grabs one or two corn cakes and comes back for another two or three. I'm kept so busy that my only task in the morning has become frying johnny-cakes. I tell Willie I think I should help her with more of the chores before we pull out, but she says she's happy to take care of everything else. She eats quite a few of the cakes herself.

I flipped my latest batch, watching the edges form a golden-brown crust over the open fire, overcome by the scent of sweet, crusty cornmeal. I thought of my life before I came here and I laughed aloud at my bizarre thoughts—one minute I'm using a microwave, the next I'm cooking over an open fire—and there was Mrs. Bea watching to see if I was indeed talking to myself. I smiled in a friendly manner, nothing doing here, and she returned the greeting in kind.

"Those are going to burn there, Duchess, if you don't watch out."

Matthew's voice snapped me back to myself. The johnnycakes were blackening and the fried smoke wafted upward. I flipped the cakes onto a plate and Matthew grabbed the darkest one.

"You don't need to eat those," I said. "I'll make some more."

"I like them a little dark. They have more flavor that way." He waited a moment for the crispy corn in his hand to cool before he finished it in one bite. He took the others, equally burned, and finished them off as quickly.

"They're very tasty, Miss Wentworth. Thank you."

Matthew made his way into the bustle of busy men as everyone readied to head out.

Willie handed me a sleeping Leticia. "She can sleep through a tornado, this one," Willie said, a warm smile for her youngest. "Hold her while I finish washing up the skillet."

"I'll do that, Willie."

"No, no. Just hold onto little Tish there."

I looked into Leticia's serene face and I noticed how much she resembles Willie. She has Willie's dark hair and green eyes, like Sally. Like Matthew. Willie nodded at the stack of johnnycakes.

"Did you keep some back for Enoch Emerson?" she asked.

"That's the last batch," I said. "Who is Enoch Emerson?"

"He's a widower here on our train. You must have seen him—

tall, gangly, always watching the ground like he's lost something. He's sure to find a wife out here if he's ready to marry again."

"When did his wife die?" I asked.

"Three weeks before we pulled out."

"How can someone remarry that soon after their spouse dies? There's no time to grieve."

"Maybe it's different where you're from, but around here folks get married again quick after their spouses die, especially on the trail. Amos says Mr. Emerson is a good man who needs some time is all. He'll jump back into the saddle when he meets the right woman. After all, Sylvester Banning got married two months after his wife died and he and Velma seem to like each other well enough."

"Two months? That seems so soon to me."

"Grief is a luxury. And so is love. Out here, you do what you need to do to survive. That doesn't mean Sylvester cared about his wife any less, but she's gone and he still has to make his way in this world. He needed someone to care for him, feed him, and clean his clothes, and Velma's an orphan who needed protection. They both wanted to go West hoping for a better life, so they got married and now they're taking care of each other. That's a good thing, Grace, believe me." She nodded at me. "You're lucky I found you, Miss Wentworth, or who knows what crude villain might have set his sights on you."

"Kidnapped into marriage?"

"It happens. All I'm saying is you never know what life has in store for you."

"No," I said. "You never do."

I searched the nearby faces, first for Takodah, then for Sylvester and Velma, but I didn't see them. Brent Hardisty's sickly bugle rang out again and hearty shouts of "Wagons ho!" echoed across the prairie. There was no time for anything but to tie Tish's cradle around my shoulders so she would stay put while I walked.

"You sure you don't mind carrying her?" Willie asked.

"I'm happy to." And I was.

Willie watched me rock Tish gently against my shoulder. "You need a baby, Miss Wentworth. I believe you do."

"I think we can leave that for a little further down the line, Willie."

We marched Westward to the rhythm of slapping feet, bellowing animals, and rumbling wagons. Several of the younger, faster men rode out front on horseback to clear a path, or at least find something vaguely crossable by our unwieldy party. Most days Matthew takes the lead with Lee Tappertit.

From seven in the morning until noon we walk. Then we noon, and then we walk again until it is nearly too dark to see. The going isn't any easier in the wagons. The wagon drivers complain of back aches, headaches, and rump aches from jostling in their seats all day and the considerable strength needed to steer the animals. Those who are driving mules need feats of near contortionism to get the mules to do their bidding. Mules will jump front, side, or center if they are scared, which is often. Riding inside the wagons might be toughest of all with the bumping, rolling, and constant bombardment of furniture, supplies, and tools. Those of us walking probably have it the easiest, though the walking is bad enough.

To say so much walking is tedious is an understatement. To say so much walking is painful is skirting the issue. Numbing. That's the best way to describe it. I've become numb—first my toes, then my legs, then my torso, then my arms, then my fingers, then my brain. I'm not sure how I keep moving, right leg, left leg, on and on, for hours, day after day. Somehow, I stay upright, most of the time, unless I trip over my own feet, which happens often.

Most days, if I can stay in the numbness, it isn't so bad. It's rhythmic, the walking, and if you can keep the cadence then it becomes mechanical, as if I've become a wind-up toy. Yesterday we pushed for 20 miles, which is great time, Hiram said proudly, but we were all too exhausted by the end and I don't think we'll be able to make that many miles in one day again any time soon. I couldn't even drag my feet to the creek to wash. I was covered in dust and grime but I was too tired to care. No one cooked. Women sliced some bacon and dry bread and passed it around to their families. Our mouths were already dry from the warmth of the day and the grit in the air, but no one seemed to notice the sandpaper-like food. Sips of water from the canteen didn't help much. Matthew didn't even eat. He slipped off Petunia, the bay mare he calls Tune, set up his tent, and disappeared inside.

The next morning was just as wearisome. As Amos pulled down the tent I shared with the children, a pitiful cry rang toward us.

"Come on, Ma!"

"No!" Mrs. Quigley's voice was firm. She leaned out of her barrow as though she meant to crawl away, back to Ohio, maybe. "I ain't going no more. I'm done, Ezra. I'm as good as gone anyhow. You all go on your way and leave me be."

"You can't stay here by yourself, Ma," Ezra said. "Besides, you haven't even been walking like the other women. You've been rolling along in your contraption. What do you have to complain about?"

"Like I said, boy, leave me be."

"But you're doing such a wonderful job with the livestock, Mrs. Quigley."

Takodah was there, kneeling besides Mrs. Quigley's barrow. She pushed her blue calico sleeves to her elbows.

"May I see your hands, Mrs. Quigley?" Mrs. Quigley complied immediately, like a child. "If your hands are hurting you from wheeling all day I might be able to help. I have a salve that works well for blisters. We can't lose you, after all. We need someone who can handle the livestock as well as you can. They listen to you."

"You're the Indian," Mrs. Quigley said.

"I'm Takodah Wetherfield."

"Hiram Wetherfield's wife," said Lenore Starkey. "We know

who you are. We saw what happened with the Duringtons'
daughter."

"Then you know she saved the boy," Willie said. "It's not Mrs.
Wetherfield's fault the girl was in the water too long."

But Lenore Starkey wouldn't be deterred. Her husband is one
of those who likes to argue with Amos over every little detail and
Lenore obviously has a similar temperament. "Where have you
been hiding, Mrs. Wetherfield?"

"I haven't been hiding," Takodah said. "I've been right here, in
the back of my wagon."

Hiram pushed his way to the front of the onlookers, his back
straight, his hand on the grip of his revolver.

"Hiram." Amos clenched his brother's shoulder.

"I'm here to protect my wife, Amos, that's all."

"Mrs. Wetherfield won't need protecting," Amos said. "Will she,
Mr. Starkey?"

Moses Johnstone and Jonas Blackwood stood behind Archie
Starkey as though forming a posse. Archie seemed startled to hear
himself called into this, but he shook his head and Hiram dropped
his hand from his gun. Johnstone and Blackwood lingered near
Archie in case reinforcements were needed after all.

Willie stood behind Takodah in a similar fashion. "Of course
Mrs. Wetherfield doesn't need protecting. Why, she helped Adelina
Trenton deliver her baby just last night. Momma and baby are
both fine." Willie stared down the other women as though daring
them to say otherwise. "There will come a time on this long
journey when one of you will need Mrs. Wetherfield's help as
well."

Moses Johnstone whispered something to Archie Starkey,
whose mouth pulled into a flat line that may have been a smile, or
constipation. The women watched carefully, stepping on each
other's toes for a better view while Takodah examined Mrs.
Quigley's hands.

"Your hands are badly blistered," Takodah said. "I can slather them with the salve and bandage them. We'll keep doing it every day until your blisters are better."

Mrs. Quigley patted Takodah's hand in a motherly way. "You seem like a nice girl, and I appreciate your help, I do, but I'm gone and done-for. I'm sorry you're already married because I would have liked you for a daughter-in-law, you're so kind. But I'm staying right here. You all go on and leave me here to die." Mrs. Quigley leaned so far back in her barrow that she nearly tipped out. Then she crossed her arms over her chest as if she were already a corpse. When Ezra went to help his mother, she swatted him away.

"You said I got old bones, boy, and won't no one contradict you. Maybe the buzzards will pick me clean and my bones will gloss in the prairie sun."

"I ain't leaving you, Ma," Ezra said.

Ezra tried to lift his mother out of the barrow, but she was heavier than him and he couldn't manage it. He yelled at her, screamed in her face, nearly pulled her thin dress right off her body as he tugged at her sleeve but her arm didn't follow.

"Come on, Ma." Ezra was pleading now. "This nice lady says she can help your hands. Why don't you let her? Or you could walk."

A horse galloped in from the distance and there was Matthew surveying the scene. He jumped off Tune, smiling at Mrs. Quigley. He leaned over Ezra's mother, who turned away like an ill-tempered toddler.

"I bet you're sincerely tired about now," Matthew said. His voice was friendly, understanding. "We're all tired, Mrs. Quigley, and since we're just a few weeks out I reckon we're all going to be a whole lot tireder before this thing's done. But we have to see it through. We've made it this far, haven't we?"

Mrs. Quigley's neck quivered and her shoulders softened. Matthew spoke to her the way he speaks to Petunia or the mules when they need to be calmed. "I think we're going to have to give it all we've got, Mrs. Quigley. I think we're going to have to push ourselves harder than we ever thought we could. But you know what? We can do it. I wouldn't have talked my family into coming if I didn't believe we had the strength to do this. And you do too. Won't you come along to keep me company? Besides, I need someone who can keep Ezra in line. I can't do that by myself."

Mrs. Quigley exhaled, long and low. "Well," she said, "if you put it like that, I suppose I got to, don't I?"

"Yes, you do," Matthew said. "And you've just made me very happy, Mrs. Quigley."

Willie gestured toward Takodah, who was still kneeling by the barrow. "Won't you let my sister-in-law tend to your raw hands, Mrs. Quigley? She can help you."

Takodah extended a hand, which the older woman accepted. Mrs. Quigley grunted as she pulled herself straighter in her barrow and Takodah helped to steady her.

"Let me get what I need," Takodah said. "I'll be back in a moment."

Mrs. Quigley nodded as Takodah disappeared into the back of her wagon.

Poor Ezra. I thought his head was going to pop off his neck. "How come you wouldn't listen to me when I said you had to come with us?" he asked his mother.

"You don't speak sense, boy, not like Matty here or that nice lady."

Takodah reappeared with a jar of salve and two long linen bandages. As she rubbed the balm into Mrs. Quigley's raw hands the older woman sighed with relief. Amos and Hiram decided that Mrs. Quigley would ride in the back of Hiram's wagon while her hands healed. Takodah would walk alongside.

"It'll be awful bumpy, Mrs. Quigley," Hiram said, "but at least you can rest while we move."

"What about them livestock?" Mrs. Quigley asked.

"Ezra can manage for now," said Amos.

She watched her son side-eyed. "I don't know, Captain Wetherfield. I don't know if you can trust that boy for nothing."

"It'll be fine, Mrs. Quigley," Amos said. "Ezra will do his job.
Won't you, Ezra?"

"I sure will, Captain Wetherfield. Haw! See! I can do it as well
as Ma. Haw!"

If Mrs. Quigley could have reached her son from where she sat,
I was sure she would have smacked him.

Amos looked at the sun, rising by the moment, and he spoke to
the men nearby in a voice loud enough for everyone to hear. "We
can't have setbacks like this. I know we're tired, but I also know we
got a long way to go and we've barely begun. Next time someone
wants to give up we're going to let you. Does everyone
understand?"

The sad-sounding bugle yowled and the wagons pressed
forward in their turn.

"There's one crisis averted," Willie said while we walked. She
leaned close and whispered. "I'm surprised incidents like that don't
happen more often. Did you hear about Elizabeth Markham?" I
shook my head. "She became a lunatic on the trail just like Old
Mrs. Quigley nearly did right there. This Mrs. Markham refused
to go any further. She sat right down and wouldn't budge. Her
husband went ahead with the children, but then he sent his son
back to fetch her. When Elizabeth arrived at the train without the
son she announced that she had killed the boy with a rock. Can
you imagine? Beating your own son like that? The father found the
boy barely breathing, and while the father was rescuing the son
Mrs. Markham set their wagon on fire."

I looked at Mrs. Quigley, who seemed comfortable enough
bundled into the back of Takodah's wagon, covered in quilts
despite the warm day.

"To be honest, Willie, I can see how someone can lose their
mind out here."

Willie looked at her own children and smiled with the depth of a mother's love. "No, no, Grace. No matter how bad things get, you have to love your children. What else is there, what else that's important?"

"You're right, Willie. Of course you are. But I also know that all this endless walking does things to your mind. It's like your brain doesn't know what to do with itself so it makes up scary stories and you're stuck inside those stories with nowhere else to go and no way out." Willie didn't respond. After a time, I said, "I wonder what became of Elizabeth Markham?"

"I'm sure she was horrified when she realized what she had done. At least I hope she was."

I watched the slow-moving wagons, the glazed resignation in people's eyes, and I hoped that no one in our train would fall to the same fate as Mrs. Markham. I searched for Matthew and saw him trotting alongside the wagon, chatting with Amos, and I found solace in his steady demeanor. In my mind, Matthew Cooper stands as a beacon of everything worth fighting our way West for —the dream of new opportunities.

Willie caught me watching Matthew and smiled. "All in good time, Grace. Everything happens in its own good time."

I shook my head. No, you've got it all wrong, I wanted to say. Matthew is...well, Matthew is Matthew. But this is a dream and he is a dream—it must be a dream no matter what my senses say. This will all go away soon. Willie took my silence for compliance and slapped my shoulder.

"Come on now, Grace. I've seen you and Matty together enough to know what's going on. You two have had a chat or two or three when you think everyone else is tucked up in their tents. One of you is always sneaking glances at the other, as if you have to know where the other one is at all times."

"Matthew watches me?"

"You didn't know? Well, now you do. You have an easy manner betwixt yourselves, better than me and Amos when we were first married. Amos doesn't have a nickname for me, but Matthew calls you Duchess. Everyone says how sweet that is."

"Everyone knows about that?"

"Everyone knows everything." She gestured toward the wide, open land. "You've seen what those tattlers are like. There's nowhere to hide out here. But here's something you ought to know." Willie dropped her voice so low I could barely hear her over the clomping hooves and groaning wagons. "Things may be different out West, but here folks think that when an unmarried man and an unmarried woman take notice of each other there's going to be an engagement announced soon. That's got their attention since like I told you some of these mothers have their eyes set on Matthew for their own daughters. All I'm saying is that if you and Matty continue to spend time together, people are going to wonder why you're not engaged or better yet married. Well?"

"Well?"

"Anything I ought to know?"

"Nothing like that, Willie."

"Nothing like that yet?" My blush was my only response. "All right, then. Like I said, all in good time. But I don't want them getting any more wrong ideas about you, that's all."

"What wrong ideas?"

"Do you really need me to spell it out for you?"

No, I didn't. I could guess easily enough. Willie and I stopped talking and enjoyed the cooling wind that blanketed the land and made the wildflowers dance and the grass sing.

CHAPTER 15

The sky is a palette, the hues the masterstroke of a Great Painter. If I had beliefs in a higher power they would be reinforced daily by the movement of color in the dome overhead. When we begin our day at dawn the sky is mellow, a yellow light along the horizon with layers of magenta and lavender reflecting gauzy clouds. As the day progresses everything softens to a pastel vision of soft pinks and see-through blues with clouds like cotton balls meandering like vagabonds until they shapeshift into faces or cats or squares. Yesterday two long clouds floated past with outstretched sides, like two people hugging, and I was sure I saw my parents.

After a long day of walking, the night fades from green to purple, and with the darkness comes flashes of luminescence. With the lack of light pollution each star is a pinpoint, like millions of sky-high candles. I had never considered the sky much before. I would admire the sunset on occasion, but I never gave the stunning kaleidoscope the consideration it deserves. Tonight, after we stopped to rest, I thought the bright clusters were so close I reached out to touch one, then laughed at my foolishness.

"I've tried it, Miss Wentworth," said little Paul as he sat next to me. "I tried to touch that one right there," he pointed at the brightest point in the sky, "but I couldn't reach it even standing on my tippy toes."

"It must be farther away than it looks," I said. "That's too bad. But there's a star that's even closer. Did you know that the sun is a star?"

"Uncle Matty told me that. But the sun's too bright, I think, and it would probably burn if you touched it." He nodded as if he had given the matter much thought. "I'd like to know what a nighttime star feels like, Miss Wentworth. I surely would." He stared into the darkness with the wisdom of a sage.

We sat together, appreciating the heavenly exhibition, while Paul sang in his sweet voice:

Twinkle, twinkle, little star,

How I wonder what you are!

Up above the world so high,

Like a diamond in the sky.

When the blazing sun is gone,

When he nothing shines upon,

Then you show your little light,

Twinkle, twinkle, all the night.

Willie, Amos, and Matthew cheered as if Paul had graced us with the greatest song yet sung. He's such a dear boy, and I found myself wishing he was mine, that Matthew, Paul, and I were a family. My cheeks blazed with the thought. From the gem-like glint in Matthew's eyes, I thought he could read my mind.

WE PASS TOO MANY GRAVES EACH DAY. PAUL AND SALLY PRACTICE their numbers by counting the impromptu tombs on the trail.

"One, two, three, four, five, six, seven…"

Today there were ten graves. Six were too small to be adults, and we were sadly reminded of Priscilla. There is little laughter and no music when we stop for the night. We're exhausted to the very sinews in our muscles. We're waiting for the next tragedy that must be coming. It has to be. Where we see the graves, along with the markers noting the names and ages of the deceased, there are notes scratched into wood or stone, warning coming trains about stampedes, toppled wagons, and poisonous roots. Stolen animals. Crushed children. Drowned men. People who disappear never to be seen again. Disease. Our tight eyes and thin lips show our worry. We don't need to give voice to it. We're too tired to say it aloud anyway.

THE TRAGEDY WE FEARED HAPPENED TODAY. THIS AFTERNOON WE were caught in a storm so all-consuming I thought we would never find our way out again. Even now, an hour after the bullet-like rain stopped and the humidity blanketed us, I'm still quivering, too unsettled for sleep. I know I need to rest, but if I lie down I'll feel helpless. After all the pounding we received today, partnered with crashing thunder and lightning strikes, and after the stampede brought on by frightened mules, all I can do is write, grateful again to Willie for gifting me these journals. I'll have them all filled before long.

I knew something was wrong from the way Matthew, Amos, and Hiram kept glancing at the sky. A storming sky is a beautiful sight, a gray ombre with gradations of silver as light struggles through the darkening lead-like layers. The very same sky I had waxed poetic over as a pastel paradise had grown into a threatening spectacle as the winds shifted and cumulonimbus clouds settled overhead like scratchy flannel.

"All right," Amos called. "Let's corral up."

"We still have a few hours to sunset," said Archie Starkey. "I say we keep going."

Amos nodded at the sky. "I'd say we've got a few minutes at best before that storm breaks."

Crash! Everyone, person and animal, looked toward the menacing sky. Thunder and another crash! The ground shuddered as though the earth would swallow us whole. Women screamed when a lightning bolt flashed overhead. Zeus himself must be angry with us, I thought, as two more zigzags lit the murky clouds.

"Everyone move into corral formation! Now!" Hiram yelled.

Men moved the wagons into our customary circle. Another crack of thunder and so much rain fell that Willie said she expected Noah and his animals to float past. Everyone piled into their wagons, though the poor animals were left to suffer the whims of the weather. Their cries were pathetic.

Amos and Matthew sat as close to the driver's seat at they dared, watching Ed, Ted, and Fred as though they were the only things in the world that mattered, and in that moment they were. Skittish mules can wreak all kinds of havoc, and it was obvious the animals were nervous by the way they flattened their ears and ducked their heads. Fred reared to the left while Ed jumped to the right. Ted pulled in both directions, and all three tried to get away from the pummeling hailstones.

"Let me get into the driver's seat and take the reins," Matthew said. "I think I can calm them."

"It's too dangerous," said Willie.

Amos watched the three mules kicking and pulling, rocking the wagon side to side. Sally screamed as the wagon tilted forward until we all pressed into the front, and then we fell back when the front wheels came off the ground.

"What will be even more dangerous is if those mules decide to make a run for it with each animal going in a different direction," Amos said. Even sitting near the front, Amos and Matthew were soaked through and held their hands over their eyes so they could see. "All right, let's do it. I'll come with you and we'll handle them together."

As Matthew and Amos crawled up front, a wild scream filled the air. Matthew and Amos jumped outside to see what the trouble was, but the evil-minded wind pummeled them from all directions and it took them a moment to figure out where the sound had come from. Amos nodded toward a wagon two vehicles behind us.

That wagon's mules were rocking their wagon just as Ed, Ted, and Fred were rocking ours, pulling the vehicle every which way while the animals nearly choked in their yokes. Their black eyes were wild while their lips pulled into maniacal grimaces. All three animals moved in unison, rocking the wagon as though it were a ship surging on the sea.

"There!" Willie cried. She pointed toward a small object dangerously close to the panicked mules and I recognized Jimmy Billings, the little boy who had given me a handful of wildflowers. I clutched Willie's hand and she clutched mine as we watched in horror. When Paul and Sally inched toward the back of the wagon for a better view, Willie pulled them toward her. "Don't you dare go near there!" She sounded angry, but it was an anger born of fear.

When all three of the Billings' mules began kicking in every direction there was another scream. Cries of "Jimmy! Jimmy!" were punctured by sharp darts of hail that sounded like bullets as they hit the ground.

"Get him out!" a man's voice called.

I couldn't see what happened next since pellets of ice blurred my vision. I didn't know how anyone could see anything out there, and the cries of the frightened animals and the anxious people grew more ominous.

As suddenly as the storm came on it stopped. A few more drops of spent rain fell, but otherwise everything was calm. The animals stopped bleating.

"Jimmy! My Jimmy!"

Takodah ran to Mrs. Billings, who was rocking her son in her arms. Hiram stepped closer, touched the boy's neck, and shook his head. Takodah backed away. We learned afterward that Jimmy had wanted to help his father, who was struggling with their mules as Amos and Matthew were struggling with ours. Jimmy thought if he unharnessed the beasts they might feel better and he ran out before anyone could stop him. Instead of unharnessing the mules he was trapped under the panicking animals' hooves and trampled to death.

"Oh, dear Father in Heaven," Willie said when we learned what happened. "Why is it always the babies?"

She pulled her three children to her chest and hugged them tighter than I had ever seen a mother hug her children. I thought of the beautiful pink wildflowers and the smile that had accompanied them and I cried.

WE PRESS ON. WE HAVE TO. IT'S NOT THAT WE DON'T CARE, BUT IF we let the grief consume us we'll do as Mrs. Quigley nearly did and we'd all lie down and never rise again. So we walk. We carry the loss in our hearts and we walk. I'm at the point now where I can hardly remember a time when my legs didn't ache and my feet didn't cramp. There are entire days when I forget I ever had another life, in this time or another.

Today our train slowed as we neared a hill in the distance, like a mirage in the flat grasslands. Desert walkers believe they see a river in the sand. We thought we imagined a blue mound in the prairie. Only we didn't imagine it. It was there, and some of the men galloped ahead and climbed the hill, hoping a trip to the top would give them a panoramic view and a sense of where we were in the world, or at least some idea of what lay ahead.

Amos slowed his wagon so he could speak to Matthew, who was trotting a bit behind.

"Do you think we should stop at that there nub?" Amos asked. "It's headed toward evening and it looks as good a place to sleep as any."

Matthew shook his head. "I took a ride out and I don't think there's any water."

"Too right," said Hiram, who was driving his wagon alongside ours. "There's no water around here to speak of, which means we can't rest here." He stopped his mules and stood, yelling as loud as he could. "All right, folks, that mound there ain't worth our time. We need to keep moving at a clip if we want to find a good watering hole where we can rest tonight." He waved everyone forward to emphasize his point.

A collective murmuring spread as though the travelers had hoped for something, even a blue mound, to put and end to the monotony. We passed the hill with little fanfare, with only a few of the boys, including Paul Wetherfield, climbing to the top to wave to their exasperated parents before they rolled back down and joined their families unharmed. Later, the men riding ahead found a nice spot with a clean stream and acres of grass to feed the animals. We pulled our wagons into our corral and settled in for the night.

I helped Willie unpack. Cookware, utensils, plates, and cups were set out and a fire was started. The men had been successful in their hunt that day and brought back armfuls of pheasants. I make myself scarce during butchering time. I'm not naïve, but I can't bring myself to watch, or help. Willie doesn't seem to mind since I make myself useful by keeping an eye on Paul, Sally, Tish, and some of the other children. I looked for Jimmy and it pricked my heart when I remembered he wasn't there.

Willie finished butchering the two pheasants Amos and Matthew brought back. She was cutting out some fillets when she toppled backwards as though her feet gave out from under her.

"Ma!" Sally cried.

Paul and I rushed to Willie's side, but she brushed us away when we tried to help.

"No, no, stop that now. I can stand on my own two feet. I'm not dead yet."

"Please, Willie," I said. "Rest a while. Heavens knows we all need it." I set my hands on Willie's shoulders and gently persuaded her to stay where she was. She had fallen into a sitting position, and she didn't seem any worse for it except for the pink spots on her cheeks, more from embarrassment, I thought, than injury.

"It's true I'm so very tired." Willie covered her face with her hands, exhaled, then sat up as if she meant business. "But that's no excuse, is it? Everyone's tired and that's no reason for me to sit here like a fairy princess while everyone else is getting their work done. I need to make supper."

"I'll make supper," I said.

Willie looked as though she would protest but she must have seen my determination and she shrugged. "If you don't mind cooking, Grace, then that's all right by me. We've got the fillets there, and I promised Paul bacon-fried bread along with his supper if he was a good boy and came down that blue hill."

"Luckily for you, I know how to make that."

I made sure the fire was high and hot and tossed the fillets into the skillet with some butter and breadcrumbs as Willie had taught me. While the pheasant was frying, I ruffled through the foodstuff for the bacon and bread. After the fillets were done I added some bacon to the pan, and after the bacon was cooked I fried the bread in the grease. I didn't realize how hungry I was until smoked, meaty scents wafted around me. Matthew sniffed the air and gave a nod of approval.

"Smells mighty nice, Duchess. Maybe you should do the cooking all the time."

"My grandmother taught me how to cook," I said.

"No one better than a granny to teach you cooking."

Willie swatted at her brother with a playful hand. She looked better. She had color in her face and seemed steadier, more herself. Amos knelt beside his wife and gave her a good looking over, as though checking her for serious ailments. He must have decided she was all right because he didn't seem concerned. Willie and Amos looked deeply into each other's eyes, and while their glances didn't have the same soulful intensity as my parents', I sensed that Willie and Amos are very much in love. For some reason, the realization makes me happy.

I watched Matthew as he took his plate of food to join Ezra Quigley and his mother. Our gazes met and we looked away as quickly. I wondered if he had received the same warning from Willie that I had. The idea that Matthew and I are simply friends would not be believed here. Men and women are not friends. They are related by blood or marriage. Anything in between lands you firmly into gossips' territory, and I have enough problems with curious eyes and prying ears. For now, it's better for me to stay out of Matthew's way. Out of sight, out of mind.

And yet.

I'll admit, only here in the privacy of these pages, that I long to be near him. I thought of Dorothy's words to Scarecrow before she returns to Kansas, "I'll miss you most of all," and I know that's how it will be with Matthew.

Only I am in Kansas. But this is not home.

When the evening meals were over the men gathered to smoke their pipes and discuss the journey while the women cleaned dishes, washed clothes, and mended whatever new scratch or tear had appeared in someone's clothing. We're all such ragamuffins already, but we still have a long way to go and it's important to keep whatever clothing we have wearable until the end.

Willie regained more of her strength after supper so she spent some time darning stockings and stitching a new yellow wannis for Leticia since she was growing out of her pink one. I sat beside Willie and she handed me the baby. I rocked Tish as I watched the men relaxing, smoking, and chatting as though they hadn't a care in the world.

"Aren't they going to help?" I nodded toward the men.

"Men? Help with the cooking and the cleaning?" The way Willie laughed you would have thought I told the world's funniest joke. "Someone would think you're from the moon with such notions."

"My father helps my mother around the house all the time. He does the dishes and he vacuums…"

"What's a vacuum?"

"Something they have in California."

"Maybe I'll see one someday. Maybe they have them in Oregon." Willie set the wannis aside, stretched her hands, and took Tish onto her lap. "Where did your mother find your father, anyhow?"

"Massachusetts."

"Really?" She smiled at Amos and Matthew, who were laughing with the other men, and shook her head. "I wouldn't go getting your hopes up, Grace. Both of my men are from Massachusetts and I've never heard of such a thing."

Marriages here are not born from romance or love—I've gathered that much. Sometimes love can grow, as it did for Willie and Amos, but for most people marriage is a contract, a business transaction. The man agrees to provide for his wife and the woman agrees to bear his children and keep his home. As Willie told me, marriage is an act of protection, especially for women. During the courting period, the prospective couple meets a few times and then a marriage proposal is made. I'm not ready to think about marriage with Matthew, not yet, and Matthew has never said anything to make me think he wants to marry me. Willie said he watches me, but being attracted to someone is not the same as wanting to spend the rest of your life with them. I know I'm drawn to him. I know he's handsome and I feel warm whenever I look into his jade-like eyes.

In my time, marriage is based on romantic love, or at least that's true in theory. Sometimes people marry because they believe it's expected of them or because they've created a beautiful illusion in their mind of what marriage will be—a vision beyond anything resembling reality. Sometimes people are lucky and their reality is better than the illusion. My parents have been lucky in that way. They have the kind of love the rest of us dream about.

Could I have that with Matthew Cooper?

CHAPTER 16

onight Hiram Wetherfield showed his uses beyond guiding us West. The brothers who played their instruments for us when we first started our journey lost heart and we've been without music for weeks. Hiram was inspired after his evening smoke and he pulled a fiddle from the back of his wagon. Willie called Takodah over.

"Takodah Wetherfield, you come over here right now and sit with us while your husband plays a tune or two."

Takodah nodded in thanks and made herself comfortable beside me on the quilt.

Hiram played some upbeat tunes while the children laughed and danced. They had such fun while the adults clapped along. As Hiram played one chipper tune after another, the children's excess energy deflated. They sat quietly, the boys with their fathers, the girls with their mothers. Hiram played another song and the others sang along:

DID YOU EVER GO FISHIN'

On a warm summer day
When all the fish
Were swimmin' in the bay
With their hands in their pockets
And their pockets in their pants
Did you ever see a fishie
Do the Hootchy-Kootchy Dance?
Turkey in the straw
Turkey in the hay
Turkey in the straw
Turkey in the hay
Roll 'em up and twist 'em up
A high tuck a-haw
And hit 'em up a tune called
Turkey in the Straw

AND ANOTHER, JUST AS WELL RECEIVED:

WELL, I COME FROM ALABAMA
With my banjo on my knee
And I'm bound for Louisiana
My own true love for to see
It did rain all night the day I left
The weather was bone dry
The sun was so hot I froze myself
Susanne don't you cry
Oh, Susannah
Now, don't you cry for me
As I come from Alabama
With this banjo on my knee

. . .

I PACED BETWEEN THE TWO WETHERFIELD WAGONS, PAINED BY WHAT I heard. When I say pained I mean in a physical way, like hundreds of fingers digging holes in my brain. I remembered clips I had seen in one of my history classes, singers in black-face singing "Turkey in the Straw" and "Oh, Susannah." And there's that ugly lyric I left out in my rendition above. My distaste must have shown on my face. When Mrs. Carson, her doll-like face pressed close to mine, her eyes wide as if in sympathy, asked whatever could be the matter, I blurted out, "Don't you know those are racist songs? How can anyone clap to them? They're horrible!"

Hiram stopped. Every head turned my way. Suddenly, I understood the term "silent as a tomb" because it was too quiet. The animals looked away to avoid my embarrassment. Even as the words came out of my mouth, I knew the word racist isn't used here, at least not the way I know it. All eyes watched me, waiting, wondering, I'm sure, if another bizarre outburst was coming. The men glanced at each other as though silently deciding what to do with me if I did indeed scream any such gibberish again.

I stood, frozen. How do I handle this? And while I worried about the others' reactions, I remembered that this is 1850, just 11 years before the American Civil War will begin. There is slavery right here in Kansas as we're passing though and there are violent disputes about where and how slavery should be expanded throughout the country.

The more everyone stared at me the more muddled I became, which must have made me look even crazier in their eyes. One of the men said, loudly enough for everyone to hear, "That squaw must be sending her voodoo magic to make that young woman say such things."

Now my dander was up, as my father likes to say. I spun toward the speaker—Moses Johnstone.

"How dare you say such a terrible thing about Mrs. Wetherfield! How dare you call her that name!" I yelled. "She's a kind person, a healer, and she has helped nearly every family on this train with one ailment or another. You can't make judgments about people like that. My uncle is Cherokee and he'd never hurt anyone!"

Silence. I should have been used to it by then but instead I grew more anxious. I watched as faces turned toward each other with consternation, amusement, or both.

Moses Johnstone has this way of smiling that reminds me of a naughty student who knows he's getting away with something behind the teacher's back. He stood, towering over me but speaking to Amos. "So she's one of them savages, is she? That explains a lot."

"No." I was confused by my own thoughts. I didn't want to explain away Uncle Chandresh, but I thought telling the truth might help. "I mean, he is my uncle, but by marriage. My Aunt Jennifer married a wonderful Cherokee man, Chandresh Mankiller, but she isn't even really my aunt, she's…" I knew I wasn't making sense so I stopped.

Moses stepped toward Amos, who watched as though he had never seen me before in his life. I was afraid of Matthew's reaction so I didn't look for it. "You best keep a handle on your womenfolk, there, Captain Wetherfield," Moses said. "She must be drunk as a fiddler. Has she been in your whiskey?" Everyone laughed. "Maybe instead of putting on airs all day long she should be taken down a peg."

"Maybe she needs a good hiding," said Archie Starkey.

God bless Willie. She put her arm around me and laughed as though I was the funniest person she knew.

"Poor girl's so exhausted she doesn't know what's she saying. Do you, darling?" I shook my head because she was right. I didn't know what I was saying.

I let Willie lead me to her wagon. She pulled the puckered cover aside. "Get in, Grace. You can rest in here tonight without everyone looking down your throat." She tucked me into the quilts as gently as if I were one of her children. I thought I would have trouble falling asleep, but I did in time, lulled by the winking stars and the knowing moonlight. They have seen everything, after all.

I OPENED MY EYES, FIRST ONE, THEN THE OTHER, CERTAIN THAT I WAS back home. I sat up, reached for the dresser near the bed and nearly rolled out of the wagon onto the rocky ground. The corral was silent. Snores and gurgles came from tents all around, complemented by snorts from the animals. Occasionally, as if the very breeze gossiped, I heard low conversations from the men on the watch.

My worst fear plagued me once again. What if this isn't a dream? What if this is real, I am here, and this is the only place I'll ever be? I burst into a heaving hysteria and sobbed until the top of my dress was soaked. After the fit of misery passed, I was too antsy to lay still so I left the warmth of my quilts. I climbed out of the wagon, ready to walk until I found my way home if I had to, until I was overtaken with fear that one of the men on the watch would mistake me for a thief and shoot first and look second. After my erratic display, I don't think anyone here would mind if I were suddenly gone.

I crept back into Willie's wagon as quietly as I could. It was late and even the snoring had stopped. Familiar footsteps crunched nearby.

"You awake, Duchess?"

My soul smiled at his whisper.

Matthew. When I was with him, everything felt all right on this long, strange journey. When I was with him, I could somehow make sense of it all.

Matthew. His easy smile. His friendly manner. His firm way of handling challenges. His eyes. His shadow loomed over me, that black silhouette I had imagined on my wall, until he crawled beside me on the tailgate. The wagon rattled with his every move.

It was dark, and I felt rather than saw him. But I could conjure him in my mind's eye easily enough.

Matthew.

I felt his weight shift as he leaned in my direction, his lips nearly touching my ear. I wanted to kiss him, but I couldn't. Not now, and definitely not here.

"I hope you don't mind the company," he whispered.

"I don't mind at all."

We glanced at each other, and even under the veil of night, I turned away, afraid he could feel the heat emanating from every part of me. We didn't say anything for a long while, but I felt better with him beside me. We stared into the night, watching the elegant shimmers of the stars.

"They're so beautiful," I said. "I never really noticed the sky before. And all along there have been these sublime constellations for me to admire every night of my life."

"Farmers know the sky pretty well," Matthew said. "We're looking for the sun and the rain. We have to guess how the weather's going to go so we can protect our crops and livestock. We have to know when a storm is coming and how long we have until it breaks. We have to know when it's going to be dry. But this sky..." He smiled as though he knew each star personally. "This is a special beauty we're privy to every night. The secret to the universe is out there. I know it."

"What is the secret to the universe, Mr. Cooper?"

"I don't know, yet, but when I discover it I'll tell you." We were quiet again, still stargazing, lost in our thoughts. Finally, he said, "What happened out there, Duchess? You seem right enough to me now, but before you sounded a little...well, I'm worried about you is all."

"Willie was right," I said. "I'm just tired."

"What does racist mean?"

He couldn't see me shrug in the darkness but I did anyway. "It means that the words of those songs aren't very nice about some people. People shouldn't say such things. It's dehumanizing."

"You're an abolitionist then?"

Abolitionist. The word sat heavy on my tongue until I remembered that I was sitting in a white-covered wagon on the Oregon Trail in 1850. "Yes, I am an abolitionist. Does that surprise you?"

"It'll take a lot more than that to surprise me, Duchess. The Coopers, the Wetherfields, we're all abolitionists. Hiram joined an abolitionist society when he lived in Kentucky. He was pretty happy when President Taylor pushed for California and New Mexico to apply for statehood. Did you hear about the conference the president had with the southern leaders?"

I thought through my American history courses but couldn't recall a conference between Zachary Taylor and southern leaders. I shook my head.

"Those southerners are dead set on growing the number of slave states. They're mad as hell, excuse my language, that California and New Mexico aren't going to have slaves and they threatened to secede from the Union right there and then until President Taylor said that anyone caught in rebellion would be hanged as fast as any a traitor."

"He sounds like a man of action," I said.

"He seems to be." Matthew leaned toward me as though trying to see in the darkness. "Duchess, if I may say so, I get where you're coming from, and so will Willie, Amos, and Hiram, especially about not judging Takodah or the man you call your uncle. But the others here? Just be careful what you say, Grace. As you can tell, they're not so understanding of anyone with different ideas, especially not a woman."

I didn't mean to lean into him, but I did. Our shoulders pressed together and I took comfort in his warmth. I felt the strength of his arm pressing into mine and I wanted to take his hand but didn't.

"Willie warned me off you," I said. "She said that if others knew you and I were friendly they'd expect a wedding announcement."

"That's generally the way it works. Is it different in California?"

"It's very different where I'm from."

"Then I bet you'll be glad to get back." Matthew's voice was small as he pulled his shoulder away, just slightly, but I felt the loss of his warmth. "Your people must be missing you."

"I miss them so much. Sometimes…"

I bit my lip, determined not to cry. I had cried enough, and crying didn't make anything better. There was so much I wanted to say but no one I could say it to. Even Matthew, as good-natured and intelligent as he is, wouldn't understand. I felt all alone, as though no one else on earth spoke my language and I couldn't communicate. I buried my face in my hands to hide my sorrow.

Matthew slid his arms around my shoulders and pulled me close to his body until my head rested on his chest. He rubbed my back and rocked me gently, the way I rocked Tish, until the wave of grief subsided. I should have pulled away but I didn't, and he didn't either. As the sun dawned in a thin yellow ribbon, Matthew jumped from the back of the wagon. Before he did, he kissed me. He kissed me easily at first, then more intensely, as though it was the most natural thing in the world.

We kissed for some time, again and again. When we came up for air the realization stung me like one hundred bees. This man beside me, with his arm around my waist, is real. His kind eyes, his gentle hands, his warm lips are real. Everything I see is real. Everything I'm experiencing is real. I'm here with this wonderful man, which makes my heart sing, but I may never see my family again.

Matthew Cooper is not a dream, and I don't know whether to laugh or cry. Both feel right about now.

CHAPTER 17

$\mathcal{W}$hen it was time to cross the Kansas River not everyone in our party came along. The Duringtons had enough of this wretched trip and they turned back, afraid of losing another child in the water. Who could blame them? Losing Priscilla and nearly losing Oliver must have knocked the wind right out of them. Reaching another raging river forced some kind of reckoning, and they chose to return home to deal with their grief without the added burden of an arduous journey.

Willie Wetherfield is a collector of lost souls, I think. She has taken in Miss Beula Durington, who continued the journey alone after her brother and sister-in-law turned back. Willie welcomed Beula into our wagon family with the same openheartedness she had welcomed me. I'm not sure about Beula, but I say nothing to Willie. I'm cordial to the newcomer, but I keep my distance. Actually, I'm steering clear of everyone who isn't a Cooper or a Wetherfield. Life is easier that way.

One good thing to happen of late is I'm finally getting to know Takodah better. There is something enigmatic about her, mystical even. She has a gentle smile and all-knowing eyes. Although

Takodah is content on her own, picking wildflowers to weave into crowns for Sally, Tish, Willie, Beula, and me, I have become her companion in searching for medicinal plants sprouting in the long grass.

I have come to enjoy our time together. Takodah has given me a small basket for my treasures, and I help her as she stoops over first one plant, then the next, pointing out what's good and what's not. Dandelions are good for digestion, she said, and they make good tea if they are roasted. Dandelions are good for salads too. Calendula is good for wounds. Unpleasant smelling mushrooms are poisonous and shouldn't be touched. Lavender is good for helping to settle people's nerves, and camomile is good for treating infections. I pick whatever she points to and set it neatly into the basket.

"I'm glad to finally get to know you," I told her.

"That's kind," Takodah said. "Most of them," she nodded toward the other wagons, "would rather I weren't here."

"I think they feel the same about me. But they're wrong about you. They don't know what's good for them."

"That's what Hiram says." Takodah watched me with eyes like citrines. There's something familiar about her I can't name. "Here's some astera. You can use them to make a poultice for sore muscles."

We stopped to add several handfuls to our baskets. As we continued walking Takodah scanned the ground for anything else that might be useful.

Takodah has become quite friendly with Mrs. Quigley, who is still traveling like a princess in the back of Takodah's wagon. Takodah continues to allow Mrs. Quigley the use of her featherbed and her softest quilts. Occasionally, as the wagon bounces its way West, something drops on Mrs. Quigley's head and an indignant "Dangnammit!" rings across the prairie.

Mrs. Quigley, for all her gruff manner, seems appreciative of everything Takodah and Hiram have done for her. Whenever anyone makes a comment about "that Indian" Mrs. Quigley isn't shy about sharing a piece of her mind about how Takodah has done more for her than her own flesh ever did.

Takodah turned her attention back to me. "What brings you West, Sarah?"

"I'm not Sarah. I'm Grace."

Takodah slapped her hand to her cheek. "Of course you are. I'm so sorry, Grace. I don't even know where that came from. Do you know someone named Sarah?"

"My mother's name is Sarah."

"Ah." Takodah nodded, as if that made all the sense in the world. "Are you and your mother close?"

"Very close."

"You miss her."

"Yes, I do."

"And your father?"

"I miss him too."

"That's right. I remember Hiram telling me. You're on your way back to your family."

I nodded. Complete thoughts, even simple words, evaded me.

Takodah's citrine eyes pierced my chest cavity, as if she had a direct line to my heart, or somewhere deeper.

"And now you've met Matthew Cooper."

I nodded.

"And Matthew is like your father."

"Yes. In a good way."

"You think of Matthew in a good way."

"How did you know?"

"Everyone here knows, Grace. Don't be afraid. Love is the same no matter when you're from."

I noticed Mrs. Brownlow and her daughter walking a bit quicker toward us as they always did whenever Willie, Takodah, or I talked. I suppose they will always need someone to gossip about, but the fact that we're always the targets is growing tiring. There was something in their manner, something about their implacable expressions, that worried me. That is, until Takodah's words screamed themselves into my brain.

"What do you mean, when I'm from?"

"You know what I mean."

"But how…?"

"It's the invisible world, dear. It's magic."

It can't be. It's not possible.

"Are you…?" I didn't know how to put my outlandish thoughts into words.

"I'm only me, Takodah Wetherfield. And yet we are all many beings, past, present, and future. You're an old soul, Grace, but so are we all. I don't know all of your story yet, but I will say that I think there's a reason you're here, on this wagon train, right now. And I think that reason is leading that horse over there."

Matthew watched our conversation as he walked alongside Tune, holding her reins. When our eyes met I felt a spark of static electricity. From the way his arm jolted, maybe he felt it too.

I looked for Willie, but then I remembered that she was riding inside the wagon. Willie has been weak lately so she's trying to rest, or at least rest as much as possible with all the jolting over the rocky ground. The children were inside with her, so I wasn't on watch duty.

"How did you meet Hiram?" I asked Takodah.

"He used to stay with my family when he made his way back and forth across the trail. He's been leading people to Oregon for about four years now. Each time Hiram passed through I came to know him a little better. When he asked me to marry him I said yes." She watched her husband driving their wagon and I felt her love emanating toward him. Takodah nodded. "It was a day of great fortune for me."

"Willie said Hiram traded a handful of buttons for you."

Takodah smiled. "My husband has many wonderful qualities, but he does like to exaggerate."

"You and Hiram are happy together?"

"He's a good man, Grace—attentive and considerate. He treats me with respect. When you find a man who treats you with respect, grab onto him with both hands and never let him go. Such men are few and far between."

I've seen enough since I've been here to know that Takodah is right. Some men here talk to their wives in a less than complimentary manner, barking orders and complaining loudly when something isn't up to their standards. They don't listen to their wives' concerns or opinions and laugh at their fears. Not all the men are like that. Hiram isn't, and Amos isn't. And Matthew. I know there are others. I can see why Takodah and Hiram, though they appear to be an odd match—he's a grizzled mountain man at least ten years older than she is—are happy together.

"You're lucky Hiram passed your way on his travels," I said.

"I don't think of it as luck. I think of it as destiny. It's our destiny to be together, Hiram and mine, and we happened to find each other at that moment. Do you believe in destiny, Grace?"

I watched Matthew Cooper hop onto Tune's back and gallop into the distance.

"I do," I said.

WE'RE NEARING ANOTHER RIVER, THE BIG BLUE, WHICH HIRAM SAID is more dangerous than the Kansas. It's nearing dark, and everyone is hungry and tired and ready to stop. We need the rest if we're to handle the dangers of the river with fortitude in the morning. The men huddle in the distance, too far for the women to hear, but we know they're deciding how to best get everyone to the other side, especially since the Duringtons' girl is still very much on everyone's mind whenever there's a river to cross. Amos joined us at our campfire, shoveling down a dinner of baked beans. He told Willie that he wanted to try to cross the river tonight since it might rise too much in the morning.

"We still have an hour of light at least," he said as he washed down his food with weak coffee. "What do you think, Matthew?"

Matthew studied the river. "I'm inclined to agree with you, Amos, but everyone is dead tired. I'm afraid if we try to cross now we'll slip under because we're too weary try to save ourselves. I don't see that one more night will make much difference and it's not raining so there's no reason to think the river will rise. Besides, I don't think we can all make it across with the amount of light we have left, and I for one don't want to be stuck in that river in the dark."

Amos nodded. "All right then. Let's stop now, get some rest, but then we're crossing at first light. We want to get to the Platte River and then when we get there we'll stop for a better rest at Fort Kearny. There should be better hunting around too. Poultry and small animals are fine, but I'm looking forward to some buffalo."

Matthew spread the news to the other men, who spread the news to the women, who spread the news to the children, and there was a collective sigh of relief. The wagons corralled for the night, and those who hadn't eaten yet had their evening meal. After that, all was still.

CHAPTER 18

*I*n the morning the bugle sounded and everyone looked as though they were sleepwalking, zombie-eyed and dead-limbed, as they went about their morning tasks. Willie made strong coffee, even giving some to the mules, while I flipped johnnycakes. All too soon, the bugle sounded again. We traveled until we stood at the edge of the Big Blue River, which ran along with a carelessness the powerful take for granted. With careful planning, we crossed without losing anyone, human or animal. After more long days like the one before and the one before, we found ourselves near the Platte River.

Amos steered the mules toward the ruts left by previous prairie schooners—a ready-made road, he called it. Willie laughed when she said she had only been hit in the head once that day, by a falling skillet, which sounded painful enough. The children stayed inside with her. I enjoy taking part in daily conversations with Willie, Takodah, and Mrs. Quigley. We're a happy little group, chatting about nothing in particular while keeping each other's minds off our painful limbs and anxious worries. I don't think I would survive this arduous journey without my friends to keep me going. Willie shouts her contributions from the back of her wagon while Mrs. Quigley shouts hers from the back of Takodah's wagon. Amos and Hiram drive near each other while Takodah, Beula, and I follow behind, engaged in conversation as though this is the most ordinary method of communication in the world.

Takodah stopped, listening.

"They're here," she said. "The buffalo."

I heard the animals before I saw them. The sound was faint at first, barely audible over the crunching wheels and pounding feet on the dry prairie ground. I gasped aloud at the sight of the majestic beasts—horned, shaggy creatures roaming the land. They munched on the plentiful grass and drank from the nearby stream. Everyone watched, especially the children, pointing out the largest animals and smiling at the babies.

We stopped at the far end of the stream, close enough to admire the golden-haired calves pressing into their mothers but far enough away to feel safe. Suddenly, I had a vision about a buffalo stampede. I don't know where it came from since the buffalo were a fair distance away and calm as could be. But in my mind I saw the huge animals scuffling past, accelerating their run until we wouldn't have time to react. The scene played out perfectly behind my eyes, from the first rumble, to the screams, to the death that surely followed.

I turned away from the others. "Stop this right now, Grace Marie Wentworth," I whispered to myself. The bison are minding their own business, not at all concerned that we're on the other side of the water. The animals are eating, drinking, resting, and doing whatever else it is that buffalo do with their time. We're of no concern to them. Stop being ridiculous.

Takodah grabbed my arm. "You see something, Grace. Tell me."

I shook my head, though I wanted to tell her. I could see in the softness in her eyes that she might believe me, especially after our previous conversation. But I couldn't bring myself to say the words. I thought sharing such thoughts aloud would make them more than a silly flight of fancy. By speaking it, I was sure I would make it real. I brushed my worries aside with a shake of my head and watched as little Paul clambered out of the wagon to stand at the edge of the stream, fascinated by the strong-looking buffalo.

"Look, Ma!" Paul shouted. "Their babies love their mommas like we love our mommas!" Paul cupped his hands into the water, staring at the herd, drinking with his eyes as well as his mouth. Willie looked like she would burst with pride for her boy. Amos jumped from the driver's seat and stood near his son.

"You're right, Paulie," said Amos. "All mommas and their babies love each other, no matter what kind of beasts they might be."

"And pas and their babies?"

"And pas and their babies. Except pas don't like to talk about it so much."

Paul nodded. He cupped his hands, dipped them into the stream, and drank some more, his eyes still glued to the animals. He smiled when he saw one particular calf being nudged toward the water by its mother. I sat near Paul, enjoying the respite from walking.

"Well, looky here at all them critters!" Mrs. Quigley called from the back of Takodah's wagon. "Ought to be able to gather enough buffalo chips to light our fires for a year!"

But our moment of joy was quickly overrun.

"Captain Wetherfield." Ezra Quigley waved his arms toward Amos. "Captain Wetherfield, we got a problem here."

Amos sighed. He patted Paul's head and joined Ezra Quigley, Archie Starkey, Moses Johnstone, Wilbur Gridley, and a few others, shouting in a heated argument. I couldn't tell what the problem was from where I sat, but they waved fists and screamed words that didn't sound particularly friendly. I could make a fair guess about the specifics by the way Beula Durington slapped her hands over Sally's ears so Sally couldn't hear. Moses Johnstone, the stronger, taller man, took a huge step toward Wilbur Gridley, whose ginger beard glowed in the sunlight. Johnstone pulled himself to his full height, Goliath to Gridley's David. But Goliath didn't have a shotgun, which Johnstone did, and Gridley had no slingshot with which to take the giant down. Not to be outdone, though, Gridley reached into his wagon and brandished his own weapon, a pistol, above his head.

Hiram joined Amos at the outskirts of the commotion. "What now?" Hiram asked, his exasperation obvious to anyone who heard him. Amos shook his head. The two Wetherfield men watched the scene play out, their backs stiff, their feet ready, prepared to jump in if needed.

"Good heavens," Willie said. "That fool Moses Johnstone is going to kill someone and Amos is right in the middle of it."

"I think Hiram and Amos are trying to settle them down," Takodah said.

Willie wagged her skillet in her husband's direction. "If Amos gets himself dead I'll kill him."

Matthew had ridden ahead to scout the terrain, and I was glad he wasn't there to get caught up in the fiasco. I've become well-versed at spotting him in the distance. He was astride Tune, shoulders back, head held high in his assured posture. He turned Tune in our direction and I could tell by the way the horse pressed faster that Matthew was heading right into the middle of it.

Bang!

Moses Johnstone lowered his shotgun. He had fired it over his head, once, and everyone froze. Those standing closest, including Amos and Hiram, watched the bullet spring into the air like a firecracker and land with a splash in the stream. We exhaled as Johnstone and Gridley said something to each other and shook hands, a far better outcome than a gunfight.

But the blast scared the bison. Their easy loitering turned into full-fledged barreling as those closest to the blast ran away as fast as they could. When the animals in the back saw those in the front galloping into the distance they followed. The ground rumbled as though the land had been hit by an earthquake and the entire herd, hundreds of them, charged toward us. Everyone stood, watching. A woman screamed, which only scared the buffalo more.

"Lord help us!" Beula Durington cried. "They're headed our way."

Amos cupped his hands around his mouth in an attempt to be heard over the commotion. "Let's make a corral like we do at night. At least there will be a barrier between them and us and they might turn away."

"We don't got time!" yelled Wilbur Gridley. "Besides, I ain't letting my horse..."

"Forget the corral!" called Hiram. "Unharness your animals! Now! Get moving!"

The mules were skittish and hard to handle. The oxen wouldn't budge from where they stood. The horses, the livestock, even the pet dogs taken along by some families, carried on like end times were here, and in that moment it seemed as if they were. Amos, Hiram, Moses Johnstone, Wilbur Gridley, Archie Starkey, and Enoch Emerson rode toward the buffalo though their horses struggled against the command. Maybe the men thought they could distract the herd and turn them away before it was too late. When I saw Matthew gallop toward the charging herd I wanted to run after him, fists brandished, and scream at him to stop. But there was no better idea. Buffalo have the weight of the behemoth on their side and if they trampled us we were done. Mothers clutched their children, husbands stood near their families, and there was a certain resignation. Everyone knew that this journey was going to be dangerous, and here was a danger that could end it all.

And then, without any reason or warning, the buffalo turned right along the stream instead of left, which is where we waited. When the animals stormed in the opposite direction everyone sighed so loudly it sounded like the very earth breathed. Most of the main herd had bounded past, forming a line as they made their way into the distance. A few of the younger, slower calves had trouble keeping up and their mothers returned to press them onward. When Paul saw the mothers and their babies, he ran into the oncoming swarm of storming bison.

Willie saw Paul and screamed.

"Paul! You come back here right this instant!"

Paul pointed at the animals. "Look, Ma! The mommas came back for their babies. Pa was right! The mommas love their babies!"

Paul ran further into the herd for a better look and found himself caught in the stampede. The animals ran recklessly and didn't notice the little boy, not that they would have cared if they did. Paul stood there, unmoving, trying to see all the animals at once. It was a miracle he hadn't been trampled yet.

Matthew, Amos, and Hiram ran to the edge. Most of the buffalo were far into the distance, but enough remained to keep Paul in danger.

I don't know what I was thinking. I wasn't thinking, really. All I knew was that Paul was in danger and he had become my family during these arduous weeks. Standing there and screaming for him would accomplish nothing, so I ran into the herd, somehow avoiding being pummeled in the process. I grabbed Paul's hand, and together we stood inside a circle of bison running toward the others. The animals were too close and one brushed my shoulder and another kicked my feet. I picked Paul up and pressed him to my chest, as if I could offer any protection. With my free hand I swatted at the beasts to try to keep them away from us. I can laugh about it now, I suppose, since Paul and I are fine, but in that moment I thought I could smack away the buffalo with my bare knuckles.

"Duchess!" Matthew paced on the other side of the fast-running bison, waving for my attention. "I'm coming for you. Stay where you are. There's only a few left and they're passing over there." He pointed to an area behind me, but I was too afraid to turn to see.

Then all was quiet. Everyone, human and animal, was too stunned. What do you say after something like that? Paul still clung to me but he was no longer weeping as we limped back to Willie's wagon. My legs convulsed as though they had been ripped away from each other, but I made it to Willie's wagon without collapsing. When I thought I couldn't take another step, Willie grabbed Paul from my arms. I stumbled and Matthew caught me. I know him well enough to recognize the panic, the frustration, and the gratitude in his jade eyes. He stood beside me, his hands on my shoulders, steadying me until I could stand on my own. Aubrey Smith, the reverend, said a prayer of thanks.

Willie could hardly contain her hysteria. "Paul Willem Wetherfield, if you ever do anything like that again you won't live to tell the tale! Do you understand me?"

Paul nodded, clutching his mother's hand as though he couldn't believe she was there. Amos ran his fingers through Paul's hair, and Sally grabbed her mother's apron as she sniffled. Beula took Sally to the creek to wash her face and give her a drink of water.

Willie wagged an agitated finger in my direction. "And you, Miss Wentworth!" She handed Paul to Takodah so she could look him over, and then Willie embraced me so tightly I had to pull back so I could breathe. She took my swollen hand in hers and shook her head. "You were so brave, Grace. All I could do was scream, but you saved my boy. I owe you my very life, I truly do."

"You don't owe me anything," I said.

"Oh, I owe you. I just don't know what it is yet." She held my injured hand close to her face. "Takodah, can you take a look here? Grace's hand is busted up pretty good."

Takodah took my left hand in hers. She flexed my fingers, and though I winced they moved when she pressed them. "Your fingers aren't broken, so that's good. I have some potatoes that haven't gone rotten yet. They'll make a good poultice." Then she moved my wrist and I screamed. Takodah shook her head. "I'll need to bind your hand after all." She turned my hand so that my fingers faced downward and I thought I would faint. She pulled my hand close to her face, examining every bone, every joint, as though she could see through my skin. "Nothing has been dislocated, but I think you have a broken bone in your wrist. It will be painful for a few weeks until it heals."

I thought I was fading away until I realized I was holding my breath. When I exhaled I started panting as though I were being smothered by two unseen hands around my throat. The wind whipped around me, blowing my bonnet from my head, and I thought I was in the herd again, trapped, and Paul would die and I would die and I would never tell Matthew...

"Grace?"

Takodah smiled, gently. "I'm going to get the potatoes, some bandages, and I have some chamomile. After I wrap your hand I'll make you some tea. It will calm you, and I think Willie and Paul could use some too. I think we all could about now."

I can't express how grateful I am for my new friend. Whether she is or she isn't, whether it's the invisible world, dear, or my own fanciful imaginings, I'm glad she's here.

And I have lived to fight another day.

CHAPTER 19

*Y*et another river crossing and more drownings. We add our own graves to the others across the rut-lined land. One, two, three, four, five...

The men make tombstones from wood or stone. Reverend Smith, who only comes out of his wagon for births or deaths, says a few words. We say some prayers, sing a hymn or two, and leave. This time, instead of one mother's screams there are many bereaved laments pummeling the night. The whispered wind becomes a haunted howl, reminding us that no one crosses this land unscathed. We are all in danger all the time, and from the silence in the night, the way everyone ducks into their tents with scarcely a word, we all know it to be true.

I struggle along with my bound, painful hand, but I have no choice. There's no time to dwell on it so I don't. There's too much to be done. Wash this shirt, fry these johnnycakes, send Paul or Sally with buckets for water for the mules or the horses or the livestock. Willie has taken it upon herself to teach me how to sew and she wonders how high-falutin' my family must be that I wasn't taught something as simple as darning. I tell her the truth, that my grandmother was going to teach me but she ran out of time. Willie thought I meant that my grandmother died and she was sympathetic as she showed me how to thread the needle and knot the thread. Willie's stitches are seamless and you can hardly tell the repair work from the original. My stitches are conspicuous, to say the least. But I can close holes in stockings and trousers and I can reattach buttons, so that has become my main mending task—sewing buttons back onto the children's clothing. There are so many tasks to get through that they prevent us from getting lost in our thoughts. Thoughts can be dangerous places to linger these days.

LAST NIGHT WAS HARD. WE DID WHAT WE COULD FOR MR. DANIELS, whose wife lost first her leg and then her life when their rotted wheels cracked and the wagon pitched onto its side, pinning Lottie Daniels underneath and ripping her limb clean away at the knee. She died not long after. After they buried her, Mr. Daniels wanted to turn back. But then, Amos told us later, he decided to go on after all.

"It's what Lottie wanted," Mr. Daniels said. "She wanted to see the Pacific Ocean so that's what I'll do."

Amos, Hiram, Matthew, and Wilbur Gridley helped Mr. Daniels chop his wagon into a handcart. He had to discard nearly all his belongings, wretched for the poor man since everything reminded him of his wife—her clothes, her dishware, her favorite desk that she insisted on bringing. First, he asked the others if they would like anything he couldn't take along. Then, when everything had been picked through, the remains were left discarded, a trash heap of furniture, clothing, and other odds and ends. Some of the furnishings were beautiful—well-polished, classical-style Queen Anne tables, a chest of drawers, and side chairs that must have been handed down for generations. Maybe those that brought such pieces wanted to retain some sense of their civilized lives back east, but now these prized possessions were left along the trail, keeping communion with their former existence. The further West we travel, the more we see such heaps—items of every kind left to rot. Most of the wagons have had to lighten their loads to ease the burden of their long-suffering animals. Whenever we pass these dumps, some of the women scavenge through the remains to see if there's anything useful to be found.

With his little handcart filled with the most basic necessities, Mr. Daniels was ready to continue his journey. He was heartbroken, but he would go on.

"At least they didn't have any children," Willie said as she hugged Sally close. "At least there's no baby crying for her momma tonight."

It was well past dark when we made our way back to our wagon. Matthew and I walked together, not looking at each other, not talking. Finally, he leaned close and said, "I'm afraid there's more tragedy to come, Duchess. I don't know what, and I don't know when, but it's coming."

As Matthew and I neared camp we saw a flock of people watching the ground with wide eyes. We drew closer and saw them staring at a wooden board with splintered edges as if it had been torn directly off a wagon. The huddled mass shook their heads, the men stoic while the women covered their mouths with their hands. Even the children were silent. Matthew and I shrugged at each other, bleak-faced. We pressed our way into the crowd and peered down. The board had one word knife-scratched into it.

Cholera.

MORNINGS ARE ALWAYS BRIGHTER. SUNLIGHT MAKES TRAGEDY EASIER to bear. Daytime brings renewed hope, at least for those of us who haven't personally experienced loss. When the wind died down, instead of phantom warnings calling dangerous days ahead, we heard whistling birdcalls and squawking geese flying north to where they'll breed, Willie told me. Paul and Sally pointed and shouted "There! There!" as cranes flew gracefully from the sand-bars in the Platte River where they rested. Amos informed Matthew, loudly enough for the rest of us to hear, that platte derives from the word flat, which the area certainly is except for the lush greenery and the river running through it.

This morning, before we moved out, Amos announced that he had had enough of a sore bottom from driving the bumpy wagon so Matthew offered to take his place while Amos rode Tune ahead to scout the trail. Willie walked behind the wagon, deep in conver-sation with Beula and Takodah. As Matthew drove, I walked alongside him, close but not so close. I was sure the rumor mill was running as fast as tongues could wag. It's easier to ignore the side-eye glances. If you don't look at people then you can't see their disapproving glowers. Besides, I was exhausted and in a devil-may-care mood. Let them watch, I thought. Let them wonder. From the grin on Matthew's face, I thought he felt the same.

Matthew didn't have much time to talk. Keeping Ed, Ted, and Fred in line was a constant struggle and he had his work cut out for him. He smooth-talked the mules, or encouraged them, or cajoled them, or told them outright that either they did as they were told or he'd sell them up at the next meat market we crossed. The mules continued to do their own bidding in their own time, certain, I'm sure, that there is no meat market for hundreds of miles and who would pull the wagon if they were gone?

No one knows that Matthew and I kissed, as far as I know. I haven't had any knowing smiles from Willie or Takodah, but the wagons have eyes, the animals have eyes, the gossiping tongues have eyes, and every eye watches every other eye to see what they are about. Matthew is a single man and I'm a single woman, an old one in this day and age, and then there are the mothers who want

Matthew for their own unmarried daughters. Matthew still hasn't shown any intention of wanting to marry me, and I still have doubts, no longer about my feelings for him, but about the truth of any of this. After we kissed I had accepted that this is my reality now. But when the glowing warmth of his lips faded, I reminded myself that I'm in the midst of a most bizarre situation. Once again, I have to wonder—is this all a dream? And if this is a dream, if this is simply a story concocted by my subconscious, then what happens when I wake up? Will I spend the rest of my life pining for this imaginary man? Then I looked at my bound hand, felt the knife-sharp pain emanating in waves up my arm, and I wondered if it was possible to feel pain in a dream, or to smell the fresh wild grass, or to hear a thunderous stampede.

The wagons ahead of us stopped and Matthew pulled back on the mules, who brayed their lack of appreciation. He squinted into the dust as Amos appeared, riding Tune toward him.

"Kearny's ahead!" Amos called, waving his arm toward a group of wooded islands in the Platte River.

Shouts of "Fort Kearny ahead!" spread throughout the train and everyone, dragging their feet a moment before, now sprang about with renewed liveliness as they squinted to make out the rugged wood-frame buildings in the distance.

The closer we came the less impressive the fort appeared. Fort Kearny is primarily a supply post and not used as a training ground for the army. The wood buildings slump around a central parade ground, but the walls aren't fortified and the buildings don't seem like they would provide much protection. The land is surrounded by cottonwood trees and beautiful white puffs brighten the landscape. Otherwise, everything is shabby and dull.

At least at Fort Kearny we could buy supplies like cornmeal and flour, at price we were told. I wasn't sure I believed that there was no profit being made here, but the others seemed happy enough to think that they could make their way across the trail without suffering the greed of others. Horses and mules, weary from the journey, could be traded for fresher animals. Amos told Willie there was once-a-month mail service here, and if Willie or Matthew or any of us wanted to send letters home, then we should do so now since we were only stopping for the night. Willie and Matthew busied themselves writing letters after purchasing some paper. I wondered who Matthew's letter was for, but I didn't ask. More than anything, I wanted to write to my parents, to let them know I was all right.

"And how might you post such a letter?" I wondered aloud.

Since I had no one to write to, or, more accurately, no way to get my letter to its intended destination, I took the money Willie pressed into my hand and bought six new journals and more pencils. The new journals aren't as nice as the embossed leather books Willie gave me. They are bound with cardboard and glue, but they'll do the trick, and who knows when I'll have the chance to buy more. I don't want to run out of paper since writing remains the only thing keeping me sane. Seeing my thoughts and feelings in gray pencil on the white paper gives me strength somehow.

"Fort Laramie is next," Amos said. "We'll stop longer there."

When others grumbled, Amos said, as he always did, "Donner Party," which quieted everyone down right quick, as Matthew would say.

There was no rest for the weary. Willie, Beula, Takodah, and I washed and darned clothing and we cooked and we cleaned, while Amos, Hiram, and Matthew helped Roscoe Cutter mend his wagon, which had tilted to the left as if it were ready to catapult itself into the sky. There were animals to shod, some to trade, tires to mend, and the children, oh the children, who always have so much energy and who are always finding new ways to get themselves into trouble. Willie looks as though she's aged ten years from her constant vigilance over Paul and Sally. Luckily, Leticia is still too small to wander away on her own. After the Duringtons lost their little girl, and after Jimmy was killed by mules' hooves, and after Paul ran into a herd of stampeding buffalo, Willie says she's ready to strap Paul and Sally right to her if she needs to, one on each leg. I have no doubt she means it.

Something about camping at the fort, even one as unsubstantial as Kearny, has cheered everyone. Chester Livingstone plucked his banjo for the first time in weeks while his brother Herbert and Hiram pulled out their fiddles and played a few tunes. I saw a few women watching me, wondering, I'm sure, if I was going to make a spectacle of myself again, but I was happy for the music and didn't recognize the songs. Children danced while adults clapped and tapped their toes to the upbeat rhythms. Chester Livingstone started calling dance moves and the adults joined in. The children, happy to see their parents smiling, joined in too.

Swing it in. Promenade. Right Grand. Left Grand. Allemande.

Matthew stood before me with his hand extended.

"Miss Wentworth, might you do me the honor of this dance?"

"I've never danced this way before," I said.

"I'm here to help."

As Chester Livingstone continued to call the moves, ladies to one side and men to the other, Matthew gestured to where I should stand and how I should turn and how to balance. He laughed, his handsome face lit by the glowing campfires, and I don't remember being happier. Perhaps I should have turned away, or looked demure, but I felt as if sparklers were lighting me up from the inside and I couldn't hide my joy. When it was our turn to join hands I held onto him as if he were the only other person in the world. There was a pop of static between us, but it didn't surprise me.

"Like fireworks on the Fourth of July," Matthew whispered in my ear. He nodded toward the other dancers. "Well, Duchess, they're watching us now for sure. What should we do about it?"

"I think we should dance, Mr. Cooper. I think we should dance like no one is watching."

The traveling is such a grind, and we still have so far to go. As long as I'm here, I have to act as if I'm staying for the long run and their journey is my journey too. If I had to struggle across every mile of the North American continent to have this moment with Matthew Cooper, to watch him lose himself in an exhilaration that looked like it would elevate him twenty feet in the air as we swung and tapped and do-si-doed, then all of this, whatever this is, will have been worth it.

If only he would kiss me again.

AFTER WE LEFT FORT KEARNY THE MURMURS BEGAN LIKE THE rumbles of an earthquake beneath my feet. Then the rumbles grew into insistent flies buzzing near my ears. Finally, the women stopped hiding behind wagons and came out in the open, staring at me, direct, defiant, as they chatted loud enough for the clouds in the sky to hear. I tried a few times to make casual conversation with a few of the women closest to me, hello, how are you, good morning, but all I had in return were cold lips and tight stares. So I ignored them, my vision focused firmly ahead, Tish in my arms or Paul or Sally clasping my apron. Willie was so fierce she looked nearly wild, her jaw pulled so far back she wore a perpetual grimace, her green eyes blazing. She looked neither left nor right but kept her focus on the western horizon as I did.

Unfortunately, Beula Durington has taken to spending the daylight hours with the tattling biddies. Time and again, Beula scurries beside us at night as we corral, but we've gone entire days without seeing her round face anywhere. Beula has become best friends with Mrs. Brownlow, her daughter, and Mrs. Starkey. I can tell by the way Willie watches them that she's noticed but hasn't said a word. Yet.

Last night while the men were smoking and the women were sewing, Beula said to Willie, "Mrs. Brownlow is worried that some of the women in our train aren't up to standard. Mrs. Starkey said the same."

"What do you mean, up to standard?" I asked.

Willie's shook her head. "I know precisely what they mean. And who might these women who aren't up to standard be, Beula?"

Beula's eyes widened more than usual. "Oh, I certainly don't know. They would never tell me such a thing. I overheard them mention it is all. I heard that some of the men brought it up to your husband since he's the captain, but he hasn't had much to say about it. They're worried Captain Wetherfield won't handle the situation properly."

"My husband will handle everything properly, Beula. You can tell them, whoever they are, not to worry."

"Oh, I don't have anything to do with it, Willie. I'm just passing on what I heard. I'm so thankful to you for allowing me to travel with your family after my brother and sister-in-law turned back."

"Why didn't you go back with them?" I asked. "When we first started the journey, you said you were going West because you had no choice. But then you had the chance to go back. Why are you still here?" I tried to keep my voice neutral but failed.

Beula smiled demurely. "You're right, Miss Wentworth. I really didn't want to go West when we began, but once we started I realized this is such an adventure. I'm sorry for the loss of my niece, of course I am. I miss her every day. And I'm sorry to be parted from my brother. But why would I want to miss the chance to find a better life?"

"Who knows?" Willie said. "Beula may even find herself a husband in Oregon." Beula's face went blank and Willie nodded. "Beula, do me a favor and catch up to Paul and Sally," she pointed into the distance where the children were walking a little too close to a team of agitated mules. "Pull the children away and bring them back here. I'd appreciate it ever so much."

"You know I'm happy to help, Willie."

Beula dropped her darning onto the quilt she had been sitting on and headed toward Paul and Sally. When she was far enough away, Willie said, "I admit, Grace, that worries me. If the wives are wagging their tongues about how we've got the wrong kind of women traveling with us, and if they get their husbands riled up, there can be all sorts of trouble."

"You mean they're riled up about Takodah?"

"Yes, Takodah. And me. I know what they say about me, that I talk back to my husband when it's not a wife's place to do so. Amos values my opinion and I give it to him whether he asks for it or not and he's never minded. I don't think that's talking back, and neither does Amos." She dropped her voice. "They have problems with you too, Grace."

"Me?"

"You and Matthew have been playing it a little loose lately, especially with that dance right there in front of everyone. Are you two engaged and haven't told me?"

"He hasn't asked me."

"Would you? If he did?"

In my heart, my answer was a ready "Yes!" I remembered what the wisest woman I know told me: "What does your heart tell you, Grace? Your heart always knows the right thing to do." My heart pounds a quick-time rhythm with love for this man. Maybe it isn't rational, but love isn't always rational. That's why people get themselves into all sorts of trouble over it.

If I can't find my way home, if I'm here for the rest of my life, could I be happy? With Matthew, the answer is yes. I would always feel the strangeness of my surroundings, but with Matthew by my side, I believe I could find meaning in it. I could find a way to make it work. Without Matthew, I don't see any point to it.

"Should I take that as a yes?" Willie asked.

"Yes, if Matthew asked me I would marry him."

"Do you love Matthew?"

"I know he's a good man who will treat me with respect."

"That's not what I asked, Grace."

"Yes, Willie, I love Matthew. And I think the respect is important too. Takodah says that when you meet a man who treats you with respect you should hold onto him with both hands and never let him go."

"Takodah is right about most things." Willie smiled. "I'll talk to Matthew."

On the one hand I wanted to dance with joy. On the other, I felt heavy and it was hard to keep moving, one foot in front of the other, right, left, right, left. Yes, I want to marry Matthew Cooper. But I also want to go home. I can only do one or the other.

I HAVEN'T WRITTEN FOR A WHILE. I HAVE BEEN IN A DAZE. Something as simple as grasping my pencil and forming letters into words has become too hard. From the height of happiness, thinking I have found my beshert, my hopes were dashed like a wagon down a precipitous ravine. Matthew Cooper will not be mine.

Willie is so mad at Amos she isn't speaking to him. Matthew makes himself scarce. He's been riding at the back with the live-stock, helping Ezra Quigley and Samuel Maylie keep the animals in line. He stays out with the watch most nights, taking the first shift while everyone in the corral settles down to sleep. When he isn't on guard duty he sets up his tent in the distance. He's a good shot and hunts well, builds his own fires, and cooks his own food.

Based on what I can piece together from Willie, who can speak in only short, snappy sentences, even to me, a group of women, including Lenore Starkey, complained to their husbands that they were worried about their delicate names being blackened by asso-ciating with women who are less than pristine in reputation. Espe-cially that one Mr. Cooper calls Duchess. Who does she think she is, Miss High-Falutin'? Just because she's educated she thinks she's better than us? Their husbands then complained to Amos about the odd assortment of womenfolk he had along for the ride, including a squaw (Takodah), a woman who doesn't know her place (Willie), and a big-bug woman with loose morals (me).

Duchess, my eye, they said. If she's a duchess, then I'm an elephant. Amos told them what they could do with their opinions about Willie, and Takodah was his sister-in-law, so don't you go grumbling about her neither.

But Amos must have reconsidered my place on the train. I know he didn't want me here in the first place—Willie's insistence brought me along—and I'm no one to him. I'm here on Willie's whim, and I have behaved in a manner considered derelict by befriending Matthew and dancing so openly with him, especially since everyone thinks I'm heading to California to marry another man.

Willie's jaw popped, her muscles were so tight, when she told me. Amos pulled Matthew aside and told him that I was trouble. Who is this young woman heading West all on her own, Amos said, without a wagon, supplies, or any man to protect her? She says she has people in California, but where are they and how can they leave her to fend for herself? What kind of people are they? Only people with an ungodly greed for gold went to California. He told Matthew the story he overheard Willie say to Mrs. Quigley— that my parents had a man in California picked out for me to marry.

"What are you doing, son?" Amos asked. "She's going to California to find her family and get married. You're going to Oregon. What is this nonsense you're on about? And her? She's educated but she don't know the first thing about how to conduct herself in company. She's not showing herself in a very good light, is what I'm saying. I worry for this man she's marrying. Someone ought to tell him his future wife is laughing and dancing and carrying on with a man she hardly knows and isn't engaged to. Why don't you find yourself a nice young lady like the widow Mrs. Carson? She's been married before, she knows what it's about, and she'll be something nice to look at when you come home from working in the field all day."

"What did Matthew say?" I asked Willie.

Willie watched Paul, who was sitting in the back of the wagon reading a book. I could see her fighting herself, as if she wasn't sure she should tell me. Finally, she said, "Matthew said, *But she's so like Gloryanna...*"

"Gloryanna Winters is the woman you and Matthew mistook me for when I first arrived." Willie nodded. "Who is she?"

Willie sighed so heavily Sally turned to see if her mother was all right. "I'm fine, Sugar," Willie said. "Ma is tired is all." Willie turned her full attention onto me. "Gloryanna Winters is the woman Matthew was in love with."

"What happened to her?" I asked.

"As far as anyone knows she disappeared. Oh, but Grace, I've never seen a man fall so hard and so fast for a woman the way Matthew fell for Gloryanna. It seemed like she dropped out of heaven. One day, there she was, and Matthew loved her the first time he saw her. She had come to Lowell to stay with her cousins, the Emersons."

"The Emersons?"

"You've seen their cousin Enoch Emerson, that tall widower who comes around sometimes for his supper."

"The one who makes puppy eyes at you?"

Willie pushed my shoulder and giggled. "He does not." She became serious. "Do you know the Emersons?"

"My grandmother's maiden name is Emerson."

"Well, I'll be. Maybe you're related to Gloryanna after all."

"Maybe I am."

"Anyhow," Willie continued, "the Emersons were our closest neighbors so we met Miss Winters as soon as she arrived. Oh, she's a beautiful girl. She looks, well, she looks like you—same blue eyes, same sweet smile. She wore her gold curls framed around her face while yours are tucked into your braid." She gestured at our simple clothing. "But that Miss Winters, she knew her own mind, also like you. She was an only child so her father taught her how to read from the day she was old enough to know her letters." The dreaminess in Willie's eyes made me think she was mistaking me for Gloryanna once again.

"I was there the first time Matthew saw Miss Winters. I thought his eyes would leap right out of his head, he stared at her so hard. She stared right back, which her cousins didn't particularly like, seeing as it was kind of forward, but at least the two young people felt the same about each other. Amos wrote to her father in Danvers for his permission for Matthew to start courting Gloryanna. Matthew spent his days in this dreamy haze and he was at the Emersons' farm nearly every night. Soon enough they decided that Amos would take Matthew to Danvers to meet her parents. And then…"

"And then what?"

"And then nothing. She disappeared. Her family disappeared. The Emersons were frantic because the parents and the daughter seemed to evaporate into the air." Willie snapped her fingers. "Just like that. Gone. No one could find them and to this day, so far as I know, no one knows what happened to them."

"People don't just disappear," I said.

"People disappear all the time, Grace. We just don't know where or why. As you can imagine, Matthew was beside himself. It was as if someone had dug into his chest, stolen his heart, and sent it wherever Miss Winters went. He spent weeks searching for her but he never did find her. Then he got the Oregon Fever and talked Amos and me into going. I already told you all about that. As we were getting ready to make our way to Missouri, Matthew said maybe Miss Winters had gone West, and if she had he would find her. I wouldn't contradict him, even if it was such a gamble. Then when we were in Independence there you were. You may not be Gloryanna, but Matthew looks at you just the same."

"I'm not sure that's a good thing," I said. "But I still don't understand why Amos said all those things against me."

"Amos is like a father to Matthew, Grace, just as I'm like a mother to him. Amos is worried the way any father would be. The fact is, you're not Miss Winters and you're going to your family in California where they have a husband set aside for you."

"You know that's not true, Willie. You're the one who made that story up to save me from Mrs. Quigley."

"I know that, but if people think you're engaged maybe it will keep some tongues from wagging."

"Those tongues have done enough damage. So you agree with Amos?"

For the first time since I met her, Willie wouldn't look me in the eye. I felt like I was going around in circles and I needed space. I wanted to run away, but where? There's nowhere to hide here, and there isn't another friendly face for me except for Takodah, but she's Hiram's wife and Amos' sister-in-law and her loyalties would lie with her husband, as they should. Instead of leaving, I faced Willie, unwilling to back down.

"Willie? Do you agree with Amos? I thought you were ready to ask Matthew if he wanted to marry me. You asked me if that's what I wanted and I said yes. I thought you were on my side."

"Of course I'm on your side, Grace, but I want what's best for everyone, including my brother. I want him to be happy. I want you to be happy too. But maybe this is too much of a coincidence. Maybe Amos is right and Matthew is drawn to you because you look so much like Miss Winters. And that's not fair on you, to be Matthew's second best because he can't have Gloryanna. Maybe it's best if you go to California like you're supposed to, and maybe it's best to let Matthew build a new life in Oregon. Who knows? Maybe Gloryanna Winters is there after all."

"Stranger things happen at sea."

"Excuse me?"

"It's something my father says. It's means things stranger than this have happened elsewhere so why can't this happen?"

Willie grabbed my hand and patted it. Her eyes and cheeks were the same pink-red and she looked more miserable than I felt.

She didn't know anything else about the conversation between Amos and Matthew, or if she did she wouldn't share it with me.

Matthew found me after we corralled for the night. He asked me to step behind the wagon, hoping for some privacy, I'm sure, though everyone, human and animal, stared at us like we were the night's entertainment, which we were. Matthew stood tall, his shoulders back like when he rides Tune. He looked first at the tents the men were setting up, then the cooking fires the women were starting with buffalo chips. He looked at Amos, who nodded as if to give the younger man strength. He looked everywhere but at me.

"You wanted to speak to me?" I said.

"Miss Wentworth."

"Are we being formal again, Mr. Cooper? I thought we were past that." I struggled to keep my voice light, which was hard since I knew what was coming.

"I'm sorry, Miss Wentworth, but Captain Wetherfield has reminded me that you and I are headed on different paths. You're going to California to your folks and whatever they have for you out there and I'm going to Oregon. I've enjoyed getting to know you, Miss Wentworth, I truly have. You've reminded me that there are fine, clever women in the world. The way you ran into the charging buffalo herd to rescue my nephew—I've never seen such gumption. I admire your spirit and I always will."

"But?"

"I think we ought to leave things here."

Without another word he doffed his wide-brimmed hat and headed into the distance where he took the first watch. As he disappeared toward a yellow-red campfire, the only light in the darkness, his familiar silhouette was surrounded by a golden aura. I stared after him, thinking he would return, hoping he would run back to me, yelling, "Duchess, I can't live without you!" But he didn't.

As soon as my life here begins to make sense the sense is pulled out from under me like a magician's tablecloth trick. Now it's here and now it's not but everything else is just the same.

CHAPTER 20

*N*avigating the steep slope of Windlass Hill was a struggle. Matthew, Amos, and Hiram chained the wheels of their wagons while others tied a small tree to the back, adding weight to slow the vehicles down. Others hoisted emptied wagons down the steep-pitched peak with ropes while children moved belongings from one side to the next. Some of the wives helped with the strenuous work of pushing and pulling when there was no one else to do it. I was so exhausted by the end, as was Willie. We both tried to be everywhere at once while keeping Paul, Sally, Tish, and ourselves safe. I'm happy to report that both Wetherfield families made it over unscathed, our wagons intact. Amos said a prayer thanking God for our deliverance. The rest of our train did reasonably well, though several families lost their wagons down the perpendicular slide. They salvaged what they could, and other families opened their wagons and their supplies to those who suddenly had nothing. Two of Hiram's cattle died in a fall, and Takodah ran herself ragged tending to the injured.

More than once, as I slipped and slid my way downward, I wished I would stumble down the other side never to be seen or heard from again. It's not losing Matthew that drags me into darkness. The truth is, I never had him to begin with. Yes, I love him, but love doesn't always work out the way you want. That's why my parents' love is so special. Not everyone finds their beshert, and Matthew is obviously not mine. I feel heartsick, but I can live with it. Broken hearts heal. In time.

No, it's more of a homesickness, like a tumor growing dangerously larger day by day. The density is killing me. I don't belong here. This is not my time. Zachary Taylor is President of the United States. There's slavery and slaughter of Native Americans and violent arguments about who gets to do what to whom. I need to find my way home; my feelings for Matthew blinded me to that simple fact. I thought I would be able to give up my real life for the love of a good man. Now that he's out of the way I can see how foolish I was and I can concentrate on my only task—getting home.

But how do I get back? There are no standing stones to pass through like in that TV show. Is there something I have to achieve before I can go home, some special line I have to cross? Is there some secret passageway, like a magical door or a yellow brick road? Is there a TARDIS lurking beyond the next river?

As I'm writing this, Takodah sits beside me. She's quiet, the whole camp is quiet since we've corralled for the night and everyone is ready to crawl into their tents. Hiram, Amos, and Matthew are sequestered together some distance away, their eyes serious, their heads pressed together in private discussion. Takodah glances over my shoulder to see what I'm writing. I should hide these very words since my current circumstances are impossible for anyone here to understand, but I'm too tired to care. If Takodah thinks I've lost my mind, then let her. Maybe I have lost my mind. Maybe I'm locked in a hospital with padded wallpaper while I'm hallucinating the trail and everyone on it. Mainly, I'm afraid I'll never see my family again.

She has read some of what I've written.

"Never is a long time," Takodah said. "You'll see your parents again, Grace."

"How do you know?" I asked.

"My people believe in a Great Spirit, Wakan Tanka. Everything around us," she gestured widely with her arms, "possesses a spirit. We should be thankful for everything we have, everything we see around us. We should worship all of it, even the smallest creation. Each of the smaller beings have their own smaller spirits, and those smaller spirits belong to Wakan Tanka, which means Great Mystery."

"That's a beautiful way to see the world," I said. "Everything is connected to everything else and we are all connected to something greater than ourselves."

"I agree," Takodah said. "It is a beautiful way to see the world. Our job is to do our best to please the Great Spirit so it will help us. Sometimes, when we're quiet and in touch with our innermost yearnings, we can send our deepest wishes to the Great Spirit and our wishes will be granted."

"You sound like Glinda the Good Witch from *The Wizard of Oz*."

"Who?"

"Never mind. But thank you, Takodah."

As I write this she is making her way to her tent. I remember that line from Hamlet, which my father has quoted a hundred times, "...nothing is either good or bad, but thinking makes it so."

I'm too tired to think any more tonight.

I've stopped looking for Matthew. It has taken some practice since I was so used to seeking him out at every opportunity. He had become my compass point, my bearing, but no more. Just as I had trained myself to look away from the prying eyes so I wouldn't see the women's puckered distaste, I trained myself to stop searching for Matthew. I'm kept well busy without him. I keep an eye on Paul and Sally and help Willie with the cooking, the darning, the washing, and whatever else needs doing. I no longer cook for the camp, which is fine by me. If I were still flipping johnny-cakes for the others I'd ask Takodah for some poisonous root I could mix unseen into the cornmeal.

The men were successful today with their buffalo hunt. They were determined, if only for the sake of saying they killed one of the magnificent beasts. But we also need the meat. No one says so, but supplies are beginning to dwindle and we may become dependent on what the men hunt soon enough. I didn't watch the lifeless carcass as it was hauled into camp. Some of the women worked together to cut the animal up for meat and remove the skin for curing. I left them to it and sat near the Platte watching the river splash. The kaleidoscope of blues, pinks, and yellows meant nothing to me. I felt hollow inside.

"I'm done with this!" I said, loudly enough to pull Paul's head out of the book he was reading. "I want to go home." I clicked my worn boot heels three times. "There's no place like home."

Nothing. I was still sitting near the bank of the Platte. I would have wept if little Paul hadn't sat beside me, running his fingers through the long grass. We've bonded, Paul and I, since the stampede, and he always makes a point of helping me with my tasks when he's done with his chores. Again, I wished this sweet boy was my son, though I pressed the foolish idea aside.

"Do you miss your home, Miss Wentworth?" Paul asked.

"As a matter of fact, I do."

"What's it like?"

"It's beautiful. We live near the Pacific Ocean in a pretty house in a pretty little town. My parents are there, and my friends. My brother is traveling, but he'll be home soon. I miss them all so much."

"Are you lonely here?"

I smiled at the little boy, who was quite serious and wise beyond his years.

"Yes, I am."

"So am I." There are many boys Paul's age, but he doesn't fit in with them. They like to jump off high rocks and frighten the mules and hide until their mothers scream for them while Paul is perfectly happy helping his mother or reading. "Maybe we can be friends," he said.

"I thought we already were friends, Paul."

Paul looked so happy. He picked a handful of white wildflowers and handed them to me. "Yes, Miss Wentworth," he said. "I believe we are."

We walked back to the wagon hand in hand. Paul, always thoughtful, watched his mother stoking the cooking fire.

"Miss Durington is gone," he whispered. I thought he meant she had died. "Not dead, Miss Wentworth. Gone. Ma says she's decided to travel with Mrs. Brownlow and Mrs. Carson. Ma says they got more social currency than we do, and Ma said she likes to position herself well, Miss Durington."

"How do you know all this?"

"I heard Ma telling Pa. What's social currency, Miss Wentworth?"

"Absolutely nothing of value," I said.

I was glad Beula was gone. I was tired of feeling her child-like eyes following me. Poor you, her tilted frown seemed to say. I had a few words I wanted to say right back to her but I never did. When I brought up Beula's desertion with Willie, Willie wouldn't even discuss it.

"Leave her be," Willie said. "It's better this way."

Later, as the sun fell in blushing hues and we were ready to stop for the day, Mrs. Quigley rolled herself over to me. We didn't say anything, but I was glad for the company. The older woman's ornery ways have continued to settle since Takodah's kindness, and Mrs. Quigley can spin a yarn like no one I've ever met, except perhaps for my father. Mrs. Quigley keeps us entertained with tales of her girlhood in Ohio. Some stories are happy, some are sad, but all are about a simple family doing the best they could in difficult circumstances. But now, she was quiet, content to roll along, her hands wrapped so they wouldn't blister.

She stopped to untie her brown calico bonnet and she tossed it into the barrow beside her. "I hate wearing that thing. Makes me feel like a horse with blinders on." I smiled, having thought much the same myself. Word came back that the scouts had found a nice spot with good water where we could camp. The wagons ahead veered off to the right and we followed.

"Miss Wentworth," Mrs. Quigley said. "Excuse an old lady for nosing her way in where she don't belong, but do you mind if I speak openly to you?"

"You can say anything you'd like, Mrs. Quigley," I said.

"Here's the thing. Those ones back there," she gestured behind us where the rather red Mrs. Brownlow and her delicate-looking daughter walked, "don't know what's what. Their coldness toward you, you know that's them and not you, right? People don't understand anything that's different from themselves. They all try to look and act and talk the same, and then someone like you comes along and you're quiet and hardworking and you do your own thing. By trying to make you feel bad, they're trying to make themselves feel better. Maybe there's something about your steady ways that makes them question what they're about. You get my meaning?"

"I do, Mrs. Quigley. Thank you."

"Don't concern yourself with them, that's all I'm saying. Let them mutter and smirk and roll their eyes so far back they got to spend the rest of their lives looking at their own brains. Nothing you say will change their minds anyhow. Self-righteous, that's what they are."

"I try to ignore them, but it's hard when we're all in such close quarters. There's nowhere to hide here."

"Darling, they're the ones who need to hide, not you. You keep on walking with your head held high. I'm sorry you and young Mr. Cooper are no longer on speaking terms. You made a nice-looking couple. I know your folks have someone set aside for you, but I was hoping it would work out betwixt you and Matty anyhow." She squinted at me, nodding to herself as though making a decision. "So then it is true what Mrs. Wetherfield said? Your parents have someone waiting for you in California?" I said nothing, unsure how to answer. "Then you really can't marry my Ezra?"

"I'm afraid not, Mrs. Quigley."

"It's none your fault, Miss Wentworth. I know he's a fool boy who ruinates everything he touches. But his heart is good as gold and I just wish he'd find himself a wife before I'm done and dusted. What's he waiting for?"

The wagons at the front had already stopped, the drivers pulling into our nighttime circle. When Amos parked Ed, Ted, and Fred, Mrs. Quigley took the kitchen box I handed her and set it on the ground where Willie had already started up the fire.

"Come on now," said Mrs. Quigley. "I'm in the mood for some potato cakes. How about it?"

"You don't need to cook, Mrs. Quigley," Willie said.

"Nonsense. Your family took me in when I needed help. Mrs. Wetherfield, your sister-in-law, I mean, gave up her place in her wagon for me when I needed a rest. The least I can do is help you with the cooking when I can."

Mrs. Quigley stripped the potatoes with a small life, removing the peel in one long swirl, cutting off any rotten pieces and grating the white flesh. She added some milk, salt, eggs, flour, and shortening into a bowl, stirred until it was smooth, then added the potatoes. She dropped small balls of the mixture into the hot skillet, flattened them with a spatula, and fried them. It was such a simple meal, like johnnycakes, but it was delicious and filling and that's what we needed after a long day. I don't think we'll have potatoes much longer though, since the ones that are left look like they'll be rotten soon. As we ate, Mrs. Quigley waved over the widower, Enoch Emerson.

"Come on now, Mr. Emerson, who you got cooking for you? I

fried up a stack of potato cakes and they're mighty fine if I do say so myself."

Mr. Emerson wandered our way. His long limbs make him look as if he's made of rubber. He always has a smile on his face, even through the worst of things. He looked shyly at Willie and addressed his words to her. "I don't want to get in the middle of a family meal."

"Nonsense," said Mrs. Quigley. "You've joined us before and we're all friends here." She handed the lanky man a tin plate stacked high with potato cakes. "Sit down and keep me company, Mr. Emerson." As they ate, Mrs. Quigley pointed her fork at me. "Do you know Miss Wentworth, Mr. Emerson? Mrs. Wetherfield tells me some of her people are Emersons."

He looked at me as though noticing me for the first time. "I'm afraid I haven't had the pleasure. You're the one whose folks are in California?"

"That's right," I said.

"I'm afraid I don't have any relatives in California, Miss."

"That's quite all right, Mr. Emerson," Mrs. Quigley said. "You just eat your food before it gets cold."

I studied Mr. Emerson, looking for some family connection but seeing none.

After supper all was quiet. Hiram and Amos were deep in conversation with a few friends, away from the other men. It looked again as though the men were forming posses—some were on Amos' side and some on Moses Johnstone's. Matthew continues to keep himself to himself. I saw him grab the copy of *The Emigrants' Guide to Oregon and California* by Lansford W. Hastings and the book by John C. Frémont and Kit Carson from the back of Willie's wagon. He set up his tent in the distance, frying his own bacon, drinking his own coffee, and reading the books. I had a feeling everyone was watching me watch him and I turned away.

It started to rain. Though the water makes the ground muddy and the going will be slow in the morning, it allowed me to escape into the sanctuary Willie created when she hung a tarp between our wagon and Hiram's. At least Willie, Takodah, Mrs. Quigley, the children, and I had somewhere dry to sit. Willie and Mrs. Quigley took up some needlework to pass the time. Takodah excused herself, saying she was tired after the long walk, and she climbed into her wagon to rest. While Willie and Mrs. Quigley talked, Paul read to Sally from *Oliver Twist*. Leticia has begun to crawl a bit, and Willie had to stop sewing to prevent the baby from making her way out into the wet night. I had time to myself, watching the storming sky change colors from dark to light to dark again, listening to the soothing rhythm of the raindrops. Such downpours can be pleasant if you're not standing in the middle of them. I found some solace thinking that this is the same sky over my parents' heads. Maybe in time, if I devise a plan, I can find my way home.

CHAPTER 21

*M*en and women, making feeble excuses, run somewhere, if there are any bushes or trees to hide behind for privacy, and come back shaking from limb to limb as though they are cold to the bone. If there is water nearby they jump in and wash off in conspicuous attempts to make their stained clothing less obvious. Children weep as they soil themselves, to the hushed tones of their mothers and older sisters soothing them the best they can. Sickly retching can be heard across the camp. Mr. Gibbons, an elderly man traveling alone, died three hours after he began feeling ill. Everyone is aware of what is happening but we're too afraid to say it.

Cholera.

I searched my memory for any knowledge of the disease but I came up mostly empty. Cholera has to do with bacteria in the water supply, I think. The water we've been drinking has a horrid smell and a worse taste, but it's all we can find so we've been drinking it. Mainly, we turn it into coffee, for us and the animals, to take away the caustic flavor. Everyone has been drinking the water, but not everyone is falling ill. Some experience only mild symptoms with stomach discomfort that passes in a day or two. For others, the disease means death, sometimes in a few days, or a few hours.

One family—father, mother, and four siblings—died within 24 hours of each other. The youngest, a year-old girl, has survived and she was taken in by another family who lost a child to cholera. Takodah helps where she can, but there's only so much she can do. Her helplessness weighs heavy on her. She slumps forward, searching the ground for some magic plant that will make this go away.

Every day we lose people. Men dig graves and bury the dead. The next day we leave the hastily made tombs behind. Every day we advance about 10 miles, though this dreaded disease makes any progress feel like a colossal leap backwards. Some cattle have died, and Takodah believes that cows are susceptible to cholera but not oxen or mules.

Fear has made some of the travelers more unreasonable than they normally are. Moses Johnstone, who had been staying largely hidden since his shot startled the buffalo, has once again become formidable in his indignant stride. He openly challenges Amos' authority, as though Moses believes he should be in charge, as though it is his task to lead us to the Promised Land. Moses' cronies seem to think the same. Whenever Moses challenges Amos on one point or another, those fools stand behind their leader, their hands on their holsters, their eyes slits as they attempt to intimidate Amos. Amos hasn't risen to the baiting that Moses and his goonies constantly inflict on him, that is, until today.

Willie and I inched our way closer until we could hear what the men were saying.

"We need to consider this carefully," Amos said. "Some of our people are sick and getting sicker. I think we need to rest for a few days and let those who will recover have some time to regain their strength. Then we'll move out."

Josiah McPherson laughed. "Ain't you the one who said we had to keep going at a clip to avoid the Donners' fate? So now you think loosie goosie is the way to go?"

"He's not being loosie goosie," said Hiram. "We have to deal with what's in front of us, and what's in front of us is some mighty sick folks. We can't leave anyone behind, McPherson."

"We've left plenty behind in them graves," Archie Starkey said. The men snickered.

"Not everyone who's sick from cholera will die," Amos said. "I'm not leaving behind the men, women, and children who will recover. What will become of them if they're left in the middle of nowhere with no supplies and no one to care for them?"

"Some other train will come along to help them," Josiah McPherson said.

"We can't count on that," said Hiram. "Who knows how far behind us the next train is?" He gestured at the empty land surrounding us and there wasn't so much as a speck of dust to hint that anyone was coming along any time soon. "Don't forget—the toughest part of our journey is ahead of us, not behind us, and people are going to need every ounce of strength they can muster to make it across alive."

"I say we go faster," said Moses Johnstone. "I say we push at a hell-for-leather pace before this damn disease stops us all dead."

Amos looked into the distance of the lonely prairie. "Some of our folks are pretty ill, Moses. They may make hell, but they won't make leather."

"They're not my folks. They're no concern of mine."

Hiram shook his head. "All right then. If you don't care about the people, how about the animals? Some of the oxen have dropped dead in their harnesses already. And I'm still worried about the newly recovered who won't be able to keep up at a fast pace. Like Amos says, we'd be leaving them to certain death. What kind of man are you that you would do that to someone whether or not they're your kin?"

Moses Johnstone spit a wad of tobacco the size of a rock at Hiram's foot. "If the people can't handle this journey then they've got no right to be here. I'm not letting some fool-ass malady stop me from getting to California. California or bust, boys, right?" The men behind Moses cheered.

Amos stood between Hiram and Moses. "All right, the both you, enough. We've been making good time and we can spare a day or two for recovery."

"Not everyone's going to recover," Lee Tappertit said.

"I know," Amos said. "And I'm sorry for it. But some will recover and they need time."

"Maybe we ought to break off and form our own group," Moses said. "Maybe we ought to find our own way West. You all," he nodded toward Amos, "are vexing me with your gormless ways."

Before I stopped myself, I searched for Matthew. I found him easily enough, standing in the background, behind Amos and Hiram, his hand on his holster in case they needed his help. Matthew glared at Moses Johnstone with the same apoplectic fury he had when I saw them that first time in Independence. Moses returned the stare, grinning all the while.

"Oh, botheration!" Lee Tappertit knocked his hat from his head in the quickness of his movements. "I'm staying here with Captain Wetherfield. You go on ahead if you want to, Moses, but you can't outrun cholera no matter how fast you move. If cholera wants you, it will get you in the end."

"If you want to go on ahead, Moses, then nobody will stop you," said Amos. "I think you're more stubborn than a mule with a temper like Beelzebub, but you've got good sense when you've a mind to it. I think we're better together, but a man's got to do what he thinks is right. Don't let me stop you."

Moses Johnstone looked every man in the eye, stroking his gray beard as he considered. He flashed a fake, friendly smile, first at Amos, then at Hiram, then at Matthew.

"We'll stay," Moses said. "For now."

"Suit yourself," said Amos.

Moses nodded. "I will."

THOSE WHO WOULD DIE OF CHOLERA HAVE PASSED ON AND THOSE who would recover have gained enough strength that we were able to travel some more. We've arrived at some of the most beautiful scenery to surround us since we began our way West. We passed Courthouse Rock, a large butte of clay, sandstone, and volcano ash rising 400 feet from the North Platte Valley, greeting travelers in an aristocratic manner. Welcome to my corner of the world, it seems to say. To look at Courthouse Rock, in all its natural glory, I see a glimpse of the Great Spirit Takodah told me about and I wonder if the rock formation has a soul of its own. Mrs. Quigley told me it's called Courthouse Rock since it reminds people of the courthouse buildings from home. When Paul first saw it, he said, "Why, that's like a lonely old castle right there along the trail, Miss Wentworth. It's like it's waiting for somebody to come visit it."

I took Paul's hand. "I believe you're right, Paul."

Jail Rock is close by since it makes sense that the jail would be near the courthouse. Some of the men ventured several miles for a closer look at the monuments and to inscribe their names on them. Paul begged Amos to be able to add the Wetherfields' name to the stone, and Amos finally relented. Amos saddled up Tune and took Paul to Jail Rock with a sharp knife in his pack. When they returned, Paul whispered to me, "Don't worry, Miss. I put the name Wentworth on there too."

I kissed the top of Paul's head in thanks.

In time we reached Chimney Rock, made from the erosion of clay and volcanic ash. I'm pleased to report that Chimney Rock does in fact resemble a chimney. For some reason, the sight of the curious narrow spire of rocks at the top of the wide hill caused a cheer to go through the train, as if passing these monuments means that we are making progress after all, even if we spend most of our time feeling like we're getting nowhere fast. Maybe we will actually make it West after all.

But I'll have to make a decision soon. If I'm going to try to find my way back to my family, do I stay with the Wetherfields and continue to Oregon or do I make my way to California to see if I can find my way home from there? And what would that way home look like, anyway?

I HAVEN'T WRITTEN FOR SOME TIME. I CAN SCARCELY WRITE EVEN now. Wretched despair cuts me sharp like rutters slicing round and round my heart. It has been too much, just too much. Everything changed so fast, but life does that, doesn't it? One day we were cheering for the progress we were making and the next we were wailing, disconsolate at our losses.

We began by cheering at the sight of the rugged heights of Scotts Bluff, which stands 800 feet above the prairieland of the North Platte River. Once again we were overtaken by the wonder that water, sun, and erosion could create such works of natural art. The hill blocked our path, but it was so spectacular no one seemed to mind. Takodah told me that the Sioux used the area as a major buffalo hunting ground, calling it "the hill that is hard to go around."

As we drew nearer Scotts Bluff another wave of cholera broke through our camp. A lot of the water we are using continues to be filthy and contaminated with animal urine from trains that have passed before us. Since the last outbreak we've been boiling our water. That's the only way I can think of to make the bacteria go away, but I don't know if it works well enough and I would give anything for a prescription of antibiotics for our whole train right now.

First Sally fell ill with diarrhea, and then Paul. Willie ran for Takodah, who agrees with my remedy of boiling any water we drink or cook with. I boiled some water and Takodah made the children some weak tea. Within a few hours, Sally was sitting up and asking for her doll but Paul began vomiting. I pressed a tin cup of cooled tea to his lips.

"Drink, Paul," I said. "It will help you feel better."

Paul struggled to swallow, but he finished his cup. He leaned into the makeshift bed in the wagon and closed his eyes. He seemed to be resting comfortably enough, but suddenly he vomited all over the quilt. Willie took him into her arms, rocking him the way she still rocks Leticia.

Her voice was melodious, pure and sweet, as she sang to her son.

AMAZING GRACE, HOW SWEET THE SOUND
    that saved a wretch like me
    I once was lost, but now am found
    Was blind, but now I see
    Was grace that taught my heart to fear
    And grace, my fears relieved
    How precious did that grace appear
    The hour I first believed
    Through many dangers, toils and snares
    We have already come
    T'was grace that brought us safe thus far
    And grace will lead us home
    Amazing grace, how sweet the sound
    That saved a wretch like me
    I once was lost, but now am found
    Was blind, but now I see

. . .

I HAD NO TIME TO FALL DOWN AND CRY SO I GAVE MYSELF A STERN talking to, screaming at myself within the walls of my mind. Grace Marie Wentworth, don't you dare fall apart now that Willie and Paul need you. I had to be fully present to do whatever I could for them. Matthew ran to the river for more water, but we weren't sure where the poisoned water came from so we boiled everything we had.

Mrs. Brownlow pressed her wide, uninvited ginger self into our camp. She wagged her finger at Willie as though damning the poor mother to hell. "You get that boy out of that cramped wagon, Mrs. Wetherfield. He needs the air. Everyone knows cholera is caused by miasma and these vapors ain't helping him."

"No," I said. "It's the water. Cholera comes from dirty water."

"Oh, Miss Big-Bug has something to say about it, does she? With her educated ways you'd think she'd know a thing or two about cholera."

I spun toward the hard-faced woman. "I know that cholera comes from dirty water. I know that we're going to keep boiling every ounce of water we drink. You do what you want. I hope your…" No. I stopped myself though there was so much more I wanted to say. I wanted to cut her down with vicious, wild words that slashed her the way she had hurt me. Willie's feeble voice stopped me.

"Takodah? Grace? He's hot."

Takodah touched Paul's wrist and stepped back. Takodah glanced at me but I was afraid to ask her what she was thinking.

Paul vomited again. Willie didn't care that she was covered in it. I dipped a cloth in boiled water that had cooled and I wiped Paul's mouth and forehead. As I touched his skin I saw that it stayed to the side where I pressed it. The poor boy was dehydrated. Takodah tried to get Paul to drink but he shook his head.

Amos knelt beside his son. "Hey there, Paulie. Now you listen to me good. You drink up all of that tea Auntie Takodah made you and you'll feel better real soon, you hear?"

"Please, Paulie." Matthew held Paul's limp hand in his. "Drink this for your Uncle Matty, okay?"

Another bout of diarrhea and Paul was so weak he could hardly hold up his head. Willie cradled him, Amos spoke soft words to him, and Matthew read to him from *Swiss Family Robinson*. Sally loitered in the distance, too afraid to watch.

When the cramping started, Paul doubled over. After the spasms subsided he asked for water, and everyone hoped that this was the beginning of his recovery. Takodah sat nearby, her face a studied blank. I think she knew. As the sun set with Scott's Bluff in the distance, my sweet little Paul slipped away from us forever, smiling in his sleep. Willie's scream alerted the camp that the worst had happened.

"It was an easy death," Takodah told me. "He slipped away peacefully in his sleep, which is the best any of us can hope for. I know that's no comfort for Willie right now, but it will be in time."

"But he's so young," I said. I didn't bother wiping my tears away. My cheeks were wet, my neck was wet, the top of my thin dress was wet. It didn't matter. The agony was too much.

"Paul was a sweet, dear boy," Takodah said. "He was an old soul. He understood more about the world than some of these adults ever will."

"That's what my parents used to call me," I said. "An old soul."

"And they were right."

Amos did as men do and pulled into himself. Matthew and Hiram tried talking to him, distracting him, but Amos puffed at his pipe and stared at the ground, oblivious to them. Takodah, Mrs. Quigley, and I did what we could for Willie but she was inconsolable. She sat on the ground, her hair and her dress covered in vomit and diarrhea, and she screamed. And she screamed and screamed, waving an angry fist toward the heavens, berating whatever God she believed in for taking her beloved little boy away.

Finally, Willie spread herself out on the ground. "Leave me here," she said. "Leave me here with my Paul."

"You can't do that, Willie," Takodah said. "You're going to keep going. You're going to keep going because of Sally and Leticia, and because of Amos, and because of Matthew. You're going to keep going because of the family right here that still needs you." Willie turned away, covering her face with her hands. But Takodah was determined. "Willie, listen to me. We believe that death is not the end of life. Paul is about to go on a new adventure, a journey for his spirit. That's similar to the Christian belief, isn't it, that people's spirits travel to Heaven to your God after they die?" Willie exhaled and her shoulders dropped. "As long as you keep Paul in your heart, he's here. He's with you. You need to hold onto that every day. He wouldn't want you to lie down and die here. He'd want you to make it to Oregon so you can have that great adventure he was so looking forward to." Takodah helped Willie sit up. "Come. Let Grace and me get you washed up. Mrs. Quigley can find you a clean dress. And then we'll tend to our dear Paul."

Matthew stood near the back of the wagon. He tried to stay stoic, but his red-rimmed eyes and his quavering voice betrayed his grief. "We need to think about the burial, Willie. Reverend Smith has come to say a few words. Do you know what you'd like him to read?"

Willie wandered away without answering. Takodah and I followed her until she dropped into a sitting position, her legs beneath her, her arms stretched out as if reaching for her son. Takodah and I sat with her while Matthew and Hiram dug the child-sized grave in the shadow of Scott's Bluff. Matthew focused on his task, shovel in, shovel out, and he moved at a frenetic pace. Amos hardly moved. He didn't speak. He stared at everything as though he had forgotten its name. He watched his brother and brother-in-law dig his child's grave with detachment. Reverend Smith said something to him, but he didn't answer.

It was fully dark by the time Paul was laid to his eternal rest. Reverend Smith talked about St. Paul, about how the apostle had hoped to visit the saints in Rome. Paul knew the dangers he would face, but he was determined to proclaim the gospel there. He did finally complete his journey, but not in the way he had planned. In the end, he gave his life to God. Now our little Paul would not be completing the journey he had set out on, but he is with God, and with God he will have eternal life. As we sang "Amazing Grace" I found myself hoping that the sweet little boy could take the song with him. Amos had come back to himself enough to create a gravestone from a large piece of clay: Paul Willem Wetherfield 8 years old. The best son any man could hope for. Much loved by his mother and all who knew him. An angel gone to heaven.

As we left the gravesite, Hiram leaned close to his wife. "We've got another problem," I heard him say. "Matthew's got it."

Takodah stopped walking. "Cholera?"

Hiram nodded.

I realized that I hadn't seen Matthew at the funeral. I stared into every face, but he wasn't there.

"Where is he?" Takodah asked.

"In his tent. He didn't want to worry anyone after what happened to Paul, but I thought you should know."

Takodah took my hand. "Come on, Grace. We have more to do tonight."

The next three days were a blur. At times I felt suspended in midair, watching myself moving on the earth below. This can't possibly be real, I kept thinking. This isn't happening.

As Takodah, Willie, and I approached Matthew's tent we heard him retching near the river. Takodah called to Hiram to bring back some water and some buffalo chips for a fire.

"We have to keep him drinking," Takodah said. "And Grace is right. We should keep boiling the water."

Seeing Matthew so ill had snapped Amos back to himself. He tried to pour some whiskey down Matthew's throat, but Willie pushed him away. I think she would have pushed us all away if she could have, pushed us right back to the time before Paul died, to the time before her family had left on the trail, even. She paced like a frenzied mule as Hiram helped Matthew back into his tent. Matthew was pale and shivering, but he didn't seem to be in too terrible of a condition. He was talking with Amos and Hiram and he even smiled a little.

As the hours passed and the eastern sky glowed like gold on the horizon he became sicker, constantly vomiting into a tin bucket. Soon he hardly noticed anyone around him. Hiram tried to get Matthew to drink some water, but Matthew shook his head. He was too sick to realize he had soiled himself.

"Out of the way, ladies," said Amos. "Hiram and I will help him."

While Amos and Hiram cleaned Matthew up, Takodah found Matthew's one pair of clean undergarments and trousers. After Amos and Hiram changed him, Takodah sent me to the river to wash his clothes. When I returned to the tent Willie was still pacing, saying, "Lord, I know you have to bring your lambs home sometimes, but do I have to lose two of mine on the same day?" Sally and Leticia sat silently to the side, their eyes wide, as if they didn't understand the catastrophes that had suddenly overtaken their lives. Sally looked half herself without her twin, and though Leticia was too young to understand, she seemed to sense that something was very wrong with Uncle Matty. I stood back, wanting to help but not sure how.

Amos and Hiram set Matthew gently back into his tent, laying some buffalo blankets over him though he was shivering. Takodah made some tea, but Matthew shook his head and refused to drink.

When it was fully day, Takodah took Willie's hand in hers. "Willie, the girls need to eat, and you need to rest."

"How can I rest when my Matty is in that tent with the very same illness that killed my Paul?"

"That's not a request, Willie. Mrs. Quigley will fry you and the girls some bacon, pour you all some milk to drink, and then you'll rest." She looked at Amos and Hiram, both worse for the wear. "Hiram, Amos—you both go too."

"But who will take care of Matthew?" Willie asked.

"We will," Takodah said. "Grace and I."

Willie looked at me and I nodded. Willie picked up Tish, took Sally's hand, and dragged herself back to the wagon, too tired to argue. Amos and Hiram did the same.

Matthew was unconscious. I tried talking to him, wiping his lips with cool water, holding his hand. Finally, I shook his shoulders. "Matthew Cooper, if you get yourself dead I'll kill you!" But he didn't respond.

Takodah and I sat with him for some time. "So now what?" I asked.

"Now we wait, Grace. There's nothing more we can do."

The camp was quiet. We were supposed to move out today, but Amos declared that the Wetherfields were going nowhere and the rest in our train decided to stay as well. Their surreptitious glances in our direction betrayed their fear that there will be more illness throughout the camp before long. Moses Johnstone and his cronies lingered outside the corral, watching, whispering amongst themselves, keeping their distance.

Takodah pinched the skin on Matthew's hand. "He needs to drink." She shook him once, and he didn't awaken. She shook him twice, three times. Nothing.

"Takodah?"

"He's only sleeping. But he's not waking up." Takodah's eyes narrowed with sorrow. "Grace, I think you need to prepare for the worst."

"Should we tell Willie?"

"Not yet. There's nothing she can do and we still need to wait and see. But I know you have feelings for Matthew," she held up her hand when I tried to protest, "and I wanted you to know."

Matthew drifted in and out of consciousness for two days. Sometimes he shuddered as if he were cold. Sometimes he doubled over because the cramps were so painful. When he wasn't in a death-like sleep he was vomiting and when he wasn't vomiting he was soiling himself. Sometimes he spoke, nonsense mainly, or he talked to Paul, or he recited passages from *The Old Curiosity Shop* or *The Pickwick Papers*. Takodah's main concern was getting him to drink. When Hiram returned to check on the patient, he was so frustrated at Matthew's refusal of water that he opened Matthew's mouth and poured the fluid right down, though Matthew just coughed it back up. Sometimes, Matthew was conscious enough to ask for water. We hoped that meant he was on the mend, but then we remembered little Paul and realized that the asking for water might be the beginning of the end. On the third night I was mopping Matthew's forehead with a cool cloth when he opened his eyes.

"Miss Wentworth. Get her here. I need to speak to her."

"I'm here," I said. "Matthew, I'm here."

Willie held her brother's hand. "She's here, Matthew. She's hardly left your side since you fell ill."

"Are you sure you don't mean Gloryanna Winters?" Amos asked.

Willie looked ready to spit daggers at her husband. "He asked for Grace, Amos. You heard him ask for Grace."

"Grace!" Matthew called. "Where are you?"

I shook his shoulders, gently, wanting to knock his confusion, along with the disease, right out of him. "I'm here, Matthew."

Matthew's eyes were so wide all I saw was white. "Willie," he said, "tell Miss Wentworth I have to speak to her, now, before it's too late." Then his head fell back and he dropped into such unconsciousness that Takodah checked his pulse. She nodded, indicating that his heart still beat.

"Grace." Takodah whispered my name. "You need sleep too."

"I'll sleep when Matthew's better," I said.

"Mrs. Quigley?" Mrs. Quigley rolled herself near the front of the tent. She and Ezra were there every moment of Paul and

Matthew's illnesses, helping however they could. "Can you please take Miss Wentworth and the girls back to their wagon and see that they all lie down?" I protested, but Takodah would have none of it. "Get some rest, Grace. I'll come for you if something changes."

"Come on girls," Mrs. Quigley said. "I think we could all use some shut-eye about now."

Mrs. Quigley took Leticia in her barrow and I held Sally's hand as we walked back to Willie's wagon. Mrs. Quigley handed me the baby and pointed at Takodah's wagon. "I'll be right there. Holler if you need me."

I promised I would and tucked the girls into the feather bed inside the wagon. I stretched out between them, rubbing their backs until they fell asleep. I felt myself drifting off until my thoughts began racing, one after another, spinning so fast I felt dizzy lying there. I remembered what I knew about myself to settle my nerves. My name is Grace Marie Wentworth. My parents are James and Sarah. I'm 22 years old. I'm on the Oregon Trail with the Wetherfields. I love Matthew Cooper. Yes, I love Matthew Cooper. And he's dying.

I climbed out of the wagon as quietly as I could. Scotts Bluff was not so far from our camp and it drew my attention, lit as it was by the brightness of the shining moon and winking stars. I should have stayed with the girls, but I was too unsettled to keep still so I sat cross-legged on the ground near the wagon, spreading my apron around me. I admired the beauty of the cosmos above my head. I remembered what Takodah told me about the Great Spirit, about how if you know what you truly want then the Great Spirit might grant it to you.

I prayed aloud since I thought my message might get through better that way.

"Hello, Great Spirit," I said. "My name is Grace. I'm sorry, I'm not really sure how to do this. We're not religious in my family. My father scoffs at the very idea, grumbling something about

Puritans, and my mother says everyone believes in their own way. But I have looked into my heart, Great Spirit, and I know what I want. I want Matthew Cooper to live. I want him to have a long, happy life. He's a good man and he deserves every good thing this world can give him. If that happy life doesn't include me, that's all right. I've learned so much since I've been here, but this is not my time. And if I'm wrong and this is a dream after all, please wake me soon.

"I leave it up to you, Great Spirit. I want you to show me the way. I want you to guide me to where I'm supposed to be. Am I supposed to be here? Am I supposed to be there? If you know, then show me. But whatever else happens, I beg you to let Matthew live."

I dropped my head into my hands, hoping I said the right words. When I looked up Willie's wagon was glowing—a smooth gold as though an ethereal sun shimmered under the white canvas cover. I checked on the girls inside and they slept soundly, oblivious to the shine that made me shield my eyes with my hand. Three shooting stars crossed overhead. Then, as soon as the incandescence began, it was gone. I stood, stretching my legs, and wondered at what I had seen.

I stared without blinking at Scotts Bluff, the 800-foot-high hill that looked like it had been dropped from the sky onto the midwestern plains. When you're feeling the most confused, that's when your thoughts are at their craziest. At first, I couldn't stop thinking of Paul, buried not far from where I sat. Then, in a bizarre non sequitur, I remembered the standing stones in that television show. I decided that Scotts Bluff was a large standing stone—a huge standing stone, in fact. Is this my portal, I wondered? Is Scotts Bluff my way home?

Forgetting any remnant of sanity I might have had, forgetting the girls, forgetting Matthew, I charged toward Scotts Bluff. I was a determined woman on a mission. I was going home. Yes, there would be people I'd miss here, and yes, I did love Matthew, but he had decided we were not meant to be and I wanted to take a shower and watch television and hug my parents. The closer I grew to the Bluff the faster I walked. It would be effortless, I thought. It might feel strange going through, but I felt strange coming here, didn't I? I was so close to the craggy side that if I reached out I could touch it. I pressed forward, unafraid, ready to meet this challenge. Like a soldier at war I charged head-first into Scotts Bluff.

It's true—you see stars when you hit your head. My forehead smacked into the side of the mountain and I was knocked backwards, landing painfully on my sit bone. Flashes of light, like fireflies buzzing around my face, were everywhere in my line of sight. At first, I was annoyed that I was still in Nebraska in 1850. And then, when the realization hit me, I was so embarrassed by what I had done I could hardly stand being in my own skin.

"Grace?" I would have turned to face Takodah but my neck hurt. "Why on earth did you walk head-first into Scotts Bluff?"

"I was trying to get home."

Takodah pulled my face close, looked into my eyes, and shook her head. "I'll have to check on you later, but I think you'll live." She sat next to me. "Your way home is through Scotts Bluff?"

"Did you follow me here?" I asked.

"I wanted to tell you that Matthew is better. I think he's going to be all right. He's awake, and he's drinking. He's even making jokes." I stayed silent. "Do you still want to go home, knowing that Matthew will likely make a full recovery?"

"I don't know what I want anymore."

Takodah nodded. Finally, she said, "I know you come from far away, Grace, farther than I can begin to imagine, and I know you love your parents very much by the way you always talk about them. But let me tell you this. Whenever you have an important decision to make, look inside your heart. Even when your head is full of thoughts, your heart knows your truth. Your heart will tell you the right thing to do. You just have to listen."

Her words took my breath away. Again, I had to ask, "Takodah, are you...?"

She pointed at the sky. "It's nearly dawn. We should both get some rest."

She helped me upright when I stumbled and we walked back to the wagons together.

CHAPTER 22

*S*ome in our train pulled out while we gave Matthew time to recover his strength, including Moses Johnstone and his followers. Mrs. Brownlow, her doll daughter, and Beula Durington followed Johnstone's new train, which pleases me to no end. It will be nice to no longer feel arrow-like eyes piercing the back of my skull. Amos has told the remaining families that we are moving out tomorrow. I think he said it to prepare Willie, and himself, since we have to leave Paul here near Scotts Bluff. Willie and I walk to Paul's grave daily. It's hard to believe that it's only eight days since my little friend died and five since Matthew nearly joined his nephew in that impromptu grave. Every morning when I wake up I look for Paul's dear face and listen for his sweet voice, and every morning it's a hard right hook to my gut when I remember he isn't here.

Matthew grows stronger each day. He's still weak, but it's good to see him smile. We're on friendly terms again, mainly small talk about how glad we are that Johnstone and his band of merry men are somewhere in the distance and not here.

"Moses Johnstone has too much of a trigger temper," Matthew

said. "That man has worried me since we were in Independence. And then when he shot his gun off like that near the buffalo and you and Paul..." Matthew closed his eyes, his grief exhausting him.

"I wish I could have helped Paul this time too," I said.

"There was nothing to be done, Duchess."

"There were times on the journey when I wished that Paul was our..."

"Our what?" I shook my head, afraid to continue. "Grace, our what?"

"There were times when I wished that Paul was our son."

Matthew took my hand in his. I gripped him tightly, my fingers entwined in his. Takodah brought him some tea, which he managed to drink despite his shaking hand, refusing help from either Takodah or me. Takodah peered into his eyes and pressed the skin on his hand aside. The elastic skin snapped into place.

"You're going to be fine, Matthew. I thank the Great Spirit for it."

"I wish Paul were here too," Matthew said.

"Paul is here, Matthew, in our hearts."

"Will that be enough for Willie and Amos?" Matthew asked. "I haven't seen either of them all day. How are they?"

Takodah glanced through the tent flap toward the wagon with Wetherfield painted in red. "They're both very still, very quiet. We're heading out tomorrow and they know they're going to have to leave Paul here. It will be hard for them, but Hiram says we need to get a move on and he's right. Besides, staying longer won't make it easier for them."

"Or me," Matthew said. "But we've got to get going again if we're to make it through the worst of the journey before winter."

"Are you strong enough?" I asked.

"I'm going to have to be."

Takodah left for her own wagon. I realized, with a hot flush across my cheeks, that Matthew and I were still holding hands. Matthew looked at our hands, smiled, and said, "Tell me more

THE DUCHESS OF IDAHO

about your family, Duchess. I want to know everything about them. I remember that your pa is a teacher."

I couldn't think of anything else to add that wouldn't sound unbelievable until I added, "My parents are very much in love."

Matthew grinned. "How in love are they?"

"They're beshert," I said. "My grandmother taught me that word. It means soulmate or destiny. It's destiny that they're together."

Matthew pulled my hands to his lips and kissed my fingers. "If I told you that's how I feel about you, Duchess, would you believe me? That you're my destiny?"

I pulled my hands away. "I don't know, Matthew. I honestly don't. I thought we were getting closer. I told Willie I wanted to marry you. Then Amos says a few words to you about how we might not be right for each other and you were just...gone."

Matthew slid his hand out so that his fingers were touching mine. When I didn't pull back, he let them linger.

"Grace, I'm going to tell you the truth about what happened and I hope you'll believe me. It wasn't Amos' words that pulled me away from you. They just gave me the ammunition I needed to stay away because I already felt guilty. You see, the reason I was first drawn to you is because you remind me of..."

"Gloryanna Winters."

"How did you know?"

"Don't you remember? You asked me if I was sure I wasn't Gloryanna when we first met. Then I asked Willie to tell me about this Miss Winters. Willie said you loved her from the moment you saw her. You were courting her."

Matthew nodded. "Her cousin is here, Enoch Emerson, the widower."

"Willie said that one day Gloryanna disappeared and when you couldn't find her you decided to come West thinking maybe she had headed this way, that you might find her in Oregon."

"Well." Matthew leaned his head against the quilt he used as a pillow. "Willie knows a lot of the story, but she doesn't know all of it. I never told Willie that I found Gloryanna, or at least I discovered what became of her."

"What happened?"

"She died."

"Oh, Matthew. I'm so sorry."

"It was too painful to talk about, even to Willie, so I kept it to myself."

"What happened to her?"

"Consumption. After she died her family returned to Salem where they had people."

I pulled my fingers away and folded my hands in my lap. "Matthew, I need to ask you something. I know how much I look like Gloryanna. Both you and Willie mistook me for her when you first saw me."

Matthew sighed. "Yes, I was struck by how much you look like Gloryanna. I already knew she had died when I first saw you, but I kept pressing you, asking if you were her because I wanted so much for it to be true. I wanted you to be Gloryanna even when I knew you couldn't be."

"Now I need to know, Matthew. When you look at me, do you see Gloryanna Winters or Grace Wentworth? Tell me the truth, please."

"The truth is what when I first saw you all I could think about was Gloryanna. But now all I think about is Grace. Talking to you, learning about you, at least what you'll tell me, watching the way you and Paul bonded, seeing your courage in saving him. Why, Duchess, I think you're the most marvelous woman I know and any man would be lucky to have you. I know Amos has his opinions, but since it's my life I think my opinions matter more than his on such matters. I called for you, when I was sick."

"I know. I was there in front of you."

"Were you? Funny. My eyes were open but I couldn't see a thing."

"You said you had something to tell me."

"It was more what I wanted to ask you. So will you?"

"You haven't asked me anything."

"You're right, I haven't. But I will. Soon. And when I ask, will you? But I need to tell you this, Duchess, and you need to think about it carefully. I promised Willie I'd never leave her, especially now that Paul is gone and she's grieving. I tried to talk Amos into settling in California, but he's set against it because he doesn't think well of the people who live there."

"He thinks I'm one of those."

"Something like that. But that means we're going to Oregon, so you wouldn't be near your parents. I'm sure once we got settled we could take a journey to California so you can see your family. Maybe they'll even come to Oregon with us."

I wheezed as though the air had been sucked out of Matthew's tent. Amos and Hiram loitered beyond the open flap and I wondered if they could hear us. My lungs froze and I couldn't breathe. Here-there-here-there—a tug-of-war was raging within me. I feel in my very marrow that Matthew is my beshert, that this man is my destiny. My place is with him. But then flashes of my parents flickered behind my eyes. What would it do to them if I vanished and never returned? They would never know what happened to me. I heard my mother's voice, "You are our miracle, Grace. You always have been." And my father's perpetual, "Good night, Gracie."

If I had met Matthew in Idaho there would be no question of whether or not I wanted to spend the rest of my life with him. But this isn't Idaho. And I still have no idea if I could find my way home from here if I tried.

Matthew leaned so close our cheeks touched. "I can see the thunderstorm behind your eyes, Duchess, and I know this is a hard decision for you. I know you had your heart set on going home. That was another reason I thought we shouldn't be together, because now you have to choose—your family or me. That's why I don't want an answer right away. I want you to think on it. All I can say to try to persuade you to stay with me is this—I will spend every waking moment for the rest of my days striving to be worthy of being your husband. Imagine me, the husband of a duchess."

When he kissed me, I was certain I ascended five feet off the ground.

Our moment of bliss was over too quickly when we heard a roaring commotion that rivaled a street fight. We stepped outside to see what was happening, and it didn't look good. Moses Johnstone and his cronies had returned on horseback, circling Amos and Hiram, fencing them in. Lee Tappertit and Ezra Quigley stood back, watching.

"Go on back to wherever the hell you came from," Hiram hissed. "You wanted to be on your own so go be on your own. No one here misses you, believe you me."

"Our supplies are here," Archie Starkey said. "We have the right to our supplies."

"No," Amos said. "You took your wagons when you left. Your supplies were in your wagons. You have no right to ours. Hiram's right. Go on your way and leave us be."

Josiah McPherson, who had returned with Johnstone, trotted toward Amos' wagon.

"You owe us, Captain Wetherfield. That time you held us up can't be replaced. You slowed us down and who knows now how long it'll take us to get through the mountains. We may not make it before the snow makes it too hard to pass."

"Nonsense!" Amos' cool resolve mutated into red-cheeked fury. "Hiram has kept us going at a clip. That's why we've been able to hold back and give some time for those who needed to recover."

Moses Johnstone stroked his gray beard. The sarcasm grated his voice. "Like your brother-in-law? Too bad you couldn't save your own boy. Sounds to me like that squaw sister-in-law of yours can't control her voodoo magic. Seems she outright kills some folks. Sounds like a hangable offense to me."

Hiram charged toward Moses, but the riders pulled their horses closer and Amos and Hiram were trapped. Johnstone smirked, protected by his own corral.

After a tense stand-off, Moses waved into the distance. "Let's go, boys. Leave these ninnies be. We've got men's work to tend to." Moses reared his horse and galloped away. His followers charged behind him into the distance, not far or fast enough as far as I was concerned.

"I had hoped we were done with them," Matthew said through clenched jaws. He trembled, but he shook me away when I tried to help.

"We are now, aren't we?" I asked. Matthew shrugged in response.

Amos, Hiram, Willie, Takodah, the Quigleys, Sally, Leticia, and I had a quick evening meal of bacon, cornbread, and weak tea. Matthew wasn't ready for bacon, but he managed a few bites of the bread and he drank every cup of tea Takodah set in front of him. No one talked. Some of the men came to Amos with their concerns about Moses Johnstone and his fools returning for those supplies, but Amos shook his head, no, they won't be back. They know we're as armed as they are. The men left looking unconvinced.

THERE'S MORE ROOM IN THE TENT WITH PAUL GONE AND I CAN stretch out more, though more headspace is no consolation for the loss of my friend. Sally sleeps closer to me, as if I help soothe the ache she must feel with her twin gone. Sally has the same affable temperament as her brother and I'm happy for her company. I watch her as she sleeps, envious of the reprieve that unconsciousness brings. Life on the trail has become nearly too much to handle. Paul dying. Matthew nearly dying. My trying to make a great escape through Scotts Bluff. Matthew recovering and very nearly asking me to marry him. Knowing that my parents are worrying about me. I wanted to pray to the Great Spirit again, but I didn't know what to say.

Suddenly, men's voices echoed across the quiet night. Sally sat up, her eyes wide.

"Are they back, Miss Wentworth? Those men?"

"I think so, Sally. No matter what happens, you stay in this tent, do you hear me?"

She nodded and I went outside to investigate. Moses Johnstone, Josiah McPherson, Jonas Blackwood, and Archie Starkey had their horses loaded with the supplies they wanted. I don't know how they managed without the watch noticing, unless our watch was in on it. The thieves also had four of our horses. Some of the men from our train yelled at the burglars, brandishing their guns, while others stood back, waiting. I searched for Matthew, afraid he would push his way into the mess despite his weakened condition, but I didn't see him.

Amos appeared with Hiram behind him.

Mrs. Quigley's voice rang out above the din. "What in dangnation are you doing, Moses Johnstone? You heard us earlier. Go on your way and leave us be!"

"How sad, Captain Wetherfield," said Johnstone. "You need a decrepit old woman to speak for you."

"Are you saying I got the decreptitude?" Mrs. Quigley waved her fist in Moses Johnstone's direction. "I got some things to say right back to you…"

Ezra pulled his mother's barrow back. "Come on, Ma. This ain't the time."

"This ain't the time? Well, boy, I'll be humruckered because if this ain't the time then I don't know when is."

Amos stepped forward. "It's all right, Mrs. Quigley. Moses, I thought you decided to go on ahead after all."

"I will. When we have what's ours."

"You already have it," Hiram said. "What you've got there," he pointed with his chin toward the stolen supplies and horses, "is ours and you ain't leaving with it."

"We want all of it," said Archie Starkey.

"You can't have what's ours," Amos said. "You can have what your people brought along and nothing more. I'm not letting your greed hurt the survival of my train."

Moses Johnstone pointed his shotgun at the full moon. "I say otherwise. What do you say, Archie? What do you say, Josiah? Jonas?"

"Not this again," Amos said. "Put your gun away, Moses."

"Who says I should?"

Amos stood toe to toe with Moses. They were of equal height and stared into each other's eyes with enough indignation to self-combust.

"I do. Gun away, Moses Johnstone, and move on out before someone gets hurt."

Moses shrugged as though it were no matter to him. Before anyone could stop him he raised his gun, pointed the nozzle, and fired. One bullet. Women and children screamed, running as fast as they could. Ezra ran, dragging his mother's barrow behind him. Hiram grabbed Takodah. Willie grabbed the girls. I felt arms around my waist.

"Get down, Duchess!" Matthew hissed as he covered me with his body.

Moses and his men galloped into the distance, leaving the extra horses behind but taking the stolen supplies. When they were gone Willie asked, "Where's Amos? What's happened to Amos?"

I don't know how much heartbreak one human can take. My dear friend Willie has been tested to her limits. Hiram found Amos on the ground, dead, a single bullet through his heart. Willie knelt beside him, shaking him, screaming in his face.

"Amos Wetherfield, if you got yourself dead, I'll kill you!"

But he was gone, and she knew it. She was too numb to cry.

She had cried an ocean for her boy and then another for her ill brother. There was nothing left in her. Ezra Quigley dug Amos' grave near Paul's. I'm not sure how much comfort it gives Willie, knowing that father and son are together. Maybe Paul and Amos know their proximity, and maybe they can rejoice in each other forever. As he has throughout the journey, Reverend Smith said a few hushed verses. Everyone else turned away, their heads hanging nearly to the ground, but Willie stayed, kneeling between the two, one hand on the mound for her husband, the other on the mound for her son. I wanted to stay with her, but Takodah led me away.

"She needs time to grieve them both," Takodah said.

After Amos' funeral, Hiram and Lee Tappertit ran their horses as fast as the animals could go. Matthew was pacing, he wanted to follow them, but he was still recovering and he didn't want to slow them down when they needed speed on their side if they were going to catch up to Moses Johnstone. Matthew learned what happened later from Hiram, though he only shared pieces with me.

"They caught him, Duchess. They caught that villain Johnstone. They told those who had stayed back at his camp what he had done, they showed everyone Amos' bloody shirt, and the people on Johnstone's train were disgusted, or at least they pretended they were. They must have known Johnstone was a scoundrel, but they chose to follow him."

"People only see what they want to see," I said.

"That's the truth. Hiram and Lee pulled Johnstone from his tent, and Hiram challenged Johnstone in front of everyone, pressing Johnstone to admit that he killed Amos in cold blood. When Archie Starkey, Jonas Blackwood, and Josiah McPherson spoke against Moses, admitting they were there and saw that Amos wasn't violent and Johnstone had no reason to pull the trigger, Johnstone saw he was finished. He wouldn't admit it, even at the end, but there was enough evidence against him and they got him."

"And?"

"And it's not fitting for a lady to hear such things. All I can say is Moses Johnstone will never trouble anyone again."

Moses Johnstone's death doesn't change the fact that Amos is gone and Paul is gone and I don't know how Willie will cope.

WE'RE MAKING OUR WAY SLOWLY ACROSS WHAT WILL ONE DAY become the state of Wyoming. Takodah warned us that the water here is dangerous because the land is poisoned with alkali. Poor mules, horses, oxen, and livestock are thirsting to death and too many have died for lack of clean water. Our own Fred, the sweet molly mule who went along with whatever was put in front of her, died during the night. Ed and Ted pull the wagon between them now and we needed to make the wagon lighter, especially since we still have to meet some of the most difficult challenges of the trail. Matthew, Takodah, Hiram, and I chose which of Willie's belongings to leave along the path since Willie is floundering in despair.

At the Sweetwater River, people and animals, of those who are left, could drink freely. Purple mountains majesty is the correct phrase for the shadows looming large from the Rocky Mountains on the horizon. Finally, we arrived at Fort Laramie, a military outpost. Upon arrival, some families toward the back realized that the Hubbles, an older couple who have been traveling with us, were nowhere to be found. Some of the men, including Matthew, rode back toward where we had started from but they found no trace of them. The Hubbles had fallen so far behind they disappeared.

As we pulled into Fort Laramie a number of people in our train gasped at the sight of the Native American families camped outside. Some people were afraid, even those who know Takodah well.

"They're just families like us," Hiram said. Some people exhaled, though others said they'd be sleeping with their guns by their sides just in case.

I'm not sure why the families outside Fort Laramie were such a surprise to the travelers. We've seen numerous tribes throughout this journey. Around the nighttime campfires, some of the men like to tell tall tales about Native Americans, about their warfare and their savagery. Takodah disappears when such stories begin. She doesn't want to add fuel to the fire, I think. But our experiences with the people have been peaceful. We haven't been stopped in our journey West, and we haven't been asked for trades. Yes, we have been watched, but we have watched them too so I suppose that makes us even.

The bugle for the soldiers' drills blasted. Fort Laramie itself is not particularly interesting—a collection of wooden houses where the officers live, a barracks for the soldiers, a post trader's store, a bakery, stables, and an open courtyard for the parade grounds.

Hiram ordered the train to make up camp. We'll be resting here for a day or two, he said. Hiram is now both captain and guide. Those who remain with us have come to trust the weathered-looking mountain man, just as they have come to rely on Takodah's quiet help with births and illnesses. They are more determined now than ever to make it to Oregon, and they believe that Hiram can help us see this journey through. No one talks about our losses. Nearly everyone on this train has lost someone along the way. Women, so quick to wag their tongues before, now glance toward Willie and shake their heads with the full knowledge that they might be next.

Willie remains hidden in the back of her wagon with Sally and Leticia by her side. She won't let the girls out of her sight. She eats and drinks just enough to stay alive. Otherwise, she lies on her featherbed, her girls clutched to her chest as though she'll never let them go while she stares at the wooden hoops that keep the canvas cover in place. Takodah, Mrs. Quigley, and I make sure the girls are fed, changed, washed, and cared for. Matthew hasn't been able to pull any more of a response from the sister who is more of a mother to him than we have. Mrs. Quigley tried cajoling something, anything from Willie, even a spark of anger, but there's nothing. I worry that we buried Willie alongside her husband and son, never to be seen again in this life.

Matthew won't give up, though. He tries gently prodding Willie to take more food, to come with me to the river to wash, to sit outside the wagon. He speaks to her in soft words, promising that she will be all right in Oregon. He will take care of her and the girls. They will never want for anything. The fact that Matthew and I were talking about marriage seems to have slipped from both our minds. Still, we make time for each other. We sit together at night around the campfire with Mrs. Quigley, Ezra, Takodah, and Hiram. But no one talks. What is there to say? One day, I'll have to address Matthew's proposal. For now, we are trying to survive.

WE REMAIN CAMPED AT FORT LARAMIE. SOME OF THE FAMILIES ARE purchasing what they can from the traders. The prices are ridiculous but you pay for what you can and do without the rest. This morning we had a visitor, which was nice since people have been giving us a wide berth since we lost Amos. Enoch Emerson came to our wagon for breakfast, said it had been a while since he had eaten my delicious johnnycakes, and I was happy to fry a batch for everyone. At least it gave me something constructive to do. Enoch joined in Matthew, Hiram, and Ezra's conversation about what was waiting for us on the other side of Fort Laramie. When he finished eating, Enoch refilled his plate with another stack of corn cakes. He said, in a gentlemanly manner, "Miss Wentworth, will you accompany me? I'd like to offer these to Mrs. Wetherfield. I know she hasn't eaten much lately, and I thought your tasty cakes might be just the thing."

"You're very kind, Mr. Emerson," I said, " but all she'll take is a bite of fried bread and a few sips of tea."

"Maybe I could try?"

He looked so earnest, Mr. Emerson, that I couldn't say no. I followed him to the back of Willie's wagon.

"Willie?" I called. "Mr. Emerson and I have some johnnycakes for you. I fried them myself."

Sally said, "Ma, may we have some corn cakes?"

"Yes, you may," said Willie. She untied the puckered cover, and though I had told her that Mr. Emerson was there, she still seemed surprised to see him.

"Excuse me for pushing my way into a family moment," said Mr. Emerson. "I know you've been hurting, Mrs. Wetherfield, and for good cause. No woman should lose her husband and son the way you did. Excuse me for saying I know a little bit of what you're feeling. When I lost my Ethel I thought the whole world had stopped. I was surprised at any sign of life anywhere. How can the world keep spinning when someone you love has died? But it does. And you'll keep going too. I know you've been hit double hard. Little Paul was a lovely child. Just like Sally and your nice baby here. But you need to stay strong, Mrs. Wetherfield. These two girls need their momma now more than ever. You need to put your grief aside and focus on the children you still have, right here next to you." He smiled at the girls. "Now what's this little one called?" He patted the baby's head.

"That's Tish," I said.

"How de do, Miss Tish. I'm Enoch Emerson. I'm a family friend."

Tish giggled for the first time in days and I was thankful for the presence of this kind man. He picked the baby up in such a tender manner I was surprised that he didn't have children of his own. Willie sat up, watching. She even ate the johnnycakes I fed her while Mrs. Quigley fetched her some tea.

. . .

AFTER WE LEFT FORT LARAMIE WE SAW INDEPENDENCE ROCK, WHICH looked like a beached whale on the Sweetwater River, or an extraordinarily large turtle. Independence Rock is less than 200 feet tall, far less imposing than some of the other monuments we've passed. Like the other monuments, though, this one was also covered in graffiti with the names of travelers. Still, this moment marks an important highlight in our journey. Most travelers like to arrive at Independence Rock by the Fourth of July in order to ensure that they would make it through the treacherous mountains before the snow made it too hard to travel.

"Well," Hiram said. "We didn't miss by much. Today is the fifteenth of July. Even with the stops we're still making good time, everyone." He glanced at Willie, who is at least spending some time outside the wagon now.

I hadn't seen so many wagons together in one place since we began our journey. There was a traffic jam by Independence Rock with a backlog of families from different trains waiting to make their way past. Many had set up camp and the area looked like a modern-day fairground. Cooking fires burned everywhere and the smell of bacon permeated the air. There was some fiddle music and a bit of dancing, but the people were largely subdued. We soon discovered why.

Matthew came back from a conversation with a man from another train with news that President Zachary Taylor has died and Millard Fillmore is now president. Hiram grumbled that he wasn't sure if that was a such good thing but he kept any other thoughts on the matter to himself. Mainly, the families stopped near Independence Rock were concerned with eating and resting for the final stage of the journey.

After our evening meal, Enoch Emerson decided to carve his name on Independence Rock. Hiram and Ezra joined him. Willie, though she had eaten with us, escaped back into the wagon with the girls. Mrs. Quigley had dozed off, leaving Matthew and me alone. We sat in companionable silence, sneaking glances at each other. Matthew touched my fingers and my whole body quivered. He nodded at Independence Rock.

"How about it, Duchess? Would you like your name inscribed there for all the world to see? They don't call it the Great Register of the West for nothing."

"Why not?"

We walked together to the swollen-looking granite, stopping at the base alongside hundreds of others looking to add their names and where they had come from. Some had chisels, some had knives like Matthew, some used pigments of paint, some used wagon grease, and a few men even used gunpowder. Everyone had the same intention: to let others know. We did this. We made a dangerous trek across a treacherous land in search of a better life. We are here.

All the space for writing on the white feldspar was taken, so Matthew climbed a bit. When he found his footing, he reached for me.

"Come on up, Duchess. The view is fine."

I climbed to where Matthew stood and looked out across the Sweetwater River, the hundreds of wagons, the thousands of travelers, and I thought it was beautiful. Matthew still had my hand in his, and I wanted him to keep it forever. I wanted him to keep me forever. I still don't know what any of this means, but if I can have this man in my life, then the sacrifices may be worth it.

"I want to show you something, Duchess," Matthew said.

"I'm here."

He reached into his pack and pulled out a small notebook. "You're not the only one keeping a journal." He handed me his notebook and nodded, letting me know it was okay for me to read whatever was inside.

"We've only spoken the once when she appeared out of the air, blown down by the heavens, it seemed. One moment I felt a presence, saw no one, but I turned back, and there she was, looking at everything at once, as bewildered as anyone I've ever seen. She looked like she was surrounded by ghosts, or maybe she was the ghost..."

"I cannot help my mind's wandering in the young woman's direction. She is a fascinating creature. Beautiful as the sunlight in the sky, because that's what she reminds me of—her hair is the sunlight, her eyes are the sky. I have learned that her name is Grace Wentworth, she is unmarried, she is going to California, and I cannot get her out of my mind. With her dignified manner and refined way of speaking, she seems like a duchess to me..."

"Every night I watch as she writes in her journal as though she was sharing the most solemn secrets. I would like to know her secrets. I would like to know the duchess better..."

"I look for her in the darkness. I know she is near and it pains me that I cannot speak to her freely. I dream of her often, but I cannot tell her. It isn't proper that I do so. I can see her golden hair, falling from her braid, fanning out under her bonnet, her wispy curls framing her face. I know it's foolish of me to even think of such things. She's educated, from a wealthy family out West, and she's too far above me..."

"Yes," I said.

Matthew stepped back. His face brightened but the light evaporated quickly. "Yes to what?"

"Yes to your question, if you ever find the courage to ask it."

Matthew swung me into the air as much as the short ledge would allow. "Here goes," he said. He knelt on one knee, my hand in his, my fingers near his lips. "Grace Wentworth, will you do me the honor of being my wife?"

"Yes, Matthew Cooper. I'll marry you."

Matthew whooped and waved his hat in the air. "Did you all hear that? I'm marrying a duchess!" And the others whooped as well.

I didn't see what Matthew had done until afterwards. We climbed one more length of the rock and he found a small space in which to carve some names. He carved Paul's name, and Amos', and Willie, Tish, and Sally. He carved his own name and next to it, in large letters, he carved Grace Wentworth, Duchess. I laughed as I threw my arms around his neck.

"Kiss me," I said.

And he did.

CHAPTER 23

$\mathcal{M}$atthew and I celebrated our engagement the best we could under the circumstances. Willie cried, hugging us both tightly, saying, "I knew it. The first time I saw the two of you together I knew it. I only wish Paul were here to see it. He would have loved having you as his aunt, Grace." We cried so much everything was blurred for the rest of the day. We had Reverend Smith along, and he said he would be happy to perform our wedding ceremony since we need something to be happy about, but Matthew and I have decided to marry further down the trail. We have some tricky points in our journey coming up and we don't want to distract anyone with wedding preparations.

Six miles past Independence Rock was Devil's Gate, another rock formation, this one consisting of a huge, narrow cleft 370 feet high. The Sweetwater River ran swiftly past. Hiram told us that wagons can't make it through the narrow space so we traveled half a mile to the south. As we hiked, Takodah told us the Arapaho legend about a powerful evil spirit with huge tusks that roamed the Sweetwater Valley. Once, when warriors attacked the beast, it thrust its tusks and ripped a huge gap through the earth, into which it disappeared, never to be seen again. None of us wanted that fate. I'm pleased to say that everyone, human and animal, made it through Devil's Gate.

I HAVEN'T WRITTEN FOR A FEW DAYS. I'VE BEEN RELUCTANT TO WRITE since I feel like forming the letters into words somehow makes it true. There's a third wave of cholera, and I worry how much more any of us can take. I worry how much I can take.

I don't want to face the reality of this, but I must. I've had to make a few discrete dashes for privacy near the river. Once I nearly didn't make it and almost soiled my dress. I want to hide the fact that I think I have it since I don't want to worry anyone. Besides, I may not be that sick. It may simply be a bout of paranoia after Paul and Matthew. I'm sure it's just a regular stomach upset— too much bacon, probably—and I'm imagining anything worse. Whenever you're surrounded by sickness you always think you have it.

THIS MORNING TAKODAH TOOK ONE LOOK AT ME AND KNEW. SHE told Willie, who struggled to maintain her stoicism once she heard. Willie told Matthew, who couldn't hide his concern. He's driving Willie's wagon now, and he keeps looking back to see that I'm all right. I feel uncomfortable, like large hands have reached into my bowels, twisting my intestines like twine, but I haven't vomited and I'm holding down the cups of tea Takodah keeps pressing into my hands. I'm well enough to write here. Matthew continues to glance back, but having survived it himself, he says I'm strong and I'll be fine. Takodah smiles at me, and she isn't tight-lipped the way she was with Paul and Matthew, which helps me feel the end isn't here quite yet.

· · ·

I FELT BETTER THIS MORNING AND DECIDED TO WALK. A HALF HOUR after we moved out my legs crumpled beneath me and I fell. Matthew stopped the wagon and gently lifted me into the back. I've vomited twice and I'm so tired. Even holding this pencil feels like too much. I'm worried that I'll never take another step along this journey again, that this is it. I'm done. I'm forcing myself to write since there are words I have to get out before it's too late. I feel the end coming for me, slowly, as if death is a plodding wagon train overtaking me. I know these words are hardly legible. Takodah helps me with the pencil but it still only looks like scribble. She reads what I have written and nods with sympathy. She says something to me, her voice insistent, but I must write.

Matthew looks like an owl, his head facing me when he should be concentrating on driving. Willie and Sally walk near the back of the wagon while Tish rides in the barrow with Mrs. Quigley. I feel the weight of Willie's fear heavy on my aching chest. Takodah waves her arms while she yells something to Matthew.

Matthew. Everything is Matthew. There's so much I want to say to him. There's so much I want him to know.

And my parents? What about my parents?

I need to tell them

CHAPTER 24

IDAHO

L. Frank Baum was right. Everything is confused when you return from the other place. You open your eyes, first your left, then your right, and then the blurry scene surrounding you comes into focus, slowly but surely. Faces you love peer down at you, waiting, worried, hoping that what they see is real yet afraid they might be imagining it. Grace tried to sit up but the fibers of her nerve endings screamed. She felt a hand under her head, helping her to lie back down. One by one she recognized the faces. Her mother. Her father. Annabelle. So it was all a dream. The dust. The wagons. The dangers. Matthew. It was all a dream.

"Oh, my God. Olivia!" Sarah cried.

Grace saw Olivia crumpled on the ground, limp as a rag doll. James rushed to Olivia's side and helped her to sit. Grace was still groggy, still coming back to herself, but she saw her father holding Olivia's hands while Olivia panted for breath.

"Grandma?" Grace called.

Olivia managed a weak smile. "Oh, Grace. Thank God. I wasn't sure it would work."

"Hallelujah," said Annabelle.

Sarah smiled at her daughter, though the smile didn't reach her eyes. "How are you feeling, Grace?"

"I'm not sure. Tired, I think. Sore. But mainly tired."

"Hand her one of those antibiotics," Annabelle said, pointing to the medicine bottle on the dresser. "That's what she needs. Fluids and antibiotics."

Everyone was quiet. Sarah wouldn't take her eyes off Grace while James helped Olivia stand up. Olivia shuddered as she balanced, and James helped her walk to the bed, where she sat beside Grace. Sarah took Grace and Olivia's hands in hers.

"We were so worried," Sarah said. "For both of you."

"I'm all right," Olivia said, her hoop earrings jingling with the shake of her head. "This is the second time I've nearly been killed by a Wentworth." She glared at James, who shrugged.

Sarah took one of the white pills from the medicine bottle and handed it to Grace with a cup of water. Grace swallowed the pill and drank the water, amazed by everything she saw. She was in Annabelle's, in the loft bedroom. Her parents were there, and Olivia, and Annabelle. And Toto too. There was Casey, the black cocker spaniel, curled into a ball on the floor, poking his head up, watching her, as though keeping an eye on her.

"Oh, Grace." Sarah covered her face with her hands while James knelt beside his daughter, studying her with a worried father's look.

"Are you sure you're only tired, Gracie?" he asked.

Olivia shook her head. "I don't know. She looks a little peaked." She took Grace's left hand and pulled it close to her face, studying it the way Takodah had. She moved Grace's fingers and nodded. "Her hand seems to have healed well, so that's something good. But I'm worried about this cholera. Maybe we should take her to a hospital."

"And what do we tell them?" Annabelle asked. "How do we explain how she got sick like this? Anyone?"

No one replied.

"We've got the antibiotics she needs. We'll make sure she takes her medicine and drinks enough. We'll take care of her. I say we leave well enough alone."

"Do you have any memory of where you just were?" James asked.

"I was..." Grace had to think. "I was..." She looked at her mother, wide-eyed as she remembered the wagons, Willie, Paul, and Matthew. "I was dreaming I was on the Oregon Trail."

Sarah sighed. "You're all right now, Grace. Olivia pulled you back." Sarah hugged Olivia, who was still pale and shaking but looking stronger. "Olivia nearly couldn't get a hold on you and it was touch and go there for a while. We weren't sure if she'd be able to do it, but here you are. And we're so grateful."

"Olivia is strong," James said. "After what she did for me? I'm not surprised she could help Grace too."

Grace's head pounded and everything she heard only made half-sense. She rested against her pillow, staring up at the ceiling and catching sight of the attic door. A vision of going up, clearing out some junk, and moving things around bounced in her memory, but the memory slipped away as soon as it arrived. She felt so weak, but she managed to say, "Will someone please tell me what is happening?"

Olivia continued to look more like herself. Her complexion was pinker and she breathed more easily. She pushed a lock of silver hair from her eyes with one hand and gripped Grace's arm with the other. "What is happening is that you have an important decision to make, dear. A decision that won't be easy either way you choose."

"What choice is that?" James asked.

"Grace needs to decide which era she wants to live in, James— this one with us or in the past with Matthew." Olivia paced to the window and looked over the stable where Daisy and Chuck munched on the hay that had been set out for them. "I've been a witch all my life, as my mother was, as her mother was, back to the beginning of our family line. I've used my magic in a positive way to promote good in the world. I've accepted all creatures, paranormal and normal, including vampires, werewolves, and ghosts. I thought I knew everything about the preternatural world. And now this." Olivia turned sad eyes onto Grace. "I've never seen anything like this before."

"But isn't this the same thing that happened to me?" Sarah asked. "I was also drawn through time to find the man I love."

Olivia shook her head. "It's similar but not the same. Sarah, when you first arrived in Salem you were dreaming about James. But Grace isn't dreaming this." Grace gasped, and Olivia put a comforting hand on her shoulder. "Grace, you weren't dreaming that you were on the Oregon Trail. You were there. You were living it." Olivia's smile was tinged with sadness. "And you may choose to go back again."

"Why would she want to go back?" James asked. "She might have died if you hadn't brought her back. I don't see how there's any decision to be made. She's our daughter. She belongs here with us. How can that not be right? After everything we went through to find her again, after our family was reunited after oh so very long. How can she belong anywhere else?"

"James." Sarah stepped toward her husband. "Grace is a grown woman. She has her own life to lead."

James shook his head. "But Sarah, listen. When we found her again in Salem…"

"Wait." Grace sat up. "What do you mean when you found me again in Salem?"

Annabelle's painted-on eyebrows raised to her hairline. Olivia turned the same expression onto James and Sarah.

"You need to tell her," Olivia said. "It's time."

"It was time 22 years ago," said Annabelle.

Grace sat up, watching her father as he paced while her mother stood near the window, watching the horses. James and Sarah kept glancing at each other, that earnest, silent communication she had seen between them so many times.

Finally, Sarah said, "My mother is right, Grace. We should have told you a long time ago, but we were afraid."

"Afraid of what?" Grace asked.

"Afraid you wouldn't believe us."

"She's your daughter, Sarah," Olivia said. "She'll sense the truth of your words." When James and Sarah stayed silent, Olivia held out her hands to them. "I can tell her if you want, but she really must know, especially now that she's discovered her own magic."

"No," James said. "I'll tell her. I'm her father and I'll tell her." He stood near the railing, his hands clasped behind his back, staring, as he so often did, into the distance. He sighed. "I don't know where to begin."

"Begin at the beginning," Olivia said. "That's always the best place to start a story."

James opened his mouth to speak but closed it again, still searching for something he couldn't seem to find. He joined Sarah by the window and looked toward the farm with the potatoes and the cows. "I remember when I used to live near cows." His voice sounded far away. "That was when I first moved to Salem. At first, I found it utterly annoying, but I grew used to them, their solid presence, and in time I was happy to see them quietly chewing the cud."

"I remember you telling me those stories," Grace said. "I used to ask you where you saw cows in Salem since I never saw any there."

"It was before you were born."

Sarah sat beside Grace on the bed and kissed her daughter's forehead. "You've always been special, Grace. When I was pregnant with you I felt you stirring inside me and I knew you would be special. Brave and strong like your father."

"I'm not brave," James said. "I've never felt less brave than I do at this moment." He brushed his cheeks with his hands. Sarah stood on her toes to see into his eyes, as Grace had seen her mother do so often.

"I'm still amazed when I see clear water in your eyes though I should be used to it by now. I've known you as human far longer than I knew you before, but for some reason I still expect to see red streak your face when your eyes well up like that."

Grace looked from her father to her mother. "Why should Dad have red falling from his eyes? You mean like blood?"

"Yes," James said. "I cried blood for a long time."

Annabelle waved her hands in the air in frustration. "Will you two please stop with this hocus-pocus nonsense and tell Grace she's adopted already."

"What?" Grace tried to crawl out of bed, but Annabelle's strong hands kept her in place. "Of course I'm not adopted. I look like both of my parents. Mom just said she was pregnant with me. It can't be both. Mom?"

"It can," Sarah said. "It is. I know exactly how you feel right now, Grace, like the ground is moving in circles beneath you feet, like there's an earthquake shattering everything you thought you knew about your life, like you'll tumble into a hole never to climb out again. I know what it feels like to want to run away screaming because you think nothing will ever make sense again. But it will. Once you learn about the invisible world, the magical world, and once you learn how to live in it, it becomes a fact of life until you don't even realize how special it is any longer. Isn't that right, Olivia?"

"You're right, dear. Goodness, I can still remember the look on your face, Sarah, when you came to the Witches Lair with your dream journal. When you realized that you were dreaming about James, I thought you were going to blow away with the nor'easter pounding the shore."

Grace dropped her head into her hands. "I don't understand what any of you are saying."

"You don't yet," Olivia said, "but you will. Promise me that you'll listen with an open mind."

Grace didn't see that she had any choice. And then she realized. When she was on the trail with Matthew, she didn't know why she was there, but she managed to make it work. She completed her chores, helped Willie with the children, flipped johnnycakes. The tragedies were nearly too much to handle, but they were real problems that she understood and she could deal with them by keeping busy, by walking, right left right left. Now, here, where she thought her life made sense, suddenly everything was confused. Even her parents were speaking in riddles. She wished she were back with Matthew, in his arms, despite the dangers of the trail.

She watched James pace, back and forth, the way he always did when he had something on his mind. Finally, he stopped. "I was born in London."

"I know that," Grace said.

"I was born in London in the year 1662."

"Dad, please. This isn't time for jokes."

"I'm not joking, Grace. I was born in 1662."

Grace looked at Sarah. "Mom? Will you please tell Dad to stop joking."

Sarah looked more serious than James. "He's not joking, Grace. He was born in 1662. And I was born, at least in that life, in 1672."

Grace stood from the bed. Despite the weakness from the cholera, despite her muscles screaming for rest, she remained standing, if shakily, and she pointed at her father. "Enough! Just say what you have to say already!"

Sarah's voice was soft, like Willie's when she soothed Tish. "I know this is hard for you, Grace. And I understand exactly how you feel right now. That's how I felt when I found out about your father in this life."

"What do you mean, in this life? You've heard this before? How can you both be so disappointing? All these years I thought you were the two wisest people I know. Now you're what, trying to make me believe fairy stories? How stupid do you think I am? And what does it have to do with my dreams about the Oregon Trail? Or my dream that isn't a dream because Olivia says it was real."

Olivia ran a comforting hand across Grace's back as if she were a child. "Remember, Grace, don't listen with your logic. Feel it with your heart. Then you'll know that what they say is true."

"You believe this too? Oh, Grandma…"

"Just listen, Grace," Olivia said. "Please."

Grace knew it was all going to be hogwash, but they were her parents and she loved them and she knew they loved her. She saw her parents through very different eyes, though. They seemed so small, so weak suddenly. She had always thought of James and Sarah as strong, level headed, able to charge through any difficulties as long as they had each other. "We're Wentworths," her mother would say. "If we can overcome our past we can overcome anything."

"Okay," Grace said. "Dad, you were born in 1662, and…"

"I know you don't believe him," Sarah said.

"Well, if you were born in 1672 I suppose you would believe him." Grace's sarcasm was really a cover for her concern. She didn't want her parents or Olivia to see the shivers creeping along her arms. She didn't want them to know that somewhere, deep inside, she felt a ring of truth to their words.

"You're right, Grace. I was there. I was…" Sarah reached for Olivia. "All these years I've dreamed of the day when I would tell Grace the truth about our family, about how special she is. Now that moment is here and I don't know what to say. How do you tell your child something like that? Then when she grew older I thought she would never believe me, and I was right. I can see it in her face. She doesn't believe me. She won't ever believe me."

"Enough!" With every ounce of strength she could muster, Grace made her way down the stairs. She wobbled and held onto the bannister as if for her very life, but she was determined to get away. When James tried to stop her, Sarah shook her head.

"Let her go, James. We're not doing a very good job explaining this. Give her time."

GRACE SAT UNDER THE WELL-SHADED TREE AND LISTENED TO DAISY and Chuck knicker as they wandered about the yard in the sunshine. She felt trapped in this odd between-world where she missed Matthew's easy, steady presence but she also missed her parents, who were there in the house with her but weren't at all themselves. She wanted to laugh at everything they had said, that Olivia had "pulled her back," that her father was born in 1662 and her mother in 1672. Something unnamed poked at her from the inside, an insistent voice, but she couldn't examine it, not yet, for fear of what it might tell her. She was still so weak, her disheveled thoughts still wreaking havoc on her unsettled mind. She closed her eyes and found herself wishing that she could fall into the deepest sleep and find her way back to Matthew. Even the difficulties of life on the trail were better than this.

She didn't open her eyes when she heard the patio door open. She didn't look when someone sat beside her. She heard her father's voice.

"Two cups of Earl Grey, and Annabelle made these blueberry scones. They're pretty good if I do say so myself."

Grace looked at her father. He looked like himself, his eyeglasses pushed back on his nose, his graying gold hair pressed away from his face. He smiled and pushed the plate of scones in her direction. Grace wasn't hungry, but she remembered Takodah pressing all those cups of tea into her hands so she drank.

James looked his daughter in the eye. "I'm sorry, Grace. We didn't make very good work of it earlier. Your mother and I are just so surprised by everything that's happened, though we really shouldn't be. It shouldn't be any surprise at all that you're touched by a magic all your own." James held up a hand as Grace tried to protest. "Please, Gracie, just hear me out. If you want to call the asylum on me when I'm done you have a perfect right to do so. But first, listen. Please."

Grace nodded. She owed her father that much.

CHAPTER 25

"I know this seems farfetched, Gracie," James said. "If I hadn't lived through it myself I'd never believe it. But I have lived it, and I swear to you it's true, every word of it. Do you believe in things you can't see, an invisible world that can't be explained by anything we know to be true?" He stopped, staring into his tea as though reading the leaves. "Do you remember that bedtime story I used to tell you? The one about the husband and wife who loved each other so much they reconnected hundreds of years later in another life in another time?"

"That was one of my favorite stories when I was a kid," Grace said.

"Was it just a story?"

Grace looked at James. The intensity in her gaze made James smile.

"Of course it was," Grace said.

"Do you remember the story? Can you tell it to me?"

"I think I know most of it." Grace recalled the first time her father told her the story. They were in Salem, sitting in Olivia's mystical shop at the edge of Pickering Wharf watching the white-foam waves lick the shore, spreading toward the horizon like long blue fingers. "Once there was a husband and a wife who fell very much in love, as if the universe itself had blessed their union. Soon their family was caught up in the madness of the Salem Witch Trials, and the wife was falsely accused of witchcraft. She was arrested and died in jail, along with the baby she carried."

Something pricked Grace's memory. She turned, expecting to see someone poking her scalp with pins, but no one was there but James pressing his back against the hefty bulk of the tree, his arms around his knees, his glasses fallen to the tip of his nose. He said nothing, giving her this time.

Finally, he said, "What is it, Gracie?"

"It's nothing." Grace's voice was hollow. She felt hollow, from her head to her toes, as though she wasn't really there, or she was somewhere else entirely.

"Continue the story. Then what happened?"

"The man lived a long, long time. And then one day she was there, his wife, standing before him again. He knew her the minute he saw her, but it took a while for her to remember him. In time, she remembered that he was her husband from their life so long ago."

"She needed help from a powerful witch to recall that past life," James said.

Sarah stood behind her husband. "The husband and wife were joyfully reunited, and though they had some difficult trials pushed their way since then, they overcame them and lived happily ever after with their two beautiful children." Sarah and James clutched hands.

Grace stared at her mother. "You know the story too?"

"I know the story, Grace. I lived it. That's the story of how your father and I found each other again."

"It's our story," said James. "But it's your story too. You were the baby we lost in 1692. We found you in this life when you were six months old. We were led to you. That's why we never told you that you were adopted. Yes, we adopted you, but you're also our child. How can you look in the mirror and doubt that you're blood of our blood?"

Olivia peered around the open patio door. When she saw that all was calm she sat next to Grace. "Everything James and Sarah are telling you is true, dear. They were together with you in 1692, and they're together with you today."

Grace didn't know whether to laugh or cry. All right, she thought. I'll humor them. For now.

"So tell me about your lives when you met the first time," she said to James.

James smiled, obviously pleased with the request. "In 1690, my father and I left England for the Massachusetts Bay Colony. I knew I could help him with his mercantile business, and I didn't want him to face the New World alone so I went with him. Shortly after we arrived we met a farmer's family also recently arrived from England. Silas Jones' daughter Elizabeth was the most beautiful woman I had ever seen." James smiled at Sarah. "But she wasn't just beautiful on the outside. Her external beauty was simply a physical manifestation of the beautiful person she was inside."

Sarah smiled back, making an obvious effort to hold back her tears. There was something in the way her parents looked at each other that made Grace pause.

"Elizabeth and I were very happy together," James said, "but the madness of the witch hunts overwhelmed everything. No one in Salem was left untouched. One night..." James stopped. Sarah pressed her head against his arm and they stayed that way a long time.

"Do you want me to finish the story?" Olivia asked.

"No," James said. He exhaled loudly and his shoulders clenched. "Elizabeth was arrested for being a witch. She was pregnant at the time and she died in jail, the baby along with her." Spark-like static flashed beneath Grace's skin. She wanted to ask questions but her mind was oddly blank. James looked across the green field where the cows languidly grazed. "I hadn't known that Elizabeth died. A man, well, a man told me he could help me. I followed him and..." James turned suddenly, his hands outstretched toward Olivia. "I agree with Sarah. I don't think Grace believes any of this."

"She's your daughter, James," Olivia said. "She knows the truth deep down. We may need to dig a bit to bring it to the surface, but the truth is in her."

"Olivia is right," Sarah said. "I remembered, and so will Grace."

"Very well." James moved closer to his daughter. "The man turned me into a vampire."

Grace shook a frustrated fist in her father's direction. "You were a vampire? Oh, Dad, you have to do better than that."

"It's well accepted that vampires are real," Sarah said. "Remember when you learned about the vampire internments in school?"

"Well, yes, but..."

"Your father was there, interned in the camp known as Camp Dracula. You probably don't remember this because you were so young, but you spotted him on the television when they were showing a news story of the vampire camps."

Suddenly, as if the pages of a scrapbook opened inside her mind, Grace saw it. She saw the television, the news report about the vampire internments, and her father. He was tall and broad shouldered as always, and he looked, no, gleaned, into the camera, a sly smile on his lips, letting them know he was okay. She saw her mother touch his face on the television screen.

"I can see it in you, Grace," Olivia said. "I can see that you remember."

Grace didn't know what to say. Her beloved father had been a vampire. "And you were a vampire too?" Grace asked Sarah.

"No, I was..." Sarah was lost for words.

"You mother is a ghost, dear," Olivia said. "Your parents' love was so strong they were reunited after years apart." Olivia took both of Grace's hands in hers. "And you, my dear, are the child that Elizabeth carried when she was arrested. Yes, you died along with her in that horrid dungeon in 1692, but just as Elizabeth was reborn in Sarah, you were reborn too. That's how you can be both James and Sarah's biological child and still be adopted. You see, you've been surrounded by magic all your life. The paranormal world is real, Grace. And I think that somewhere inside you've always known that you were special, different from everyone else." Grace nodded. "Do you feel the truth of what we're telling you?"

"I don't think..."

"Don't think," Olivia said. "Feel. What do you feel about what we're telling you?"

"I think this should all be nonsense, but you're right—I feel the truth inside me. But none of this explains where I've been."

"Where you've been?" James asked.

"I think she's referring to the Oregon Trail and Matthew Cooper."

Everyone turned toward Annabelle. She had come out of the house so quietly no one realized she was there.

"How do you know about Matthew?" Grace asked. When no one answered, she held onto the tree as she pulled herself up until she was standing. "How do you know about Matthew?"

"We know everything, Grace," Sarah said. "We know you've been on the Oregon Trail. We know you've fallen in love with a man named Matthew Cooper. We know that little Paul died of cholera, and Matthew nearly did, maybe even you, if Olivia hadn't managed to pull you back."

"But how do you know?"

"The journals, dear," Olivia said. "Your journals, the ones you're writing on the trail? They're here, in Annabelle's attic in that trunk you found. I'm not quite sure how it happened, not yet, but my best guess is that when you started reading the journals you were touched by magic and transported back to that time to reunite with Matthew."

"No! No!" Grace waved her hands at the invisible terrors everywhere around her. She was sure she looked like a madwoman but she didn't care. "You have lied to me all my life! All of you!" Fury consumed every part of her, every thought she ever had, every love she ever felt. Even the weakness brought on by cholera was no match for her furore. She wanted to run fast and far away.

"Grace, we..."

"No, Dad, you've lied to me every single day of my life. You never told me you were a vampire, or that you and Mom have been intertwined for generations. You never told me that I was adopted, or whatever the hell you think happened to bring us together as a family. And now you've been letting me think that my time on the trail was real..."

"But it was real," Sarah said.

Grace pointed an accusing finger at Annabelle. "If it was real then you knew what was going to happen to me! That's why you taught me how to make johnnycakes and how to churn butter and why you wanted to teach me darning. So I'd be ready. And you never told me!"

Annabelle shrugged in surrender. "You're right, Grace. I should have told you. But I wasn't entirely sure it was you, and..."

"But what about my journals? Didn't you read my journals?"

"No, I never did. It all seemed too crazy to be true, but based on what I knew, I wondered..."

Grace would have wept but she was so weary. Whatever excess energy had propped her up a moment before was gone. "Oh, my God." Grace slapped her hands to her cheeks. "All of it is real. Matthew is real! Oh, my God." Sarah reached for her but Grace pushed her mother away. Grace dragged herself back inside and up to the loft where she could lie down. She couldn't face any of them anymore.

· · ·

Grace slept, a long, dreamless sleep. She was disappointed when she opened her eyes in Annabelle's loft. She had hoped she might find herself reunited with Matthew. But she was still in Idaho. Casey slept on her bed, and Grace took comfort in his soft warmth. She thought she should have been confused, or sad, or even mad, but even after a long sleep she was too exhausted to feel anything else.

"Take one of these." Annabelle was sitting in the chair next to the bed and she pressed a white pill into Grace's hand along with a cup of water. "You need to keep up with the antibiotics or they won't work."

"We could have used some antibiotics on the trail."

"You're right, of course. As far as I knew, Sarah and James had adopted you, so I wouldn't allow myself to believe that you were the family member in the legend. I had my suspicions, yes, because of the photograph, but I wasn't certain."

"You don't strike me as the type to believe in legends, Annabelle."

"That's the truth, Missy. And that's a big reason why I never trusted that any part of that story could be real. It had to be a fairy tale, or some strange coincidence. I tried to convince myself that things like that don't really happen."

Annabelle poured more water into Grace's cup from the pitcher on the nightstand. "Come on now, drink up. You need to stay hydrated." When Grace finished her cup, Annabelle set it aside. "So do you want to know the legend or not?"

"Why not? I can file it away with the rest of the nonsense I've heard today."

"This one's maybe a little less crazy than some of the things Sarah and James have been telling you. Story goes we had an ancestor who kept a journal on the Oregon Trail. While traveling the trail she fell in love and she married and settled with her husband here in what later became Idaho. But it wasn't just that the journals were a record of her thoughts. The legend says that the journals are imbued with magic and if one of the lovers finds their way back to the books the couple will be reunited."

Grace pet Casey's ears while she considered. When the dog had his fill of attention, he jumped off the bed and wandered downstairs. Grace watched him leave. "That does sound like what happened to me, except that Matthew and I never had a chance to marry. But I don't understand. If I traveled the trail in 1850, how am I here with all of you? Is my life then or is my life now?"

"That sounds like something you ought to ask your other grandmother. Olivia seems pretty in tune with the mystical world. That's not really my comfort zone, if you get me."

"I can't talk to her right now," Grace said. "I can't talk to my parents either. I'm so mad at them. How could they lie to me about who I am for so long?"

"People have different reasons for keeping secrets, Grace. Sometimes it's to protect themselves. Sometimes it's to protect someone else."

"It's a horrible thing to do to someone you love."

"Maybe it is and maybe it isn't." Annabelle's painted-on eyebrows came to an arc over her nose. "So do you love this Matthew Cooper?"

The thought of Matthew lit Grace up like sunshine. "Yes, I do." She looked around the old-fashioned house, the one she thought so odd when she first arrived in Idaho, and she smiled. "Did Matthew build this house then, Annabelle? You said our ancestors settled nearby."

"As a matter of fact, this is Enoch and Wilhemina Emerson's house."

"Enoch and Willie?"

"You haven't gotten there yet, I suppose. Spoiler alert. Willie Wetherfield marries Enoch Emerson. Get it? Emerson?"

"Yes, I get it. I wondered when I saw him if he was any relation."

"Well, he is. Or he will be. That there," Annabelle pointed

toward the square of the house, "is part of the original structure they built in the 1850s, though it's been moved around and fixed up quite a bit over the years."

"And the red barn? You said it belongs to cousins."

"That's where Hiram and Takodah settled. Of course, their house has been remodeled a lot over the years like this one. Their family lives there to this day. I'm surprised you didn't see the Wetherfield sign hanging from their door when you were there."

"I don't remember noticing it. I just thought it was a nice barn." Grace smiled, knowing what was in store for her friend.

Annabelle looked around as though searching for a cigarette pack. When she didn't find one, she folded her hands in her lap. "Now back to this Matthew Cooper. If Olivia can manage it, will you go back to him?"

"I don't know, Annabelle. I want to. I miss him so much. But I worry about Mom and Dad."

"Your parents are adults and they've had their own lives to live, rather long lives from what I can gather. Now it's your turn to live your life. So I ask you again—if Olivia can arrange it, will you go back to Matthew?"

"It's funny because if you had asked me before I came back here, I would have second-guessed my decision to stay with him. But being here, being without him, it's helped me realize that I want to be with him, even if life is more difficult then."

"Life has always been difficult, Grace. It's just difficult in different ways now." Annabelle leaned toward Grace, squinting. "And you're going to tell Mr. Matthew Green-Eyes that you're from the future?"

"Of course not."

"Why ever not?"

"He'll never believe me. It's too ridiculous for words. He'll think I'm crazy and he'll never look at me the same way again and…"

Annabelle crossed her arms over her chest, her victory playing as a high smile across her cheeks.

Grace sighed. "All right, yes. I understand why my parents were afraid to tell me the truth."

"Good. Now put them out of their misery, will you? And Grace?"

"Yes, Annabelle?"

"Tell them the truth about your decision. You owe them that. Whatever mistakes they might have made, they made them for the right reasons. They wanted to protect you, which is what all good parents want to do for their children. Sarah and James love you so much. I've always seen that in them, their unconditional devotion to you."

"And I feel it for them. Which is why it's going to be so hard to leave."

Annabelle nodded. She scanned the floor and said, "Where's that dog?" She said it with such warmth, and Grace knew how much Annabelle loved Casey. Grace wondered if Annabelle ever felt lonely.

As if she had read her thoughts, Annabelle said, "I was wondering, Grace, you know, only if you want to, but I thought maybe you might call me Nana. I can see how much you all love Olivia and how much Olivia loves all of you, how much she's done for you over the years, and I couldn't compete with that even if I wanted to. You call Olivia Grandma and so you should. Instead, I thought Nana might be nice. It's more family-like than calling your own granny by her name."

"Of course, Nana. I'd be happy to."

Annabelle looked away as though she were afraid her stoic demeanor would desert her completely. "That makes me happy, Grace. I'm sorry to lose you now after finally getting to know you after all these years. You've turned into a fine young woman, indeed."

"Thank you, Nana."

Annabelle huffed. She left so quickly she nearly evaporated into dust.

. . .

Everything was silent in the night but Grace couldn't sleep. She felt well enough to move around and she made her way downstairs to the kitchen. She pulled the water jug from the refrigerator and took great joy in the clean, fresh-tasting water. She glanced around, noticing that the old house seemed different. Instead of looking out of date and unfashionable as it had when she first arrived, now it seemed positively luxurious. She went to the window and watched the night, searching for answers in the stars as she had seen her father do so many times. So much made sense now—her father's nocturnal habits, her parents' deep concern for her, their knowing glances at each other. She believed in their magical world because now it was hers too.

She was living her own version of her parents' love story. James and Sarah had fallen into a love so deep that it transcended time. And she had the same with Matthew.

She watched the nightclouds, still white in the moonlight, as they muted the stars. How many thoughts, fears, and dreams had her father had when he was a preternatural man? Everything he had seen, everything he had done over all that time. Grace could scarcely stand to count the number of years he had been alive and longing for her mother.

"My Sarah." Grace had heard her father say those words to her mother with such meaning. "You are my Sarah."

And now she understood since Matthew was hers in just the same way. My Matthew. What was she to do? That here-there-here-there tugged at her heartstrings again.

If Olivia could do as Annabelle said, if Olivia could send her back to 1850, she would likely never see her parents again. Could she stand that?

She went back to her bedroom, pulled out her composition book, and did what her logical father always told her to do when she had a decision to make. She made a list of pros and cons. She folded one of the pages in half, wrote Pros on the left side and Cons on the right. And then she thought. What were the pros of living in 1850? Matthew, of course. And Willie. And a strange new life that made her feel more alive than she had ever felt before. But what were the cons? Missing her parents, and Olivia, and Johnny, and now Annabelle and Casey. Then Olivia's voice, and Takodah's, came to her, loud and strong.

"Follow your heart," they had said. "Whenever you need to make a decision, listen to your heart. It always knows what to do."

Suddenly, Grace knew. She loved her parents so much. But this was the beginning of her life and she needed to live it her way. With Matthew. She was sure of it. She didn't have to follow her heart to Matthew. He was her heart. All of it.

CHAPTER 26

*G*race was only half-surprised to see Olivia at the kitchen table with a cup of tea in front of her and Casey by her side. Olivia stared hard into the formica floor, pondering the mysteries of the universe, Grace thought. Olivia smiled when she noticed Grace.

"It's chamomile, dear. Would you like some?" Grace nodded. Olivia poured some of the steaming liquid into a porcelain mug and handed it to Grace.

"I have to be honest, Grandma," Grace said. "A lot of this still doesn't make sense."

"I agree." Olivia tapped her temple with her finger as if trying to jog a memory. "For years you believed you were from another era, didn't you?"

"That was childish nonsense."

"Was it? You said you were searching for where you belonged. Maybe this is it." Olivia looked far away. Whenever she seemed distant like that, Olivia always said afterwards that she was in touch with the spirits. Grace used to think it was a joke. Who gets in touch with spirits? Now, she wasn't so sure. "We'll get to the bottom of this. Don't you worry."

Grace paced to vent her nervous energy. She felt so electric she wouldn't have been surprised if lightning flashed from her eyes. "You're right, though, Grandma. I did always say I was from another time. And now this. Did I really know Matthew in 1850? Did I really write the journals that ended up in the attic? But I'm sitting here with you today. How can I be in both places at the same time?"

"Technically, you're not in both places at the same time. You're not in 1850 at the moment, are you? You're here. And remember, you were in Salem in 1692 when your mother was carrying you and you're here now."

"But how?"

"It's the invisible world, dear. It's magic." Olivia laughed. "I believe you have a friend who says that as well." Grace thought of Takodah and smiled. "And that's only accounting for a small fraction of time. Where were you between those two lives? What were you up to then? That's what I want to know."

"I wasn't up to anything. I wasn't anywhere."

"Weren't you?"

Casey wandered over to Grace. She picked him up and sat him on her lap, the dog content to have his black curls combed by Grace's fingers. "Where could I have been?"

"You could have been anywhere, Grace. Everyone's soul is somewhere at all times, even if you can't remember in your current life."

"Are you talking about past lives?"

"As a matter of fact, I am. Could you have been on the Oregon Trail in a previous life?" Grace didn't answer, and Olivia took her hand. "Come, dear. There's something I want you to see."

Olivia led Grace up the stairs to the loft then up the stairs to the attic. Grace's grip tightened when they passed the finely carved trunk, but Olivia stopped near another trunk, this one perhaps as old but not as well made as the one containing the journals. Olivia pushed open the top and pulled out an old-fashioned photograph in a filigree frame. Grace took the daguerreotype into her hands and gasped.

There she was, Grace, in a plain, homespun dress, her hair pulled into a severe bun. She wasn't smiling as she stared directly into the camera, but there was a contentedness behind her eyes. Even through the grainy black and white tintype it was obvious she was happy.

"This wouldn't happen to be the photograph you told me about? That vision you saw of yourself in the past?" Grace nodded. "Annabelle showed me this after you disappeared."

"Then Annabelle did know this was going to happen to me. I asked her, and she hedged quite a bit."

"Yes, but you know Annabelle. She's too practical for her own good. She saw it with her own eyes when she saw that it was you in that photograph, but she still wouldn't allow herself to believe the truth of it. Don't hold it against her. She did the best she could under the circumstances."

"Are you telling me I wrote myself those journals knowing I would end up here in Annabelle's attic in another life ready to return to Matthew? Are you saying this was predestined?"

"I'm not so sure about that. There's still a lot I have to figure out. Besides, I'm not a fan of predestination. And your father? Don't even get him started. He hates the idea of predestination, having lived among the Puritans the way he did. James detests the very notion that people's lives are determined before they are born. He thinks we have control over the outcome of our lives, and so do I." Olivia put a motherly hand on Grace's shoulder and squeezed. "I'm sorry, Grace."

"Why? None of this is your fault."

"I know, but your parents and I should have done a better job preparing you for living in the magical world. It's quite a thing to come up against when you're not ready for it."

"I don't know how anyone can prepare you for time travel." Grace managed a weak smile. "I still don't understand how I ended up in 1850."

"Welcome to my world, dear. When you engage with the supernatural every day, you come to terms with the fact that there are some enigmas so powerful you may never learn the truth of them. In time you'll come to accept the unexplainable." She squinted at Grace. "But you're not ready to accept that, are you? You still want to know how you ended up in 1850."

"Was it being in Annabelle's that sent me back in time?"

"I don't think so because you're still here. If it was the house that caused your time-travel you would have disappeared the moment you walked through the door. No, it's something else. Something…" Olivia shook her head as though trying to rearrange her thoughts. And then she smiled. "After you disappeared, Annabelle told me that the family legend says the magic is in the journals."

"Yes," Grace said. "She said the same thing to me."

"I think that's right. Isn't that when you slipped into the past, when you sat down to read the journals?"

Grace closed her eyes as she struggled to remember. Her thoughts were so easily jumbled, and her life before the trail was blurry. "I went to the attic, found the journals, sat down to read them, and that's the last thing I remember from here."

Olivia's smile was triumphant. "Then Annabelle's family legend was right. The magic is in the journals."

"But how?"

"I can't explain how—not yet anyway. I'll need to do some research. Maybe some of my magical friends can shed some light."

"But Grandma?"

"Yes, Grace?"

"Do you think that if I read the journals again I would go back in time? I would go back to Matthew?"

"If the magic is indeed in the journals, then yes, you'll return to

1850. But I'm afraid I wouldn't be able to pull you back to this time again. The only reason I managed it the first time was because you were ill, and I certainly don't want you to be ill again. I also think we had some luck on our side with the timing. But to do it again? I'm not sure, Grace. I'm not as young as I used to be."

"You must be one of the most powerful witches in the world."

Olivia held up her hands in a gesture of surrender. "I do what I can, Grace, which is all any of us can do." She nudged Grace's arm, a sly smile on her lips. "So? Tell me about this Matthew Cooper. From your description in your journals he sounds handsome enough. But what else? What haven't you written down?"

"He's kind, and strong. I don't mean physically strong. He is that, but I mean he's strong enough to handle whatever comes his way. And he'll help anyone. And he likes to laugh, he can see the funny side of things, but he feels deeply. It's a hard time to be alive, Grandma. Death is everywhere. On the trail you can't escape it. Around every bend, across every river, it's there, and none of us know what's in store for us next."

"So this Mr. Cooper finds himself in need of a wife?"

"It seems he does."

"And are you still sure about the feelings you had for him when you were writing in your journals? Are you still in love with him?"

"Are you asking me if he's my *beshert*?"

"I suppose I am."

"Yes, he is. I know it. I'm listening to my heart, like you told me to, and my heart tells me Matthew Cooper is the man for me."

"Well then. Maybe the explanation we're looking for is right in front of us. Your parents are *beshert* and their love transcends time. It seems to me that you and Matthew are *beshert* and your love transcends time as well. You know, Matthew sounds a bit like your father."

"Don't say it, Grandma."

"It's normal, of course, for a girl to want to find a man like her father, that is, unless her father is an immature loser who can't keep a job to save his life. Or something like that." Olivia shrugged. "Never mind me. That was my first husband I was referring to. But for you, of course you would want a man like James. Men like that aren't easy to find, and it seems you've found one. So the question becomes, now that you've found him, what are you going to do with him?"

"I want to be with him. I can't wait until I see him again. While I was on the trail I'd search for him because I wanted to know where he was all the time. I'd grow giddy at the sight of him, looking like a centaur, he sits so tall on his horse. I pretended not to notice him, and I tried to look anywhere else, but I always knew where he was, who he was talking to, whether he was smiling or frowning. When Matthew and I became closer I learned to recognize his footsteps. I heard his laughter from a mile away. And as much as I love all of you, being with you, being with Mom and Dad, all I can think about is how much I want to go back to him."

"It seems to me you've made up your mind." Grace nodded. "I wish I could travel back with you and meet him, Grace. I wish we could all travel back with you." Olivia clasped her hands together. "Should I try? I've never time-traveled before. Who knows? It might be fun."

"You wouldn't say that if you've been through what I've been through."

"I've read your journals, Grace. I know how hard it's been. But if your heart tells you that you belong with Matthew, then that's where you need to be. It will be hard for you, for all of us, but your parents will accept your decision."

"Even though it will break their hearts?"

"They'll accept it, Grace. Believe me. They'll accept it because they've lived it themselves."

. . .

GRACE WAITED FOR HER PARENTS DOWNSTAIRS. OLIVIA AND Annabelle were oddly absent. Even Casey was gone. Grace guessed they meant to give her time alone with James and Sarah.

Sarah appeared first. She was still in her nightgown, her loose bathrobe hanging from her shoulders. Her graying curls framed her face, and though her eyes were wet she smiled.

"Are you going back to Matthew?" Sarah asked. Grace nodded. "Do you love him?"

"I love him so much, Mom, I think my very soul will burst. As strange as it sounds, I think he's always been in my heart. He fit right inside from the first moment I saw him."

James came out of the bedroom and sat on the stairs. He looked as though he had hardly slept. Sarah looked at James, who nodded in acknowledgement. He heard.

"Of course, we understand, Grace," Sarah said. "I know how I would feel without your father. I couldn't bear it. But are you sure this Matthew Cooper is worth the sacrifice? We'll never see you again."

"Is Dad worth the sacrifice?" Grace looked at James. "Or Mom? Is she worth the sacrifice?"

"Of course she is," said James, "but so are you. Your mother and I mourned your loss until the day we found you. We don't want to lose you again."

Grace looked at Sarah. "How did you know Dad was worth the sacrifice?"

"The love your father and I share is intense, Grace. Dad and I have been intertwined for centuries. That's a good place to start."

"Matthew and I are intertwined too."

Sarah took her daughter into her arms. "My heart will be broken without you, Grace Marie Wentworth, don't you doubt that for a minute. But I want you to follow your heart, not mine, and not your father's. You need to live your own life. Your father and I will always be here for you however we can. I don't know what that might look like with the time gap, but Olivia always finds a way."

Olivia joined them near the stairs. She was already dressed, her long gray gypsy skirt sweeping the ground, her white peasant blouse flowing to her waist. "Am I disturbing you? I can leave if you need more time alone."

"Of course not, Olivia," Sarah said. "Who else would we want in this conversation but you? I was just telling Grace that though my heart will break if she goes, she needs to live her own life. You can find a way for us to keep in touch, can't you? You are one of the most powerful witches."

Olivia shook her head. "I just wish I understood more about what is happening with Grace."

"This is Grace's way of finding her way back to her one true love," Sarah said.

"Do you think she got her lines crossed when she came back to us?" James asked. "Do you think she was headed back to 1850?"

"Oh, no, James. Grace was destined to find you and Sarah again. I have no doubt about that. But she's had other lives, like Sarah, like all of us, really." Olivia gave Sarah a long, hard stare. "Do you remember any other lives besides the one you shared with James in 1692 and the one you have with him now?"

Sarah shook her head. "Are there others?"

Olivia laughed. "You sound like your daughter. We never looked for any of your other lives because your lives with James are the only ones that matter now. But you've had other lives. And so has Grace."

"Wait." James rubbed his eyes under his glasses. "That name that Grace mentioned in her journals. That woman Matthew was in love with, the one he mistook Grace for."

Grace nodded. "Gloryanna Winters."

"That's it. This Gloryanna looked so much like Grace. Matthew even thought Grace was Gloryanna. Is there some connection there?"

"Perhaps," Olivia said. "But if you don't mind, dear, I like to take my mysteries one at a time. We'll save that one for another day."

Grace didn't know what to say. She saw the redness in her mother's eyes, the white streaks on her cheeks. She wondered if she would be able to leave her parents after all. Sarah sat on the step below James and looked at Grace, hard, the way only a mother could, as if Sarah could see through Grace to something beyond.

"It's okay, Grace. It will be very hard, but I'll support you, and so will your father."

"And so will I," said Olivia.

"I hate the thought of never seeing any of you again, but I feel like there's this line pulling me back to Matthew. It's like that invisible string you always said bound the Wentworths together."

Sarah nodded. "I can see that, Grace. It's obvious whenever you speak about him. That must be what I look like when I speak about your father."

"And when Dad speaks of you. But I understand now. I know why you two have always been connected the way you are. Everything makes sense now."

"Are still you mad at us for not telling you sooner?" Sarah asked.

"Not anymore. I was, but Nana helped me see sense."

Sarah looked surprised. "Nana?"

"That's what I call Annabelle now."

"It's a good name," Sarah said.

"But I understand why you were afraid to tell me. It's a crazy story after all."

"We're Wentworths," Sarah said. "No story is too crazy for us." Her smile was tinged with sadness. "Will you be able to come back to us in this time?"

Grace looked at Olivia, who shrugged. "I can't promise that," Olivia said. "I wish I could, but I nearly didn't get her back the first time."

Sarah put her arm around Grace's shoulder and leaned her

head against Grace's. "You know that your father and I have only ever wanted you to be happy. You're our miracle. Now you know why. You're the Grace we were missing. But now it's our turn to let you go so you can make your own way, and your way is with Matthew."

"So you're not mad?" Grace asked.

"Of course not. I will miss you every day for the rest my life. I will never stop trying to reach you. But you have to go, and you can take my blessing with you."

James stepped silently into the rectangle of the house. He closed the guest room door behind him.

"Dad?"

"Give him time, Grace," said Sarah. "He'll come around."

"I don't think I'll be able to leave if he's upset with me."

"Your father understands your pull to Matthew. He just needs to adjust to the idea of your leaving. I think we both hoped you'd find the love of your life a little closer to home."

Grace hugged her mother with every ounce of strength she had. "I'm going to miss you so much, Mom. I don't know what I'm going to do without you."

"You're going to return to Matthew, you're going to build a beautiful home, and a beautiful life. And you're going to live your life to the fullest, knowing not to take anything for granted, as your father and I learned the hard way. It's all we can do in this life and any other lives we may have."

Grace couldn't let go of her mother. "I wish things were different. I wish Matthew lived down the road from here. I wish I didn't have to choose between then and now. It's too hard."

"It is hard, but you can do it. You can do anything you set your mind to. I've never had any doubt about that." Sarah brushed a blond curl from Grace's eyes. "Now I think you should go talk to your father."

"What should I say?"

"You'll know, Grace. Just start speaking. You and your father have always been two peas in a pod." Grace hesitated. "He'll come around, Grace. I promise."

Grace kissed her mother's cheek, went to her parents' room, and knocked on the door. When there was no answer she pushed the door open and found the room empty. She wasn't surprised to find her father outside under the tree, petting the dog, staring toward the cows.

"It still must seem strange to you," Grace said, "being awake during the day after living at night for so long. At least now I know why you've always been such a night owl." James said nothing. He wouldn't look at her. "When you and Mom first told me the truth it sounded so bizarre, but Grandma Olivia is right. I've always known that I was different somehow."

"Have you come to tell me you're determined to go back to 1850?"

"Yes." Grace took James' hand. "Will you give me your blessing, Dad? Will you give Matthew and me your blessing?"

James sighed. "I really ought to meet this Matthew Cooper in person and give him the third degree. I mean, I've never set eyes on this young man and yet I'm supposed to entrust the welfare of my daughter to him during a time more dangerous than this one?"

"First of all, I don't need my welfare entrusted to anyone. I can take care of myself."

"Things are different then, Grace. You've seen it."

"You're right, I have. But you were there, weren't you? You were alive during that time?"

"Yes, I suppose I was, or at least as alive as I could be."

"Where were you then?"

James closed his eyes as he remembered. "In 1850, I was... Goodness, Grace, when you've been around as long as I have the years blend together, but I believe I was in England in 1850."

"Did you go home to London?"

"London hasn't been home for a very long time. But yes, I lived in London for a while, and then I moved to Scotland when I taught at St. Andrews."

"Could you visit Idaho? If I went back to Matthew, and you're alive then anyway, could you come to see me?"

"Oh, Grace." James looked as if he were being sliced in half. "If there was anyway I could be there with you I'd be there in a minute, you must know that. But I don't know how to make that happen. How can we communicate with my past self so that I would know where to find you or even that you existed?"

"I bet Grandma Olivia could find a way to make it happen."

"If anyone can, it's Olivia. She's pretty determined when she sets her mind to something."

"So do you give us your blessing?"

"Of course I do, Grace. I wish you and Matthew every blessing for your whole lives. I just wish we had more time together. I feel like after all these years we've only had you back for a little while. Twenty years feels so short when you've been alive since 1662."

"I love you, Dad. I wouldn't have you any other way."

"I'm so proud of you, Gracie. Thank God you took after your mother."

"I always thought I took after you."

"You do in more ways than you know. I'm glad you're experiencing your own eternal love story. Your mother has brought such great joy to my life. I know what it is to wait for the one you love. I know what it is to have that anticipation, waiting to see them again. It's breaking my heart into a million pieces, but I want you to be happy. So go be happy with Matthew. But promise me that you'll stay safe."

"I will, Dad. I promise."

GRACE HAD BEEN BACK AT ANNABELLE'S FOR A WEEK, BUT WHO KNEW how time passed in other eras and she was afraid that Matthew was worried about her. How could she explain her sudden disappearance? She told her mother that she was ready to go, but no, she wasn't ready to go. She'd never really be ready. But she had to return to Matthew, and maybe the longer she waited the harder the parting with her parents would be.

There was a quietness, a peacefulness in Annabelle's that day. Grace, James, Sarah, Olivia, and Annabelle spent the day roaming through Boise, taking pictures on the Capitol steps, drinking coffee at the funky coffee shop. They enjoyed a picnic lunch at the rose garden, fully bloomed in white, blush, and crimson under the summer sun.

When they arrived back at Annabelle's Grace called Johnny. She caught him as he was leaving his hostel to explore Paris. He sounded upbeat and in high spirits, his good humor overtaking any concerns about the difficulty of his vagabond trip through Europe. She realized, as they spoke, that she would never see Johnny graduate from university, never see him marry and have children, never see anything else life had in store for him. She would never see him again, and the thought made her so sad, but she didn't want to alert him to any problem. All she said was she was going on a journey of her own.

"Maybe we'll meet in Europe," Johnny said.

"Maybe we will." When she ended the call, she cried.

As the day passed a frenetic energy overtook everyone inside Annabelle's. Even Casey seemed on edge, wandering through the rooms, wagging his stumpy tail, watching everyone.

Grace still had so many questions. Even Olivia, one of the most powerful witches, was stumped to her very core about this strange time-traveling phenomenon that had caught Grace in its grasp. But Olivia, in consultation with other witches, had some ideas about what they could do. She sat Grace down on the sofa and gave her some pointers about how to communicate with them. They showed her how to locate the area of Annabelle's house and how to locate the hulking tree in her yard.

"This tree is nearly 300 years old," Annabelle said, "so it will be here when you're in 1850. Not as big, of course, but it will be here."

James carved Grace's initials, a huge G W, into the tree.

"You can leave us messages here by the tree and we'll find them," Olivia said.

"Will it work?" Sarah asked.

"I don't know for certain," Olivia said. "But it might." She held Grace close to her, squeezing, as if she wouldn't let go. "I will do everything I can to find out what this magic is, Grace. I will discover it, I will learn how to work with it, and I will help you. I will do my very best for you, dear. Don't you ever doubt that, not for a minute."

"Can you really find a way to understand this magic, Grandma? It seems crazy even to me, and I'm living it."

"Magic can be understood if you're willing to open your heart to what the eye can't see."

Grace wouldn't let go of Olivia. "You've read my journals, Grandma. You've read about Takodah. Are you?"

"I don't know, Grace. I've never done a past life regression on myself. I always felt like I'd find out what I needed to know when I needed to know it. But if it's true, and I am Takodah, then I'm so glad I'm able to be there for you however I can. Actually," Olivia smiled, "it makes me happy to think I'm there with you. It seems fitting if I do say so myself."

"I don't know how we would manage anything without you, Grandma."

"Oh, my dear. You're about to find out that you can manage on your own very nicely with that handsome husband by your side."

"I hope you are Takodah, Grandma. I feel your presence when she's there."

"That must be a sign," Olivia said.

"Grandma, do you...?"

"Yes?"

"Do you know my whole life? How much did I write in those journals?"

"We don't know your whole life. We only know what you wrote up to the time you were taken ill with cholera."

"What does that mean?"

Olivia's smile was so bright it lit all of Idaho. "It means you get to write the rest of your story, dear. Make it a good one."

GRACE SPENT SOME QUIET TIME THAT EVENING WITH HER PARENTS. They didn't say much. What do you say when someone you love is going away and it's likely you'll never see them again? Words seemed extemporaneous somehow, hollow platitudes we say to make ourselves feel better when really there's a chasm in our hearts that the most perfectly constructed sentences can't heal. Instead of speaking they held hands. When it was fully dark, Grace kissed her parents, first her mother, then her father.

"It's time for me to go," she said. James and Sarah nodded.

Everyone followed Grace to her bedroom—James, Sarah, Olivia, Annabelle, even Casey. Grace had to remind herself to breathe. Olivia smiled through her tears as she handed Grace one of the white leather-bound journals that she had been writing in on the Oregon Trail. Touching them again made her skin spark. She sat on the edge of her bed and opened one.

"Wait!" Sarah's anguished voice pierced Grace's heart. She knelt by Grace's side and took the journal from her daughter's hands, and then she took those hands into hers. "I love you, my most darling daughter. I love you. Just be happy. Even when we were trapped in that horrid dungeon together, I prayed that you would have a happy life. That's what I still wish for you."

"I pray that you'll have a happy life too, Mom. I'll always love you."

Grace looked at her father. His eyes were small, his lips thin. Finally, he pressed the open journal into her hands.

"Say good night, Gracie."

"Dad…"

"Say good night, Gracie."

Grace thought a butcher's knife was carving through her heart. "I can't."

"Yes, you can. Say good night, Gracie."

With all of her love for her parents, for Olivia, for Annabelle and Casey flooding through her, making her lightheaded with joy, joy that she loved these amazing beings, and joy that she had their love in return, she smiled. She turned her eyes towards the words she had written and exhaled.

"Good night, Gracie."

CHAPTER 27

GRACE

I want you to know that I'm here. I'm all right and I'm here.

During my journey back I felt myself levitating, as though I were being air lifted to another planet until I was flung about and I saw myself spiraling down a vortex. The spinning stopped as suddenly as it began. I found myself bent over, my hands on my knees, my eyes closed to keep the dizziness away. When I was able to stand upright I tried settling my breath enough so I could think coherent thoughts. This time, at least I knew where I was.

A river flowed nearby, and I felt the dust from hundreds of wheels, animals, and people kicking the dry ground. The air was heavy enough to hold in my hands. I stood there, gathering my bearings, watching the wagons head into the distance. I looked behind me and saw no one. If I was going to find Matthew, I had to catch up with that train.

I picked up the hem of my dress and ran. I was breathless, afraid I was too far behind, but finally I stumbled across the men keeping the livestock in line at the back.

"Hey! Miss Wentworth!" Ezra Quigley waved his floppy hat in

my direction. "I can't believe it's you! We thought we lost you for good. Wait til Matty sees you!"

He left the livestock to Sylvester Banning and raced his horse toward the front of the train. He was back to me in a matter of minutes, stopping his horse and swooping his arm down to help me. "Come on now, Miss Wentworth, hop on. Matthew's driving the wagon and he can't turn around so I'm to bring you to him."

I hopped onto the back of Ezra's horse. Finally, I saw it—the wagon with Wetherfield painted in red. Matthew kept turning back, but I was too far to read his expression. I wasn't sure if he wanted to shout with joy or shake me with frustration. When Ezra pulled alongside Matthew's wagon, Matthew stopped so I could climb into the front seat with him.

"Thanks, Ezra," Matthew said.

"Of course, Matty." Ezra tipped his hat toward me. "I hope everything's all right, Miss Wentworth." And he trotted toward the back to the livestock. Matthew kept one eye on the two mules and one eye on me, checking me over from head to toe, making sure I looked all right. When there was nothing wrong that was visible to the eye, he turned away. I could see he didn't know what to say. Should he be relieved? Furious? Both? He was about to speak, but Willie poked her head out from inside the wagon.

"Grace Wentworth, I don't know whether to strangle you or kiss you. Where on earth have you been? We were afraid you had fallen so far behind we'd never see you again."

I didn't know what to say. How could I explain where I had been? I was home, with my family, saying good-bye. But I couldn't tell them that for all the reasons I shared with Nana. Maybe secrets have their place after all. Instead, I said, "I'm not sure what happened myself."

"You were sick with cholera," Matthew said, his voice hard. "You were in the back of the wagon, you crawled out like you were on fire, and then you disappeared." He snapped his fingers. "Just like that."

"I couldn't have just disappeared," I said. I hardly knew what I was saying since I was making it up as I went along. "I climbed out of the wagon, but I fell so far behind and I was ill and I didn't have the strength to search for you. Luckily for me, another train came along and the people helped me recover and got me back to you."

Matthew looked around but there were no wagons he didn't recognize. "So where are they?"

"Who?"

"The folks who rescued you?"

"They brought me as close as they could but then they headed down another path."

"What other path?" He shook his head. He's no fool, Matthew, and he knew there was a lot missing from my story—like the truth. I wanted to tell him, but how could I?

"I only know what I know, Matthew. I was sick and some people helped me." I took his hand. His grip tightened on the reins, but he didn't pull away from my touch. "And I know that I want to be here with you."

"You say that like you've just come to realize it." Matthew's hurt cut me deeply.

"I knew it before. But I had to be sure."

Matthew gazed at me side-eyed. "And now you're sure?"

"Forget all that for now," Willie said. "You were pretty ill, Grace, when you fell behind. Are you sure you're all right? Should we get Takodah?"

"They had good medicine where I was," I said. "I'm better, Willie. I promise."

"I wish we had some of that good medicine for my Paul," Willie said.

"So do I, Willie." I gripped my friend's hand. "So do I."

Sally climbed into the driver's seat and sat on my lap. She smiled at me and I realized how much I had missed her. I stroked her hair, dark like her mother's and her uncle's, and she leaned into me, ready for a nap. Seeing Paul in her face made me happy.

"Looks like Sally is happy you're back," Matthew said.

"And you?" I asked.

"Duchess, if you're sure you want to be with me, if you're sure you have no doubts, then I couldn't be happier for anything in all the world. You missed some of the excitement, though."

"What kind of excitement?" I asked.

"Just the most terrifying part of the journey," Willie said. "Once we got here along the Snake River, we passed Fort Hall, and then there was a narrow break in the rocks called the Gate of Death."

"The Gate of Death? I'm glad I missed that."

"Not as glad as I am that everyone made it through safely." I was relieved to see Willie looking more like herself.

As if he read my mind, Matthew said, "And you missed the other excitement. Willie is engaged to Enoch Emerson."

"I'm so happy for you, Willie." I hope I looked surprised.

Willie turned away. "I'm sure you think it's too quick."

"My opinions on a lot of things have changed since I've been here, Willie. I know it's hard for you without Amos and Paul..." My voice cracked when I said my favorite little boy's name. "And Enoch Emerson is a good man."

It was the first time I had seen Willie smile since Paul and Amos died. "He is a good man, Grace. He cares about me, and he cares about the girls. He said he'd take me as I am, broken in places. Enoch says that wherever it is you're broken the most that's where you grow back strongest and he thinks we could be even stronger together if we help each other heal. How could I say no to that?"

"You couldn't."

She looked meaningfully at Matthew, then pulled Sally into the back with her. She pulled the puckered cover closed to leave us some privacy.

"We've been thinking about where to settle," Matthew said. "Do you still have your heart set on California?"

"No," I said. "My family knows that my place is with you."

"You told your family about us?"

"I was able to communicate with them."

Matthew nodded. "We heard from some settlers at Fort Hall that there's some good, fertile land not far from here along Reed's River."

"I thought you wanted to go all the way through Oregon," I said. "You had your heart set on it."

"I had my heart set on all sorts of things, Duchess, but life isn't always what you think it's going to be, is it?"

"No, it certainly isn't."

"What I want is to start a new life in a new land. This is Oregon Territory, after all. That's close enough for me. If we settle nearby, then that leaves something for another time, doesn't it? And if the area doesn't suit us, or we want to move closer to the ocean, or even down to California to be nearer your folks, we can always move on. There's always a new adventure to be found."

"Ha!" Willie pulled the cover aside. "I've warned you once, Grace, and I'll warn you again. My brother has an adventurous heart and I don't see him staying in one place for long. Are you sure you're ready for that?"

"Yes, Willie, I'm ready for it. I'll follow him wherever he goes. Apparently, I've developed a taste for adventure too."

"You two belong together for sure." Willie closed the cover and I heard her laughing with the girls.

Matthew and I sat close as I pressed my arm into his, my hand over his on the reins. We glanced at each other, then glanced at each other again. Matthew grew serious.

"I thought I was never going to see you again, Duchess. After you disappeared I rode up and down all day and night searching for you. When Hiram insisted that we had to leave I rode Tune so far back I lost sight of the train. You were nowhere to be found. It was like you vanished." He looked at me, hard, waiting for me to say something. "I reckon you're not going to tell me what really happened while you were gone?"

"Not yet. But I will. One day."

"But you're sure you're all right?"

"I'm fine, Matthew. I promise."

"And you want to be with me? No regrets?"

"Not one." I touched my hand to his cheek and he leaned into my touch. "I choose you, Matthew Cooper."

"Good, because I choose you too. And I will thank God every day for the rest of my life that I found you again. The thought of suffering through the rest of my days without you was too hard, Duchess. It was just too hard."

Matthew and I were married along the Snake River. Friends in our train were generous. Several of the women combined their ingredients and made us a cake while others gifted us linens and dishware from their own supplies. Willie reminded me of the blue cotton dress she had found me in and we pulled it out so I could wear it at my wedding. Reverend Smith performed the ceremony with a few Bible readings. Then Takodah shared a blessing with us.

"You are good to us, Great Spirit," she said. "All your creatures need a partner. Each wing needs a mate. Each feather needs its likeness." She gave one feather to Matthew and one to me, which we held close to our hearts. "Now we carry a feather. It is close to our hearts. In secret there is its likeness and it is close to a heart. Matthew and Grace Cooper will now have a life together. Your song will be in them. Your happiness will live in them. And they will praise you."

After the ceremony, with our feast of bacon, beans, fried bread, and our wedding cake, Takodah pulled me aside. She handed me this very journal and the others I've been writing in.

"Your love for Matthew is in these books," she said. "You discovered your love for him through writing these words."

"How did you know?" I asked.

"Because writing is thinking, and through thinking you were

able to discover your feelings. After you discovered your feelings, you found your heart. First, we think the thoughts that flood our brains. Then, we feel the movement of our hearts. Listen to your heart, Grace. It always knows what to do. And this is what I'm going to do." Takodah held the journals high above her head, chanting. She turned once, twice, three times, waving the journals, spinning, spinning, weaving a whirlwind around Matthew and me. Takodah said, "And they will praise you," and she handed me the books.

"What have you done?" I asked.

"I think you already know. But I've captured all the love you and Matthew feel for each other and pushed that love into these journals. The journals are infused with your eternal connection to one another. When this life is done, as you return in other lives in other times, whenever one of you engages with the journals you'll be pulled back to each other." I nodded, unable to speak because now I know where the magic has come from. "You and your husband are attached forever, Grace. Your souls are intertwined, and you'll always be together in one way or another. Beshert."

I laughed with such uninhibited joy that everyone surrounding me joined in.

My life is a mystery, a secret within a secret, a life within a life, but so is everyone's. I live within the puzzle of my heart, cloistered off and protected from a harsh world that neither knows nor cares what hidden depths I have within me. I am my secrets, and my secrets are me.

There's still so much I don't understand, and maybe I never will. Maybe my job in this moment is to feel the simple joys of the sun on my face with my husband's arm around my waist while having a laugh with Willie, who will also be a bride soon. Maybe my job in this moment is to become the person I was meant to be. And I take joy in the continual discovery of her.

· · ·

YOU ALREADY KNOW THAT WE SETTLED NEAR THE TRIBUTARY NOW called Reed's River but will someday be the Boise River. You already know where Hiram and Takodah Wetherfield settled—in the house that will eventually be converted into the red barn near Annabelle's—and where Willie and Enoch settled—they built Annabelle's house. The scenery is the same as you see, even if the area is hardly populated now. Matthew found a nice stretch of land with close access to the river and acres of rich, brown soil and a lovely view. After the wedding, the rest of the train continued West, determined to find their way to the Pacific Ocean. It was a tearful good-bye. When you've crossed hell with people, even people who began as strangers, you become connected in ways you can't explain.

I don't regret my decision, not for a moment, but I wish it hadn't come at such a high price. I think about all of you every day. I wish more than anything that you could know Matthew. He's a wonderful man, and I know you would love him, and he would love you all just the same.

I feel as if I'm saying good-bye, but I'm not, not really. Somehow, in the deepest recesses of my heart, I know I will see you again, all of you, and this is not the end. Instead, I will say good-bye for now.

With all my love.

Forever.

Grace Wentworth Cooper,
Duchess of Idaho
1850

AUTHOR'S NOTES

As I finished writing *The Duchess of Idaho*, I tried to think of some wisdom-filled words that would help me make sense of the experience of writing this book, but the only words that feel right are thank you.

Thank you to the many readers who began following me after *Her Dear & Loving Husband* was published. Thank you to the Wentworth superfans who insisted that the story could be more than the trilogy I originally meant it to be. Thank you to the lovely readers who contact me through my blog or email to let me know how much they enjoy my stories.

For those of you who like to know when my next books are coming out, in Autumn 2022 there will be another book featuring James, Sarah, and Grace in a story set around the Salem Witch Trials called *And Shadows Will Fall*. *The Duchess of Idaho* is just the beginning of Grace's story. Look for the next book, *The Princess of Painted Skies*, which will appear in 2023.

In case you're wondering, Casey is based on the real-life black cocker spaniel Casey Allard, who was a very good boy.

I lived in Idaho for year between 2002-2003. I know from a friend who still lives in the area that it has grown quite a bit since I lived first in Nampa and then in Boise. The descriptions are based on memories from two decades ago.

One of the most challenging parts of writing historical fiction is being true to the era when referring to people's attitudes toward and language about those who are different from themselves. I was not comfortable using the words squaw or savage to describe Native Americans knowing that such words were used with dehumanizing intentions. I believe that when we choose to write historical fiction we should be true to the era we are writing about, or why write historical fiction? I also believe that we have to face the tragedies of the past, including the use of language and violence as weapons against other human beings, before we can hope to do better. Takodah is not meant as a representative of Native Americans in 1850. She is, in her own words, only herself. Or, maybe she's…

My intention with *The Duchess of Idaho* was not to write a treatise on the Oregon Trail. My intention was to bring Grace Wentworth's story to life. As a result, there's a lot about the Oregon Trail I didn't cover. I didn't cover the Mormon Trail, the California Trail, and I didn't do justice to the experiences of the Native Americans. My hope when I write historical fiction is that readers will become interested enough in the history that they'll seek out nonfiction accounts so that they can learn more about the era.

If you're looking to learn more about the Oregon Trail, I can recommend starting with the following books: *The Oregon Trail: A New American Journey* by Rinker Buck, *Covered Wagon Women: Diaries and Letters From the Western Trail Volumes 1-5* by Kenneth L. Holmes et al, *Pioneer Women: The Lives of Women on the Frontier* by Linda Peavy and Ursula Smith, and *The Pioneers* by David McCullough, which isn't specifically about the Oregon Trail but gives wonderful insight into the pioneering spirit. And the Oregon Trail video game is pretty cool too.

ABOUT THE AUTHOR

Meredith Allard is the author of the beloved bestselling paranormal historical *Loving Husband Trilogy*. Her sweet Victorian romance, *When It Rained at Hembry Castle*, was named a best historical novel by IndieReader. Her other books include *Christmas at Hembry Castle*; *Down Salem Way*, the prequel to the *Loving Husband Trilogy* set during the Salem Witch Trials; *Victory Garden*, a novel of the American women's suffrage movement; *Woman of Stones*, a novella of Biblical Jerusalem; *That You Are Here*, a contemporary sweet romance; *The Window Dresser and Other Stories*; and *Painting the Past: A Guide for Writing Historical Fiction*, named a #1 New Release in Authorship and Creativity Self-Help on Amazon. She loves books, cats, and coffee, though not always in that order. When she isn't writing she's teaching writing, and she has taught writing to students ages five to 75. She lives in the hills of Southern Nevada near Las Vegas. Visit Meredith at www.meredithallard.com.

If you'd like to read more about James, Sarah, and Grace Wentworth, you'll enjoy the following books: *Her Dear & Loving Husband*, *Her Loving Husband's Curse*, *Her Loving Husband's Return*, and *Down Salem Way*—all available from Copperfield Press. Another book featuring James, Sarah, and Grace, entitled *And Shadows Will Fall*, will be available Autumn 2022. The second book in the Grace series, *The Princess of Painted Skies*, will be available in 2023.

If you enjoyed *The Duchess of Idaho* <u>you can sign up for free updates from Meredith here.</u>

ALSO BY MEREDITH ALLARD

READ AN EXCERPT FROM HER
DEAR & LOVING HUSBAND

Chapter 1

Sarah Alexander didn't know what was waiting for her in Salem, Massachusetts. She had moved there to escape the smog and the smugness of Los Angeles, craving the dulcet tones of a small town, seeking a less complicated life. Her first hint of the supernatural world came the day she moved into her rented brick house near the historic part of town, close to the museums about the witch trial days, not far from the easy, wind-blown bay. As the heavy-set men hauled her furniture inside, her landlady leaned close and told her to beware.

"If you hear sounds in the night it's ghosts," the landlady whispered, glancing around to be sure no one, human or shadow, could hear. "The spirits of the innocent victims of the witch hunts still haunt us. I can feel them stirring now. God rest them."

Sarah didn't know what to say. She had never been warned about ghosts before. The landlady peered at her, squinting to see her better.

"You're a pretty girl," the old woman said. "Such dark curls you have." She still spoke as if she were telling a secret, and Sarah had to strain to hear. "You're from California?"

"I moved there after I got married," Sarah said.

"Where's your husband?"

"I'm divorced now."

"And your family is here?"

"In Boston. I wanted to live close to my family, but I didn't want to move back to the city. I've always wanted to visit Salem, so I thought I'd live here awhile."

The landlady nodded. "Boston," she said. "Some victims of the witch trials were jailed in Boston."

The landlady was so bent and weak looking, her fragile face lined like tree rings, that Sarah thought the old woman had experienced the hysteria in Salem during the seventeenth century. But that was silly, Sarah reminded herself. The Salem Witch Trials happened over three hundred years ago. There was no one alive now who had experienced that terror first hand. Sarah wanted to tell the landlady how she believed she had an ancestor who died as a victim of the witch hunts, but she didn't say anything then.

"Yes, they're here," the landlady said, staring with time-faded eyes at the air above their heads, as if she saw something no one else could see. "Beware, Sarah. The ghosts are here. And they always come out at night."

The landlady shook as if she were cold, though it was early autumn and summer humidity still flushed the air. When Sarah put her arm around the old woman to comfort her, she felt her skin spark like static. She rubbed her hands together, feeling the numbness even after the old woman pulled away.

"It's all right," Sarah said. "I won't be frightened by paranormal beings. I don't believe in ghosts."

The landlady laughed. "Salem may cure you of that."

For a moment Sarah wondered if she made a mistake moving there, but she decided she wouldn't let a superstitious old woman scare her away. She thought about her new job in the library at Salem State College—Humanities I liaison, go-to person for English studies, well worth the move across the country. She saw the tree-lined, old-fashioned neighborhood and the comforting sky. She heard the lull of bird songs and the distant whisper of the sea kissing the shore. She felt a rising tranquility, like the tide of the ocean waves at noon, wash over her. It was a contentment she had never known before, not in Boston, never in Los Angeles. She was fascinated by Salem, looking forward to knowing it better, certain she was exactly where she needed to be, whatever may come.

Sarah's first days in the library were hectic since it was the start of an autumn term. She spent her shifts on the main floor, an open, industrial-style space of bright lights, overhead beams, and windows that let in white from the sun and green from the trees abundant everywhere on campus. Across from the librarians' desk, a combined circulation and reference area, was a lounge of comfortable chairs in soothing grays and blues where some students socialized using their inside voices while others stalked like eagle-eyed hunters, searching the stacks or the databases.

By Wednesday afternoon, as she saw the short-tempered rain clouds march across the Salem sky, Sarah thought she would have to buy a car soon. After driving and dodging in nail-biting Los Angeles traffic for ten years, she liked the freedom of walking the quiet roads from home to work, watching in wonder as the leaves turned from summer green to an autumn fade of red, rust, and gold. But she had been living in the sunshine on the west coast for ten years, and she had forgotten about the sudden anger of New England thunderstorms. They could appear just like that, a crack of noise overhead, then a gray flannel blanket covered the sky as fast as you could blink your eyes, water splashing all around, wetting you when you did not want to be wet, and she was caught unprepared. She held out her hand and shook her head when she felt the drops splash her palm. Jennifer Mandel's voice sang out behind her.

"Need a lift?"

"Please."

Sarah wiped her palm on her skirt, grateful once again for Jennifer's assistance. Jennifer had been the head librarian at the college for five years, and she had taken Sarah under her wing, showing her where everything was, introducing her to the rest of the staff, answering her questions. There was something almost odd about Jennifer's intuition—she always seemed to know when Sarah needed her, like a clairvoyant magic trick. They sprinted to the parking lot, trying to avoid the sudden splats of rain soaking their thin blouses through, and they clambered into Jennifer's white Toyota, laughing like schoolgirls jumping in puddles. Jennifer drove the curve around Loring Avenue to Lafayette Street, the main road to and from the college.

"I remember from your interview that you're from Los Angeles, right?" Jennifer asked.

"I lived in L.A. for ten years. I worked in the library at UCLA."

"A small town like Salem must seem dreary after living in the big city."

Sarah looked at Jennifer, saw the compassion in her eyes, the understanding smile, so she said just enough to make herself understood. "I'm recently divorced."

Jennifer held up her hand. "You don't need to explain. I have two ex-husbands myself."

They drove quietly, letting the sound of the car's accelerator and the rain tapping the windshield fill the space. As Sarah watched the small-town scene drift past, she thought it might not be so bad to drive in Salem. Everything back east, the roads, the shops, the homes, was built on an old-time scale, narrower and smaller than they were out west. But here people slowed when you wanted to merge into their lane and they stopped at stop signs, so different from L.A. where they'd run you over sooner than let you pass.

"Why don't you come over tomorrow night?" Jennifer asked. "We're having a get-together at my mother's shop." She leaned closer to Sarah and whispered though they were alone in the car. "I should probably tell you, and I'll understand if you think this is too weird, but my mother and I are witches."

Sarah studied Jennifer, her hazel eyes, her long auburn hair, her friendly smile. "You don't look like a witch," she said.

"You mean the kind with black hair and a nose wart that fly around on broomsticks? We're not that kind of witch."

"You're Wiccan?"

"Yes, I practice the Wiccan religion, among other things. I'm the high priestess of my coven. I'm also licensed to perform weddings here in Massachusetts, in case you ever need someone to preside over a wedding for you."

Sarah laughed. "I just got divorced. I won't be getting married again any time soon." She paused to watch the drizzle slip and slide on the windows. "I'm surprised there really are witches in Salem."

"Ironic, isn't it? The city known for hanging witches is now a haven for mystics." Jennifer shook her head, her expression tight. "Is this too much information? I don't usually tell someone a few days after I've met her that I'm Wiccan, but you have a positive energy. You don't seem like someone who's going to assume I'm a Satanist who loves human sacrifices."

"I don't mind. I'm just surprised. I've never known a witch before."

"There are all sorts of interesting people you could meet around here." Jennifer nudged Sarah with her elbow. "So will you come tomorrow night?"

"I don't know, Jennifer."

"You don't need to participate in the rituals. Come make some friends. I think you'll like the other witches in my coven. They're good people."

A Wiccan ceremony did sound odd, Sarah thought, but she had always been fascinated by different religions and cultures. Librarians had to keep learning—a healthy curiosity was a job necessity. And it would be nice to know some people in Salem, even if they were witches.

As they continued down Lafayette Street, Sarah saw the sign for Pioneer Village and she added it to her mental to-do list. "I haven't had a chance to see much of this part of town since I've been here," she said.

"How about a quick tour then?"

"What about the rain?"

Jennifer turned right down Derby Street. "I've lived here my whole life. A little water doesn't bother me."

Jennifer drove down one tree-lined street, then down another street, and another until Sarah didn't know where she was. Though Witch City was small, Sarah was still learning her way around. She tried to gauge her surroundings and saw the tall, white lines of the Peabody-Essex Museum close to the brick, colonial-looking Salem Maritime National Historic Site. As she watched the history flip past, like a stack of photographs from time gone by, she noticed a house she thought she knew though she was sure she hadn't been down that way before. The house had wooden clapboards, diamond-paned casement windows, and two gables on the roof. It was old, though it didn't seem to be a museum as the other old buildings were.

"What is that house?" she asked. "It looks familiar."

"James Wentworth lives there."

"Do you know him?"

Jennifer's answer was stilted, as if she considered each word, weighed it, measured it, decided yes or no about it, before she let it drop from her lips. "He teaches at the college. He—his family—has owned this house for generations. It's over three hundred years old, one of the oldest standing homes in Salem."

Jennifer slowed the car so they could get a better look as she drove past. "Does it still look familiar?"

"Yes. Even that crooked oak tree in front seems right. I can picture the man I dream about standing in front there kissing me."

"What dreams?" Jennifer gripped the steering wheel more tightly and her eyes brightened. "My mother's friend Martha is great at dream interpretation. She's done a world of good for me." She winked at Sarah. "And you dream about a man? Is he a good looking man?"

Sarah pulled her arms around her chest, wishing she could take back her casual reference, afraid she had already said too much.

"Do you have a lot of dreams?"

"Yes," Sarah said. But that was all she could manage. When Jennifer had waited long enough and Sarah had to offer something more, all she could say was, "It's not a big deal. I just thought I knew the house from somewhere."

"A lot of houses around here look the same," Jennifer said.

Sarah looked at the houses, the tall, Federal-style ones, the Victorian ones, the brick ones, the modern-looking ones. Suddenly, as they drove around the green of Salem Common, the rain cleared, the sun brightened, and the clouds flittered away across the bay.

"That must be it," she said.

She lowered the car window so she could smell the wet air. Though she missed the rain when she lived in Los Angeles, at that moment she was glad to see the serene blue reflection of the northeastern sky again.

They drove the rest of the way in silence.

Printed in Great Britain
by Amazon